JUNIPER RISE

ANNE LUCY-SHANLEY

JUNIPER RISE
Copyright © 2022 Ninth and Aries Publishing
EBook ISBN: 978-1-7366907-2-7
Paperback ISBN: 978-1-7366907-3-4
Editing by EnCompass

Look for Anne online at: www.AnneLucyShanley.com

Henry Wadsworth Longfellow quote from *Evangeline: A Tale of Acadie* (public domain) can be found at: https://www.hwlongfellow.org/poems_poem.php?pid=273

For Almie, who is my home

CHAPTER ONE

"THREE HUNDRED SIXTY-FOUR FUCKING DAYS."

Raindrops pelted against the plexiglass skylights, making the usually dim warehouse even dimmer. The interior was shrouded in shadows. Ghostly. But Sofia was accustomed to that now. The rows of floor-to-ceiling shelving stood like soldiers in formation, the dust-covered forklift facing them resembling a stern drill sergeant.

Squinting at the newest hash mark she'd scribbled on the concrete wall, Sofia capped the Magic Marker. She pinched her lip between her teeth and chafed her arms for warmth.

Three hundred sixty-four days in seclusion, not daring to depart the confines of her haven. No human interaction. Sweltering temperatures during the summer. Arctic conditions in the winter. Mornings spent pacing the aisles, sure she was losing her sanity. Reading the magazines she'd taken from the employee breakroom aloud just to hear a voice. Eating tinned soup straight from the can. Washing with a rag in the staff restroom, the water freezing.

A crack of thunder reverberated, then bursts of lightning illuminated the warehouse through the skylights like a strobe light. It jolted Sofia back to the present. Hefting her plastic crate from the shipping and receiving counter, she climbed the metal stairs to the manager's office—Howard's office—which overlooked the hushed warehouse. The stacked pallets that served as her bed were situated between the desk and the wall. Sofia lowered wearily to it. Draping her tattered foil blanket around her shoulders, she sniffled from both cold and emotion.

Was anyone alive out in the real world? What if she was the only survivor? The crates of food would spoil before she could eat it all. Then what? Starvation?

Rubbing her hands to create friction for heat, Sofia reflected. She had tried contacting her friends repeatedly, her cell charging in the outlet behind Howard's desk. Her calls and texts went unanswered. Sofia had been certain that after a couple of days things would blow over. That Mama and Daddy would phone to let her know they were booking a flight. They hadn't.

For a while, the internet functioned though her social media platforms were down—Sofia had no way to connect with her followers. She scoured the results of her searches. News outlets were apparently defunct. Instead of articles and broadcast news, Sofia found shocking MeTube videos. Uploaded by a panicked populace, they highlighted anarchy—looting, disorder, lawlessness. Random violence. Brawls over resources. Once victorious, the winner abandoned their battered adversary on the pavement, their wounds leaking lifeblood that flowed into the gutter like a scarlet river.

What if somebody saw the entrance to Spenser Suppliers and, nosy, broke in to investigate? Once they realized it was filled to the brim with nonperishable foodstuffs, Sofia would be in grave danger. They'd see her as merely an obstacle. She'd be as disposable as the people in the videos. The thought terrified her.

Why hadn't she had the foresight to comb Daddy's den for his gun before driving to the warehouse?

Sofia had watched in horror, biting her knuckles to keep from shrieking at the savage inhumanity unfolding onscreen. When she was sure there was nothing worse to be seen, more recordings were uploaded that left her blinking in disbelief.

Vloggers, dumbfounded, editorialized and documented *the dead awakening*.

Bodies supine on the streets lurched to their feet. Their faces lifted to the heavens. They loudly snuffled the air. Then, they stilled. Squatted. The creatures launched up as they fixed on a target in the crowd. People scrambled to evade them, trampling those unfortunate enough to lose their footing. The slowest of the bunch were picked off first.

Before long, there were no more uploads. Sofia refreshed the screen obsessively, desperate for more information. It was almost a blessing when her phone stopped finding a signal.

The warehouse, first Sofia's salvation, became her prison. Submerging into a profound depression, she'd curled up on the carpeted floor in Howard's office and slumbered. What else was there to do but sleep and hope that when she woke the nightmare would be over? Hours blended into days which stretched to weeks, the hash marks on the wall the only confirmation of the passage of time.

One day, Sofia dreamed of Mama.

"I didn't raise you to give up, *querida*," Mama whispered softly, patting Sofia's cheek. "This won't last forever. You're resourceful. Strong. You'll survive. You have to."

The dream roused and renewed Sofia's determination. As she scribbled her sixtieth hash mark on the wall, she vowed to take her car, to look for others. There was plenty to share at the warehouse.

Weaponless, Sofia took a nine iron from the golf bag in the corner of Howard's office, intending to hunt for the keys to the lobby entrance.

She'd never heard any indication that what happened to the dead online had happened to Howard the Creep, but Sofia decided to be wary.

Metal double doors led to the lobby, where she'd left his

corpse. Gripping the golf club, she tentatively opened one of the doors, her heart beating hard in her sternum. The sun shining through the plate-glass windows facing the parking lot was blinding. Gagging against the sickening stench that drifted to her, Sofia put a hand over her mouth and peeked into the lobby. Shuffling, a clack of teeth, then a flash of movement.

"Gah!"

Howard barreled toward Sofia, the sunlight encompassing his form in a gilded aura. He traversed the lobby in seconds. Stinking of rotted meat, his flesh was mottled. His once brown irises were now milky white.

Releasing her golf club, Sofia used both hands to force the door shut. It wouldn't latch. Howard rammed against it. It smacked Sofia's forehead. Stunned, she lost purchase, her feet skating across the floor. She clung to the doorknob as she stumbled.

Howard's fingers slithered around the edge of the door jamb. Snatched at her. Sofia screamed, recoiled. Clambered to get her bearings. Put her shoulder to the door and used her body weight. The door bounced against the jamb.

Why wouldn't the damn thing close?

The golf club's handle was in the way.

Sofia kicked at it but missed. Howard's icy fingers touched her wrist. He was milliseconds from getting in! Doing the only thing she could think of, Sofia let the door go. Positioned herself in the opening. Bringing up a foot, she booted Howard in the family jewels. He teetered back.

The club! The toe of Sofia's sandal connected with it, and it skittered into the lobby. She slammed the door just as Howard rebounded, his fingers curling around the jamb. Red-black blood sprayed Sofia's dress as his fingers were sliced clean from his hand. The digits plummeted to the concrete floor near her feet.

Stomach heaving, she bent. Vomited. Wiping her hand against her mouth, Sofia straightened. Tears and snot tracked down her face as she bawled. Howard struck the metal doors. Would he get in? If he did, she was dead.

Like an automaton, Sofia unbuckled the belt from her dress and tied it around the doorknobs. She prayed it would be enough to keep him out.

The doors rocked in their frames. Sofia backed away.

Moments lasted an eternity but Howard quieted, his interest waning. Sofia sensed him pressed against the metal. Swallowing, she tiptoed over and brought her ear to the door. He snuffled as he sniffed at her scent.

A goose egg was forming on Sofia's forehead—her brain felt muzzy. There was a bulky wooden shelf overflowing with office equipment and printer apparatus. Inching the shelf over until it blocked the doors, she then sagged against it.

Howard possessed the keys to the lobby entrance, the only logical egress. Although there was an exit by the shipping counter, Sofia was leery about traipsing all the way around the perimeter of the building to the parking lot. More of those things could be out there—she'd be too vulnerable. Plus, no keys meant she couldn't secure the door behind her.

Howard had become her prison guard, keeping her incarcerated. Sofia wouldn't be going anywhere anytime soon. Tears in her eyes, she cursed her weakness. Her fear.

Dejected, she went to the restroom to wash.

ELECTRICITY HAD QUIT WORKING on day sixty-seven, the boiler along with it. The summer had been awful, but winter was interminable. Agonizing. Teeth chattering, Sofia had shivered as she layered up in every outfit from her suitcase. A foraging exploration netted a first aid kit with a throwaway foil blanket. It proved inadequate. Suffering terribly night after night, Sofia questioned whether she'd live to see another day. Her only companion was her sore rib cage from an unrelenting, barking cough.

Now, the cusp of spring pledged a reprieve from the frosty temps, along with the first anniversary of her confinement. Something in her bones told her Mama and Daddy were dead. That everyone she'd known was dead. She didn't know *how* she knew, *but she knew.*

Sofia was an orphan. She wore the crushing melancholy and loneliness like a weighty shawl.

Sitting on her pallet bed with her legs crossed, Sofia toyed with the last present her parents had gifted her—a charm bracelet, crafted from Ecuadorian gold mined from the village where her mother had been born—and remembered Mama's words.

Expression determined, Sofia took a cardboard packet from the plastic crate. Unwrapping the chocolate iced Little Sallie snack cake, she said, "Happy twenty-first birthday. You're gettin' out of this place. Soon."

CHAPTER TWO

THERE WERE NO IFS, ANDS, OR BUTS ABOUT IT. SOFIA *MUST* GET THE keys. No way would she leave the door by shipping and receiving accessible. The warehouse was hers. She wasn't going to make entry easy for any scavengers that may discover the place.

The keyring was probably in Howard the Creep's trouser pocket or on the front reception desk. He'd have to be *dealt with*. Once he was, she could take the direct route outside to the parking lot through the lobby. Again, she regretted not bringing Daddy's gun.

Maybe she could bash in Howard's cranium with one of the golf clubs? But that meant she'd have to allow him within arm's reach. Sofia's mouth pinched in distaste. Could she do it? She wasn't sure.

That night, Sofia bit her nails to nubs as she attempted to envisage a plan, to rally courage. Slaying Howard was a mandatory litmus test, one she couldn't fail—she was liable to come across other bloodthirsty creatures outside. If she couldn't put Howard down, how could she possibly hope to stay alive?

Sofia's posh life hadn't prepared her for this—she'd never had to *fight*. Anxiety caused her tummy to burn, her legs to shake. When she did doze, it was in fits, and she was awake long before dawn.

Pacing the length of the office, Sofia psyched herself up. Bravery eluded her until she thought of Mama's words in her dream. They galvanized her into action.

You're resourceful. Strong. You'll survive. You have to.

Sofia propped the eight iron from the golf bag against the cinder block wall. Hunkering down, she put her back to the supply shelf obstructing the double doors. She used her legs to scooch it. It screeched as it dragged across the concrete.

Pausing to catch her breath, she heard the unmistakable shuffle of Howard approaching the metal doors. Then, the warehouse echoed as his fists beat against them.

"This may be the dumbest idea you've ever had, Sofia," she muttered as she considered her belt on the doorknobs.

With a steeling breath, she unknotted the belt and let it drop.

Sofia twisted the doorknob. The door cracked open. Swiveling, she seized the golf club. Retreated. Keeping to her plan, she dashed to the shipping counter. Waited. She mustn't get boxed in.

Hinges squeaked. Howard appeared. He shouldered the door further ajar, huffing the air. The early morning shafts of sun flooded the corridor through the opening. Dust motes swirled around his pudgy profile like stardust.

His footsteps were halting. Then, the snuffling ceased, and Howard's teeth crashed together. *Clack-clack-clack-clack-clack.* The door banged closed. He squatted.

"Oh shit..." Sofia exchanged the eight iron for the fire extinguisher she'd placed on the shipping counter.

Howard sprang up and forward, like he was on a pogo stick.

Hands sweaty, Sofia grasped the pin on the handle. Fumbled. She yanked it out. Aimed the nozzle. When Howard was almost on her, she squeezed the handles together and sprayed the thick foam directly in his face.

Disoriented, he paused. Faltered.

With a war cry, Sofia threw the extinguisher at Howard's head. It ricocheted off his temple and hit the floor. He staggered.

Clutching her club, Sofia swung with all her might. With a hollow clunk, it connected at Howard's brow bone, the momentum of it taking him from his feet.

"Oh fuck, oh fuck," Sofia gasped as she pummeled him with the eight iron. His revolting blood splattered her clothes, her skin. The smell inundated her sinuses, making her eyes stream. "Ugh!"

The force of her blows had bowed the eight iron. Dizzy, Sofia dropped it, slumping to her knees. Would she faint?

Howard's flattened head on the concrete sickened her. Bits of brain tissue and slivers of bone littered the floor, clung to her hair. Sofia swiped at the strands, feeling defiled.

"Don't freak out... don't freak out... don't freak out..." She scrabbled back like a crab until her spine connected with a wall. Half-shrieking and half-sobbing, Sofia covered her face with her palms and howled.

When her sobs had reduced to hiccups, she used the hem of her shirt to dry her tears. As much as she disliked the man in real life, she'd never wanted to physically injure him... Was she now a killer?

Sofia shook her head. No. Howard wasn't Howard anymore. Feeling much older than her years, she stood. After washing in the restroom, she climbed the stairs to the office to change her clothes and fetch the seven iron. She'd packed a tote bag with snacks, water, and the miniature fire extinguisher from the staff breakroom. It waited on her pallet bed.

Slinging the straps over her shoulder, Sofia returned downstairs. Quivering with adrenaline and wobbly-legged, she contemplated digging in Howard's trouser pocket to search for the keys. Repulsed, she opted to check the reception desk for his keyring first.

Sofia timidly opened the metal door leading to the lobby. Howard's stink lingered, watery sunlight saturating the room with radiance. Curious, she went to the plate-glass windows. Her car was where she'd left it. Howard had driven a company car, a hybrid. Electric cars were one of Daddy's green initiatives. Last year, Sofia had plugged the car into the solar-powered charging dock next to Howard's parking spot—just in case.

Her gaze scanned the blacktop, the surrounding forest. Mother Nature had begun to reclaim what was rightfully hers— the grass had grown three feet tall. Unchecked, glossy vines stretched across the parking lot like greedy tentacles. A crow flew past, landing on a tree limb. It was wild but unnaturally still.

"Strange," Sofia whispered. Wearied by her sleepless night and grossly overwhelmed by the quest that lay ahead of her, she worked her neck muscles with her hand.

Howard's keyring was on the reception desk beside the computer. Pulse thrumming, Sofia tucked her club under her arm and shifted the tote. Keys in hand, she marched to the entrance.

It was too late to second guess herself now.

Closing her eyes momentarily, she summoned strength then located the correct key. Legs shaking, Sofia unfastened the deadbolt and stepped outside.

CHAPTER THREE

A BREEZE RUFFLED THE VEGETATION. SONGBIRDS TWITTERED. SOFIA'S breath vaporized in the air, but the sun was cheerful. Warm. It revived her. Fortified her.

A year had elapsed since Sofia had last been outside. She resisted the urge to soak in the solace the rays offered. Instead, she kept to the task at hand and bolted the lobby door with efficient, decisive actions.

Sofia didn't bother with her vehicle—the battery would've died months ago. She unlocked Howard's car, tossing her belongings on the passenger's seat. Biting her lip, she put the fob in the ignition and rotated it.

Silence. Plugging the car into the solar dock hadn't been enough to keep everything charged.

"Well damn," Sofia said. "Plot twist."

The plan was to stop home first. The gun was there, along with so much more. Sofia's armpits prickled with dread as she deliberated journeying on foot with a golf club and a compact fire extinguisher as her sole defense.

How the fuck could this be real life? Hysteria engulfing her, Sofia angled her neck against the headrest and cackled.

She debated retreating. Going back to her pallet bed and

curling into a ball. Succumbing to what would be easier. But Mama's words niggled Sofia. *I didn't raise you to give up.* She could almost hear Mama scold, "*Ay Dios mío.* Put on your big girl panties!"

The flimsy sandals were Sofia's only shoes. No doubt they'd shred her feet after a hundred yards. Obviously, hiking boots and sturdy jeans were a necessity. And a flannel shirt over a tank top that she could take off if she got too hot. The filmy, flowery blouse and linen capris she wore were more suitable for a garden party.

With no other option, Sofia gathered her things and got out of the hybrid, her mouth pursed. The sun rose in the east, right? Highway 7 ran in front of the warehouse, making that west. Sofia's house was northwest of Spenser Suppliers, a few hours' walk away. She'd stay parallel to the road. The last thing she wanted was to become disoriented and get lost.

An hour later, Sofia's clothes were damp with perspiration, and her feet hurt. Other than scattered abandoned vehicles along the highway, she was alone. Dense shrubs and steep ditches lining the roadway forced her to tread on the pavement. Parched, she rifled through her tote bag for a bottle of water.

From the corner of her eye, the weeds rippled in the ditch. Time halted as Sofia frowned, wheeling to inspect the brush. A toddler dressed in a corduroy jumper, her wispy blonde hair held back by a pink barrette, thrust through the overgrowth. She stumbled and fell face first into the thicket.

"Oh honey," Sofia breathed, discarding her tote bag and club, "what are you doing out here by yourself?"

Sliding into the ditch, Sofia bundled the child in her arms. She registered the odor clinging to her a millisecond too late. The milky eyes, the blotchy flesh—she was a creature! Her jaw snapped open and closed as she dove for Sofia's neck.

"Jesus!" Horrified, Sofia flung her into the bushes. Careening up to the pavement, she retrieved her golf club from where she'd left it.

There was snuffling from the undergrowth. Sofia held her breath. Trembled as she extended her club in readiness.

The creature reappeared, her head emerging from between the woody reeds. Brambles tore at the jumper as she crawled on her hands and knees up the bank. Sailing toward Sofia, she nipped at her ankles like a yapping dog. Sofia shrieked, shaking her off and leaping away.

Like a boomerang, she flew at Sofia again. Sofia kicked the creature away. The toddler tumbled down to the weeds, then, righting herself, lunged back up to the pavement.

Swallowing a whimper, Sofia put her foot out to hold the child in place. Whacked her with the club until she no longer twitched.

Aghast, Sofia wouldn't, *couldn't*, fathom that she'd slaughtered a baby. Perhaps *she* was the monster. Woodenly collecting her belongings, Sofia persisted on, the incident with the toddler playing over in her mind. It'd be a long time before she'd make peace with the callous aggression the new world exacted.

Was that the hum of an engine?

Sofia's instincts squawked *caution*. She bailed, hiding in the thicket at the bottom of the bank among the razor-sharp reeds.

A rusty pickup zoomed past, the exhaust belching sooty smoke. The truck bed was weighed down with rough-looking men holding shotguns. Sofia waited an extra five minutes after they passed to be sure she hadn't been seen.

When she got back on the asphalt, Sofia's knees shook. Abrasions from the reeds marred her skin, and her clothes were streaked with dirt. She'd been out but a scant couple of hours, and she'd already had her fill of exploring.

Sofia's belly demanded sustenance. She ate beef jerky as she hiked. Constant vigilance for more people, dead or alive, wore her out. Her sandals rubbing her toes and heels slowed her. She'd acquired blisters the size of Mount Vesuvius.

It was past lunchtime before Sofia spied the winding

driveway to her house. Bone-melting exhaustion pulled at her like an undertow as she set foot on the paved drive.

Circumventing the closed security fence at the entrance to the property, Sofia waded through the overgrowth to the access gate. Using her key, she unlocked it and forced it open. The canopy of the weeping willows cast shadows. She quavered from cold and nerves.

Before relocking the gate, Sofia ran her gaze over the grounds. The lawn, which once had been religiously trimmed twice a week, was now a scraggly hayfield. Desolate. Deserted. But no obvious signs of a breach were apparent. And what of the house? Despite being on the outskirts of town and set back from the road, it didn't seem possible that it remained unscathed.

Had the metal fencing been enough to deter intruders? And the creatures. Could they scale six-feet-tall fences? What if there were squatters in the house? What if they were armed?

Stifling the whirlwind of questions, doubts, and fears threatening to devour her, Sofia held tight to her golf club as she trudged across the lawn.

A snake slithered over her foot, and she flinched, clapping a hand over her mouth to squelch her scream. She swept her seven iron across the grass before each step the rest of the way. It was laborious. At the driveway, Sofia leaned on the club to catch her breath.

The house was an expansive stone ranch sitting atop a knoll. Nostalgia swelled in Sofia's breast as she drank in the sight of the gracious home. It was where she had taken her first footsteps, learned to ride a bike, and posed for photos with her prom date. Chest wracking, Sofia surrendered to her tears.

The interior was gloomy, stinking of mildew and neglect. Intuition told her the place was unoccupied—a layer of dust coated every surface. The house was as Sofia had left it.

Dabbing away the remnants of her tears with the hem of her shirt, she went to the dining room and took one of the silver candelabras from the buffet, lighting it with matches stored in a drawer below. Hauling the fire extinguisher from her tote bag, Sofia inserted it into the waistband of her capris. Golf club raised in one hand and candelabra in the other, she scoped out each room to ensure she truly was alone.

Deflated pink-and-gold balloons lay pitifully on the carpet. Streamers and a banner remained strung across the marble fireplace—20 On The 20th Happy Birthday Sofia. So much for her golden birthday, Sofia thought. The virus had put the kibosh on her party. How disappointed she'd been at the time. Now it mattered little. She stuffed the decorations in the trash before sitting on the sofa.

Pulling her sandals off with a groan, she considered building a fire in the fireplace to dispel some of the chill in the air. The living room windows showed the swimming pool, blooming with a profusion of neon green algae. The barbeque grill. Sofia could use it to heat a can of soup for dinner. A warm bed and cooked food for the first time in a year—what a heady notion!

With a wrenching noise from the pipes, discolored water flowed from the kitchen faucet, reeking of sulfur. Eventually it cleared, and Sofia scrubbed her filthy hands and face with the frigid water, drying with a tea towel from the cabinet.

Yawning, Sofia went to Daddy's den. The key to the closet lockbox was in the desk. She opened the lockbox. The detective's special .38, the revolver Sofia had learned to shoot with, was there along with a box of bullets. She pushed the cylinder out and loaded the six empty chambers with bullets.

Sofia held the gun in her grip, weighing it in her palm. She prayed she'd never have to fire it.

CHAPTER FOUR

ONCE IN HER BEDROOM, SOFIA BOLTED THE DOOR AND PUT THE candelabra on her desk. Setting her club and tote bag on the floor beside the bed, she carefully placed the gun and ammo on her bedside table.

What she wouldn't give for a hot shower. Shivering, she stripped down, finding a pair of gray sweats in her bureau. She dressed, pitching her dirty clothes in the hamper. Her feet throbbed. Sofia eased down on her bed and slathered them in scented lotion then pulled on fuzzy slipper socks.

Her mattress tempted her—it looked cushy, inviting. Eyelids heavy, her hunger forgotten, Sofia bunched the fluffy duvet around her body and snuggled in.

If a creature broke through the door and slaughtered Sofia in her bed before she could aim her revolver, so be it. She was spent beyond the point of caring.

WHEN SHE WOKE, the candles had long burned out. Filmy predawn light filtered through the window blinds. Panicked, Sofia sat up abruptly, pulse racing. Where was she? Then it all came rushing back. The apocalypse. Her house. Her bedroom. Her bed.

The house was quiet. She was still alone.

Settling back on the mattress, Sofia stifled a sneeze and laced her fingers under her pillow. Her bed linens smelled musty, but they were heaven after her year of sleeping rough on a pallet bed.

While she came fully alert, she strategized. Daddy's weekend driver—a muscle car—was parked in the attached garage. Cars were Daddy's hobby, and he'd taught Sofia about them. He stored the vehicle in the garage over the winter months with the battery disconnected, but Sofia knew how to connect it. And if the battery needed a charge, there was a jump pack in Daddy's tool chest. Sofia knew how to use that, too.

After sitting for a year, most gasoline blends would've gone bad. Daddy's car, Blue, ran on recreational fuel with no added ethanol, which lasted much longer. Sofia was positive she remembered Daddy filling his portable gas can with fuel last spring. How many gallons did it hold? She'd have to investigate after breakfast.

If Sofia could get Blue started, she'd drive to the warehouse. Load the car with provisions and return to the house. That way she'd have access to staples in two locations. After recuperating the rest of the day and sleeping in her bed that night, she'd foray out in the morning.

The sun rose, bathing the room in brilliance. Slipping from her bed, Sofia snatched up her gun and unbolted her door. There was a driving atlas in the den.

The atlas spread open on Daddy's desk, Sofia found Highway 7 and trailed a finger along the paper to the intersection nearest the house. Pulling a pencil from the drawer, she drew a circle equidistant to ten miles, the house at its center. Then Sofia found the approximate location of the warehouse and did the same. Unwilling to venture too far from food and shelter, she'd do her best to not stray beyond the limits of those circles.

Sofia's tummy rumbled, reminding her she must eat. She chose cans of baked beans and Vienna sausages from the pantry.

After emptying the beans and sausages in a pan, her revolver in her waistband, Sofia unlocked the French doors in the dining room. Her hand froze on the doorknob. The house was secure, but outside danger lurked.

Acknowledging the fine line between conquering fears and downright recklessness, Sofia shrugged off her misgivings and strode out to the patio. She'd just have to be attentive. A hot meal would be worth it.

The grill clicked as it struggled to ignite, then *whoompf,* flames caught. She set the pot on the grate, thinking how lovely a cup of tea would be.

After grabbing another pan from the house along with a mug, bottle of water, and a tea bag from the canister in the kitchen, Sofia heated water on the grill.

Revolver next to her on the chaise, Sofia sipped her tea. The sun hit the budding leaves on the trees flanking the pool, making them shimmer in the wind. A juxtaposition of light and shade flickered on the cement like a mosaic. A dun wren serenaded her. Sofia's esophagus thickened with emotion.

The steaming drink gladdened her soul. Made her feel human. As she ate breakfast, Sofia marveled at how much she'd missed life's simple pleasures—things she'd not valued before. She'd never be so cavalier again. This, she realized, was *living*.

Sofia's teeth were fuzzy. She touched her matted hair and her caked-with-grime skin. What if she boiled tap water on the grill and filled the bathtub? There were bottles of shampoo, conditioner, and bodywash in the shower. Surely they were still usable after a year of sitting. What an indulgence it would be to be clean again.

Two hours later, the bathroom misty with humidity, Sofia hunched down in the bathwater, rinsing conditioner from her hair. She used a washcloth and soap to scrub her skin and cuticles. The water clouded brown. When Sofia got out and toweled off, she pulled the plug, shaking her head at the filthy ring left around the tub.

Dressed in her gray sweatsuit, Sofia took scissors from the kitchen junk drawer and trimmed her hair to shoulder length. Running her fingertips through the strands, she scraped them into a ponytail. Revolver in her waistband, she selected a backpack from her closet. Transferring her belongings from her tote bag to it, she headed to the garage.

Popping Blue's hood, Sofia made quick work of connecting the terminals to the battery. She checked the fluids—transmission fluid, oil, coolant. The portable gas can in the corner of the garage was full. She wheeled it to Blue and filled the gas tank with fuel.

Her belongings stowed in the car, Sofia stood on a stool, pulling the string hanging from the garage door opener. Then, she hefted the door open, pausing to scrutinize the yard. Everything looked alright. Blue's keys were on a keychain attached to the pegboard over the workbench.

It was the moment of truth.

Getting behind the wheel, Sofia put the key in the ignition. Grinding. Sofia pumped the gas. Blue roared to life, and she punched the air in victory. "Yes!"

Now, how to get the gate at the bottom of the driveway open? Just when Sofia triumphed over one challenge, another reared its head. There must be a manual override on the gate. She'd throw some tools in the backseat and drive down there.

She parked Blue in front of the house, then hopped out to pull the garage door closed before she continued to the gate.

The control panel's cover was attached with screws. She removed the cover with a screwdriver from the backseat. Green circuit board and wiring. Nope. That wasn't the answer.

There was a black metal arm on the gate. Sofia stooped down. Examined it. A plastic flap was situated on the far side of the arm. Using the screwdriver, she pried the flap up. A lock. Sofia ran back to Blue and unhooked her keychain from the loop on her backpack. The key that fit the walking gate fit the lock on the main gate. Once unbolted, the gate glided open.

Repeating her earlier routine, Sofia pulled Blue past the gate, parked, then ran back to secure the gate. She was awed by how she'd taken electricity for granted before the end of the world. Without it, every task took twice as much effort.

Blue's engine was loud in the silence. Jarring. Worried she'd be heard, Sofia put her foot down on the gas and drove fast, weaving around the automobiles on the road. The faster she got to the warehouse, the less chance of being spotted.

Avoiding Howard's corpse, Sofia tramped from Blue to the bowels of the warehouse and back. She loaded the trunk and backseat with crates of water, cases of canned food, cartons of jerky, and dehydrated fruit.

An hour later, she was whipping down the highway toward home. Going through the process of unbolting the gate, parking inside, then closing the gate again, Sofia stopped to wipe away a bead of sweat. Each moment she'd been out had been fraught with apprehension.

Blue returned to its spot in the garage, she split up the staples. Half went in the kitchen pantry. The other half she hid in the basement wine cellar. Needing a breather, Sofia took a snack out to the patio. She plunked down in her preferred chaise longue and unwrapped a cereal bar.

A stirring in the distance snagged her attention. She blinked. Squinted. Was it a mirage? A group of six people stood outside the fence in the far corner of the backyard.

CHAPTER FIVE

Jumping to her feet, Sofia swiped her revolver from the end table. How long had they been there *watching her*? Not knowing what else to do, she shifted from foot to foot.

Was one of them beckoning her? Yes, a lean figure waved an arm, entreating Sofia to join them at the fence line. Should she?

Sweaty palmed, Sofia bit her cheek. Her legs were jelly. Would they buckle beneath her? Again, the figure waved, insistent. The group began striding along the fence, nearing the house.

Briefly, Sofia considered fleeing inside and locking the door. But, to what end? If the people wanted in badly enough, *they'd get in*, and then any goodwill would be gone. Advantageous to present herself as friendly. To feel the situation out.

Shoulders squared, with a finger on the gun's trigger, Sofia picked across the lawn.

They wore camping packs. Three men. Two swarthy with dark eyes, likely related, wearing pistols in holsters and toting shotguns. The third man was blond-haired and blue-eyed with a compound bow slung over his shoulder. Solidly built. Handsome. His eyes watchful. A woman around Sofia's age with greasy blonde hair was weaponless. There was another lady who held a machete. She was older—early sixties and dark-complexioned—a grandmotherly type, petite with soft wrinkles and snowy hair. Sofia's gaze caught on the final person. A boy grasping a tire iron. He was the one who'd waved at her. Shaggy ebony-hued hair. Almond-shaped eyes. Scrawny, emaciated frame.

Sofia gasped as recognition sparked. "Zac Kim? Is that really you?"

His chin dipped shyly. "Hey, Sofia."

Sofia had babysat then-sixth-grader Zac for a whole summer when she was in high school. His family owned the Chinese buffet in Crestview. "I can't believe somebody I actually know is alive! Where are your parents? Grandfather Bao?"

Zac shook his head.

"Oh." Sofia swallowed. "Of course. Sorry."

Grandma cleared her throat. "My house was down the block from Zac's. We banded together, keeping each other alive… scavenging. We came across the others two weeks ago." She flashed Sofia a warm smile. "Safety in numbers, you know. We were in the area, so Zac suggested your place."

Sofia's focus skittered back to Zac. "Why would you do that?"

He shrugged, mumbling, "You brought me to swim during summer vacation. There was always lots to eat here. Almost as much as the restaurant."

That was true. Mama had grown up poor. She'd tended to stockpile non-perishables once she had the budget to.

The taller of the swarthy men said, "You don't look like you've missed a meal, buttercup."

Grandma scolded, "Be polite, Kyle."

"What?" Kyle laughed. "I like fat girls. They're juicy."

"My brother, the chubby chaser," the shorter one chortled.

Blondie seemed mortified. She shushed them, scowling. "Don't encourage him, Tucker."

"More cushion for the pushin'," Kyle said slyly, his eyes raking Sofia and hovering at her ample breasts.

Sofia bristled, intersecting her arms over her chest. *Asshole.* "I don't have a lot of provisions left."

"Betcha you got more than we do," Tucker snorted.

"Can't you help us? Just a little?" Zac implored, and Sofia softened. He was dirty and obviously starving. When had he last eaten? Her memories of Zac were sweet. She hoped he hadn't changed too much from the kid she'd once known.

Wary, Sofia styled her face impassive. Grandma was probably harmless. Blondie too, but appearances could be deceptive. The men were another story altogether. Alarm bells clanged like claxons. In addition to the fact they were clearly jerks, the brothers had the potential to become menacing. And what of the hunk?

She met Hunk's eyes. They were sapphire. Hooded. He hadn't spoken, hadn't flexed a muscle. Could *he* be trusted?

"Why don't we keep this cordial?" Kyle asked Sofia.

"Wouldn't want things to get ugly," Tucker agreed slyly. "I sure do hate having to take what I want *by force.*"

Ice flooded Sofia's veins at his not-so-veiled threat. Mouth parched, she gulped, unable to summon words.

Grandma volleyed the brothers a censuring glare and shook her head in aggravation.

Blondie mouthed "Sorry" to Sofia.

For the first time, Hunk's gaze swung away from Sofia and landed on the brothers. "Why don't you two jabronis shut the fuck up for once?"

Sofia expected Kyle and Tucker to draw their weapons on Hunk, but their body language revealed that Hunk was the alpha of the group. His voice was deep, authoritative. Unconcerned. *So he knows he can get away with speaking freely. Interesting.*

"What do you say, Sofia?" Zac asked quietly. "We had to fight a group of Zs back there, and I'm thirsty."

There were splashes of red-black viscera on their clothes. The wind altered course, and Sofia caught a whiff of the putrid odor which accompanied it. "Zs?"

"That's what we call 'em. The zombies," Grandma explained. "There are less now, but they're still around."

"And they could be anywhere," Hunk pointed out shortly. "Not smart to stand around too long and tempt fate."

"I'm Cora." Grandma smiled. "And I'm just plain too old to keep standing. My dogs are barkin'.'."

Hunk deliberated the darkening sky. "Clouds are telling me a downpour is imminent. You going to let us in?"

Sofia hesitated. Hunk had a commanding presence. Would he, along with the rest of the group, be capable of reining in Kyle and Tucker?

Hunk seemed to read her mind. He pinned the brothers with a glower. They looked like they wanted to say something but bit their tongues. Hunk's eyes caught Sofia's and held them. "In this world, a man's worth can be measured solely by his words and actions. Miss, if you open your home to us, you have my word that no harm will come to you."

Sofia sighed. Though wedged between a rock and a hard place, for some inexplicable reason she believed the man's pledge. "I better not regret this. Alright. Walk down to the gate by the garage. I have to get the key to unlock it."

As she hurried to the French doors to go inside and fetch her keyring, Sofia muttered, "This is crazy."

They waited at the gate when she came back outside. As she rotated the key in the gate's lock, Sofia saw a creature—a Z—in the distance. Supercharged, it headed in their direction, cutting through the overgrowth like a knife through butter.

"What's wrong?" Hunk had detected the change in Sofia's demeanor. He twirled around to where Sofia gawked. "More Zs out here than I anticipated. I got it."

Sofia's hands were unsteady. She fumbled with the key.

Hunk stepped away, his jaw tightening. His face transformed into a study of intensity. With fluid motions, he slid his bow from his back and plucked an arrow from the quiver. Nocking the arrow, he brought the bow into position. Aiming, he pulled the bowstring. The arrow smoothly arced through the air and implanted in the Z's temple. The Z slumped to the ground.

Hunk gave Sofia a lazy grin, revealing a dimple in his cheek and an impeccable set of teeth. The tempo of her heart rate increased, her reaction nothing to do with the close call with the Z. Hunk was a *hunk*. Wow. Attraction flared low in Sofia's abdomen, a delectable ache.

She broke her gaze from his, worried he'd decipher her thoughts. Sofia concentrated on the lock, and it clicked open. While the group filed into the yard one by one, Hunk jogged through the weeds to the Z and yanked the arrow from its head. He wiped the arrow on his jeans as he came back to the gate.

A cough covering her discomfiture, Sofia backed up to allow him passage through the gate.

He paused as he made his way past, causing Sofia to crane her head back to meet his eyes. He loomed over her by a foot. A raindrop plopped on his aquiline nose, then another. There was a clap of thunder. Lips crooking in a ghost of a smile, Hunk murmured, "I'm Ben, by the way. Pleasure to make your acquaintance, Sofia."

CHAPTER SIX

THE STRANGERS PEERED AT THE INTERIOR OF THE HOUSE, THEIR curiosity blatant. Ben had his hands on his hips, expression thoughtful. Shrewd. The set of his face told Sofia he was sizing things up. Assessing usefulness. His gaze meandered over Sofia in an identical fashion.

Sofia's tongue cemented to the roof of her mouth. Small talk seemed odd under the circumstances. They weren't intruders, but they weren't truly invited guests, were they?

Ben placed his bow on the dining room table and his pack on the floor, then unzipped his black hoodie. The others began shedding their weapons. Sofia gaped in disbelief as they undressed. "What are you doing?"

Blondie shimmied from her jeans and rooted in her pack. Her skin was heavily tattooed, a stylized songbird on one shoulder. She held up a bar of soap for Sofia's perusal. "Bath time."

"Ohhh." Sofia averted her gaze but not before noticing Ben's sculpted pecs and abs. Bolts of lightning struck the ground outside, highlighting his tawny chest hair. Wicked scars on his side blemished the otherwise flawless contours of his physique. She pretended to find the floor tiles fascinating as the group went back outside, wearing nothing but their undergarments.

They took their weapons along and leaned them against the stonework, apparently unwilling to leave them with Sofia.

Thunder rumbled, making the windowpanes rattle. Raindrops bounced on the cement patio. The group lathered up, the deluge rinsing them clean. Ben's briefs clung to his firm backside. His thighs were corded and his calves finely muscled. Sofia squirmed. When he turned, she gasped as she got an eyeful of the outline of his impressive package.

What the fuck was she doing gawping? What if he saw?

Too late. As Sofia cut her eyes away, she registered Ben's amused smirk. Her skin tingled, flushed with embarrassment mingled with bone-melting desire. She backed away from the door, out of sight.

What is wrong with me?

Their mouths moved. They were talking, but Sofia couldn't puzzle out their words. Were they plotting something, or was she paranoid? What about the atlas on Daddy's desk with her notations? Blue parked in the garage?

"Horny idiot," Sofia whispered, chastising herself. She needed to keep her wits about her and guard her secrets instead of becoming a drooling feeble-minded simp. Revolver still in her waistband and her keyring in hand, she rushed to the den. Sofia stashed the atlas in a desk drawer under a pile of manila folders. What about her bedroom? No, she wouldn't concern herself with that room—there was nothing of importance there. Plus, it only bolted from the inside. The service door leading to the attached garage was at the end of the hall. Sofia locked the knob with the house key on her ring, along with the deadbolt.

She peeped into the dining room. The storm was letting up. The strangers were finishing their ablutions. Sofia tucked the keys under her bra strap and hastened to the linen closet across from the guest bath. Arms heaped with towels, she arrived back in the dining room as the group straggled in, dripping water.

"Thanks," Blondie muttered as she took a towel, apparently unbothered that her sports bra and underwear were plastered to her body. Perhaps modesty in the apocalypse was a frivolous pretension. Although Sofia credited herself as confident, she doubted she'd ever be at ease stripping down in front of others.

They all were gaunt and raw-boned, except Ben. He was broad-shouldered and barrel-chested. Solid. He'd evidently had access to proper nutrition. How had he managed that on the road?

There was something exceptional about him.

Sentience crept up her spine, tickling. Who was watching her so raptly? Sofia panned over everyone's faces. Kyle. He leered as he toweled off, giving extra attention to his crotch and making sure Sofia saw. Creep! She returned her gaze to the tile.

"I saw firewood behind the garage. That fireplace functional?" Ben asked, indicating the marble fireplace visible through the arched opening to the living room.

Sofia nodded. Glistening rivulets of water trickled down the column of Ben's neck. What was it about him that tugged at her? She could scarcely look away as he pulled his t-shirt over his head.

"I'll get a fire going," Ben said as he zipped his hoodie, "if I can get volunteers to help me bring in the wood."

Zac offered, "I will."

Tucker combed his fingers through his hair, slicking it back. He buckled his holster around his hips, lobbing Sofia, Blondie, and Cora a smarmy smile. "You ladies go rustle up some grub."

Fully dressed, Kyle eyed the drinks cart on the opposite side of the room. "Well, well, well. Lookie here, bro." He lifted an amber-tinted bottle. "We got us genu-wine French cognac."

"Jackpot," Tucker said, joining him. He picked up two cut-glass tumblers and blew the dust away.

Sofia squelched a protest. That pricey brandy was Daddy's, and it didn't seem right that the brothers help themselves without asking.

Cora sidled to Sofia and put a gentle hand on her forearm. "Let them have it. It'll keep them occupied."

Ben and Zac went outside, closing the French doors. As Tucker and Kyle walked past the women to go into the living room, Kyle smacked Blondie's butt. Blondie cringed. "You heard Tucker. Go make my grub, foxy."

Sofia shared glances with Cora. Cora lifted a shoulder. "Come on."

The window over the sink spilled gray light into the darkened kitchen. Blondie closed the pocket door to the dining room, complaining, "I can build a better fire than any of those guys. Why do we always get stuck with menial work? The division of labor fucking sucks."

"Best we choose our battles," Cora answered evenly as she opened cabinets. She asked Sofia, "You still have running water here?"

"Yeah, but I don't trust it for drinking. It's foul." She leaned a hip against the kitchen island, observing the two women. "I suppose we can boil it on the barbeque grill outside. To sterilize it? I've been drinking bottled water."

"You must've had a lot of it to last this long," Cora commented as she pulled a stockpot from the hanging rack. "Boiling the tap water should be enough to make it potable, but it's a pity we don't have a filter, too."

"Oh, we do! The house has a water filtration system," Sofia said, explaining, "because it's well water."

"Then we're okay. Do you have any bleach? We'll use tap water to wash the dishes after eating—we can add bleach to sanitize them."

"I'm sure there's a jug in the laundry room. Let me see." Sofia was happy to be assigned a task. Having a passel of people around after a year of solitude was peculiar. Surreal. She didn't know how to act or what to say.

The laundry room was off the kitchen, adjacent to the walk-in pantry. It was difficult to see in the windowless room. Sofia ran a hand along the detergents on the shelf above the washer. There it was—an economy size container of bleach. Sofia brought it back to the kitchen and sat it beside the sink as Blondie went into the pantry.

With efficient movements, Cora filled the pot using the filler faucet above the range. "This is a gas stove. Did you know you can light the burners with a match?"

Sofia shook her head, feeling stupid. "I didn't."

"That's okay. I just didn't want you to be lugging pots of water to the grill unnecessarily. You have matches? Ones on long sticks?"

"By the fireplace." Sofia went out to the living room. Kyle and Tucker sprawled on the sectional sofa, their bare feet on the coffee table. Tumblers discarded on a side table, Tucker took a swig of the brandy straight from the bottle then handed it to Kyle. Zac stacked logs on the grate. Ben twisted newspaper for kindling, his expression inscrutable.

"This wood's kinda damp," Zac said, worrying at his lip as he shoved a lock of hair from his eyes. "I don't know if it'll burn."

"It'll burn," Ben assured him quietly. "But it'll smoke."

"Uh, excuse me," Sofia said as she reached up to the mantle for the decorative tin of matches. She took a handful.

"Why don't you come set down on the couch and keep us company, sweetness?" Kyle wheedled, patting the sofa cushion.

Sofia sneered as she ambled by. *No thanks, asshat.*

Blondie had unearthed some boxes of penne and jars of pasta sauce from the pantry. Cora smiled when Sofia handed over the matches. "These'll work perfect. Watch."

She switched the burner on and struck a match, demonstrating how to ignite it. Blue flames caught and licked the bottom of the pot.

"How long should we let the water boil before adding the pasta?" Sofia asked Cora, but Blondie answered.

"At least a minute at a rolling boil, or we'll end up with the trots." She crossed her arms, her solemn gaze on Sofia while they waited for the water to heat. "I'm Lark."

"Nice to meet you," Sofia said.

Cora slouched against the counter. "We really appreciate your hospitality. Have you been here the whole time?"

"Yes," Sofia lied, heeding her intuition.

"You're clean. You've been warming water on the grill to wash?" Cora asked.

Sofia nodded. "It'll be easier doing it on the stove now."

"This house is a nice little hideaway," Lark mused. "The fence prevents Zs from getting in?"

"So far."

The water began to boil. Sofia counted to sixty under her breath. Cora sprinkled salt into the pot then poured in the penne. "Not many places are safe nowadays."

"I'll bet," Sofia said. Lark handed Cora a wooden spoon to stir the penne. Sofia asked Lark, "Is Tucker your boyfriend or Kyle?"

"Sort of," Lark replied in an evasive way, not meeting Sofia's gaze.

Sofia frowned, then comprehension dawned. They were *both* Lark's boyfriend. "Oh."

"Don't judge me with those big doe eyes of yours," Lark snapped. "You don't have a clue what it's like out there."

"I—"

"Not everyone has a fancy house in the country with a fence and unlimited food and water. Not everyone is privileged," Lark said bitterly. She stalked across the kitchen to the door that led to the side yard and went outside, banging the glass storm door.

"Whoa." Sofia spun to Cora where she pulled a colander down from the pot rack and set it in the sink. "What did I say?"

"Don't take it personal," Cora advised. "Lark's had it tougher than most."

Sofia put her hands up. Lark's venom smarted. "Should I... go apologize?"

"You didn't do anything wrong. Leave her be. She'll work out her snit at her own speed."

"But she doesn't have a weapon."

"She'll have a knife."

For several minutes, Sofia surveyed Cora. Inwardly, she wrestled with her emotions. Seeing the woman at her mother's stove triggered lots of flashbacks—Mama loved to cook. A lump formed in Sofia's windpipe. Tears stung her eyes. She longed for her parents. Needed their guidance. She felt ill-equipped to plot a course in this scary new world.

When the pasta was done, Cora drained it in the colander then poured it back into the pot. She added the jarred sauce to the pot, sprinkling herbs from the spice rack and letting it come up to temperature. "A hot meal sure is a blessing."

Sofia got bowls from the cupboard, setting them on the counter along with forks.

As if putting out feelers, Cora said, "This place may be a decent one for us to stay at a while."

Sofia wisely said nothing.

CHAPTER SEVEN

SOFIA LIT CANDLES FROM THE DINING ROOM, ARRANGING THEM ON an occasional table beside the pot of pasta. The group ate in front of the blazing fire, covered in blankets. Outside, the sky was overcast, smudged pearl-gray with undertones of pewter. At intervals, the rain pelted then tapered to a drizzle, but the violent wind never slackened. It whistled, buffeting the roof, sparking embers up the fireplace grate and into the chimney flue.

Sofia's *guests* scarfed their penne then heaped seconds into their bowls. Kyle and Tucker had made a significant dent in the bottle of cognac, which mellowed them. After eating, Ben drew the drapes over the windows, and they lounged, yawning.

"Any chance we can uncork some wine?" Cora asked Sofia. "There was Chianti on the cart."

"That's dry," Lark protested. She'd rejoined Cora and Sofia in the kitchen in time to serve the dinner, seemingly in an improved mood. Sofia hadn't said anything to her—she was prickly as a cactus, and Sofia didn't quite know how to approach her. "How about a white? Not overly sweet. A Riesling?"

Sofia smiled. Being cuddled up in front of the fire was cozy. Sitting there, it was almost believable that everything was normal. Sated and lids drooping with lethargy, she allowed pleasant memories to flood back. Slumber parties. Silly pranks. Giggling. Gossiping about boys. Buttered popcorn by the handfuls. She could almost imagine there had been no virus, no mass deaths, no zombies. That she was among friends. Almost. Cracking an eye open, she nodded. "Go ahead. Corkscrew's in the buffet."

Cora was soon back, handing a goblet to Sofia.

"What about me?" Zac asked from the club chair where he was under a quilt.

"You're too young," Sofia objected.

"I'm seventeen!"

"You're not much older than that yourself, are you, Sofia?" Ben asked drily from his own chair, waving a careless hand. "Let the kid have a glass. He's earned it."

After serving Zac his wine, Cora asked Ben, "What about you? Red or white?"

"Neither. One of us should remain sober."

Sofia sipped her Riesling—a vintage her parents had brought back from a trip to the Rhine. Even at room temperature it was crisp and delicious, tasting of pears and apples and summertime. "Cora mentioned she was Zac's neighbor in Crestview. Where are the rest of you from?"

"Our folks had a farm outside Mergenville," Tucker said, interlocking his knuckles and putting them behind his head. "Got run over with Zs in the early days."

"Wasn't enough of us left to fight 'em off," Kyle added. "Wasn't safe to stay there."

"So you became…" Sofia paused, trying to think of the right word. She had to keep reminding herself which brother was which—Tucker was the shorter of the two, but that didn't help when they were seated. Their personalities were equally indistinguishable and equally unpleasant. Even their voices were similar. They were two sides of a coin. "All of you became… nomads?"

"Essentially," Cora conceded. "Not ideal, at least not for me.

I'm old and riddled with arthritis. I'd rather stay put. But when you have Zs breaking down your door and chasing you..."

Sofia murmured, "At least you had company."

Cora, who sat parallel to Sofia on the sectional, examined her. "Zac and I were fortunate to have each other, to be able to team up. Fact is, neither one of us would've made it if we hadn't. What's your story, hon?"

Her stomach curdled, the pasta weighty as a sizzling boulder. Sofia wondered if perhaps it had been a mistake to broach the subject of histories. She wasn't sure she was an adept liar— they'd likely see right through her. She must stay vague but as close to the truth as possible. "I was a sophomore at St. Belfridge University in Henley, and I was home for spring break—"

"College co-ed, huh?" Kyle winked. "Sorority girl?"

Tucker chortled. "Part of the Omega-Mu."

Kyle enunciated a drawn-out exaggerated "Moo," and the two cackled uproariously.

"Cut it out," Ben snapped, which muzzled them.

"God, you guys are assholes," Zac grumbled, throwing an apologetic look at Sofia. "Sorry."

Doing her best to disregard the brothers, Sofia said, "I was heading back to school—my parents left for a cruise earlier in the week—when they phoned me from the ship. My dad said to lock myself in. So I did."

Zac sat up straighter in his chair. "You've *never* been outside the fence?"

"I did walk along the highway," Sofia admitted. "Just to see, you know?"

Lark sat her empty goblet on the coffee table. "You come across Zs?"

Sofia nodded.

"The ones nowadays are more savvy. Advanced. At first, they could only hear and smell us. Now, some can make out shapes, too. Evolution, I assume," Cora said. "Still, the first time you gotta dispatch one is always the toughest."

"Especially if it was someone you loved," Zac replied, his eyes focused on the fire.

Cora said, "We've all had to do things to survive, Zac."

"Anyone have to bludgeon their two-year-old to prevent him from murdering you, like I did?" Lark demanded in a harsh tone. "That wasn't particularly *fun*."

There was a moment of silence, then Cora gently reprimanded her with a soft, "Lark."

"You said I should talk about it. Tackle my trauma."

"Not like this."

"I'll book an appointment with my shrink tomorrow, shall I?" Lark whirled to Sofia, her lips contorted in a facsimile of a smile. "Cora was a therapist. Old habits and all that crap."

Sofia remembered the toddler in the thicket, and thought of Mama and Daddy. If her parents had become bloodthirsty Zs intent on massacring her, would she have had the courage to put them down? Would biological instinct for self-preservation have been enough to spur her into action? Shuddering, she bit her lip. "I'm convinced everyone I knew is dead. That's why I was so taken aback seeing Zac."

"You don't think your folks are alive?" Cora asked her.

"My gut says they aren't."

"No other family?"

"Not really. You?"

Cora replied, "I have—I had—two children. They were both happily married. I had four grandchildren. Like you, I'd know if any of them had survived."

"If the Z virus didn't kill them, the Zs did," Zac said, matter-of-fact.

Sofia toyed with a loose thread on the woven throw over her knees. "So you don't find many survivors?"

"Few and far between," Ben said. He stood abruptly. "Nightfall is coming. I suggest we bring in more wood and stack it next to the fireplace so it dries. Then figure out where everyone plans to sleep. I'll take the first one-hour watch shift. Who wants the second shift?"

"I can take it," Sofia offered.

It was only later when she and Lark went to wash dishes that Sofia realized Ben was the only person who didn't share anything about his past—he'd skillfully evaded volunteering a single shred of personal information.

CHAPTER EIGHT

"You know, I owe you an apology."

Sofia finished drying the bowl with a tea towel and waited expectantly for Lark to speak.

"You're a nice girl," she said with a shrug, not meeting Sofia's eyes. "You don't deserve to be my punching bag."

"*Girl*? Aren't we... similar in age?" It wasn't the only time somebody had remarked that Sofia was young. Did she give the impression of naïveté? Of immaturity? The idea disturbed her. Sofia may not have rambled across the countryside slaying Zs like a badass from a disaster movie, but she'd weathered her own storms, hadn't she? Lark's laissez-faire dismissal irked her.

"I got a couple years on you. Anyway, I tend to be rough on people." She faced Sofia, unflinching. "I know it's toxic."

Sofia scanned her. Lark possessed well-formed features and an hourglass figure. One could even posit she was gorgeous. Everything about her was youthful, except her time-worn hazel eyes. "I'm sorry about your son."

Lark nodded, sniffed. Her hands shook as she passed Sofia another bowl to dry. "A woman next door operated an unlicensed daycare. It wasn't the best place for Ty, but she didn't charge much. I was working so many doubles, I was just relieved to have a place for him. He contracted the virus there. The kids got sick one after another—like dominoes falling."

"I-I'm sorry," Sofia said again, her own eyes misting at the raw grief etched on Lark's face. Words were inadequate. Her sadness was too intimate. Sofia felt like an intruder.

"Didn't mean to tell you that. I don't want sympathy. Not from anyone. I—" Lark wiped a tear away with her forearm, her chin quivering. "The point is—what's done is done. Just because you had it easy doesn't mean I should treat you shitty."

"*Had it easy*? You don't know anything about me—"

"Look, can we let it go? I know it's not your fault you come from money any more than it's my fault I was born into poverty."

"Lark—"

Cora poked her head in the kitchen. "You two almost done in here? We need to get sleeping arrangements sorted out."

"Yep," Lark said, pulling the sink plug and drying her hands on her jeans. Before Sofia could say anything further, Lark pivoted on her heel and followed Cora.

In the living room, firewood was piled in a tall row beside the fireplace. Sofia asked, "Is that all the wood from behind the garage?"

"That's it," Ben said. "Thankfully, warmer weather's coming."

Cora gathered the blankets, folding them and placing them on an arm of the sectional. "Sofia, how many guest rooms do you have?"

"There are two, plus my room and the master but—"

Lark interrupted, speaking quickly, "I want to sleep with Cora."

That garnered a reaction from Kyle and Tucker. Sofia rolled her eyes at their guffaws and rude comments. She couldn't blame Lark for avoiding sharing a bed with either one of them. She nibbled at the inside of her cheek. "I was saying... I don't feel comfortable with anyone using my parents' bed."

"That's alright," Ben said with a casual hand gesture. "I'll take this sofa, and Kyle and Tucker can have the other guest room. I prefer to be here. That way I can keep an eye on things through the night."

"I thought we were taking watch shifts?" Sofia asked, one eyebrow raised.

"Everyone will." Ben's lips curved into a grin. Warmth sprouted in Sofia's solar plexus, and her pulse jackhammered. She couldn't resist returning his grin.

"I'll sleep here, too," Zac said.

"There's a pullout in the den that can be all yours, Zac. The bedrooms are down there." Sofia pointed to the hallway, and everyone headed to the other wing, leaving Ben and Sofia alone.

"Go to bed. I'll wake you in an hour."

"Why bother? I'll hang out with you until it's my turn. You have to tell me what's involved in keeping watch anyway."

"It's simple." He bent to rifle through his pack, which was beside the sofa, and pulled out a book. "Most of it I was planning to sit here and read."

"What's that?"

Ben held it up so she could skim the cover. Sofia strained to make out the writing. *Guide to Alcohol Fuel Conversion for Gas-Powered Engines.*

"Looks boring. Plus, hard on your eyes trying to read by candlelight."

"Lucky to have candles." He sat the book on the folded blankets. "I'll step outside every fifteen minutes and listen for anything untoward—starting with the beginning of my shift. Want to tag along?"

Sofia trailed him to the French doors in the dining room that led to the patio. "At least there's a moon."

Ben took hold of his bow. "Damn straight. Nights when it's pitch black? Those are the scariest ones. How can I fight what I don't see?"

Sofia had expected it to be chilly outside, but it was balmy.

The wind whipped her hair into her eyes. She pulled the elastic from her hair and redid her ponytail. The sky was starless, but the moon threw Ben's profile into relief, blurring the edges of his square jawline. "What if Zs get into the yard?"

"We hightail it inside, batten the hatches, and hope to hell we make it to daybreak. By that time we'll be able to see. Or they'll have lost interest and wandered away."

Awareness tinkled as Sofia sensed Ben's gaze on her. Her breath exited her lungs, painful and thick, but her nerve endings vibrated. Being near him made her vitally *alive*. Fingers itching to touch him, she balled her hands into fists. What was it about him that pulled her in? Did his blood run as swift and hot as hers?

He whispered, "Why do I feel you have secrets, kiddo?"

Kiddo? Well fuck. Friend-zoned. Sofia pursed her lips. It was confirmation that she was no different than Zac in Ben's estimation. She probably looked ten with her hair pulled back. Her baggy sweats were frumpy, too. She narrowed her eyes. "Don't we all have secrets? Why don't you tell me some of yours, Ben?"

CHAPTER NINE

Ben chuckled. "You'll find I hold mine close to my chest, kid."

"I'm *not* a kid," Sofia interjected. It came out shriller than she intended.

"You are to me."

So, was he acknowledging the attraction humming between them but letting her know from the outset that he wouldn't entertain it? Sofia was baffled—she'd always been able to read when men fancied her, specifically ones who didn't feel it was socially acceptable to get a hard-on for a fat girl. But who cared about conventions in the apocalypse? What would he do if she planted a kiss on him? Too chickenshit to try, Sofia chewed a nail and stared meditatively into the darkness instead, as if her questions could be answered there.

From a nearby tree, an owl hooted. The wind tossed a tendril of hair into Sofia's eyes. Ben was a puzzle she wanted to solve. Tucking the strands behind her ear, she cleared her throat and said, "How about a little *you show me yours and I'll show you mine*?"

For a second, Ben was still, then he broke into laughter. "What?"

"I tell you an interesting tidbit about my life pre-Armageddon, then you tell me one."

"*Quid pro quo?*" Ben shook his head, but the light from the moon hit his face, revealing his smile. "My life was humdrum. You wouldn't be riveted."

Sofia slumped against the house, cocking one knee and putting the sole of her sneaker on the stone wall. "Why don't you let me be the judge of that?"

"If you insist," he said, shrugging. "I... grew up on a farm. My father was a gentleman farmer, but the entire family helped run it. See, boring."

"What's a *gentleman farmer*?"

"It just means that my father farmed for pleasure rather than profit. He had success in business and retired early, buying acreage and farming it. My mother practiced law. Estate planning and wills. And your folks?"

"My dad was in business, too. He owned warehouses. My mother came to the US from South America, and she worked for him. That's how they met."

"You were an only child?"

"Yeah."

"Happy home?"

Sofia nodded. "Was yours?"

"The best. A big family." Ben's voice turned cynical when he added, "Made me want the same for myself someday."

"Not anymore?"

"No."

Sofia wanted to probe Ben for more, but the set of his spine told her now wasn't the time. "You know I was a student. What did *you* do... before?"

"I was an attorney. Public defender."

"Really?"

"You're shocked," Ben said lightly, his eyes searching her.

"N-no. It's... noble. Kinda fits. You seem articulate. Educated. Wily."

He snorted. "I've heard charming, boyishly handsome, and affable but never that."

"The way you look at people... you're trying to figure out what makes them tick."

A cloud drifted in front of the moon, shadowing Ben's face and obscuring his expression. "Huh. Amazing how we never fully recognize how others perceive us." He hesitated. "Aren't you curious what I see when I look at you?"

Sofia's breath caught. She swallowed around the lump in her esophagus. "What?"

"A pretty girl. Big-eyed. Innocent. Comes across as coy, but she's also wily."

"Is she?" Sofia asked weakly, heart skipping.

"As she should be. Where'd you get your street smarts, Sofia?"

She chose her words with care. "My parents doted on me, but they taught me a lot, too. My mother had been undocumented before she met my dad. She traveled all the way from Ecuador by herself when she was much younger than I am now. And Dad... he had the ability to get along with all types. He was personable. Approachable."

"I can see those traits in you. You're easy to open up to. God knows I haven't talked this much about myself in a long time. Did you have a lot of friends?"

"I did. But not many close ones. I had more online than in real life."

"Social media?"

"Uh huh. They were more followers than friends."

"Followers?"

"I had almost five hundred thousand at one time, but I was taking a hiatus. Trying to reconnect with friends from high school—actual people. The trolls were really tearing me down. It fucked with my head."

"Five hundred *thousand* followers? How'd you manage that?"

The disbelief in Ben's voice caused Sofia to giggle. "It wasn't that many. Some influencers had millions." She lifted a shoulder. "I posted videos of what I was wearing that day. Did makeup tutorials. I advocated for fat acceptance. Later, for animal rights. People admired my confidence. Most people anyway."

"Keyboard warriors got ugly?"

"Yeah. I'm sure plenty were bots, but there were some legit posters. Mostly guys. Some females, too. Catty little bitches. They didn't like that I wasn't ashamed to be a big girl. That's alright though. Confidence is alluring."

Ben scratched his eyebrow. "Oh?"

"Mama always said there's a lid for every pot. Why should I be embarrassed that I have an insatiable appetite for food and cock?"

Ben *rowred* and wiggled his eyebrows. "Who am I to argue with that?"

Sofia laughed. "There's that trademark charm."

"You are full of surprises, Sofia. By the way," Ben shifted, propping his arm against the house, "I'm impressed with the way you handled Kyle and Tucker."

"My skills were honed over years of interacting with twatwaffles. Pisses them off when they don't get the reaction they want."

"The brothers needle new people. Push boundaries. You know, adolescent garbage."

"They're bullies," Sofia sneered.

"I'll give them their due. In the three or so weeks since we teamed up, they've shown merit—they keep the group fed. They know how to hunt and fish. And they're valuable fighters. Hand-to-hand with Zs? Highly skilled."

"That's enough to keep them around? They're repugnant."

"I tolerate them for Lark."

Hmm. Does he have a thing for Lark? Sofia felt a zip of jealousy at the thought. Striving for nonchalance, she said, "Lark's attractive."

45

"What does that have to do with anything? I care more about a person's character than their appearance."

"But it sure doesn't hurt, does it?"

Ben dismissed Sofia's comment with a wave of his hand. "She's rough around the edges but..."

"At first, I thought she had a chip on her shoulder. Now, I empathize with her. She's obviously working through shit. I think I like her."

"To coin *my* mother? Lark's a good egg."

"Zac and Cora apparently are, too. Jury's still out on Kyle and Tucker, counselor," Sofia replied, smothering a yawn.

Ben stiffened, and she copied him, listening. The French doors cracked open. Voice hoarse from sleep, Cora said, "It's got to be past time for me to keep watch."

Sofia's eyes widened. Did she and Ben just chat for over two hours?

CHAPTER TEN

Sofia sat up. Sun streamed in the window. It had to be mid-morning. Why hadn't anyone woken her?

Lazing in bed for a minute, she contemplated her and Ben's conversation the night before. Sofia thirsted for more, guessing what she'd learned about him was merely the tip of the iceberg.

She padded into the ensuite and washed. Running a brush through her hair, she decided to leave it loose. Finger tapping her lower lip, Sofia considered the rows of clothes in her walk-in closet. No baggy sweatsuit today. She pulled on a ruffled blouse in a shade of apricot that flattered her olive-toned complexion, along with a pair of skinny jeans.

Revolver tucked into her waistband at the small of her back and her keychain in her pocket, Sofia unlocked her bedroom door and stepped into the carpeted hall. Voices floated from the living room.

The group was seated in the same furniture as the night before—Ben and Zac in club chairs and Tucker, Kyle, Cora, and Lark on the sectional. Dirty dishes were stacked on the coffee table. The drapes were open, allowing dappled sunshine into the room.

"There you are," Cora said warmly when she caught sight of

Sofia in the entryway. "Thought we'd let you sleep in. We don't punch a time clock nowadays."

"Rice and beans on the stove," Lark added.

Sofia nodded, feeling Ben's gaze on her. She turned her head and met his eyes. In the bright light, they glittered like sapphires. He smiled at her, and her cheeks heated. Hiding her own smile, she asked, "What's on the agenda for today?"

"Mister Industrious over there wants to take advantage of the weather," Kyle groused, hitching a thumb toward Ben.

Tucker said, "We'd rather kick back with a bottle of booze. Instead, we'll be setting up snares."

"Snares?" Sofia asked blankly.

Ben said, "For rabbit. I'll be deer hunting."

"I'm going with Ben," Zac piped up from his chair.

"And Lark and I will be hunting, too. For berries. Probably just strawberries since it's too early for raspberries and blueberries," Cora said. "You can come with us. Do you have any old ice cream pails? Even grocery sacks will work."

AN HOUR LATER, Sofia locked the gate behind them, and the group split, going in opposite directions. The air was perfumed with damp soil and rough vegetation. Sofia cautioned, "Be careful. There are snakes."

"We've become experts in foraging." Cora raked her machete through the tall weeds as they combed the forest just out of eyeshot of the house. "Strawberry patches will be the easiest to find, but we'll watch for morels and wild asparagus, too."

"Morels? Oh, right. Mushrooms," Sofia murmured, her eyes on the horizon for any indication of Zs. "Lark, are you sure you're okay without a weapon? Maybe you should've taken that golf club I offered."

Today Lark's long blonde hair was piled on the top of her

head in a messy bun, accentuating the graceful line of her neck. "Got my switchblade lashed to my ankle."

"But using a knife you have to let the creatures—the Zs—get super close," Sofia argued.

"I had an ax, but the handle broke when we were fighting off the Zs the other day. I'll be fine—we don't come across swarms of them anymore. Just scattered ones."

"Have you noticed rain disorients them?" Cora asked.

"Spraying a fire extinguisher in their face does, too. That was what I did. Then I used a golf club to bash its head in," Sofia told them. "But lugging a fire extinguisher, even a small one, gets old."

"Canny of you not using the gun. They're only for emergencies," Cora said, shuddering. "I'd only use one if I hadn't anything else."

Sofia asked Lark, "Don't you like guns either?"

"I don't have a problem with them, but put yours away. This ain't the OK Corral." Lark nodded at the revolver in Sofia's grip. "You fire that and any Zs in the vicinity will melt outta the woodwork."

Sofia stuck the revolver back into her waistband. "But Kyle and Tucker are armed to the teeth."

"Kyle and Tucker have micro pricks," Lark drawled, and Cora snickered.

Cora glimpsed at Sofia where she straggled behind her and Lark. "They know better than to shoot willy-nilly. They'd find themselves in a heap of trouble."

"Motherlode!" Lark pointed to a dewy ditch with knee-high green stalks.

"Asparagus?" Sofia asked.

"Correct." Cora descended the shallow bank. "We've been eating it a lot lately, but we're mighty grateful for it. We'll harvest enough for two days' worth now. We can always come back later for more."

They filled Cora's ice cream pail then continued on, seeking strawberries but mindful not to stray too far from the house. They found a patch a short distance from the ditch. Soon, Sofia's bucket was full. "Do you really think we need this many berries?"

"You've seen the way the guys pack it away." Cora appraised the sky, swabbing perspiration from her face.

"No mushrooms," Lark said, "but I give up for today. I'm hungry."

"So am I," Cora replied. "Sun's high in the sky. We need to meet back up at the gate."

Tucker and Kyle waited for them, lounging against an elm near the security fence. Kyle chewed on a blade of grass. The bowl in the crook of his elbow was mounded with morels and strawberries, a handful of aromatic chives across the top. Sofia smelled onion from where she stood.

Tucker whooped, "We're gonna eat like fuckin' kings tonight!"

Two figures emerged from the woods. Sofia said, "Ben and Zac. No deer."

"Not out long enough," Tucker replied.

Kyle straightened, throwing the grass blade on the ground and starting for the gate. "We'll check our snares tomorrow. Expect we'll get some rabbits."

"There are tins of luncheon ham in the pantry. If we pan fry them, we can sauté the mushrooms and asparagus in the grease. Finish with a sprinkle of chives," Cora said, and Sofia's stomach growled.

Ben adjusted his bow and put his palms up in concession as he and Zac approached. "The only thing we saw was a lady Z. Sorry."

Sofia's mouth parted. "A lady Z?"

"Ben took care of her," Zac said, offhand. "No biggie."

When they entered the house, Tucker beelined for the drinks cart. "Tequila or rum, bro?"

"Tequila."

Lark rolled her eyes and took the bowl from Kyle before trailing Cora into the kitchen. Ben called after them, "I'll cook."

"Sofia," Zac asked, "is it alright if I read one of your dad's books? There's a Sir Arthur Conan Doyle on the bookshelf in the den."

Sofia volleyed him a quick smile. "Sure. Help yourself."

Leaving the brothers at the dining room table, Sofia went into the kitchen where Ben had lit a stove burner. Cora rinsed mushrooms in water she'd sterilized the day before while Lark snapped the woody stalks from the asparagus spears.

"What can I do?" Sofia asked.

Ben said, "Open the ham and slice it up."

After completing their tasks, Cora and Lark sat at the breakfast bar. They'd found a deck of cards in a drawer and played gin rummy. Sofia planted a hip against the counter and watched wordlessly as Ben cooked. He seemed completely at ease as he sautéed the asparagus and added a dash of pepper from the spice rack. "Any chance it'd be okay if I borrow a razor? I'm not a beard guy." He swished his wrist against the wiry golden hairs of his scruff for effect.

"There's likely a razor in the master bath. I was thinking... there's no reason to enshrine my parents' bedroom. You may as well sleep there. If any of my dad's clothes fit, they're yours. It's what he would want." Sofia turned to address Cora and Lark, "Maybe you can use my mom's stuff?"

"Fresh clothes would be a blessing, but are you sure, hon?" Cora asked as she put a card down.

Ignoring a pang of sorrow, Sofia gave a slight nod.

"Soup's on," Ben said. "Who's dishing up?"

After eating, the group loafed in the living room, replete.

"Tomorrow I'll fix rabbit stew," Tucker said, yawning. "It's my specialty."

"Don't count your chickens," Ben drawled. "We may be feasting on tuna casserole instead."

"I have an excellent hunch about the snares," Cora said. "The flour in the pantry has bugs, but there's an unopened packet of biscuit mix only three months out of date. I'll make 'em to go with the stew."

Sofia's gaze bounced between her guests. Life now seemed consumed with procuring meals. She was about to open her mouth to comment on that when Zac asked, "How about a song, Lark?"

Lark's fair cheeks flooded with rosy color.

Cora coaxed, "The one Patsy Cline sang… you know. The one about seeing pyramids and silver planes and tropic isles?"

"You Belong to Me," Lark said.

"Come on," Zac cajoled.

Lark waggled her hand. "Alright, alright." Taking a breath, she launched into a poignant folk-rendition of the song. Her voice was an evocative vibrato and achingly exquisite. The lyrics hit Sofia like a sledgehammer. Tears sprang to her eyes. She thought of Daddy and Mama and how alone she was without them. Blinking away the moisture, her throat clogged with emotion, Sofia attempted indifference.

When Lark finished singing, they applauded. Tucker passed her the bottle of tequila, "Here, songbird."

Lark took a swig and gave it back. Kyle stood, lifted his arms over his head and stretched languidly, saying to Lark, "How about you and me head into the bedroom for a *nap?*"

The way he said it made his intentions clear—what he wanted had nothing to do with napping. Lark lowered her eyes, her posture displaying reluctance. "Now?"

"Yup. Hop to it."

Zac lumbered to his feet, protesting, "Hey—"

Kyle wheeled, jabbing him in the breastbone with a stubby index finger. Zac fell back into his chair. "Mind your business, Jet Li."

Sofia's intestines twisted as she took in the scene unfolding before her. She'd always had a healthy libido, but even after a yearlong dry spell, Sofia couldn't imagine sleeping with the brothers. How could Lark stand doing it? "Hold on. You don't have to do anything you don't want to, Lark."

"She knows the score," Kyle said. His brows lifted, he gave Lark a look that challenged her to refuse.

Lark seemed to shrink. A mournful expression splashed across her face, but it was fleeting. It was replaced with abject resignation. "It's fine. I'll go."

"No, it's not *fine*," Sofia argued.

Cora reached over and placed a hand on Sofia's forearm. "Lark's an adult. She's got to make her own choices."

"He's not making it a choice," Sofia snarled. She got up. "Coercion isn't consent. Lark—"

"*I said I'm fine*," Lark retorted, her hazel eyes wrathful. "I don't need anyone to fight my battles for me, princess."

Sofia swiveled to Ben. Mouth compressed, he shook his head. Dismayed, Sofia dropped back to the sofa. Her hands shook. She clasped them in her lap.

Lark went to Kyle, lasering everyone in place with a defiant glower. Kyle laughed, triumphant. He grabbed Lark around the waist possessively, his hand sliding up to cup her breast. She jostled him away, muttering, "Let's just get this over with."

Sofia watched in horror as Tucker stood, tequila bottle in his grip. He licked his lips in an exaggerated way. "I love a spit roast for dessert."

Lark paled, but she permitted the brothers to lead her toward the hall to their bedroom.

CHAPTER ELEVEN

Outrage choking her, Sofia looked from Zac to Cora to Ben. They said nothing. Zac and Cora glanced away, but Ben held her gaze. Sofia smacked the sofa cushion. "How can you let them do this to her?"

"You don't think we've been through this before, Sofia?" Ben asked.

"I don't know, Ben. Have you?" Sofia bit out through gritted teeth.

"The answer is yes. Yes, we have," Ben replied calmly.

Zac sighed. "We don't like it. But what can we do?"

"You were witness to how antagonistic Lark was when you interceded," Cora pointed out, her expression hinting at her distress. "When we've spoken on her behalf before, she digs her heels in. *I'm fine* is her standard comeback."

"Lark's a realist. Unfortunately, it's how things work now—"

Sofia whirled on Ben. "Come on. It's how things have always worked, isn't it? If Lark said no to them, would you have her back?"

"Of course. But she didn't say no."

"Sofia." Cora put her fingertips on Sofia's arm. "Lark has been very transparent about her wishes."

Blood rushing in her ears, Sofia shrugged Cora's hand off. "An idiot could tell that she didn't want to go in there! How can you condone rape?"

Uninvited memories flashed. Shane throwing Sofia on his ratty couch. Backhanding her, then putting the tip of his knife to her clavicle. Whispering in her ear that if she didn't shut up and comply he'd slit her from ear to ear. Lip busted open, Sofia had gagged on the coppery taste of blood. She'd shut her eyes. Allowed her mind to retreat.

Strangling a sob, Sofia lurched to her feet. She staggered her way through the dining room and exited the kitchen door to the side yard, hyperventilating.

Sagging to the concrete stair, she put her head in her hands, then remembered she ought to keep an eye out in case any Zs had breached the fence. Bleakly, she deliberated if death was preferable to this hell. Maybe it would be an escape.

There was the creak of the door opening. Ben lowered beside Sofia, extending his jean-clad legs and intersecting them at the ankles.

Sofia sniffled, shooting him a blistering look. "Isn't it the responsibility of the strong to protect the weak?"

Ben smiled, but he seemed morose. "It's been a long time since I've met someone so idealistic."

"Idealistic? Is that a diplomatic way of saying naïve?"

"It's refreshing." He worked a hand at the back of his neck, sucking air between his teeth. "However, not everything is black and white, Sofia."

"Shit like that is. It always will be, for me."

"Fair enough. What do you want to do?"

Suddenly deflated, Sofia bit her lip, studying him. The sun was setting, ushering pinks and oranges to turn Ben's skin and hair to gold and emphasizing fine wrinkles around his eyes. He was smoking hot. Why did he have to be honorable, too? It would be easier to fight her attraction if he were a jackass like Kyle and Tucker.

The overgrowth muffled everything except the buzz of cicadas, insulating them from the outside world. Seconds dripped into minutes. Their gazes dueled. What *could* she do?

Her voice knotted, Sofia whispered, "I'll talk to Lark."

TUCKER AND KYLE sauntered into the living room wearing smug expressions. Kyle had the nearly empty tequila bottle. Lark surfaced later, her face flushed, hair mussed, and eyes vacant. The tension in the air was like encroaching fog. Weighty and oppressive. In unspoken agreement, everyone pretended nothing had happened. Little was said. By candlelight, they read old magazines or dealt solitaire.

When Lark went into the kitchen for a drink of water, Sofia tailed her, closing the pocket door behind them. With nightfall, the room was swathed in shadows. Sofia put her hands out and used the wall to guide her to the breakfast bar, where she took a seat on a stool.

"Oh, here we go," Lark said caustically as she dipped a cup in the tepid pot of water on the range. "I'm not in the mood for a sermon from you."

"I can make them leave, Lark."

She snorted. "You and what army?"

"They can take whatever food we have left and be on their merry way. You don't need them to survive. *We* don't."

"Don't underestimate them."

"What's their hold on you? I don't understand."

Lark slammed her cup on the counter. "It doesn't matter if you understand!"

Scalp prickling, Sofia took a breath and charged forward before she lost her nerve. "I was raped a few months into my second semester of college."

The words hovered between them, then Lark groaned, coming to join her at the breakfast bar.

"I met him on a dating site—an actual *dating* site, not a hookup app," Sofia said stiltedly. "We went for coffee and hit it off. He invited me back to his place. Once he had me inside… it was like Jekyll and Hyde." She snapped her fingers though the way they wouldn't cooperate made it difficult. "Flipping a switch. A different person."

"Christ."

"He locked me in. Took my purse. My car keys and phone were in it. When he was done, he released me, but not before threatening me and my family."

"I am sorry," Lark whispered.

"All I could do was comply. Is that how you felt earlier?"

"Our situations aren't equivalent. Not in the fucking least."

"Aren't they?"

"I can refuse any damn time."

Sofia didn't bother to disguise her incredulity when she huffed, "Sure, Lark. I believe that."

"I can!"

"Then why didn't you tonight? Because I know you didn't want to be *spit-roasted* by those two assclowns!"

Lark stuck her chin out, not answering.

"You're stubborn as hell."

"Just keep your goddamn nose out, princess. You'll only make it worse."

"Alright. You're on your own."

"That's the way I like it."

CHAPTER TWELVE

THE FOLLOWING DAY, KYLE AND TUCKER WENT TO THE LOCATION where they'd set their snares, returning with three rabbits. Kyle skinned them, and Tucker prepared stew. Cora mixed biscuit dough. Lark sat poolside in the backyard, writing in a journal. When she came inside to eat, she was polite but aloof. Sofia granted her space, not wanting to disrupt their shaky truce.

Days melded together as the group lolled between the forays for berries and veggies. Sofia dug out board games from the hall closet, and they played Monopoly and Parcheesi to pass the hours. Nightly, she and Ben stood watch outside together, often with their backs against the house in comfortable silence. The others seemed content with the living arrangement. Perhaps it was because they hadn't been able to linger in one place up until then, but the lack of permanence chafed Sofia. They were in limbo. No promises had been verbalized about sticking together, and she certainly didn't trust them enough to confide about the warehouse.

One night a week later, everyone except Ben and Sofia had retired to their rooms, lending a sleepy feel to the home. The living room was lit by a single pillar—they'd begun to conserve candles—and it wasn't cold enough for a fire. The muted light blurred the edges of the room and camouflaged the dust. Sofia straightened the couch cushions and took dirty cups to the kitchen sink while Ben fetched his textbook from his bedroom.

When he hadn't returned by the time she'd poured them glasses of room temperature sun tea, Sofia went to see what had delayed him. The hall was lengthy and windowless. Using the wall, she navigated to the master bedroom, finding Ben at the bed, his backpack on the cedar trunk at the footboard. Head bent, he peered at something in his hand. The object radiated a green glow over the contours of his profile.

"What's that?" Sofia asked, coming to his side.

If Ben was startled, he didn't reveal it. He lifted the object for her perusal.

"A watch? Why would—"

"Curious about the date." Ben grinned and took his finger from the tiny button mechanism. The display went black.

"Why?"

"Curiosity isn't reason enough?"

Sofia thought of her hash marks on the concrete warehouse wall. His excuse was plausible but flimsy. She narrowed her eyes. "What's the date?"

Moonbeams through the window silhouetting him, he leaned to put the watch in his pack and get his book. "We're already into June, can you believe it? C'mon, let's go outside. I don't feel like reading yet."

Why was Sofia's intuition niggling at her? She thrust her suspicions away, saying, "Alright."

When they were seated outside with their tea, Sofia tipped her head back and pondered the star-studded sky.

"Silently, one by one, in the infinite meadows of heaven, blossomed the lovely stars, the forget-me-nots of the angels," Ben murmured.

Lava flowed through Sofia's veins, puddling in her loins and throbbing dully. Lust. She squirmed and took a drink of tea then cleared her throat. "Did you write that?"

He was amused. "I wish I were so talented. Longfellow."

"The poet?"

"The one and only."

"Beautiful."

Now Ben was the one to clear his throat. He set his tea on the patio. "Can I say something?"

Sofia nodded.

"You know that expression *cabin fever*? I think you've got it, kid."

"Don't call me that."

"Sorry, forgot. Listen, you've been isolated here, so it's understandable if you're... itchy."

"Apparently I'm not proficient in concealing my thoughts."

He sucked his teeth. "Want to discuss it?"

"It—it's just... is *this* the way we live now? Lying around doing nothing once we have our next meal or two arranged?"

"Monotonous, right? But being transient that's precisely what people pray for. Someday *you* might."

Sofia nodded.

"What exactly do you want, Sofia?"

I want you. Her words evaporated on her tongue before she could utter them. Instead she asked, "What do you mean?"

"For the future."

"Just—more. I know how lucky I've been... here. Is it wrong to yearn for more?"

"No, of course not."

"I had this vision in my head of what it would be like when I found other survivors," she confessed, faltering.

"Ah. So that's it. We aren't living up to your expectations. Did you fantasize we'd sit around the campfire and roast weenies and marshmallows on twigs? Make s'mores? Sing *Kumbaya*?"

"Shut up."

"I can learn the lyrics for you."

Sofia put her glass down and swatted his arm.

After a moment, he became serious, urging, "Tell me."

"It's stupid." Pausing, she said, "I'd hoped to regain some of what was lost. To start over. I missed having people around... a community... work beyond subsistence. Work that fed the soul."

"Self-actualization?"

"Yeah, sure. Maslow's hierarchy crap. It wouldn't be famous if there wasn't something to it, right?"

"Careful, you sound like a college student."

"Very funny, counselor. You think I am romanticizing?"

"Maybe." Ben lifted a shoulder, sought Sofia's eyes, a gentle smile playing on his lips. "But the world needs more dreamers, especially these days. Don't you *ever* fuckin' change. It'd break my heart."

Maybe it was the way the stars shone on his face, turning the curve of his cheekbone into finely carved ivory or how he smelled of musk and moonlight. Sofia's inhibitions loosened. She leaned over and planted her lips on his.

That was all it took. Ben seized her and slammed her hard against his torso so she straddled him, his fingertips snaking up her spine to cup her head and knot in her hair. With a groan, Ben traced her lower lip with his tongue, then plunged it in her mouth, the tip tangling with hers. Sofia ran her palms down his muscled abs, searching for the hem of his shirt. He tugged her hair just enough to make her scalp tingle, and she arched her back, moaning as he bit the exposed expanse of her neck.

Sofia's soft cry brought Ben to his senses. Exhaling a breath, he shook his head. He gasped, "Fuck... What am I doing?"

The sizable ridge of Ben's erection strained his jeans. She ground her crotch hungrily against it. "Don't stop."

He gritted his teeth, cupping his hands over hers where they roamed his taut flesh. "I'm too old for you, Sofia."

"No, you're not," she panted against his mouth, gyrating her hips. "And I don't care anyway. I need this."

With a guttural grunt, he slipped from under Sofia, and she

tumbled to the patio. Springing to his feet, Ben raked a hand through his hair, leaving it in spikes. "I am. Not only am I ten years older than you... I-I'm in love with another woman. It's not fair to you. I apologize, Sofia."

He went inside.

Sofia shakily smoothed her blouse and tightened her jaw. Mortified by Ben's rejection, she blinked back hot tears. She wasn't going to let him see her bawl, dammit.

With as much dignity as she could, Sofia got up, opening the French doors. Ben was in the living room, his gaze on his textbook. She strode past him and down the hall to her room. Locking the door, she stripped her clothes and got into bed, putting her gun under her pillow.

She swiped at the tears tracking down her face and into her ears. Sniffled. "Cool it. No man is worth bawling over," she whispered fiercely to the empty room.

Restive, Sofia eventually dozed. Scratching in the hall woke her. The moon was gone, gray mist in its place. It was hours from sunrise. Who was in the hall? Could it be Ben? Had he changed his mind?

Caution had her reaching under her pillow for her gun. Sofia stayed still, listening. Yes, somebody was messing with her doorknob. There was a click, and the door swung inward. Her belly clenched, anxiety making it churn. Palms slippery with sweat, Sofia positioned her gun at her side with her finger next to the trigger. She pretended to be asleep while fixating on the shadow in her doorway.

Kyle, in nothing but jockey shorts tented with a hard-on. "Want some company, sweetness?"

Trachea thickened from sleep, Sofia's words came out husky. "When have I ever given you that impression, asshole?"

"Don't think I ain't noticed them fuck-me looks."

"Get out."

Kyle laughed. Latched the door. Took a step toward the bed.

"You're a dick-tease with all them low-cut shirts. You know what motorboating is, sweetness?"

The blood roared in Sofia's eardrums. She steeled herself so her voice wouldn't wobble. "How about *I* ask a question? You know the thing about double-action revolvers, Kyle? I don't have to cock the hammer... I can simply pull the trigger and shoot holes in you like Swiss cheese. Tell ya what though, although I'm getting awful sick of you and your brother's bullshit, Mama taught me courtesy." She lifted her revolver, aiming it at him. Drew the hammer back and cocked the gun to illustrate her words. "My finger is on the trigger. What are you going to do now, spanky?"

Kyle put his hands up and edged toward the door.

"First thing tomorrow, I'm assembling a meeting about this stunt," Sofia called as he opened the door and slinked out.

Relief surged in waves. Sofia leaped from the bed. Her knees were weak, and she stumbled to the door, slamming it and depressing the lock with her thumb. "God."

What if he came back? Sofia wedged the sturdy wooden chair from her desk under the doorknob. She set the gun within arm's reach and found a nightie, hastily dressing. Gaze fixed on the door and ears tuned to any sign of Kyle returning, she slumped down on the edge of the mattress.

Sofia's head snapped up—she'd fallen asleep. Her eyes burned with fatigue. Swirls of pink and purple were in the sky visible through her window. Dawn.

An engine revved, then tires squealed on pavement. *What the fuck?* Sofia snatched up her gun and hustled to the door, yanking the chair and hurling it aside. Ben and Zac met her in the hallway, Cora and Lark not far behind.

"What was that?" Ben had his bow. His eyes were smudged from slumber.

The service door at the end of the hall was unlatched. Sofia gasped, "Holy shit. The garage. Blue!"

"Huh? Sofia, wait! Let me—"

Ignoring Ben, Sofia flew to the door, whipping it open. The garage door was ajar. Blue was gone. She ran outside and along the driveway until she could see over the hill to the entry gate, the rest of the group on her heels. The gate stood open.

In the distance, Blue raced down Rural Route 9.

CHAPTER THIRTEEN

Sofia flushed at the others' scrutiny.

"The whole time you had a fucking car?" Lark growled. "What else are you hiding?"

Zac wiped crusty sleep from his eyes, looking baffled. "What just happened?"

"Was that Tucker and Kyle burning rubber out of here?" Cora asked. "How'd they know about your car?"

Sofia lifted a shoulder, sheepish. "I guess during their watch shift they got snoopy and jimmied the lock to the garage. Blue's keys were hung up on the pegboard. I'm an idiot for leaving them there plain as day."

Ben's body language was apathetic, but his eyes rested cannily on Sofia. "They know how to hotwire an ignition. Not having keys? Wouldn't thwart them." He shrugged. "I say good riddance to bad trash."

Sofia turned to Lark, worrying at her lip. Would she be upset the brothers left her behind? Or relieved?

Lark scowled and snapped, "What?"

"Did I say anything?"

"I know you're dying to make a remark, Sandra Dee."

Sofia pulled a face. "Huh?"

"Girls," Cora interjected, "quit your fussing. We've got bigger issues to contend with right now."

Ben jerked a thumb toward the highway. A half-dozen Zs had materialized from the woods. "Revving from the engine must've drawn 'em."

"Are they too far away to sniff us out?" Zac asked.

Sofia gasped, "We've got to shut the gate before they get in!"

"No." Ben moved in front of her. "If they catch our scent, they'll be up here in seconds. We'll go inside and monitor from the dining room window. Once they roam away, I'll shut the gate."

"But—"

"Now, Sofia," Cora coaxed, her tone hushed. "Ben's right. If they don't smell or hear us, they'll lose interest. Why borrow trouble?"

They reversed into the garage.

"Should we close the garage door?" Zac whispered.

Ben scratched his eyebrow. Addressing Sofia, he asked, "Does it screech as it goes down?"

Eyes wide, Sofia shook her head. "I-I don't think so. Not usually."

"Jesus. Let's stop discussing it and just do it." Lark stretched, extending an arm to the overhead door. Gliding silently on its tracks, it thunked as it latched.

"You're trembling, hon, but we're gonna be okay," Cora soothed, clasping Sofia's hand and urging her inside.

Ben held the service door. "Hurry." He led them to the dining room window. The figures remained glued to the pavement. "I've seen them stay in place for days... if they don't mosey along, none of us will be sleeping tonight."

"But," Sofia said, "you guys said they'd lose interest!"

"Normally they do," Cora replied, her brow furrowed.

Panic rose in Sofia's sternum. She imagined the Zs swarming the house. Breaking in. Chasing her like Howard did. Their icy fingers clutching at her. "We cannot leave the gate that way!"

Ben angled his head, examining her.

Sweat beaded on Sofia's lip. It was impossible to focus. Her breaths came out rapid and shallow.

Cora gently took the revolver from Sofia's hand and set it on the table. "You're hyperventilating."

"Don't spiral. Get yourself under control," Lark said, her concentration on the window.

"She doesn't have our experience with Zs. Don't be so rough on her," Zac chastised Lark.

"I'll take care of it, Sofia." Ben's eyes softened as he met her gaze. "I'll go out back and use the Z from when we arrived here. Then I can go to the road, fell the Zs, and lock the entrance. Where are your keys?"

"O-on my bedside table..." As Ben sped to her room to get the keyring, Sofia turned to Cora. "What does he mean *use the Z?*"

"If you smear Z blood on your clothes, it'll cover your scent," Cora replied.

"It's nasty. We try not to do it often because it's like toxic waste," Lark added.

Cora pursed her lips. "Makes me vomit."

Ben was back with Sofia's keyring.

"Want help?" Zac asked.

"I got it." Bow slung over his shoulder, Ben gave Sofia a reassuring smile before he went out to the backyard through the French doors.

Sofia, Zac, Cora, and Lark waited in terse silence for several minutes.

"There he is," Zac cried, pointing. Ben stalked along the outside of the metal fence. They tracked his progress. He picked through the weeds and down the hill, disappearing from view then reemerging. Jumping across a narrow drainage ditch, he landed on the highway shoulder. Twenty yards from the Zs, he nocked an arrow and drew it back. It whizzed through the air and into the closest Z's forehead. Ben took each Z out in quick succession, then went to recover his bows.

Sofia's lungs burned from holding her breath. The man was a sight to behold. She exhaled, saying, "I can't believe it—he did it!"

Ben jogged to the entrance gate, fastening it before climbing the hill. Once in the front yard, he sat his bow on the grass and peeled off his bloodied t-shirt. He chucked it into the weeds, the sun sparking the perspiration on the musculature of his pectorals and making them glisten.

Sofia fidgeted, spinning away from the window. Ben had seen her verging on a panic attack. Taking pity on her, he'd put himself in harm's way to dispatch the Zs. Maybe they were a legit threat, but he'd clearly chosen to act to assuage *her* fears. She must seem a weakling. A head-case. Still, Ben's overt masculinity was hot as fuck. Equal parts embarrassed and worried that the others would ascertain her attraction for Ben, Sofia squeaked, "You know, it occurs to me that Kyle and Tucker might've cleaned out the pantry."

"Shit, I'll bet they did," Lark said. "Those asshats."

She marched to the kitchen, and Sofia, Cora, and Zac followed. The pantry was stripped of all canned items and bottled water. Lark kicked an empty bin. "Even that package of votive candles is gone!"

"I was really getting used to having candles," Zac said, slumping dejectedly. "No more reading during watch."

There was the jangle of Ben unlocking the front door, then he appeared in the kitchen doorway. He set the keyring on the counter and his bow on the floor. "Pinched all our stock, didn't they?"

"Uh," Sofia said, raising a hand to get their attention. "I've got more rations squirreled away. Enough for at least two weeks."

Ben grinned, dimple surfacing in his cheek. "You never cease to amaze me, Sofia."

She felt a blush spread across her face, conscious for the first time of the skimpy nightie she wore. Of the fact she didn't wear a bra and that her nipples had pebbled against the fabric. That Ben's greedy gaze swished over her and dawdled at her cleavage.

Sofia's mouth watered. Ben's naked torso made logic elusive. All she could think about was taking the tip of her tongue to his neck and licking off his salty sweat. She avoided his eyes, afraid he'd read her mind. "My mother always told me *don't keep all your eggs in one basket.*"

"My mom said that, too," Zac said. "It was smart of you not telling us before—not 'til we proved ourselves."

Sofia admitted, "I'd have been a fool to trust Kyle and Tucker. I didn't dare mention anything around them."

"You're a cagey one. Very tricky, sis." Lark gave Sofia a look of grudging respect. "I never would've guessed you had it in you."

"I was planning ahead. That's all."

"Thank the Lord for that," Cora said.

"Boxes are in the basement wine cellar."

Ben propped against the door jamb and crossed his arms, his biceps bulging. "I've been biding my time."

They turned to him.

He elaborated, "Waiting for an opportune moment to shed the brothers. It took all I had in me not to murder them in their sleep."

Lark chewed her fingernail. Stared at the tile.

"And?" Sofia prompted. "What stopped you?"

"Let's lay it on the line," Ben said earnestly. "Would you all want to continue together as a unit? Permanently? All for one and one for all?"

Sofia considered everyone in turn. Cora beamed. Zac bobbed his head. Lark nodded. They surveyed Sofia expectantly.

Ben's fair eyebrows went to his hairline. "No pressure or anything, kiddo."

ANNE LUCY-SHANLEY

Sofia's gaze washed over Ben's handsome features, and her heart squeezed. She liked him. Wanted him. Ached for him. He wanted her, too. She knew that for certainty. But he was too noble—he saw her as a child. Plus, his heart belonged to someone else. It would pain Sofia being near him, not able to touch him. Torture. She swallowed her misgivings. "Yes."

"Congratulations," Ben said. "You four have passed my vetting process. I extend you a cordial invitation to Mayfly Hollow."

CHAPTER FOURTEEN

"MAYFLY WHAT?" SOFIA ASKED. "VETTING PROCESS?"

"Yeah," Zac added. "Like she said. What's Mayfly Hollow?"

"My home." Ben smiled. "It's a self-sustaining compound on the outskirts of Colliers Junction."

Cora asked, "Self-sustaining?"

"We have animals and gardens and orchards. Solar panels which provide electricity. Hot showers. Tasty cuisine. Tall fences and security cameras."

"Hold up." Lark gave a short laugh. "Forgive my skepticism, but that sounds too fuckin' good to be true."

"If you live in some sort of utopia then why are you here? Why leave it?" Sofia asked, unable to keep the frown from her face.

"You have questions. I have answers," Ben said. "Why don't we pop a squat in the living room where we can be comfortable?"

When everyone was seated on the sectional, Ben pulled a club chair up, facing them. "I was invited to Mayfly Hollow by a friend. Her sister and brother-in-law had been doomsday preppers. When they passed on, my friend took the reins with her husband." He met Sofia's eyes. "She had her own vision for what she wanted the future to be."

Sofia swallowed. "A commune?"

"We are simply a like-minded group of survivors who've chosen to band together and form a family. To do our best to thrive in these unprecedented times."

"Please tell me it isn't modeled after Jonestown," Cora entreated, her eyebrows pleating. She put a hand to her cheek and shook her head. "Because that did not end well."

Ben grinned, his eyelids crinkling in amusement. "I promise it's *not* a cult."

"Seems hinky to me—when things sound too unbelievable to be true, they usually are. How do we know this isn't a sex thing? Or that you don't lure unsuspecting people into a den of cannibals where they become dinner?" Lark glared at Ben, her expression savage.

Ben said, "You don't. But trust is a two-way street, right? You won't be forced to return with me if you don't wish to. And we won't detain you there against your will."

"Right," Lark drawled, winking in an exaggerated fashion.

"I'm leaning towards going," Zac said, nodding. "What do I have to lose?"

"Your life! Jesus. You'd probably be the first to volunteer to drink the Flavor-Aid, too. You won't make it to eighteen," Lark scoffed. "You're too damn gullible."

"I might only be seventeen, but I'm not dumb, and I'm *not* gullible! Ben's treated me like a son. He listens to my opinions— like an equal," Zac told Lark, his face reddening. "I didn't see you offering to kill those Zs. You rolled your eyes when Sofia was freaking. Why not do something constructive for a change? Like Ben. He was the one who took charge. He put himself in danger to protect us all. But you're all talk, aren't you, Lark?"

Sofia observed the interchange, mouth gaping. It was the most she'd heard Zac say the entire week.

Lark sat up, sputtering, "Now see here, you little shit—"

"Let's not get heated, folks," Cora said.

"No," Zac declared, motioning impatiently with his hand. "She's flapped her gums before about wanting to settle some-place. *Make a life*, she said. You complain about the arthritis in your knees from walking all the time, Cora. Sofia, you talked about how it's great not to be alone anymore. Why not give Ben a chance? He deserves it."

Ben cleared his throat, and Sofia's attention skittered to him. She wasn't sure what she'd expected, but he looked pleased. "It's okay, buddy. Suspicion and distrust are natural and predictable reactions. I'd be more concerned if everybody agreed right off the bat. Everyone contributes at Mayfly Hollow. We work hard. Self-defense and weapons training are compulsory. It's a sweet setup, however, compared to the alter-native. Sometimes, outsiders get the not-so-bright idea that it's up for grabs." He quirked a shoulder, pragmatic. "We're prepared to defend what's ours. You'd be required to vow the same."

Sofia asked, "So your role there is… what? Recruiter?"

"Yes. I share that role. We go out for six weeks at a time. Meet up with survivors, gauge whether they'd be a fit. Invite them back."

"Is that why you were looking at that wristwatch?"

"That's right. I'm due at a rally point Friday with anyone who wishes to go before our council."

"Council?" Lark's hazel eyes narrowed. "What kind of fresh BS is this?"

"We have to pledge fealty?" Cora asked. "You sure this isn't a cult?"

Zac grazed a lock of hair from his face. "What's *fealty*?"

"When a knight swears allegiance to royalty," Sofia said, thoughts racing.

"It's not like that, but they do have final approval. Don't fret. Everyone's kind at Mayfly Hollow. You won't be cross-exam-ined, but there will be a conversation. It's imperative that we're selective. We've gotta be careful who we permit in. Surely you can understand that after allowing us into *your* home, Sofia."

She tilted her head in assent. "How many survivors are there?"

"Any my age?" Zac interrupted.

With a chuckle, Ben said, "No. We have less than twenty right now, including me. There are some younger than you, but most are my age or older."

"Younger than Zac?" Cora asked.

"Elementary school aged. And a baby."

Lark asked, "*A baby?*"

"I can't recall the last time I saw a little one," Cora murmured, her voice thick.

"A beautiful, healthy girl named Maggie. Her first birthday is coming up." Ben smiled, his chest puffing out as if he were a proud father.

Sofia's spirits sank. What was next? Would Ben tell them he was married? "Is Maggie yours?"

"Nope, but I've unofficially adopted one of the older kids. Nora. Eleven years old. Her father was a farmhand at Mayfly Hollow, but she lost him—and her mother—last year to the virus. I'm anxious to return to her. She isn't a fan of me scouting. Luckily, we have an *it takes a village to raise a child* mentality at the farm, or I'd not leave her."

Ben was a father. That threw Sofia. She tried to wrap her head around the new sliver of information, speculating what else he'd reveal. "You said that you scout for six weeks at a time?"

He nodded.

"Then you meet up at a rally point with someone from Mayfly Hollow?"

"Yeah, my friend Adam. If I can't get back this Friday, he'll return every Friday for a month."

"But what if you're delayed for more than that?"

Ben shrugged. "Then I try to get back to the compound on

my own. We don't venture too far when scouting so it's doable to hike back."

"But fraught with danger, I'm sure," Cora said.

"Part of the job. Gas is in short supply these days. We can't waste our reserves locating missing people. You've seen me reading the textbook, right? We plan to convert our engines. Lots of work to be done yet." Rubbing his hands together, Ben then laced his knuckles and stretched, popping them. "Well, I'm going to grant you all an opportunity to decide about whether you're coming along. I'm leaving Thursday morning. You're welcome to join me. The plan is to walk toward River Heights. I know of an empty cabin we can camp overnight in. Adam'll be waiting for us Friday noon, rain or shine, at the designated spot."

CHAPTER FIFTEEN

THURSDAY MORNING, WEARING JEANS, A TANK TOP, AND HIKING boots, Sofia bid farewell to her childhood home. It wasn't guaranteed she'd return. Perhaps she never would.

Her gun placed in her waistband, Sofia had on a backpack and pulled an oversized suitcase on wheels. Along with a sleeping bag, she'd found a sturdy metal garden wagon in the garage and packed food and water. Zac had offered to take charge of it.

As they hiked down the driveway, Ben said, "If we were driving, it would only take us fifteen minutes."

"It won't take a full day to get there on foot," Cora pointed out, binding the straps on her backpack which held her rolled up sleeping bag. "Why not leave tomorrow morning?"

"We need to allow for contingencies," Ben explained. "Adam won't hang around all day. God forbid we end up missing him and have to do the trek again next week."

"This house you referred to… the one that we're going to spend tonight at. Where is it?" Sofia asked, her eye on the horizon.

"River Heights."

Lark said, "Kyle and Tucker and I passed through there a couple months ago. It's toast. You sure the cabin is still there?"

"Yeah. Should be. We use it every scouting mission. It's actually on the periphery of town, a five-minute hike from where we'll be collected."

At the base of the driveway, Sofia used her key to unlock the gate. Once they were outside, she slid it shut, making sure it bolted. Clipping her keyring to the hook attached to her backpack, she took a shaky breath. A tear teetered on her waterline and splashed on her dark tank top. She'd been an emotional wreck since waking, but she didn't want the others to notice. Clenching her teeth, Sofia gripped her golf club, gaze on the scrubby overgrowth lining the drive. She wouldn't get weepy, dammit.

"I suppose we should stay on the highway," Zac said, "rather than cut through the weeds."

Sofia was reminded of how she had dived into the overgrowth during her trip home. How could that have been just two weeks ago? The abrasions she'd received from the reeds had healed since but itched dreadfully during the process. She didn't relish enduring that again. "The reeds are like razors."

"Pushing through would be too exhausting. And dangerous," Ben said as he led them to the end the of the drive and turned left on Rural Route 9. They picked around the corpses of the Zs he'd put down the day before. The pavement stretched before them, misty and carpeted with mayflies. Their boots crunched on their exoskeletons as the group walked in taut, heedful silence.

An hour into their journey, Cora shared a bag of beef jerky. They passed deserted vehicles, treading over faded contents of suitcases strewn in their path. They didn't encounter Zs. Mid-morning, the sun warming their backs, they turned left onto Route 65.

Ben said over his shoulder, "Won't be long now."

They followed as he took the first right on Leoch Road. A

rough-hewn log cabin with flaking green paint was surrounded by pine trees, an outhouse a short distance away. There was an old-fashioned well with a hand crank beside the porch. It was covered with a piece of warped plywood. The cabin's windows were boarded and the door fastened. Covered in spongy lichen, the structure had a vacant, forlorn feel.

Climbing the steps to the wide front porch, Ben shifted his bow and pulled a switchblade from the side pocket of his back-pack. He motioned for Sofia, Zac, Cora, and Lark to remain on the porch. Unlatching the door, he kicked it ajar with his foot and sidled inside. A moment later, he called, "Come in. It's empty."

Sofia's nose twitched at the reek of mildew and rot as she trudged over the threshold. She stifled a sneeze, surveying the one-room cabin. Light spilled through the slats of the boarded windows. An iron bedstead with a decomposed mattress sat in one corner alongside a rocking chair. The opposite corner was fitted with primitive kitchen cabinets. A thick layer of dust and mouse droppings coated every surface. Ben put his pack and bow on the dinette in front of the cabinetry. Cora helped Zac pull the garden wagon inside then latched the door.

Ben's smile was rueful as he swept a hand. "Home sweet home."

"We won't be sleeping on that bed," Cora said, wiping at the sweat dripping down her face. "We'll have to move the table and chairs aside to make space on the floor."

Zac plucked the neckline of his t-shirt from where it stuck damply to his collarbone. "It's going to be too hot inside our sleeping bags."

"I'm sleeping on top of mine," Ben said.

A daddy longlegs scurried across the toe of Lark's hiking boot. She shook off the spider then stomped on it, cautioning, "Creepy crawlies'll be all over us."

"True," Cora said. "Phew. It's sticky already. It'll be boiling in here with sleeping bodies."

Zac plopped down on the rickety rocking chair. "We can sit on the front porch during watch. Be cooler there."

"With the brothers gone, we'll do longer shifts to cover the whole eight hours," Ben said. "I can take the first. You want the second, Sofia?"

She nodded.

"Third," Lark offered.

Cora perched on a kitchen chair, stroking her knee and grimacing. "I may as well do the next."

"That leaves me with the last shift," Zac said.

Lark selected a bottle of water from the wagon and looked through the stacks of cans. "Well, I'm hungry. What should we have for lunch? Looks like spaghetti rings are the easiest since they have pull tops."

She handed out cans of the spaghetti rings and plastic forks and bottles of water to everyone, then sat on the floor with her legs crossed and popped her can open.

"It's dark in here. We won't be able to read the books we brought," Cora said after she swallowed a bite of pasta.

"There's a camping lantern in a kitchen cabinet. And some candles and matches. Once it's dusk we'll have to extinguish them, however. The light will show through the window slats," Ben explained. "Not worth the risk."

The afternoon passed slowly. Sofia unrolled her sleeping bag, taking her gun from her jeans and placing it on the floor. She lay on her side and read the novel she'd brought along until her hip ached, then she flipped on her back.

They turned the lantern off once it was dark, and Ben went to sit outside with his bow for his scheduled watch. Sofia curled up beside Lark, who fell asleep within minutes. Cora, restless, finally drifted off. Zac snored from the other side of the room. Sofia listened to the night noises—the echo of the crickets and a nearby owl. She was still awake when Ben came in ninety minutes later to let her know it was her turn, passing her his wristwatch so she could keep track of time.

Outside was blissfully cool compared to the confines of the cabin. Gun in her waistband and golf club in her fist, she closed the door softly and took a seat on the top porch stair. It was the first she'd been outdoors by herself at night.

A lump swelled in Sofia's windpipe as she searched the darkness for any movement. The Zs' teeth would clack to alert her of their presence, wouldn't they?

Sofia consulted the watch often, only to learn mere minutes had elapsed. Clouds floated, veiling the moon. A fox screamed, a lonely, haunting shriek. Suddenly chilled, Sofia's flesh spiked into goosebumps.

When it was finally Lark's shift, Sofia's head pounded with a tension headache. She went inside and gently shook Lark's arm. Lark took the golf club and Ben's wristwatch and stole groggily out the door.

Sofia put her revolver on the floor beside her zippered sleeping bag. Ben slept on top of his own bag, which was unfolded beside hers. With a sigh, she took care not to disturb him as she settled on her side, tucking her hand under her cheek to pillow her head and shutting her eyes.

When she woke, it was hours later. Ben spooned her, his arms caging her—one under her neck, the other thrown over her hip, his fingers cupping her left breast. The even inhalations and exhalations revealed he was in deep slumber.

Scarcely breathing, Sofia squinted at the colorless light filtering through the window slats. It was perhaps an hour until sunrise. Lark was back from watch and asleep. Zac still snored from across the room. That meant Cora was sitting her shift.

Feeling wicked, Sofia scooched into Ben, nestling her backside into his groin and wiggling ever so. He mumbled in his sleep, the heat from his breath teasing her earlobe. Did he say her name? Ben's grip tightened on her breast, and he kissed the shell of Sofia's ear.

Teeth on her lip, she squirmed, feeling the answering twitch as his arousal became obvious. He flexed his hips, grinding into her, his hitching respirations telling her he was no longer asleep.

Hand leaving her breast, he pushed the neckline of her tank aside, then the cup of her bra. His fingers found her nipple, and Sofia gasped, arching her back and rotating her bottom against him.

From the fringes, Sofia was aware of Zac rustling from his bed. She stilled, kept her eyes closed and pretended to sleep. Ben must've heard him, too. He pulled hastily away and turned to his other side.

Yawning, Zac got to his feet. He shuffled out the door. Sofia waited to see if Ben would say anything or flip back over to resume his explorations. Just when she opened her mouth to speak, there was the sound of screaming from outside.

CHAPTER SIXTEEN

Ben was up with bow in hand in seconds.

Befuddled, Sofia shook Lark awake and scrambled to her feet, fixing her shirt. Where was her golf club? Lark had left it on the dinette. It was hard to see in the dim light. Nearly stumbling over Cora's sleeping bag, she seized the club as Ben cautiously opened the cabin door.

"What's going on? Where're Cora and Zac?" Lark asked huskily from behind Sofia, fumbling for her knife.

"I don't know!" Sofia's pulse thudded in her neck. Her knees knocked. She put a steadying hand on the kitchen cabinet.

"Flank me," Ben ordered, nocking an arrow. "Keep your backs to the cabin."

Once on the porch, Sofia scanned their surroundings, but the predawn mist obscured everything. Outlines of trees were barely visible. Mayflies blanketed the porch. Ben's watch lay on the top step. Sofia bent to pocket it.

The trio waded down the mayfly-covered stairs and slogged through the overgrown grass. Lark stayed on Ben's left side and Sofia on his right as they sidestepped around the perimeter of the cabin.

Sofia heard chewing and wet gasps as they rounded the side

of the cabin where the outhouse stood. Hackles rising, she whispered, "Oh my God."

Cora kneeled over Zac's sprawled body.

Weapons at the ready, they neared. At their approach, Cora started. In slow motion, she bounced up, her legs springs. Then, she crouched. Bloodstains painted her lilac blouse. Zac's blood. Cora's teeth clacked.

Comprehension registered. Lark shrieked, "She's a Z!"

As Cora launched toward them, Ben aimed and released his arrow. It went through Cora's eyeball, and she crumpled. Ben ran a hand down his face. "Godammit!"

This can't be happening! Sofia hastened to Zac's side. His shirt was drenched with metallic-scented gore. He was alive but in appalling condition, his thorax shuddered unevenly.

Discarding her club and diving to the ground, Sofia evaluated his injuries. Tattered skin hung from his neck. He convulsed and gurgled.

Sofia gulped as realization hit—his ragged respirations were agonal—a *death rattle*. These were Zac's final moments. At a loss for what else she could do to bring him comfort, she skimmed his hair from his brow, murmuring words she hoped were soothing. He tried to talk, and Sofia shushed him, one eye on Lark. The woman paced in an agitated manner to the outhouse and back.

The sky was slowly transitioning. It became lighter by degrees with each moment. Sofia's gaze sought Ben. His eyes were fixated on the edge of the yard near the road. "The Z that got Cora can't be far away... I think something's moving over there."

Zac took his last breath.

Then, he was gone.

Tears dribbled down Sofia's cheeks, and she blinked. Surely, she'd wake soon from this nightmare. All she needed was someone to pinch her.

Ben's attention was still on the fringes. Lark had dissociated.

Was unreachable. She sobbed in earnest but resumed pacing.

Somebody must take charge.

Voice wobbly, Sofia demanded, "Lark, give me your knife."

Snagging Lark's wrist as she passed, Sofia pulled her close. She pried the knife from Lark's fingers. Lark sank to the ground and put her knees to her abdomen, swaying back and forth.

Sofia took a second to marshal courage. Both hands wrapped around the hilt of the knife, she brought the tip between Zac's eyes. With a grunt of revulsion, she forced it into his nasal cavity. Lark was now watching Sofia, her expression horrified. Her sobs became thin wails.

"Shh," Ben commanded edgily, but it was like Lark didn't hear him. From the corner of his mouth, he hissed, "Sofia, shut her up. I see a shitload of Zs over there!"

Robotically, Sofia clambered over Zac's body. Letting the knife go, she drew Lark into her arms. Pliant, Lark quieted, babbling incoherently. Sofia urged, "Keep it together, Lark. We have to get up now. C'mon."

Sofia assisted Lark to her feet. From the road, there was the discordant melody of teeth crashing together. Ben aimed his bow. "There's gotta be fifty of them!"

His words pitched Lark into a frenzy. Her body bowing, she shrieked. Sofia clapped a palm over Lark's mouth to silence her. "There's no way you can hold them off, Ben. We've got to retreat!"

Ben seemed loath to fall back. He struggled to aim, but there were too many targets.

Sofia thought fast. They were in crisis. Ben was outnumbered. Lark was a liability. Sofia must step up and assume leadership—there was no one else to do it but her.

Mind made up, she took her hand from Lark's mouth. Remembering the trick Ben used before, Sofia bent and retrieved the knife from where she'd left it in the weeds. Yanking Lark along, she crawled to Cora's corpse. It stank distinctly of the Z virus. Gagging, Sofia dragged the blade along Cora's midsection, then wiped the blood on her jeans. She dipped the tip into Cora's guts once again, spreading the viscera on Lark's pant leg. Lark recoiled, but Sofia restrained her, yelling, "Ben, over here *now!*"

As the Zs squatted and sprang up, Ben tore through the grass to join Sofia and Lark. His gaze lasered on the approaching Zs, he didn't appear cognizant of Sofia swabbing Cora's red-black blood on his clothes.

"We're sneaking back to the cabin," Sofia stated as calmly as she could. She inserted the hilt of the knife in the crook of her armpit and linked her arm with Lark's. "Help me with her, Ben."

Growling with frustration, Ben did as Sofia requested. Half-carrying and half-dragging Lark, they dashed around the corner of the cabin, the Zs in pursuit.

By the time they got to the porch, the Zs had faltered. Slowing to a stop, they snuffled the air. Towing Lark inside, Sofia let her go and sagged in relief.

Ben shoved the door firmly closed. Shambling footfalls landed on the porch. He wheeled to Lark, who was screaming incoherently. "You're drawing 'em. Quiet!"

Sofia sat the knife on the floor and bundled Lark into a snug embrace, tucking the woman's face into her shoulder to mute her screams. Conscious of the Zs on the other side of the cabin door, Sofia patted Lark's back and whispered, "It's gonna be okay... It's gonna be okay..."

CHAPTER SEVENTEEN

BRACED AGAINST THE CABIN DOOR, BEN HAULED A HAND THROUGH his hair. In the shadows, Sofia noted the rigidity in his stance. The way his teeth were gnashed, causing his jaw to tick. His ferocity. Lark no longer cried. She clung to Sofia like a petrified child.

Would the Zs break into the cabin, or would the viscera Sofia had smeared on their clothing conceal them?

Perspiration trickled down Sofia's spine. She held her breath. The Z blood on their clothes perfumed the cabin, making her want to heave. Potent, it imbued her hair and skin. Permeated the soft tissue of her sinuses and smarted. The porch floor creaked. Then, there was a crash as ancient floorboards buckled. Lark squeaked, and Sofia put a finger to her lips, cautioning her.

Not daring to move, they remained in position. Sofia's hamstring cramped, and she shifted her weight. After what seemed forever, when nothing further could be heard outside, she asked, "Do we dare crack the door? I think they've left."

Arms crossed, Ben's stubbled chin rested on his chest. With a sigh, he slowly straightened and rolled his head, stretching. "Fuck," he muttered as he considered Sofia's request. "Alright."

Sofia, toting Lark along, tiptoed to Ben's side. He swallowed.

Put his hand to the latch. Carefully, he opened the door, and they craned their necks. Half the porch had collapsed, but the area in front of the door stood, as did the stairway.

In the weed-choked front yard, two dozen Zs loitered. Some were immobile. Others lurched about, their noses to the air. Ben gingerly closed the door and locked it, wincing at the *click* of the bolt.

Leading Lark to their sleeping bags, Sofia gestured for her to sit. She meekly obeyed. Distressed by Lark's chalky complexion and wide, empty stare, Sofia snatched up Cora's sleeping bag. She draped it around Lark's shoulders then grasped Lark's clammy fingers in hers, chafing her wrists. "You're in shock."

Ben bent over the dinette, hands flat on the tabletop. He shook his head as if attempting to digest everything but failing. He muttered disbelievingly, "What. The. Fuck."

Gaze panning between Lark and Ben, Sofia reasoned, "Cora obviously got surprised by a Z. Maybe she nodded off during watch. Or was attacked when she went to use the outhouse. Who knows?"

"And when Zac went outside, she'd already turned. Tackled him. Poor fucker didn't stand a lick of a chance," Ben finished, lamenting, "What a goddamn waste."

"How did she turn so quickly?" Sofia asked.

"Sometimes they do."

"I didn't realize. The Z must've wandered away afterward... but not far enough. The ruckus we made lured it back, along with others." She bit her cheek to keep from weeping. In the thick of the action, there had been no opportunity to think, to dissect what had happened. To process it. Now, in the silence of the cabin there was nothing to do *but think*.

Lark's face was buried in Sofia's shirt, her knuckles white on Sofia's arm. Head bowed, Ben hadn't budged from his spot at the dinette. His bearing was that of a broken man. Inconsolable.

Sofia had only really known Zac as a sixth grader and Cora hardly at all, yet their absence stung. Left an empty hole. She couldn't make sense of the deaths. She reeled from the suddenness. The unfairness. Gone was Cora the pragmatic peacemaker, and Zac the boyish optimist.

Fury at the ugliness of the way life was now bubbled in Sofia's stomach. The new world was *evil*. Vile. She clenched her fists to contain her rage. The absurdity of how swiftly two decent people could be taken—their existence snuffed out with ease—was something she just couldn't wrap her mind around. It was cruelty she couldn't bear. A teardrop escaped the corner of Sofia's eye, and she let it skim down her cheek.

She lifted her chin and squared her shoulders. Quelled her misery. Their group was fractured, the dynamic changing as a result. Ben floundered in his role as leader. Lark had been driven past the brink.

Sofia must be their strength.

The cabin was sweltering, but Lark shivered. Sofia rubbed Lark's back until her teeth quit chattering. Sitting up, she croaked, "Thanks. I'm better now, Sofia."

Sofia studied her. The color had returned to Lark's cheeks though her expression revealed despair. "Why don't we get you situated in the rocking chair? You can rest. It's still hours 'til Ben's friend is due to pick us up."

"We won't be leaving this cabin unless the Zs disperse," Ben said flatly from the dinette.

"Everything is out of our control. We'll just have to play it by ear." Fishing a bottle of water from the wagon, Sofia set it on the table within Ben's reach, encouraging him to drink. Unscrewing the lid off another bottle, she took it to where Lark perched on the edge of the rocker. She held the water to Lark's lips. "Sip."

Once Lark had enough water, Sofia brought the bottle to her mouth and gulped thirstily. She found chocolate bars in the wagon and gave one each to Lark and Ben. Glimpsing at it dispassionately, he said, "The last thing I feel like doing is eating."

"You need the sugar. We all do," Sofia insisted as she

unwrapped a bar for herself and popped a square in her mouth. Stealing to the door, she unlatched it and peeked out. The sun had risen, glimmering on the speckled dew and masses of mayflies. The Zs hadn't left the vicinity of the cabin, though they'd ambled further afield.

As Sofia bolted the door, Lark asked, "W-well?"

"Still there."

"What'll we do?"

Sofia looked to Ben, but when he didn't answer Lark's inquiry, she said, "I think as long as most of them leave, we'll be okay continuing on. We might have to put fresh Z blood on our clothes though."

"I-I wish we could give Zac and Cora a proper burial," Lark whispered. "Don't we owe them as much?"

Anguish made Sofia's trachea smart. "They'd understand."

Sinking onto a dinette chair, Sofia noticed her hands for the first time. They were tacky, stained livid crimson with Zac's blood. She flung her chocolate on the table, unable to tolerate another bite. Digging in her pocket for Ben's watch, she depressed the button on the side to illuminate the dial.

Six hours until they must leave to meet Adam. Would the Zs permit their departure?

Lark dozed in her rocker. Ben retreated, slumping in a chair across from Sofia, his head in his hands and his face an inscrutable mask. Whenever Sofia spoke to him, she received one-word answers or shrugs. Did he blame himself for Cora and Zac's fate? Was he angry? Grieving? Sofia could only guess. He steadfastly refused to open up to her.

Ben's withdrawal both concerned and saddened Sofia. She thought they were close, that they'd forged a bond. That she couldn't penetrate the walls he'd put up drove home the harsh reality—no matter how many moonlit confidences they'd shared, she and Ben were but strangers.

Sleep was not possible. Instead, Sofia performed busywork. She tidied their belongings. Rolled their sleeping bags and optimistically tethered them to their packs. Organized their rations. When there was nothing else to be done, she took a seat and counted down minutes under her breath. At intervals, she checked the status of the Zs outside. The passage of time was everlasting. Excruciating.

At twenty to twelve, Sofia stood and strode to the door. It was the moment of truth. If there were too many Zs cutting off access, the trio would miss their ride to Mayfly Hollow and be trapped in the cabin at least another night.

She crossed her fingers for luck and unbolted the lock.

CHAPTER EIGHTEEN

"Screw it," Sofia decisively told Ben and Lark over her shoulder. Three Zs staggered by the porch. Faces to the air, they rooted, perceiving Sofia's scent but unable to fully track it. "I say we go for it."

Ben joined her at the door. "They're whipped up. We're invisible now, but they could fix on us unexpectedly."

"Yeah." She turned and met his eyes. "You'll have to cover me while I go to Cora's body. I'll add more Z blood onto my jeans then on yours. I'll bring the knife to the cabin for Lark's."

Hesitating, Ben nodded. "We gotta shake a leg."

"Get your bow." While he went to the table for his bow, Sofia grabbed her knife, saying to Lark, "Put your pack on. Be ready to leave in two minutes."

Arrow nocked, Ben skipped down the porch steps. Sofia followed. She jumped from the bottom stair, knife readied. Heart pounding and gaze darting, she sprinted around the cabin. A handful of Zs milled through the tall weeds. Some concluded their aimless lumbering and came to attention. Others meandered into Sofia's path, creating an obstacle course. Swallowing a yip of terror, she veered around them.

Bending at Cora's corpse, Sofia squelched her disgust and

dipped her blade into the guts. Painting her jeans hems with the fresh blood, she signaled Ben. He shifted his bow from Z to Z while Sofia wiped viscera on his pant leg. She retrieved her golf club from where she'd left it. Then, plunging the knife into the corpse once more, she nodded to Ben. They power walked back to the cabin.

Lark stood uncertainly on the portion of the porch that hadn't collapsed. She'd placed Ben's and Sofia's backpacks on the landing, and her fingers were around the handle of Sofia's rolling suitcase. At their approach, she mouthed, "I put water in our packs, but I couldn't manage the wagon."

"It's okay," Ben said, maintaining a low tone. He deposited his bow on the step and slipped into his pack. "Leave it."

Once Sofia wiped the bloody knife on Lark's jean cuff, she shrugged into her backpack. Lark handed her the suitcase and closed the cabin door. Sofia gave Ben his wristwatch. Stooping for the golf club Sofia had set by her hiking boots, Lark mimed she was all set.

They tramped single file through the verdant overgrowth adjacent to Route 65, avoiding the Zs on the roadway. Ben was at the front with Lark sandwiched between him and Sofia. The Z blood proved an effective disguise, but noise seemed to alert the zombies within hearing distance. Taking care to keep as soundless as possible caused their pace to lag. Ben frequently looked back to gauge Lark and Sofia's progress. Sofia noted the way his mouth was compressed into a grim line. She knew what vexed him—although he'd said the rally point was a speedy five-minute hike from the cabin, he was apprehensive they'd miss Adam. Sofia couldn't imagine such a thing—it was unthinkable.

They *had to make it.*

Her suitcase was cumbersome. Sofia had packed the oversized case until it was practically unzippable. She tugged it through the weeds, suppressing a roar of aggravation, her teeth set. The wheels snagged on scrub brush, costing her precious seconds as she paused to right them. She debated abandoning the suitcase, but the knowledge that it held all her worldly possessions toughened her resolve. Sofia soldiered on.

Skirting Route 65 until no more Zs were in sight, they stepped onto the faded asphalt. All three were breathless. Humidity frizzed Sofia's sable-colored hair. She pushed a tendril from her eyes and groaned.

Ben consulted his watch.

"Are we gonna make it?" Sofia panted.

"It'll be a close shave." Steps purposeful, Ben shepherded them to a T in the road. He bore right onto Calloway Avenue. A minute later, they emerged from the heavily forested area they'd been traveling. In the distance, River Heights loomed. Knowing they neared the rally point was enough to provide a second wind. They increased their stride in a final push.

"I-I'm dizzy," Lark gasped, her face flushed deep red. "Low blood sugar."

Ben pointed a quarter mile ahead to a sedan next to a scarred welcome sign splattered with red-black blood and tagged with graffiti. *River Heights—A Little Town With A Big Heart. Population 6,000.* "I use that car if I'm early. The seats are comfortable."

Sofia was desperately thirsty. Once they made it to the sedan, she could drink. It was an oasis in the desert. A shining beacon.

"Almost there," Ben said. "Watch for Adam. Black minivan."

The midday heat was relentless, and Lark was clearly flagging. Sofia wound an arm through Lark's, supporting her. Lark thanked her with a grateful smile.

The four-door car was tan and stippled with orange rust. Its nose faced the welcome sign. The beige interior was stained but looked cushy. Somebody had emptied it of trash, dumping the debris on the berm.

Sofia helped Lark remove her pack. Ben opened a door to the front passenger seat, ushering Lark in as Sofia rummaged in her pack for bottled water.

After taking a long draw of water, Lark passed it back to Sofia. Sofia took a swig, then offered it to Ben. Lark mopped her forehead. "I put a pouch of peanuts in your backpack, Sofia. Could I have them?"

Sofia found the peanuts and handed them over. Leaving her backpack on the gravel, she pulled the back door open and sank into the plush upholstery. Shutting her eyes, she tipped her head back on the headrest, trying to cool down. Ben sat in the driver's seat. He and Lark munched hungrily on the peanuts. When Sofia was presented with the pouch, she shook her head. As ravenous as she was, the concept of food was revolting—she hadn't washed her hands yet.

Lark sighed, sounding beat. "At least I feel more human after eating. I'm dying for a shower."

Sofia said, "Me, too. A freezing cold one."

"Like clockwork," Ben murmured, "but why is he coming from that direction?"

The unease in his voice had Sofia opening her eyes and sitting up. Ben glanced in the rearview mirror. Sofia spun in her seat, her gaze locking on a black minivan bearing down on them.

Swiping a hand against his mouth, Ben said, "Get your packs. I can't wait to blow this town."

The van screeched to a stop. It had a pink stylized cupcake logo on the side which said *Buttercream Bakery, Clayton's Corners*. A fit dark-skinned man with close-cropped hair sat behind the wheel. He motioned for them to get in. Ben opened the back door for Sofia and Lark then stowed their belongings and his bow on the furthest bench seat.

Ben shut the sliding door and climbed into the passenger seat beside Adam. The back window was missing, crudely replaced with a cloudy sheet of plexiglass. A classic rock CD played softly over the speakers. AC vents blasted frigid air, and Sofia exhaled with relief. She caught Adam's eye in the rearview mirror and smiled tentatively.

"Seatbelts on," Adam commanded, his voice deep and low-pitched. He accelerated, peeling away. The inertia flattened Sofia and Lark to their seat backs. Once past the welcome sign, he hung a U-turn and drove eastbound. At Felling Parkway, he turned left.

The parkway was tunnel-like. Each side of it was lined with sloping hills crowded with towering emerald-green conifers. Sofia wondered if perhaps it had been a logging thoroughfare in the past. The speeding van left billowing dust in its wake. Occasionally, a shaft of sunlight threw a lace-patterned design on the dirt road ahead, but Felling Parkway was plainly little-traveled.

"If you've chosen Felling rather than the other routes," Ben said tautly, "that means bad news."

Adam nodded, his manner grave. "I came across a horde on our regular course. We've got to stay on backroads, even if it takes a little longer to get home."

Ben swore under his breath. "A horde? It can't be the Canadian migration from last year returning, can it?"

Adam lifted a shoulder, exchanging a dismal look with Ben. Lark's clammy fingers clutched Sofia's forearm. She tried to find words to reassure Lark, but her guts clenched.

Mass migration? Hordes? What the eff is this all about?

CHAPTER NINETEEN

"WHAT DO YOU MEAN *MASS MIGRATION*?" SOFIA DEMANDED. HER palms were slick with sweat. She wiped them on her jeans, leaving streaks of blood behind.

Adam grimaced, meeting her eyes again in the rearview mirror. "You don't know about that?"

Ben made a dismissive hand gesture. "She's been secreted in her home outside Mergenville since the virus."

"Ah, I see," Adam said as he took a right at a stop sign. "Well, Zs congregated in massive numbers around this time last year. Nobody understood why. Then, they traipsed north, presumably to Canada."

"And now," Sofia said slowly, "they're migrating back. But wait. Not all of them left. I saw some this spring."

"No," Ben agreed, "not all left. Just the majority of 'em."

"Autumn through winter, we barely came across *any* Zs. We were able to voyage out and obtain numerous provisions for the farm. We ran our vehicles almost nonstop for weeks." Adam elaborated, explaining, "Kate was troubled things could turn pear-shaped if the Zs returned. She wanted us prepared to lock down indefinitely if necessary."

Sofia thought about the warehouse and all of the foodstuffs

there nearing expiration. If Mayfly Hollow were to be her new home, she must consider sharing with her hosts. Were they worthy? Time would tell.

Lark asked, "Who's Kate?"

"She owns the farm, along with her husband Teller. Didn't Ben explain? She's a hell of a woman. Preparedness is her mantra, and it's saved our bacon more than once."

"He didn't mention many names," Sofia murmured, her gaze volleying between Adam and Ben. Did she detect Ben's posture stiffen? Something about Kate being introduced unsettled him. Disconcerted, Sofia contemplated the passing scenery outside the window while Adam and Ben quietly chatted.

Lark whispered in Sofia's ear, "You don't think we're making a mistake here, do you?"

Little late now, isn't it? Sofia bit her lip. "I'm not getting any alarm bells going off, if that's what you mean."

"I'm scared, Sofia."

Her gaze roamed over Lark. She did indeed appear scared. Her hazel eyes were wide, her face pinched. Sofia wavered for just a moment, took a breath, then confided, "If Mayfly Hollow sucks, we'll leave. I know a place we can go. It's somewhat remote and relatively safe."

Lark turned bemused. "Why is this the first time I'm hearing about it?"

"Why do you think? Because I've decided you're trustworthy." Sofia raised an eyebrow. "Don't make me regret it."

Squeezing Sofia's arm, Lark nodded.

Adam turned onto a narrow lane bordered by trees and a profusion of vegetation. A minute later, they approached a tall entry gate that made the one at Sofia's house look puny. There were floodlights on metal poles every fifty feet along the slatted metal fence line. A sophisticated-looking surveillance camera was pointed at the entry. Adam pressed a remote clipped to the van's visor, and the gate opened.

Once pulled through, Adam waited for the gate to latch, then bore right, following the curve of the lane. An 1800s brick farm-house was on the apex of the ridge, surrounded by assorted outbuildings. A large red-painted barn stood behind the house. Sofia thought it all looked ordinary. Unpretentious.

The van crunched on the gravel for about an eighth of a mile before a row of three log cabins with solar-paneled green metal roofs came into view. Adam idled in front of the middle cabin.

Ben regarded Lark and Sofia over his shoulder. "You two each want your own cabin? Or do you want to share this one? Your choice."

Lark spoke up at once. "If it's okay, I'd like to be with Sofia."

Sofia nodded. "We'll stay together."

"Alright. This'll be your place, for now anyway. There are cans of soup in the kitchen cabinet and water in the fridge. Why don't you relax, eat, take a shower, nap. Feel free to explore if you're up to it. We used to quarantine, but we figure by now everyone is immune to the virus. Tomorrow morning at six, come up to the house, and you can meet Teller and Kate."

"Alright," Sofia said. There were things she wanted to say to Ben, questions she wanted to ask, but not with Lark and Adam there. She hoped she'd get the chance later to find him alone.

Ben unloaded their packs and Sofia's suitcase, leading Lark and Sofia up the stairs to the minuscule porch. Opening the unlocked door, he accompanied them inside the cabin. It smelled dank but was immaculately clean. Essentially one large room, there was a compact kitchenette tucked in one corner which butted up to a bathroom. There was a wooden desk and chair in the other corner. A queen-size bed, nightstands, and an over-stuffed chair and ottoman dominated the living area.

"I'm itching to get up to the farmhouse to see Nora. There's a walkie-talkie on the kitchen counter. Let us know if you need anything," Ben said before leaving.

A wall-mounted unit with options for heat or AC was across from the bed. Sofia set her knife on a bedside table and went to flip the switch on the wall unit to the lowest cool setting. It hummed to life.

Lark lingered at the foot of the quilt-covered bed while Sofia surveyed the room. It was sparse, but whoever had decorated it made meticulous choices. The walls were restful lavender, coordinating with the purple-and-gray tiled floor and the patterned curtains on the windows. It was worlds apart from their accommodations the night before.

The bathroom was basic. Toilet. Wood vanity topped with an oval mirror. White fiberglass tub stocked with soaps and shower gel. Floral shower curtain and matching floor mat. Fluffy lavender towels were stacked in a metal rack opposite the toilet.

Sofia washed her hands before returning to the main room. Gaze roving over the kitchenette, she suggested, "Why don't you shower first? I want to scope out the outside of the cabin."

Almost shyly, Lark leaned her golf club against the wall and shouldered her pack. Going into the bathroom, she shut the door.

Sofia walked around the peninsula countertop, where two stools were under the lip of the counter, and into the small kitchenette. She found canned soup a month from expiration in a cupboard by the apartment-size fridge. Popping the top on the soup, she rummaged in a drawer for a spoon.

There was a wrenching screech from behind the kitchen wall. Sofia stiffened. It was only Lark turning on the shower faucet. Shaking her head, Sofia breathed, "Phew. Jesus. Jumpy much?"

She fetched her gun from where she'd stashed it in her backpack, putting it into its usual spot in the waistband of her jeans before letting herself outside.

There was a pair of green plastic chairs on the porch. Wearily, Sofia perched on the edge of one. She shoveled room temperature soup into her mouth, her gaze on the landscape.

It was a typical summer afternoon. Warm and humid, with cotton candy fluff clouds in an azure sky. Farmyard noises drifted to Sofia's ears. Peoples' voices, along with a dog's bark, cut through the buzzing drone of insects by the cabin. A passel of goats came into view, nibbling grass on the hillside facing the cabin. It all seemed so... innocuous. So *normal*.

Weird, Sofia thought, setting the empty can on the floorboards. She got to her feet, noting the colorful clematis vining the porch railings. Descending the stairs, she circled the cabin. Sweet-smelling pink peonies drooped along the side. Her favorite. Pausing to choose a bloom, Sofia brought it to her nose, inhaling deeply.

She recalled how Cora had once advised her during a conversation to stop and smell the roses whenever possible. What would *she* think of Mayfly Hollow? Sofia envisioned her commenting on the wedding ring patterned quilt on the bed or reveling in being able to shower with hot water. And Zac. If he were here, he'd have insisted on tagging along with Ben like an eager pup, raring to meet everyone today rather than tomorrow.

Grief was slippery—hard to contain. If Sofia didn't take painstaking care, it would circle her neck and envelop her like a hefty cloak. Suffocate her. No. She couldn't allow that. Sniffling, Sofia coughed away her sorrow.

Peony stem dangling from her fingertips, she rounded the corner of the cabin to the backyard. The metal fence was set into the gently sloping hill behind it, swathed in the shadows from the canopy of pine and fir trees. Unremarkable. Sofia returned to the front porch. Standing with her hands on her hips, she surveyed the gravel lane, which curved around a bend and vanished. Various outbuildings dotted the hillside above. The brick farmhouse was visible, but she didn't see anyone about.

Lark opened the cabin door, her hair dripping from her shower. "Sofia, what are you looking at?"

"Nothing much."

"You should come inside and get cleaned up."

Burrs stuck to the hems of her jeans. Zac's rusty blood

smudged her knees. Dried perspiration had crusted white along the neckline of her black tank. "You're right. I guess I'll have to wait to explore more."

CHAPTER TWENTY

THE ALARM CLOCK RANG AT FIVE THE FOLLOWING MORNING. Silencing it, Sofia flicked on the bedside lamp and sat against the metal headboard, yawning and rubbing her eyes.

"Just because I spazzed out yesterday doesn't mean I'm a wimp."

Sofia squinted at Lark where she was cross-legged next to her on the mattress. Even in the wee hours, with her hair mashed and her cheeks creased, she looked pretty. "What are you talking about?"

Lark flipped the slumber-tousled strands from her face in a defiant sort of way. "I'm *not* embarrassed."

"Did I say you ought to be?"

She declared as if Sofia hadn't spoken, "You needn't worry. I'm not a nut job."

"Everyone is entitled to vulnerability," Sofia replied mildly, putting her hand to her mouth to smother another yawn.

"I don't like being vulnerable. Gives people the impression I'm weak. I'm not."

"It means you're human."

"Hmm."

Sofia laughed. "Delighted to see you're yourself today. Brimming with piss and vinegar, as my dad used to say."

Lark didn't answer.

"Listen. I don't think any less of you. Actually, quite the opposite."

After weighing her response, Lark finally said, "You're a sweet girl. Too sweet for this world."

Snorting, Sofia protested, "I'm not *that* sweet."

"Well, too kind, maybe."

"Why do you say that?"

Ignoring Sofia, Lark got out of bed. She thumbed through her pack for a clean shirt and jeans. Sofia recognized the floral blouse as one of her mother's, and her heart twanged.

"I suppose we'd better hotfoot up to the farmhouse for our appointment with the *council*. See if we pass their examination," Sofia said drily more to herself than Lark. She found a cotton sundress and sturdy leather sandals in her suitcase and went into the bathroom to change and brush her teeth. When she came out, Lark was fully dressed.

"I was a bitch to both Cora and Zac," Lark admitted as she combed her hair. "I shouldn't have been. And I shouldn't have made that smartass remark about Zac not reaching eighteen either. I've gotta live with that now."

Sofia sank to the upholstered ottoman. Her brow furrowed, then she nodded. "Ah. So that is what's really eating at you this morning. They didn't hold it against you, you know?"

Scraping her hair into a ponytail, Lark avoided Sofia's eyes. "I don't wanna be so hard. I wanna be soft, like you... But I've just spent so many years in a shell... I don't know how to shed it."

"This is a start. This conversation."

Lark sniffed. Lifted a shoulder.

They were silent for several minutes, each lost in their own thoughts. Sofia deliberated the floor tiles, feeling her face heat and relieved it wouldn't show in the lamplight. "You think you're too hard... I think I'm too soft. Too naïve. That's why I'm sensitive when people point out how young I am."

Lark tossed the hairbrush on the nightstand, giving Sofia a keen appraisal. "Yeah. Sure. Sometimes you're a bit innocent and naïve, but you're clever. And sharp-witted. Don't undersell yourself."

Sighing, Sofia entwined her hands in her lap. "I have a lot to learn about how to survive."

"Hey. I was the one falling apart yesterday," Lark replied, "and you were the one who was a grade-A badass."

Lark was right. Pride buoyed Sofia's spirits.

"We wouldn't have made it here without your quick thinking." Lark scooped up the golf club. "Although I'm not convinced this place is all it's cracked up to be yet."

"Yeah."

"With that frilly dress you're wearing, you won't have a place to put the gun. You carry the golf club, and I'll take the gun. We aren't going weaponless, that's for goddamn sure."

"Okay." Sofia took the club from Lark and stood. "Let's get this over with."

THE WOMAN WAS around Ben's age with a no-nonsense attitude. Kate. Possessing a dancer's body, she was willowy, with coltish legs and a modest bosom. Her long chestnut hair was woven into a braid which extended to the hem of her patterned shirt. Sofia squashed her instinct to squirm under the piercing jade gaze.

Sofia's golf club against a wall, she and Lark sat on a bench at the rustic trestle table in the farmhouse kitchen, untouched mugs of coffee before them. They faced Kate, who was seated with Adam on one side and a slim, unconventionally handsome Stetson-wearing cowboy on the other. Both men deferred to Kate. She apparently ran the show.

"Ben says you two will fit in well here at Mayfly Hollow," Kate said.

Sofia's gaze strayed from the bright white cabinetry to the oiled butcher block countertop where a roaster was plugged into an outlet. She recognized the yeasty scent mixed with cinnamon and sugar as French toast—her favorite. The walls were a shade of robin's egg blue, and the appliances looked brand new. Expensive. It was a comfortable room, airy and bathed in early morning sunshine, but that did little to dispel Sofia's jitters. It took a concentrated effort not to fidget. She kept her hands laced in her lap and her mouth shut.

"Where's Ben?" Lark asked shortly. "Shouldn't he be present?" Whereas Sofia was nervous, Lark came off as petulant.

Adam answered in an even tone, "It's common practice that whoever recruits abstains from the interview portion. Conversely, he'd be present if I recruited you."

"He's already filled us in. Vouched for y'all. But him not bein' here grants a measure of distance," the cowboy drawled. "Lessens any inherent bias. I'm Teller, by the way. Kate's husband."

"So the council is you four?" Sofia asked.

"Correct. Me and Teller, with Adam and Ben alternating." Kate's eyes lost some of their chill. "You can relax, Sofia—we don't intend to interrogate you. I know I'm intimidating. I don't mince words, and I'm not one for small talk, but this farm is a peaceful, welcoming place."

"I don't mince words either," Lark said. "If Mayfly Hollow is so *peaceful and welcoming*, how do you explain the bullet holes in the outbuildings? And the others in the brick exterior of this farmhouse?"

"Dang, lady, you're as tetchy as my wife," Teller commented without rancor. He threw Kate an easy grin. "I reckon you've met your match with this gal."

Kate gave him side-eye but didn't reply. Instead, she said to

Lark, "Last summer a motorcycle gang tried to oust us. But, this is *our* home. We won't surrender it without a fight."

"If," Adam interjected, "you elect to remain here, there are certain conditions."

Sofia was rattled by how adeptly Kate had identified her anxiety. Weakly, she asked, "Conditions?"

"Participation in weapons and self-defense training. Learning various drills designed to be used in case of raiders. You'd have to be willing to defend Mayfly Hollow, and the other survivors, at significant personal peril," Adam said, his dark eyes sharp. "And then there are the mundane daily tasks involved in running an operation this size."

"Chores—feedin' livestock. Machinery maintenance. Weedin' in the garden. Preservin' veggies," Teller stated. "And so on. Sure can get tedious."

"Everyone pitches in and pulls their weight. That's the only way this can work." Kate sipped her coffee. "What did you do before the virus, Sofia?"

"I was a student," she said. "Undergrad, finishing my liberal studies courses. Once I completed my bachelor's, I intended to enroll in the Doctor of Veterinary Medicine program. I worked part-time at a vet office in Mergenville during summers. Not much hands-on stuff, but I was supposed to begin as a vet assistant there last summer break."

"I could tell you liked animals by the way you greeted my mutt," Teller said, referring to his Australian shepherd, Ace, who sat obediently at his feet.

"I was excited to see a dog for the first time in over a year." Sofia explained, "We went on a lot of trips, and my dad was allergic to dander so I was never able to have pets growing up, but I've always loved animals."

"I never would've guessed you wanted to be a vet," Lark said.

"It's not something I talk about. In fact, I don't even think about it anymore." Sofia shrugged, then looked into Teller's blazing azure eyes. "I didn't get the opportunity to learn much about treatment or pharmacology, but I'm willing to help in any way I can."

"A person's vocation can divulge a lot," Teller said sagely. "If you were ponderin' vet trainin', that suggests you're compassionate. Intelligent. Not afraid of sullyin' your hands. You got an iron stomach and a steady nerve in an emergency?"

"She does," Lark said. "Sofia can handle a crisis."

"And what about you?" Kate asked, her gaze skating over Lark. "What did you do before?"

"Whatever blue collar job I could get—bartending, cleaning hotel rooms, short-order cook in a diner," Lark said.

Kate perked up. "You know how to cook?"

"Sure."

"We could use someone who knows their way around a kitchen," Kate said, "besides me."

"You were a cook?" Sofia asked.

"Bakery owner." There were footfalls above their heads. At Sofia's inquisitive expression, Kate smiled. "That's the kids getting up for breakfast."

"So... what now?" Lark asked.

"I approve." Kate gave Teller, then Adam, a probing look.

"We don't coerce folks to join us," Teller said, unfolding his long limbs from the bench. He went to stand behind Kate, resting his work-calloused hands on her shoulders. "But you're welcome to become part of Mayfly Hollow."

"Lark is ambivalent," Kate said astutely. "How about we give you a few days or a week to evaluate us? See how we operate before committing?"

Sofia regarded Lark. The woman had a world-class poker face. When she didn't respond, Sofia spoke up, "Great. Thanks."

CHAPTER TWENTY-ONE

Lark and Sofia stayed for breakfast and were introduced to the kids. There was Nora, Ben's adopted daughter. She was a diffident, somber child. Her white-blonde hair in neat pigtails, her cornflower blue gaze was intent on the other children huddled around the table. She fussed over them like a mother hen, specifically with an Indian boy called Ravi.

Her baby daughter Maggie on her lap, Kate explained that since there were too many people to fit in the kitchen at once, the children always ate first. While they had breakfast, the adults did chores. After eating, the kids' day commenced with school, which was taught by a retired schoolteacher, Edna.

Lark wanted to wander around the farm after she finished her French toast. Sofia remained, meeting the rest of the group when they came in after choring. She scrambled to memorize all of their names.

There was Rob, a balding ginger-haired physician in his forties. Fritz, a pudgy farmer who wore overalls, was super chatty. A wiry-framed guy with brown hair, Josh, hardly spoke. He didn't make much of an impression on Sofia. She kept forgetting his name. And then Bella and Milo, a hipster couple in their twenties who were friendly enough.

"Where's Ben?" she asked Kate while helping clean the kitchen after breakfast.

"He spent yesterday with Nora, but once she was in bed, he went to Juniper Rise and slept there. He often needs solitude after bringing recruits back… to decompress, you know?"

Sofia wiped the trestle table with a dampened sponge. "What's *Juniper Rise*?"

"It's his homestead in the back forty."

"Homestead?"

"Yeah." Kate started the dishwasher and dried her hands with an embroidered tea towel. "Last autumn, he was ready to have his own home. We didn't want to lose him, so Teller and I encouraged him to claim a plot on the acreage and build a cabin. He chose one in the pasture a ten-minute walk from here."

"Your pasture is fenced?"

"With barbed wire. We actually extended the security fence last year to include the area Ben selected. It was a colossal undertaking—an all-hands-on-deck sort of thing. We never would've been able to do it if the Zs hadn't migrated north."

Sofia placed the sponge on the lip of the sink, and Kate handed her the tea towel. "Because it would've been too dangerous to work out in the open?"

"Well, yeah, but mostly because we had the freedom to drive wherever we needed to without any hindrance. I found a file in my brother-in-law's office with paperwork from the company that installed the fence. It was in Upper Bremer. So we went there, and I rummaged around in the manager's office until I located the address to their warehouse. We borrowed a tractor trailer and ferried supplies."

"Wow… but how did you figure out how to install the fence?"

"Trial and error. There were manuals, of course, but the language was uber technical."

Once her hands were dry, Sofia folded the towel and set it on the counter. "That's amazing. I'm not sure I could've done any of that."

Kate's eyes drifted over Sofia's face. "You'd be astonished what you can accomplish if you put your mind to it—I didn't even know how to fire a gun before shit went south. Ben said you lived on your own since the beginning?"

Sofia nodded.

"That takes a heck of a lot of grit."

"There were times I wasn't sure I'd make it through the night," Sofia admitted.

"I think I would've gone insane. I always fancied myself a loner, but the loneliness would've gotten to me."

"That was tough, too." Sofia swallowed. "Did Ben tell you about the two people we lost the other day?"

"Yes, but he didn't go into detail. I know he's ruminating over it."

"Would you point me in the direction of his house? I'd like to visit there and see how he's doing."

TWO AFFABLE NANNY goats trailed behind Sofia as she strolled on a footpath behind the farmhouse. Trotting up to her, they flanked Sofia, one on each side. They took turns cheerfully bleating and nudging her in the hip with their heads until she scratched their ears.

Distracted by a patch of berries, they stopped to chew on the fruit, and Sofia left them behind. She passed a row of cabins similar to the one she and Lark stayed in, then there was open terrain. Deep ruts were carved into the soil, perhaps from tires, and there was evidence of a narrow trench that had been dug up and refilled.

Remaining parallel to the fence as Kate had instructed, she could tell where new segments had been linked up with old. The newer panels were indistinguishable except that they were black rather than gunmetal gray. Fifty feet on, she came to a barbed-wire barricade, which Kate had explained led to the pasture proper.

Sofia lifted a metal stake and moved it aside, scooting inside the enclosure. She put the stake back where it belonged before sidestepping stones and random cowpats.

Kate had assured her that the livestock were now pastured in a different area and she wouldn't stumble upon them, but Sofia kept a wary eye out for anything that could be construed as a threat. Even with a tall iron fence, she didn't want to get lulled into a false sense of security. Better to remain vigilant at all times.

The tire tracks led to Ben's homestead. It was in a shallow, valley-like area to Sofia's left, on a slight rise and surrounded by foliage on three sides. Larger than she'd anticipated, it was a one-story house in shades of brown and tan and topped with a dark metal solar-paneled roof. A set of prefab concrete steps led to a wraparound porch with cedar pillars. Decorative brick skirted the house, coordinating with the siding. Although there was no walkway, juniper bushes were planted in rows leading to the steps, forming a path.

How had Ben constructed such a place?

Sofia climbed the steps and rapped on the door. It was cedar with decorative stained-glass inserts. There was movement inside, then Ben opened the door.

"Sofia, what are you doing here?"

"I just wanted to say hi." Sofia searched his face. He needed a shave and looked tired, with pouches under his eyes. "Can I come in?"

"Sure… sorry," he said, backing up to let her in. He was barefoot and wore basketball shorts and a wrinkled tee. "I don't know where my manners are. Welcome to Juniper Rise."

They stood in a small, tiled foyer. Directly ahead was a living room with a fieldstone fireplace. Sofia slipped off her sandals so she wouldn't track dirt, then walked forward to the carpet, putting her golf club by the fireplace.

Open concept, the living room connected to a kitchen and

eat-in dining alcove. A smartphone on the counter streamed the dulcet melody of Van Morrison's *Tupelo Honey*. There were no appliances or furniture other than a card table and folding chairs next to the kitchen. "You *built* this house?"

"Not exactly." Ben sounded entertained, and Sofia turned and caught his sapphire gaze. She wanted so desperately to kiss him. Her heart gathered momentum with the realization, and she glanced away, afraid he would read her thoughts. "It's a manufactured home. While out last summer, I encountered tractor trailers loaded with sections of this house. By late fall, I was able to bring the sections here and set them in place."

"How'd you do that?"

"Teller drove the tractor trailer down the lane to the entrance gate—it was a tight squeeze coming down the lane—and along the west side, where there's room to navigate within Mayfly Hollow's fence line."

Feeling overheated, Sofia feigned interest in browsing around the living room and kitchen to detect seams. There were none. "But in sections, you said. How did you place them?"

"Crane we took from a building site. It's parked in the pasture along with the tractor trailer. The machinery is useless now unless we can convert the engines. Teller brought a couple double-wides in case we need more housing in the future."

"Kate and Teller really do plan ahead," Sofia murmured. A blush had crept across her décolletage, and she hoped Ben wouldn't see it.

"That they do. Some may even call it going overboard, but you know that saying—preferable to have and not need." He indicated the card table and chairs. "Care to sit?"

Sofia gladly pulled out a chair and sat, arranging the skirt of her sundress ladylike over her knees, aware of Ben's gaze on her. She tucked a strand of hair behind her ear, self-conscious.

"Sorry it's so warm in here. There's a central air unit, but I haven't had much time to get electricity hooked up. Truthfully, I'm still figuring it out. Adam's been a big help—he's a plumber and a jack-of-all-trades—but neither of us are electricians. Actually, every step of setting up has taken twice as long as it should."

"Understandable," Sofia said, tongue twisted.

"Now that I'm home, I'm going to devote all the time I can to finishing up. I want to move in before fall."

"Nora will live here, too?"

"Yeah. You met her this morning?"

Sofia nodded. "She's a solemn little thing. Likes to mother the other kids. She made their plates and fed them. Wiped their faces when they got syrup on them. The whole nine."

Ben smiled, the corners of his eyes crinkling, then he turned more serious. "How'd the council meeting go?"

"Fine. Lark's not quite sure about staying yet. Kate said we can take a week and see how we like it here. She's... nice." Sofia checked Ben's face to see if his expression changed at Kate's mention, but it didn't. "I didn't think cowpokes like Teller existed. Thought they went out of style with Spaghetti Westerns."

Chuckling, Ben said, "What you see is what you get with Teller."

Space stretched out between them. The air became charged. Taking a gulp, Sofia blurted out before she lost her bravado, "Aren't we going to talk about what happened at the cabin yesterday morning?"

CHAPTER TWENTY-TWO

BEN'S EXPRESSION SHUTTERED, TRANSFORMING INTO A BLANK façade. "What's to talk about?"

A whoosh of irritation zipped up Sofia's spine. *So that's how it's gonna be.* "Are you joking?"

Ben picked at his thumbnail nonchalantly, not answering.

"Nuh-uh," Sofia said, frowning at him. "You're not withdrawing like yesterday. Not again. I won't let you, Ben."

He met her eyes and scowled.

The French toast sat like a rock in Sofia's digestive tract, but she charged forward, insisting, "We need to discuss Cora and Zac."

"We both know," Ben faltered, coughed, and continued, "I should've had the foresight to prevent it."

"How could you have? How?" Sofia leaned forward in her chair. "Accidents happen. People get complacent. Careless."

He massaged the back of his neck. Jutted his chin out mulishly. "It could've been prevented if I'd been thinking with my brain instead of my cock. The truth is... you're a distraction I just can't afford, Sofia."

Scoffing, she asked, "I'm a *distraction*, am I? I wasn't aware I was such a seductress. Wow. That's a backhanded fuckin' compliment if I've ever heard one, Ben."

"Don't talk like that. Flippancy doesn't suit you," he said quietly.

Into the Mystic began playing over the smartphone, but Sofia barely noticed. "I want to be clear. Are you blaming me for Cora and Zac, or yourself? Because both options are straight up bullshit."

"Of course it's not your fault. I assume full responsibility… for everything! In fact, I owe you an apology for feeling you up." Ben sighed. "I took advantage of your drowsiness. I should've kept my damn hands to myself."

"Okay. Knock off the self-flagellation. I get it. You have principles, and you're a stand-up guy even though I welcomed you," Sofia simulated air quotes by waggling her fingers, *"feeling me up."*

"I'm just trying to do the right thing. Sometimes, it's a battle. I'm fallible. Nevertheless, I do try."

"Congratulations on being Mister Honorable." Sofia couldn't keep the scorn out of her voice when she demanded, "What's the big fucking production about anyway? You want me. I want you. God!"

"Sofia—"

She waved her hand to silence him. Getting up, she went to the window, which overlooked the backyard. The view was lovely—a meadow dotted with wildflowers and sheltered by conifers. A fat russet squirrel chased another up a tree trunk. Sofia's hands shook. She clasped them. "Why are you making this complicated?"

Ben came to stand behind her. "I've learned the last year that I'm a complex man, Sofia. I don't want to be. I just am. I'm sorry."

The warmth of his body radiated to hers, infusing the air with his scent—something spicy and woodsy—that left her weak-kneed. It would take no effort whatsoever to turn and put her lips to his. How would he respond if she did? "I'm not seeking an apology."

"Then what," Ben retorted, "are you seeking?"

Sofia threw her hands up and whirled around. He was close enough for her to make out the tiny flecks of amber in his irises. To smell the toothpaste on his breath. "I don't know. Not this—not an argument."

His gaze softened as he scanned her face. "You deserve so much better than me."

"Don't do that," Sofia said. "Don't pull that self-effacing paternalistic crap on me. I decide what I deserve. *I do.*"

"There are too many years between us. Too many dissimilarities. Most importantly, I'm not in the appropriate headspace for a relationship."

With a huff, Sofia slanted her head back to brazenly meet his eyes. When he didn't speak further, she asked, eyebrow raised, "*A relationship*? When did I say anything about expecting that?"

"Experience has taught me that strictly sex arrangements don't work. Lines invariably get crossed."

"I've never found them problematic." She put her hands on her hips. Narrowed her gaze. "If you don't want me, just come clean."

Ben exhaled, closing his eyes. His hands were balled at his hips.

Sofia stepped into him. Ben's breath hitched when their chests made contact. The golden wiry hairs on his forearms stood up in gooseflesh. Smiling in satisfaction, Sofia went on her tiptoes and whispered in his ear, "Tell me you don't want me. I dare you."

Ben's eyelids fluttered open. His pupils had dilated. He rasped, "God help me, I can't."

His arousal poked Sofia's belly. He groaned. Started to pull away. Sofia wouldn't let him. She twined her arms around Ben's neck and dragged his mouth to hers.

"Oh, fuck it," he growled against her lips in surrender.

Ben's kiss was urgent. Cupping her bottom, he rubbed his pelvis against her. The only barrier separating them was a few thin scraps of fabric.

Sofia moaned, and Ben backed her up until she was pinned to the wall. His lips left her mouth, suckling her collarbone and the cleft between her breasts. He went to his knees before her, his nails lightly scraping as he hooked his fingers around the elastic of Sofia's underwear. A rough tug had them skimming down her thighs.

Mesmerized, Sofia panted as she watched him lift the hem of her dress and disappear under her skirt.

Grasping her behind a knee, he brought her leg up to his shoulder. His whiskers delicately abraded her inner thigh. When the tip of his tongue touched her clit, Sofia gasped, bucking her hips. Head flung back, she concentrated on the sensations of Ben hungrily tasting her. His tongue lathed her swollen lips then circled her throbbing nub. When his teeth grazed her there, electric pleasure tinkled from her center to the soles of her feet. He slid one finger in her slit, working her with calculated precision, then added another finger.

Tension mounted. Sofia's muscles clenched. She cried out her release as waves of sensation surged from her core. Ben's movements didn't cease—he prolonged every last second of her ecstasy until Sofia wilted against him, spent, using the wall for support.

Removing Sofia's calf from his shoulder, Ben positioned her foot on the floor. He got up, his chin glistening with moisture. After licking his lips, he swept his hand across his mouth to wipe it. "I've wanted to do that for a long time. That was... incredible."

"My turn," Sofia breathed, her fingers finding the waistband of his shorts.

He placed his palms over her hands, stilling her. His sternum rose and fell rapidly as he caught his breath. "Sofia..."

She glimpsed at his face, her heart skipping at his bleak expression. "What's wrong?"

"We need to stop," Ben said, regret tinging his tone.

Sofia stared stupidly. "Why?"

"We can't—I shouldn't have—I got carried away—"

Confused, she shook her head. Real life rushed back. "Oh, come on. Are you freakin' kidding me?"

"You have every right to be angry. I-I've got zero willpower. I'm a louse…" He brought his hand to Sofia's face and caressed her cheek, his eyes entreating her.

Sofia wrenched away. "You're ruining my afterglow."

"Please try to understand—"

"Oh, I understand." Sofia bent and seized her panties from the carpet, scanning Ben's crotch as she straightened. "You've got major issues."

"Yes. That's exactly why I've got to stop this—us—before we get in too deep."

Sofia stepped into her underwear, pulled them up, and smoothed her skirt. She pointed to his raging hard-on. "It's obvious how turned on you are right now, yet you'd rather deny yourself. Torture yourself. That's screwed up."

"I want you, Sofia. But part of being an adult is—"

"Shut up." Sofia snatched her golf club from where she'd left it. "You're only hurting yourself. It's… perverse."

A look of panic flew across Ben's face, and he put his palms up.

She clapped a hand over her mouth to contain her mirth. "I'm not going to brain you, idiot. I'm not even that mad."

"You're not?"

"Why would I be? I'd be pissed if you'd used me for a blow job or something, but I got mine."

"Sofia…"

She strode to the door and stepped into her sandals. Ben followed. "You wanna know what I really think?"

He looked at her mournfully.

"You've gotta get your shit together. Cope with your hang-ups. You're too uptight."

"I—"

"It's a shame, 'cause a mind-blowing suck job might've mellowed you." Sofia opened the front door, saying over her shoulder with a mocking grin, "But anytime you want to slap me against a wall and make me come without demanding anything in return, I'm down for it. Adiós."

CHAPTER TWENTY-THREE

"I don't buy it."

Sofia found Lark by happenstance after leaving Ben's house. She rambled further along the fence, ignoring the wetness between her thighs and the way her dampened panties stuck to her. She hadn't fibbed when she told Ben she wasn't mad, but... Sofia was perturbed.

She rolled her eyes.

Fucking men.

Approaching the double-wide trailers Ben had referred to, Sofia saw movement in her peripheral vision. Hand up as a visor to shield her eyes, she squinted. Lark leaned against a weeping willow near the security fence. Calling Lark's name to get her attention, Sofia waved and went to join her.

The tree was on a patch of grass beside an outcrop of craggy boulders. A small spring bubbled from the depths and spilled onto the rock below, draining into the fissures and puddling on the ground. The earthy smell of loam permeated the air. Sitting down under the willow, Lark crossed her legs at the ankle. At her invitation, Sofia dropped beside her and, needing a friend, confided what occurred at Ben's place.

The bubbling of the spring was comforting, lending to the

companionable mood, but Lark's comment stymied Sofia. Brooding, she plucked a thin blade of grass and shredded it over her knee. Scooping the shreds, she brought her palm up and blew, scattering them into the wind. "What do you mean, *you don't buy it?*"

"You say you're not bothered by him rejecting you. I don't believe it for a second."

"I mean, nobody likes being rejected, no," Sofia replied. "But there's no reason for the drama. I'm a modern woman. A friends-with-bennies set-up would be perfect. He doesn't seem to understand that."

"Because we say that all the time while secretly wishing for a relationship. Ben's skeptical. Most men would be." Lark shrugged. "You sure you're not fallin' for him?"

"How could I be? I don't know him."

"Infatuation," Lark said with a knowing look. "So, how was it? He rock your world?"

Sofia's cheeks stung, but she laughed. "Hell yeah."

"Old Ben's secretly a beast who likes going downtown, huh? Don't know why that shocks me." Lark bit her thumbnail, contemplative. "He's hot enough, but his good guy persona does nothin' for me. Not my type—I'd friend-zone his ass."

"What's your type?"

"Muscles. Tattoos. Attitudes. The kind that ends up fucking your mother behind your back."

Sofia asked, "Seriously?"

"Yep. *I'm just helping your mom unclog her sink* was his single biggest lie besides *your child support check is in the mail.*"

"I know another lie."

"What?"

"*Just the tip, baby.*"

Lark snorted. "I misjudged you. When we first met, I thought you were a fuzzy bunny."

"What's a fuzzy bunny?"

"It's,"Lark flailed her hand, "an insult. You know, a girly-girl. Frou-frou. Bit of a princess. Now, I'm seeing you're a cool chick."

"Why can't I be both a girly-girl *and* a cool chick?" Sofia deadpanned, "People tend to be multi-dimensional, Lark."

"What can I say? Rushing to judgment is one of my countless character flaws." She paused. "I had a chat with Adam."

"Oh?"

"Misjudged him, too."

"How so?"

"He spews a lot of five-dollar words. I thought he was a stuffed shirt."

Sofia gave Lark side-eye. "Are you holding it against him that he's well-spoken?"

"No. I just didn't realize he's alright." Lark smiled in a conspiratorial way. "He told me that he and Josh grow weed. I don't know about you, but I'd *love* a joint."

SOFIA AND LARK meandered to the farmhouse in time for lunch. It was Rob's turn to cook, which meant simple fare—meat sandwiches on hearty, dense whole wheat bread and raw veggies with dill dip. The kids had already eaten and were sent outside to play while the adults lingered in the kitchen. Ben was conspicuously absent.

"I don't know how much of the farm you were able to see so far," Kate said, "but do you have any questions about anything?"

"Just general stuff," Lark replied. "Are you going to give us a tour?"

Kate shook her head. "Not yet. I will once you decide to stay. Nothing against you two, but we don't like to let strangers know all our inner-workings."

"Can't say I blame you." Sofia swallowed her last drink of

iced tea. "Mayfly Hollow is a sizable operation. How many acres is it?"

"Just over three hundred. The land isn't particularly suitable for farming, but we grow hay for our livestock and enough wheat to make flour."

"I was wondering about the bread," Lark said, "since flour would've spoiled by now. Is there a mill nearby?"

Teller smiled, shifting baby Maggie on his lap. "Grindin' flour conjures visions of gristmills, don't it?"

"We have an electric countertop mill," Kate explained. "It's a quick process to grind wheat berries into flour, but we mill it right before baking bread since oxidation lessens the nutritional benefits."

Sofia marveled, "How do you guys know all this?"

"I learned a lot from my sister—she and her husband were doomsday preppers," Kate said. "They also collected a library's worth of reference books in the den."

Adam, who had silently listened to the conversation until then, said, "The key to everything is electricity. Heat, air conditioning, sanitation. If we lose our power grid, we'll be living in the eighteen hundreds."

"Yeah, that's been my experience this last year. Not fun," Sofia said. "I don't know how I survived without hot water, AC, and delicious food."

"We took those small luxuries for granted pre-apocalypse. Not anymore. We can do without them, if we have to, but they make us feel human," Kate said. Her expression intensified, as if she were passionate about what she was about to say. "We'll do our damnedest to hold onto them—we don't want to merely survive here. Having a fulfilling life is our goal. Living well. Thriving."

"Amen to that," Teller injected. He kissed Maggie's plump cheek before passing her to Kate. When Kate smooched her, Maggie cooed and clapped her hands. "Anyhow, Josh and I got some work to do this afternoon. Best we get hoppin'."

Wordlessly, Josh stood, and Lark followed, saying, "If it's okay, I want to look around more. Sofia, you coming?"

"Dinner's at six," Kate told them as Lark and Sofia cleared their plates and loaded them in the dishwasher. "I'm cooking pasta. I could use help with the salad."

"Sure," Sofia said. "We can do that."

"Afterwards, it's movie night." Kate called as they trod down the hall to the back door, "There'll be popcorn!"

The screen door swung shut behind them. Sofia turned to Lark. "I like it here. What do you think?"

"Maybe." Lark descended the stairs and was met by Teller's dog, Ace. She stroked his ears. "I'm going to loop around the farmhouse and down the lane on that side of the property. See what's over there. It probably leads back down to the entrance. Alright?"

"Yeah."

In the side yard, the kids played tag with Ben, who was *it*. He chased Ravi, his laughter carefree. With a bark, Ace trotted off to join the fun.

Stepping around the free-range chickens pecking at the gravel, Sofia and Lark sauntered along the lane. Feeling Ben's gaze on her as they passed by, Sofia studiously avoided looking in his direction.

CHAPTER TWENTY-FOUR

THE FOLLOWING WEEK AT BREAKFAST, SOFIA TOLD KATE AND TELLER that she had chosen to make Mayfly Hollow her home. When asked, Lark, who was more reserved in her admiration of the farm than Sofia, assented that she too would remain there.

Other than a smattering of polite exchanges, Sofia and Ben barely spoke since their interlude at his house in the meadow. Feeling stubborn, Sofia resolved to let *him* come to *her*—she would *not* be the first to reach out. He obviously required space to get his head on straight, to acknowledge there was something singular between them. Rare. Maybe he never would acknowledge, but she'd proceed with her life regardless.

Still, despite Sofia's pragmatic stance, their attraction persisted over the subsequent weeks. It was hard to disregard the pull. It was an invisible yet pulsating tether linking them together whenever they were in the same room. Sofia suspected Ben felt the connection as well, but he was stealthy at veiling his emotions.

The ranch proved to be a happy place. People were friendly. Laid-back. Although the chores could be demanding, even tiresome, they were also gratifying. Sexual frustration notwithstanding, Sofia was content.

Appointed to kitchen duties, Lark switched off with Kate to prepare dinner, which was their biggest daily meal, and baked bread and preserved food. The others alternated preparing breakfast and lunch. Each member was in charge of their own laundry. Housecleaning and the children's laundry were delegated on a rotating schedule. Edna, the retired schoolteacher, was primarily tasked with school activities. Sofia adored her, a gentle soul reminding Sofia of her Auntie Alice, who'd lived in an assisted living facility before succumbing to the virus. Sometimes, in the evenings, Sofia sat at the kitchen table with Edna and chatted while preparing lesson plans or craft projects.

Everyone helped outdoors in some capacity, principally weeding or watering the garden. While Adam, Ben, Teller, Fritz, and Josh mostly saw to crops and general farming responsibilities, Milo and Bella enjoyed caring for the goats, fowl, and other livestock, including those pastured. In addition to beekeeping, Rob grew herbs and flowers outside his cabin. Even the children were assigned simple jobs.

Without fail, Monday, Wednesday, and Friday afternoons were reserved for weapons training or combat drills. These were Sofia's least favorite activities—although she'd mastered archery effortlessly enough, she didn't care for one-on-one sparring with swords or knives. It didn't come naturally to her, and she was often paired with Ben, which was awkward. Sometimes, Sofia got the feeling that Kate analyzed her, as if trying to gauge her strengths and weaknesses. It was unnerving.

At the end of July, when she and Lark had been at Mayfly Hollow nearly two solid months, Kate casually said one night while they sat on the front porch, "Adam is departing soon for a six-week recruitment trip."

Sofia's bare feet rubbed against the plank floor as she rocked, but Kate's words slackened her speed. "But... didn't he say that the zombie horde is coming back? Won't that be risky?"

"Adam'll head home if it turns dicey. I have faith in his skills. He lived out there alone for a long time." Kate lifted her tumbler of iced tea to take a lengthy drink, then said, "What I was considering was sending you out with him."

"What?" Sofia gasped, putting her feet flat on the floor. "Adam may be skillful, but I'm not!"

"That's precisely why I'd prefer you to go." Stretching over to Sofia's rocker, Kate placed a steadying hand on her forearm. "I've heard how courageous you were when your friends were attacked. Both Lark and Ben sung your praises. You can do it, Sofia. You just need to gain self-confidence."

Gulping, Sofia grappled for an excuse. No, she did not want to leave the sanctuary of Mayfly Hollow. Beyond the gates was hardship. Adversity. If she had her choice, she'd never leave again!

A wail came over the baby monitor on the wicker end table flanking Kate's rocking chair. Kate exhaled tiredly. "Maggie's cutting an upper incisor. Poor lamb will be miserable for her birthday tomorrow. I'll fetch her a fresh teething ring from the freezer." She stood. "Have a think. We'll talk."

Plagued with apprehension, Sofia did not sleep that night. She tossed and turned in bed until Lark snapped, "Sofia! Will you quit wriggling around for crying out loud?"

"Sorry."

Slipping on her tennis shoes and grabbing her golf club, Sofia went outside. She'd take a twilight stroll. A low dew point made it pleasantly warm out. It was pitch black except for the solar pathway lights along the lane. Thirsty for a glass of icy lemonade, she opted to head to the main house.

A velvety breeze blew, ruffling the lace hem of Sofia's chaste cotton nightie. The climb up the hill winded her, but the breeze was blissful. A light fixture by the hayloft illuminated the barn, chicken coop, and the kitchen steps. Caught unaware, Sofia recoiled as the barn door squeaked open, and a figure appeared around the corner. It was Ben, wearing dusty jeans and a gray sleeveless tee which highlighted his brawny biceps. He wiped his hands on a faded bandana.

When he saw her, he asked, "What on earth are you doing out at this time of night? It's gotta be after midnight."

"Couldn't sleep," she murmured. "What are *you* doing in the barn this late?"

"Hunting for a part."

"You look as parched as me."

"I am. I'll get us a drink if you want to wait for me on the porch."

Nodding, Sofia ambled around the house and up the three stairs to the porch while Ben went inside through the kitchen door. The moon cast just enough of a glow to make out the rockers and the swing. Pausing, she eyed the swing, which had room for two to sit. Curious which seat Ben would choose, she got comfortable on the swing.

Ben exited the house through the front door, carefully prodding the screen door open with his hip, a tumbler in each fist. He loomed above Sofia in the semi-darkness, silently handing her one. To her surprise, he settled on the porch swing beside her.

Sofia raised her glass to sip and coughed. "What is this?"

"Bourbon whiskey with a splash of lemonade. You like?"

"Packs a punch." She swigged greedily. She'd never tried bourbon before, but the drink was tasty. Heat seared her breastbone, trailed to her tummy, then pooled, smoldering like cinders do before unexpectedly reigniting.

The soporific cadence of cicadas and the piquant fragrance of the phlox bordering the porch made Sofia languid. She wrapped her hand around the chain suspending the swing from the ceiling and propped her head against it, already buzzed. *Talk about a cheap date!* "Are you trying to get me drunk so you can take advantage of me, counselor?"

As soon as she uttered the query, she regretted it. Reminding herself that the easy relationship they once shared was gone, Sofia waited anxiously for Ben's response. She anticipated a stilted rejoinder, but he merely chuckled. "Do I need to get you drunk to take advantage of you, brown-eyed girl?"

They were in treacherous territory now. Awareness constricted Sofia's thorax. Vined its way to her loins and unfurled. *In for a penny, in for a pound.* "You know you don't."

"Possible that the liquor wasn't a wise choice... especially since I've been successful distancing myself over the last weeks. Gotta keep my wits about me," he mused.

"Is that so? Why?"

"You know why. It's taxing enough not touching you when I'm stone-cold sober."

"Still wrestling with your lust, I see," she drawled.

Ben lowered his eyes. "I'm a fool. Playing with fire like this. Why am I here?"

Sofia's head swam, but she took another drink anyway. "Are your dark urges threatening to overpower you at the slightest provocation? Is your control dangling by a thread?"

"Dark urges? I'm Benjamin Cassidy, Esquire. Mild-mannered lawyer. Even labeled *Mister Honorable* if I remember correctly."

"That was sarcasm."

"It flattered me. Lawyers usually get a bad rap. Accused of being the lowest of the low. Disparaged as slugs, roaches, vermin. Preferable to amoebic dysentery or leprosy... You know, you can interrupt me at any time."

"Hey," she said mildly, "I'm just waiting for you to list something that I don't agree with."

Ben laughed and put a hand to his heart. "Ooo. Ouch."

Sofia giggled. Shutting her eyes, she soaked in the nighttime sounds. Thoughts turned to what Kate had said earlier. Opening one eye, she faced Ben. "Did you know Kate thinks I should go out recruiting with Adam?"

Ben's demeanor changed. He sat up abruptly. "*What?*"

"She says I'm capable. But I need to gain self-confidence. Should I?"

"Hell, no," he ground out, "do I want you leaving with Adam for six weeks. Putting yourself in jeopardy like that. Absolutely not. I'll tell Kate my opinion in no uncertain terms."

Sofia laughed. She didn't imagine for a minute that Ben doubted whether she could handle being in the real world. His display of machismo tickled her. Maybe it was the bourbon urging her to poke the bear, but she said slyly, "Hmm. That got a reaction. Careful or I may think you're actually jealous of me spending time alone with another man."

Ben seemed to chew over his response.

"Adam has a crush on me," she said sweetly. "You're not the only guy around here who's partial to chubby chicks."

"What," Ben cleared his throat, "makes you think he has a crush on you?"

Sofia bit back an evil grin. "It's little things... the ogling of my cleavage. The lilt of his speech when he speaks to me. A lady just knows, Ben."

He dragged a hand through his hair. "How can you sit there in that nightgown all innocent and virginal and tease me?"

Feeling wicked, she finished her drink and murmured, "He is attractive. And I do have an itch that must be scratched."

"Don't be cruel. You're twisting the knife. Punishing me."

Sofia shrugged. "You should know that I won't wait around for you forever." She couldn't see the fly of his jeans, but the way he shifted uncomfortably told Sofia he was aroused. It made her feel powerful, which was addictive. "If I got up, lifted my nightie, and straddled you... you wouldn't refuse me, would you?"

Ben gulped audibly.

"I'm not wearing panties. And, did you know there's no reason to hassle with condoms because I have an IUD?" She whispered, "I'd just hitch my skirt and ride you until you come inside me."

In a strangled tone, he gasped, "Sofia..."

"Don't worry, counselor." She stood. The liquor rendered her tipsy. And brash. Placing her empty tumbler on the wicker table, Sofia bent to Ben's ear. Nipped it. He jumped. She laughed. "I won't seduce you. It's up to *you* to take what you want. Just don't wait too long."

Seizing her golf club from where she'd left it, Sofia glided down the porch steps, leaving Ben to stare after her.

Once tucked back in her bed, she fell asleep instantly, a smile on her face.

CHAPTER TWENTY-FIVE

The following evening after Maggie's birthday celebration, Kate inquired whether Sofia would recruit with Adam. Sofia studied the woman's face. Had Ben spoken to her as he'd vowed? She'd seen Kate and Teller whispering in the garden the other day before lunchtime, their gazes speculative while they watched Ben, Sofia, and Edna converse. Once Sofia had noticed, they played it cool, but what had they been discussing? Were they gossiping about her and Ben? "Uh, I don't feel quite ready. Is it okay if I sit this one out?"

"I'm not a dictator. I won't insist," Kate replied, her green gaze solemn. "But I do advise that you take the next opportunity which presents itself. How else will you grow if you don't challenge yourself?"

Sofia nodded, feeling vaguely ashamed. A flush washed over her. "You're right, of course. I will."

Kate patted Sofia's arm before unbuckling Maggie from her highchair and removing her sparkly party hat. Still running a low-grade fever from teething, Maggie's eyelids drooped. "Let's go have a bubble bath and scrub off that cake so you can go to bed, sweetie."

She left Sofia and Lark alone in the kitchen. Pressing the

button to run the dishwasher, Lark said, "She must not know about my freak out during the trip here, otherwise she'd suggest I go with Adam."

"I'm timid. You're not, so you don't need to test yourself that way. I do."

"Oh," Lark said airily, "you'd be fine. You've built it up in your head is all."

"Hmm."

Folding a tea towel and placing it beside the sink, Lark sidled to Sofia. She brought her hand to her mouth, putting her middle and index fingers together with her thumb to simulate a toking gesture. "The celebrations continue tonight with a bon voyage party for Adam behind the barn."

"Who'll be there?"

"Milo, Bella, Fritz, and Josh. Naturally, Adam. Rob may stop by later, as well as Teller and Kate. Edna'll stay back with the kids if they want to hang out." She wiggled her eyebrows, adding in a wheedling voice, "I've got jugs of wine chilling in the fridge."

"What about Ben?"

Lark didn't suppress her smile. "Adam says when Ben's not with Nora he's working at his house. That's why he wasn't at dinner. He's trying to get his wiring fixed."

"Oh." Shrugging, Sofia said, "Well. Why not?"

AFTER SHOWERING, Sofia took extra care with her appearance. In truth, she was excited about Adam's party. She coiled her sable-colored hair into a clip and selected a floral-printed sundress with a halter tie, one of the few dresses she'd packed in her suit-case. Golf club in hand, at twilight, she made her way up to the farmhouse.

Folding lawn chairs were set up on a cleared patch of grass behind the barn, tiki torches and strings of fairy lights strung on fence posts. Bowls of popcorn and homemade chips were on a rectangular folding table beside glass tumblers. A galvanized tub was half-filled with ice and held a variety of wine and spirits. Classic rock streamed from an iPod hooked up to freestanding speakers.

Lark, Adam, Milo, and Bella lounged on lawn chairs off to the side of the refreshment table. Adam lifted a hand, beckoning Sofia. "Hey, pleased you could make it. Can I get you a drink?"

Sofia perched on a chair, smiling a greeting at the others then pointing to Adam's glass. "What's that you have?"

"It's called The Four Horsemen—the ultimate libation for the apocalypse. A mix of four whiskeys. You game?"

Sofia recalled how the lemonade-spiked whiskey had affected her. She'd slept like a rock and woke with an aching head, faintly scandalized by her naughty behavior the night before. "Oof. Better not. Wine?"

"Dandelion or rhubarb?"

"Surprise me.

"You got it."

Fritz and Josh arrived. In his introverted way, Josh dipped his chin when Adam welcomed them. Fritz shook his hand. They fetched their beverages, and Adam led them back to the group, where they all chose seats. Adam gave Sofia a tumbler of dandelion wine, and she murmured her thanks.

Lark took a sip of her Four Horsemen then toasted Adam, "To safe travels!"

"To safe travels," they repeated.

"Bottoms up," Fritz boomed, taking a healthy guzzle.

"Shots next," Bella said. "There's vodka and tequila."

"This is strong enough for me. It could strip paint," Lark said. "I'm on my second round."

"One is good, two is the most. Three, you're under the table. After four... you're under the host," Fritz quipped, then chortled, his bulbous belly jiggling.

Lark snickered at his joke then grinned. Sofia's gaze oscillated between Lark and Adam. Was *he* the host? Maybe Lark wouldn't mind hooking up with him. Sofia hadn't lied to Ben—she had noticed Adam's interested glimpses, but she wasn't attracted to him. As far as she was concerned, Adam was a friend and could sleep with whomever he wished.

"Should I make a bonfire?" Milo asked, pushing his horn-rimmed glasses up the bridge of his nose.

"I'd love one," Bella enthused. "What do you guys think?" Although it was a warm night, they all voted for a bonfire.

Fritz set his beverage on the ground and hefted from his chair. "I'll help ya, Milo."

While everyone chatted, Fritz got a metal ring from the barn, centering it in the grass. He and Milo brought armfuls of seasoned wood from where it was stacked along the side of the barn, mounding it in the ring. Milo arranged twigs for kindling. Fritz struck a match, and flames licked the wood.

They gathered their chairs around the fire. Sofia was content to nurse her wine and listen to the others converse while staring into the flames. The smoke drifted in her eyes, and the heat flushed her skin, but she enjoyed the crackling of the embers and how the coals glowed crimson. Occasionally, the lowing of cattle wafted from the barn.

"You zoning?"

Lark's voice pulled her from her reverie. "Just relaxed."

The moon's position implied that the hour was late. Josh and Fritz had left, and Bella and Milo stood, saying they ought to head to their cabin.

After they were out of earshot, Lark said, "Bella and Milo have been handsy all night. They're in a hurry to bang. Everybody is so horny here."

Sofia stiffened, waiting for Lark to bring up her and Ben's names. She hadn't confided everything, but Lark knew enough.

Lark added, "Kate and Teller are constantly sneaking off to the bathroom for an after-lunch quickie. They think they're crafty, but they ain't foolin' me."

Adam shrugged. "They're newlyweds."

"Oh," Sofia said, "I thought they've been married a while. They have a daughter and all."

"Actually," Adam replied, "Maggie is Kate's niece."

Lark tilted her head to the side. "What happened to Kate's sister and brother-in-law? Ben said they died, but he didn't provide details."

Adam took a deep breath, his face grave. "It's... it was a horrible era in the history of Mayfly Hollow."

"We don't mean to pry," Sofia reassured him. "You don't have to relive it if it's too..."

"No, no. I'll tell you." He stood and went to the refreshment table. "But I need another drink first."

CHAPTER TWENTY-SIX

"I'd been transient since the virus decimated the population. The Zs were more sensitive to human scents than now, but supplies weren't as scarce then." The firelight hit Adam's dusky features, making them shine. His mouth turned down. "Trade off, I suppose. Still, I found just enough to subsist on—I was skin and bone. Sometimes, I'd find a group to forage with. I'd teamed up with two other guys. We were in Mergenville, scavenging. We bumped into an MC. It was... ugly. They tied us up. Dragged us behind their bikes. I barely got away with my life. They only released me, so I'd let folks know that Mergenville was theirs."

Sofia thought back to Kate mentioning a motorcycle gang when Lark asked about the bullet holes in the farmhouse brick.

"I did my best to avoid them, and a short time later, I stumbled upon Kate and Teller. Little did I know, they'd witnessed what went down in Mergenville and recognized me. After we talked, they invited me here. Finally, a place to call home. I was immensely appreciative."

"But what about Kate's sister?" Lark prompted.

"Hold your horses," Adam scolded, pausing to take a drink. "Her name was Connie. I didn't know her well, but she was decent. Fair. Worked hard as anyone I've ever met. Even nine months pregnant, she labored in the garden."

"And her husband?"

"From what I learned from Teller, Seth suffered from mental illness and was off his meds. He'd been acting erratic. Spouting Bible verses and bullying people." Adam scoffed, "What's the zombie apocalypse without a trite Jesus-freak?"

Lark snorted. "Such a cliché."

"Right? Anyway, Connie sent Seth away on an errand. When he never returned, everybody assumed he died."

Sofia asked, "Assumed? So he was still alive?"

"Apparently, Seth teamed up with the MC during his absence from Mayfly Hollow. He was on a quest for retribution against Connie and Kate for casting him out. *He* brought them here, intent on raping and pillaging."

"Holy shit," Lark breathed.

"Yeah," Adam said. "Luckily, we'd prepared for attack and had a strategy in place. There was a shootout. With home field advantage, we prevailed but still took a beating. Lost a lady. Nearly lost Nora." Adam swallowed and gazed meditatively into the bonfire, which had burned down to ashes.

"Connie... was shot?" Sofia asked.

"Seth stabbed her. She bled out. Kate took Seth out then cut Maggie from her sister's womb."

There was silence for several beats, then Lark said, "Whoa."

"No wonder everyone holds Kate in such high esteem," Sofia murmured. "She's a warrior."

Adam nodded. "She does what's necessary, even when unpleasant."

"Rob told me that she was bitten by a Z," Lark said. "He was in awe that it didn't kill her."

Sofia's mouth dropped open. "Kate was *bit*? I didn't know about that."

"Before the MC altercation," Adam replied. "She was treated with an antibiotic we had on hand, and Teller tended to her."

"I've never heard of that happening," Lark said. "Bitten and lived?"

Adam bobbed his head. "Me either. It was... miraculous. So, you can see why Kate's a legend around here."

With sudden clarity, Sofia remembered when Ben claimed he was in love with another woman. Was *Kate* that woman? He'd known her pre-virus, and she had invited him here, after all. Sofia had caught Ben's attentiveness whenever Kate was around and had observed the deferential way he spoke to her. Sofia had dismissed it as just close friendship, but they must have a past.

Well, fuck.

It was an unsettling notion. Sofia gnawed at her cheek, her earlier contentment waning. Ben had provided a laundry list of reasons why they couldn't be together. He was too old. They were too different. He was complicated. She deserved better.

After last night, Sofia assumed she'd begun to find the chink in Ben's armor. To penetrate his defenses. But him pining away over Kate... that was something Sofia couldn't do anything about.

Lark said, "How about some weed to lighten the atmosphere?"

"There's an idea." Adam unfolded from his seat and went over by the refreshment table. He bent and grasped a zippered pouch that Sofia hadn't noticed before from behind the cooler.

Pulling a joint from the pouch, along with a lighter, Adam returned to his chair. He placed the joint between his lips, lighting it. Inhaling, he held his breath then passed the joint to Lark, who took a puff.

When Lark presented it to Sofia, she accepted without hesitation, taking a protracted hit. She needed a respite from thinking. It had been ages since she'd last smoked—it burned her lungs, and she had to smother a cough—but she waited until her lungs were protesting before slowly exhaling. Reclining her head, she closed her eyes and surrendered to the sense of well-being crowding out all else.

Lark took the joint from Sofia, asking Adam, "What is it?"

"It's a sativa-dominant strain called Jem Euphoria. THC levels are important, but I won't sacrifice quantity for quality."

Giddy, Sofia brought her fingertips to her mouth and pantomimed a *chef's kiss*.

They were on their second joint when Lark was overcome by the giggles. "I do declare. That there is some satisfactory Mary Jane."

Sofia tittered. "Maui Wowie."

"Ganja," Lark replied.

Sofia said, "Grass."

"Buuuud," Lark rejoined, drawing the word out and causing Adam and Sofia to cackle.

Sofia had tears in her eyes. "Devil's Lettuce."

"Having fun?" Ben asked from the other side of the now extinguished bonfire, and they quieted.

"Don Juan himself," Lark intoned slyly.

"Lark, hush," Sofia hissed, glaring at her.

Lark put her palm over her mouth.

"Hey, man. Were we too loud?" Adam asked as Ben approached.

"You're okay." He had a rectangular contraption in his hand. "I've figured out the issue connecting up my solar panels. Faulty DC disconnect."

"What's that?" Lark asked, offering Ben the joint.

"Thanks." Ben sat down on a chair beside Sofia, taking a drag. His narrowed gaze scanned her, but his words were directed at Lark when he exhaled. "It's a switch that facilitates DC electricity flow. It goes between a solar panel array and the power inverter."

Her reservations vanishing at the heat in Ben's eyes, Sofia fluttered her lashes at him. "Fascinating."

"I don't know about that," he replied easily, "but it's an essential component."

"We don't have more of them in our stockpile?" Adam asked, his forehead wrinkling.

"Believe it or not, nope."

"That is a dilemma."

"Not only for me, Adam, but for the entire farm if one needs replacing elsewhere."

A zing of alarm sobered Sofia. "You aren't suggesting what I think you're suggesting, are you?"

Ben smiled crookedly. "What am I suggesting?"

"That you're gonna leave Mayfly Hollow on a mission for more of those switch thingies."

"That's my plan. And you're tagging along, brown-eyed girl."

CHAPTER TWENTY-SEVEN

"Oh am I?" Sofia asked pertly. "You sound rather certain of that."

"A little birdie told me that you promised Kate you'd venture out at the next opportunity," Ben reminded her, hitching his thumbs to point at his chest. "I'm your man."

Their gazes clashed. The majority of their interactions consisted of Sofia in a dominant role. His assertive attitude was a switch up. *Hot.* Tendrils of desire lapped at Sofia's groin. She moistened her lips with her tongue. "Uh huh. Plan on breaking me in, do you?"

"Gawd, get a room, you two," Lark said.

Not severing her gaze from Ben's, Sofia raised her eyebrows, daring him to reply. To rebuff Lark's comment. To deny the palpable charge in the air. He lifted an unconcerned shoulder. *Interesting.* Usually, Ben would treat her like a kid sister when they were in the presence of others. His boldness was a novelty. Had her warning last night about not waiting forever gotten through his thick skull?

"I won't let anything happen to you. Don't you trust me?"

Sofia blew a raspberry. She trusted Ben, but she did *not* feel comfortable leaving Mayfly Hollow. Period. The gravity of what lay ahead subdued her. How could Adam and Ben be so blasé about it? She planted her hand on her hip. "Am I the only person in this compound that's concerned about the horde? You," she wheeled in her chair to regard Adam, "act like it's *nothing*," she faced Ben again, "as do you!"

"That's not accurate, Sofia," Adam objected. "Yes, we're sheltered here inside the fence, but we're hardly cavalier while outside it. We exercise caution in all arenas, I assure you."

Ben added, "If the horde is returning, the longer I wait, the worse it'll be."

"If? Adam saw evidence of their arrival two months ago! They're likely all back by now," she growled. "It's—it's foolhardy!"

"Here." Lark held the joint. "Puff the magic dragon before you spontaneously combust."

"No," Sofia said, getting to her feet. She was in a fit of pique. Attraction and worry and annoyance warred, vying for her attention. She was wretched company in this mood. "I'm tired. Just leave the mess here. I'll clean it tomorrow."

"No, I'll do it," Lark said. "You have breakfast duty and have to be up at the butt crack of dawn. I don't. I'm sleeping in."

Sofia went to where Adam sat, bending to hug him. She felt her skirt rise, exposing her panty-covered backside. Ben would get an eyeful. *Let him.* "Have a good trip. Be safe."

"I wanna smoke this joint. Catch ya at the cabin, Sof," Lark said with a wave.

Ben stood. "I'll walk you."

I bet you will, Casanova. She picked up her golf club. "I don't require an escort."

"I know." He bid Adam and Lark goodbye, trailing Sofia.

She rounded the corner of the barn, treading briskly on the gravel road. "When are we leaving?"

"Wait up. What's the rush?" He increased his pace until he was abreast Sofia. "So you're coming with?"

Read the room! "Do I appear ecstatic? I don't have much

choice in the matter, do I? Empress Kate has decreed it, so I shall."

"Don't be that way. She meant well."

"Why are you defending her? When she wants something done, she's as subtle as a steamroller."

"It's for your own benefit. Listen, nobody is gonna shove you out of the compound against your will." When Sofia didn't answer, Ben gripped her wrist, halting her. "Sofia, what's going on with you?"

Her eyes pricked with tears. How could she verbalize the emotions roiling in her gut? She felt like bawling. Maybe a meltdown was exactly what she needed. She blinked the tears away, thankful the inky darkness concealed her.

Tone soft, he cajoled, "Talk to me. This isn't like you."

"Role reversal," she murmured, swallowing away the lump in her esophagus. "Usually I'm trying to get *you* to open up to *me*."

"Honestly… it's throwing me for a loop. You're typically so damn feisty. I'm not familiar with this side of you."

Sofia resumed walking, mentally shrugging.

"I don't know what to say," Ben admitted, maintaining step with her. "I thought you'd want to be alone with me."

"It's not a date, Ben."

"I *have* to locate that part. There's no other alternative. You want to stay? Stay."

The lane curved. The lit porch fixture on Sofia's cabin came into view. She sighed. "How long will it take?"

"Overnight is always a possibility. Depends. Probably a couple hours."

When they reached the cabin, the mood was strained. Sofia climbed the porch stairs. Hand on the doorknob, she faltered, turning. Ben loitered on the road, visible only in silhouette. "It's not that I don't trust you… it's… nerves. That's all. Do you *want* me to go with you?"

Ascending the stairs two at a time, he stepped into Sofia until she was flattened against the door, the outsoles of his work boots meeting the toes of her sandals. She tipped her head to search his face. The gold bristles of his five o'clock shadow made him appear harsher. Eliminated his guy-next-door veneer. Lent intensity. Broodiness. Ben whispered, "Yes."

He scraped his knuckles against her cheekbone. Sofia shut her eyes. Nuzzled her face against him. Her heart sang at his jagged intake of breath. She smiled. "Alright."

Ben cupped her cheeks with hands calloused but tender. He sought her lips. His kiss was sweet as honey. Gentle. Undemanding. Sofia wound her arms around his neck, burying her fingers in his hair. She slipped her tongue in Ben's mouth, deepening the kiss.

He broke contact, his voice gruff. "Throw some clothes into a backpack. We'll depart after breakfast. 'Night, Sofia."

BEN CAME DOWNSTAIRS as the children finished the scrambled eggs, bacon, and home fries Sofia had prepared. He wore faded Levi's, a long-sleeved black tee, his tan work boots, and a somber expression. His slicked-back hair was damp from a recent shower. Sofia wiped the counter with a dishrag, smiling in welcome. He returned her smile. His gaze skimmed her coral-hued crop top, lingering on her bare waist, before he sat at the trestle table beside Nora.

"Adam get off okay?" he asked Kate, who fed Maggie on her lap.

"He did. Left ninety minutes ago. Had bags under his eyes. You guys must've partied into the wee hours."

Yawning, Sofia found a seat at the table, a cup of coffee in her hand. Her attention skittered between Ben and Kate, trying to detect anything simmering beneath the surface of their conversation, but it seemed unremarkable. "We missed you and Teller."

"Maggie was restless all night. She's still fussy, but at least her fever broke."

Ben put an arm around Nora's slight shoulders, quietly explaining that he must leave Mayfly Hollow for a replacement part for the solar panels at their new home.

"No!" Nora cried. Tears swam in her cornflower blue eyes. "I don't want you to. You said you wouldn't again for a long, long time!"

"I know, honey." Ben brushed away a tear that skated down Nora's cheek. "But don't you want to move into the house? You're thrilled to have your very own bedroom, right?"

"Y-Yeah..." Nora sniffled.

Ben tugged Nora's blonde pigtail. "We can't stay here until we have functioning electricity, silly."

"We can! We can use candles."

Ben shook his head indulgently. "How would we cook food or take a bath? C'mon, Nor, try to be understanding."

"Tell you what, kid," Kate said from her spot at the head of the table. "You and I'll visit the pole barn and choose furniture and stuff while Ben's out. Would you like that?"

Nora sulked but nodded in a reluctant sort of way.

"You have furniture in the pole barn?" Sofia asked.

Kate explained, "We cleaned out stores in Fenton last year of everything we'd possibly need—furniture, decorations, house-wares, appliances."

"Everything except a DC connector switch," Sofia said.

Ben conceded, "Except that."

"I want unicorns in my bedroom." Nora no longer snuffled, but she moped, her lower lip protruding. "Are there any blankets with unicorns in the pole barn?"

"Maybe," Kate replied. "We have to sort through the bedding sets out there. When are you leaving, Ben?"

"In a minute. Sofia's accompanying me."

Nora glowered at Sofia, her face reddening. "Why's *she* going? That's not fair. Why can't you take me?"

Oh. Sofia worried her lip with her teeth and pretended her cup of coffee intrigued her.

"Don't be rude, young lady," Ben admonished. "We've discussed this. You're only eleven. Once you're older, you'll have your chance. Now apologize to Sofia."

She mumbled, "Sorry."

"Forgiven," Sofia said, smiling politely. Nora sneered and glanced away. Inwardly, Sofia groaned. Apparently, she was the girl's adversary, seen as competition for Ben's affections.

Edna appeared in the kitchen doorway. Her gray hair was in a bun, and she wore a flowered button-up and polyester stretch pants. She didn't wear spectacles, but she was otherwise every inch a stereotypical schoolmarm. "Ready for morning lessons, children?"

"Better run along, guys. The others are due for breakfast shortly. Put your dishes on the counter," Kate told them. After the kids left, she stood. "I'll tidy the kitchen, Sofia. You and Ben go now if you wish."

Sofia took a deep breath. Her backpack sat in the corner of the kitchen. "I'm ready anytime."

"If you gather rations, I'll prepare the flasks," Ben said, "and then we're off."

Kate went to change Maggie's diaper. She reappeared as Ben filled metal flasks with water, and Sofia zipped her pack, saying, "Hey, I just noticed the camera feed is goofy on the monitor in the office."

Ben screwed the lid on his flask and stowed it in his backpack. "Goofy how?"

"The screen's blank for the camera posted by the entrance gate. If it's non-operational, it'll have to be replaced ASAP."

Ben shouldered his pack. "I'll have a look-see on our way out and report back. Do we have replacement cameras?"

"There's a carton of them on an office shelf," Kate said, shifting Maggie on her hip.

Ben nodded, saying to Sofia, "Switch your golf club with a

weapon from the armory. Either an ax or a sword is best. And a knife along with an ankle holster. I'll be outside."

After Sofia exited the converted bedroom used as a pantry and makeshift munitions store, she locked it and went out the kitchen door. Ben was behind the wheel of a gunmetal gray 4x4 pickup.

She got in the passenger side. Ben's bow was in the backseat. "Driving? Isn't fuel in short supply?"

"It is, but it's too far to Calhoun to go on foot. Worst case scenario, we'll park on the outskirts and hike in."

At the entrance gate, Ben used the remote control on the visor, pulling through and putting the 4x4 in park. He slid out of his seat, staring up at the camera. "Hmm."

Sofia got out of the truck, using her hand as a shield against the sun. "What?"

"The lens is busted out. Maybe a bird flew into it?" He kneeled, examining the gravel lane beside the gate. "But I don't see evidence of a dead bird, only these tiny fragments of broken lens."

Foreboding swept over Sofia. "If somebody hurled rocks from the lane to smash the lens, we wouldn't be able to tell, would we?"

CHAPTER TWENTY-EIGHT

AN ANVIL SQUISHED SOFIA'S DIAPHRAGM. PANIC. THE COMPULSION to insist they flee to the safety within the fence was downright overwhelming. What if the person who destroyed the camera lurked in the bushes?

"I know you're spooked, but," Ben cautioned from where he kneeled, "don't let your imagination run rampant."

She wrung her hands, her gaze darting. "I-I think—I made a-a mistake…"

"You're hyperventilating." Ben got up. Dusted off his jeans. He came to Sofia and enveloped her hands in his, forcing her to peer up at him. "Breathe, Sofia. In through your nose, out through your mouth."

Heat blossomed on Sofia's cheeks, but she did what he instructed. The pressure on her diaphragm eased. The panic dissipated. Still, she was mortified. How would she ever manage the trip if, at the first whisper of trouble, she balked? Retreated? "What if someone really is canvassing the compound? What can we do?"

"People don't happen upon us haphazardly. We're hidden. Plus the cameras are high enough off the ground to discourage interference." Ben sucked his teeth, as if mulling something. He released her hands and went to push the button on the intercom mounted beside the gate, buzzing the farmhouse.

A moment later, Kate's disembodied voice replied over the speaker, "I'm here, Ben."

"Lens is trashed. Don't know how. Could be a bird. Regardless, camera's toast."

"I'll ask Josh to replace it today."

"Kate?"

"Yeah?"

"Might be prudent to fabricate metal cages to house the cameras… and to monitor the live feed more often."

"Wait. You think a *person* may be to blame for the camera?"

"No trace of a person, but in an abundance of caution…"

"Gotcha. I'll discuss the camera cages with Fritz. And I'll send one of the guys to patrol twice a day. You two don't dally. Return home as quick as you can. *Capiche*?"

"Yes, ma'am."

They climbed in the truck. Sofia held her breath as Ben maneuvered down the overgrown lane and turned left on the highway, but there was no inkling of anything odd—it was identical to when Sofia arrived at Mayfly Hollow two months prior. No amassed Zs. Perhaps she was being idiotic. She exhaled, saying, "Thank you for listening to me. For not making me feel childish. It's just… I'm a coward, I guess. It's humiliating."

"I remember feeling the same, you know? After finally reaching the farm, I wasn't keen to rush out and be vulnerable again." He shrugged. "You're *not* a coward, Sofia. You were fearless that morning at the cabin. You're a braver woman than you realize."

Noting Ben referred to her as a *woman* rather than a *kid*, Sofia recovered a modicum of her usual humor. "Oh, I was brave way before Armageddon. You know those stern *Do Not Remove Under Penalty of Law* tags on pillows? Ripped them off with reckless abandon. I was quite the rule-breaker when it came to fashion, too. I even," she lowered her voice, "wore white after Labor Day."

"How plucky of you," Ben said, chuckling. "You'll be okay. It's first-time butterflies."

"First-time butterflies?" she asked. "So you'll help pop my cherry?"

Ben threw her one of his signature grins. "That's the Sofia I know." He coughed. "Speaking of, uh, fashion... I like that ruffly off-the-shoulder deal you're wearing."

She considered her brief blouse with its frilled short sleeves and a plunging neckline. Held up with thin spaghetti straps, it bared her midriff. It was one of Sofia's favorite summer tops—the coral shade suited her. "Glad you approve, although I did pack a sweatshirt to put on later."

"I didn't want to say anything," Ben said, "but it's probably impractical to have too much skin exposed."

"You know, you're proficient in the art of distraction, counselor."

He blew on his fingernails and rubbed them on his tee like he was polishing them. Sofia laughed.

Over the subsequent minutes, they were absorbed by their journey, gazes sharp on their surroundings. Ben traversed secluded backroads. They rolled their windows down to listen, but there was no noise other than the steady drone of insects over the hum of the engine. Ben piloted the 4x4 around the occasional discarded automobiles in their route. Any decomposed bodies littering the pitted blacktop were treated as speed bumps.

"Where are we driving? You said Calhoun?"

"Yeah, the shop's called Calhoun Solar. It's downtown."

The trek to Calhoun city limits took fifteen minutes. A once bustling municipality with a population of sixty thousand, it had served as the county seat. Every direction showcased destruction. Fleshless corpses lay on the streets and on the sidewalks, the scraps of ragged clothing draping them flapping in the breeze. Sofia murmured, "Resembles a movie set for a horror film."

Fire had consumed half the business district. Torched patrol cars sat like sentinels outside the charred remains of the police station. Shards of glass from blown windows crunched under the tires as Ben cruised past. Soot had been carried by the wind, dusting onyx powder on the buildings that hadn't perished. There was no sign of life apart from a murder of cawing crows outside the courthouse. Sofia said, "Reminds me of *The Raven*. Creepy."

"It is. We won't dawdle."

"And it reeks here. But it's... distinctive, isn't it?"

"You're right. I'm used to that piercing Z blood stink that makes your nose sting and eyes water. I've never smelled this before. Sort of rotted and cloyingly sweet."

Calhoun Solar was at the end of State Street. Ben stopped the truck, shifting the engine to park. "It doesn't seem as if it's been looted. Hope the door isn't locked. If I have to bust in, it'll create a helluva racket."

Sofia took her sweatshirt from her pack and pulled it on before jumping from the pickup, the ax from the armory in her fist. A flicker of movement snagged her gaze, and she frowned, squinting. "Ben?"

A Z shambled a block up near the post office.

"Where there's one, there's more. We'll use the Z blood trick."

Sofia unsheathed the knife holstered at her ankle over her jean cuff. "I'll do it." She hurried to a Z sprawled face up on the sidewalk, and bent, dipping the tip into its bloated abdominal cavity. The putrefied tissues collapsed, and noxious gas discharged. Eyes streaming, Sofia retched, then held her breath as she smeared blood along the hems of her and Ben's jeans.

"Phew. C'mon." Bow in one hand and an empty duffle bag in the other, Ben led her to Calhoun Solar. The door was not bolted. He used his foot to prod it ajar.

Shafts of light from the plate-glass window lit the dusty shop, which appeared unoccupied. Shelves of battery packs, mini-panels, and inverters lined the perimeter. Index finger under her nostrils to curtail a sneeze, Sofia said, "They have solar lanterns. Those would be pretty on your front porch. Should I grab a bunch?"

"Please." Ben surveyed the smaller display racks of components in the middle of the store. "Here are switches. There are a range of brands. We don't have time to be choosy." He tossed boxes into his duffle. Lapping the store, he added any items he deemed of merit before zippering his bag.

Her arms loaded with packages, Sofia had her ax tucked in her armpit. Sweat beaded down her spine. "All set?"

"I'll make sure the coast is clear." Strap of the duffle in the crook of his elbow, Ben hoisted his bow and made for the door. He ducked his head out, checking left then right before murmuring, "It is. Let's load up and split."

Ben opened the passenger side back door, standing by as Sofia stacked the lanterns on the floorboard. "See? This hasn't been so terrible."

Sofia was about to agree when a shout rang out from behind them. They whipped around. At the opposite end of State Street, a raw-boned teen with a shaved head thrashed her arms. She ran toward them, screaming, "Help! Help!"

There was stampeding of feet. A throng of Zs rounded the intersection of State and Virginia Avenue, hot on the girl's tail.

CHAPTER TWENTY-NINE

Sofia beseeched, "Ben, we have to save her!"

With a slight bob of his chin, he motioned to the girl, pointing to the back passenger seat. He put his fingers to his mouth to amplify his words over the din of the zombies, yelling, "Hurry! In!"

Sofia bent into the truck and chucked the solar lights and Ben's duffle across the floorboard to make space before unlatching her door. Shedding her backpack, she hopped into her seat.

Sofia watched in horror, expecting the gap between the girl and the Zs to shrink. For the Zs to engulf her. But the girl was fast—by halfway down the block, she outpaced them. Sofia's fingers shook as she clicked her seatbelt. She urged, "Ben, start the truck now so we can take off once she's inside."

Leaving the back door gaping, Ben sprinted around the front bumper, yanking open the driver's side door. He situated his backpack and his bow between their seats and slid behind the steering wheel. He put the key into the ignition. The engine purred to life. Jamming it in gear, he glimpsed over his shoulder, assessing the girl's progress. "Come on! Hurry…"

The girl threw her sharpened walking stick in the truck bed

before vaulting into the backseat. She slammed the door, nose-diving across the bench seat and gasping, "Go! Go!"

Ben mashed his boot on the accelerator and reversed into the street, bumping into a car. Flinging the shifter into drive, he rocketed down the block, weaving between stalled cars.

At the stoplight at the end of State Street, Ben's gaze volleyed to the rearview mirror. The mob of Zs were giving chase. He took a left. The path ahead was unobstructed, but a handful of Zs milled about on the sidewalk, their faces to the sky.

One stilled, then, within seconds, sprang at the truck. He landed heavily on the hood, the impact causing the chassis to buck. His knees slipped from under him, but he scrabbled back up the hood, finding the windshield wipers. He clutched at them, smooshing his face to the glass. Sofia shuddered and squeaked—his crazed eyes were *trained directly* on her. "Oh my God! Eye contact! Get him off, Ben!"

"Hold on tight, you two!" Ben accelerated, and the engine roared. He stomped on the brakes. The Z lost its grip, cartwheeling to the blacktop. The wipers stuck out at right angles, one snapped in half and dangling.

The struts creaked as Ben steered over the Z.

There was a dull thump from behind.

Sofia twisted in her seat. "Um, Ben..."

Another Z was on the bumper. Only his fingers were visible where they clung to the top edge of the liftgate. Three more Zs hurtled toward the truck.

"I see," Ben said. "I'll try to shake him. If he or his friends climb into the bed, we're screwed."

Pedal to the metal, Ben maneuvered the steering wheel from side to side. The 4x4 shimmied, the rear quarter panel hitting a parked station wagon, then fishtailing. The Z fell off, rolling into the others like a bowling ball knocking into pins.

The girl didn't have her seatbelt secured and hadn't had the opportunity to remove her bulky backpack. Thrown violently across the bench seat, she smacked into the window. As Ben sped forward, she tumbled off the seat, landing on the floor-board behind him. She wheezed, "Omph!"

"We lost him. He's off." Sofia put a palm on the girl's splayed leg where it rested cockeyed on Ben's headrest. "Hey, are you alive?"

After a second, the girl responded, "Y-yup."

Ben didn't slacken his speed until they were outside Calhoun on a deserted expanse of highway beside a shady grove of pine. Shifting into park, Ben rotated in his seat and held out a hand to the girl. Clumsily, she grasped it, allowing him to haul her up. She collapsed against the seatback. Unsteadily rubbed her face. Her grime-caked skin was chalk-white with a dusting of freckles. The odor of unwashed body wafted through the pickup cab. "I might've crushed your stuff when I went ass over teakettle."

Ben said, "I'm more concerned about you. You injured?"

"More shook up than anything. My pack insulated me." Her cautious baby blue gaze slid from Ben to Sofia. "Thank you."

"You're welcome," Sofia said. She took a canteen of water from her backpack at her feet. "Here, drink. What were you doing in Calhoun?"

The girl drank thirstily. "Hunting for food and resources. What else?"

"Why not stick to houses on the outskirts?"

"I ain't an imbecile. I have been. I'm workin' my way south and couldn't pass Calhoun up. I knew it could be chancy."

Sofia handed her a bag of homemade granola. "I'm Sofia Spenser." She inclined her head toward Ben. "And that's my boyfriend, Ben Cassidy."

Ben raised his eyebrows but didn't refute Sofia.

"I'm Mikayla Chalmers—Mik." She popped a fistful of granola in her mouth. As she chewed, she said, "Them are the slowest roamers I ever came across."

"They didn't seem slow to me," Sofia replied, brushing perspiration from her brow.

"This ain't my first rodeo." Mik scooped another handful of granola. "Y'all noticed they're changing?"

Ben's gaze narrowed. "Changing how?"

"Besides bein' slower and slower every day? Takes them longer to notice people. They don't clack their teeth no more—not that they got many teeth left. How 'bout their eyes?"

Sofia gasped. "Oh shit, she's right. Usually Zs' eyes are milky and bloodshot. The one on the windshield had normal-looking irises! Remember, I said he made eye contact with me?"

"Yup," Mik said, nodding. "Told ya. They're seeing stuff now. And their skin's becomin' less blotchy, too. Something is up with them motherfuckers."

Ben and Sofia digested Mik's revelations as she finished the granola and drained the canteen. Sofia asked, "Are you all by yourself?"

"Yup." She straightened her thin shoulders. "But I can take care of myself."

She couldn't be more than fifteen or sixteen, reminding Sofia of Zac. Her heart panged as she thought of how delighted he'd be to know another teenager. She met Ben's gaze, a plea in her eyes. Almost imperceptibly, his body language communicated his consent. "We live at a farm outside River Heights. Would you like to come back with us, Mik?"

"I figured you guys are doin' good. Y'all are hella clean. Naw. I'm better on my own." Mik set the canteen on the seat, her fingers at the door handle. "I appreciate your help all the same."

Sofia rolled her window down as Mik exited the truck. "Are you positive?"

"I'm positive." Mik stood on her tippy-toes and retrieved her walking stick from the truck bed, then came to Sofia's door. She scratched her shaved head before turning to leave, saying, "Thanks anyhow, Sofia."

"Wait," Sofia said, digging in her pack for more zipper bags of snacks. "For you."

Mik pocketed the bags, flashing a quick smile. Her teeth were yellowed and chipped, some rotten. "Y'all are nice. I owe ya."

Waving a hand in farewell, Mik disappeared into the woods.

"YOU'RE UPSET," Ben said as he drove them home.

"I'm... unsettled. We shouldn't have let Mik go off again on her own. It's not right."

"She wouldn't have tolerated us insisting she come to Mayfly Hollow. Would've fought us tooth and nail. You can't rescue the unwilling." He reached over and laced his fingers with hers.

"I know."

"You handled everything perfectly in Calhoun. I'm proud of you, Sofia."

Warmth spread across Sofia's solar plexus at Ben's praise. "We'll have to pass along what we learned about the Zs to Kate and Teller soon as we get back."

Ben returned his hand to the steering wheel and careened around a pile of corpses in their path. "Agreed."

"And what about Adam? He could be in danger."

Quiet for several seconds, Ben murmured regretfully, "Nothing to be done about that."

Once home, Ben parked behind the farmhouse. Kate was in the garden harvesting tomatoes for lunch, Maggie attached to her chest in a baby sling. Sofia loitered by the kitchen door while Ben fetched her.

Arm looped through a wicker basket heaped with tomatoes and cucumbers, Kate joined Sofia. Ben headed for the barn. She explained, "He's bringing Teller."

Sofia unearthed a pair of clean jeans from her overstuffed pack and went to the bathroom to change and wash up. When she came out, Kate had unloaded her basket and gotten a pitcher of iced tea from the fridge. "BLTs and cucumber salad for lunch. Grab some glasses for this tea, will you?"

Kate sat Maggie in her playpen in the corner of the kitchen. She handed the baby a colorful board book to occupy her, then settled at the table, pouring the iced tea.

Sofia put her elbows on the table, propping her chin on steepled fingers. She told Kate about Mik while they waited for Teller and Ben.

"Well," Kate said with a benevolent smile, "if she's survived on her own this long, she must be tough. She'll likely be alright."

"True. Just feels wrong to leave her."

There was the screech of the screen door, and Ben came into the kitchen, Teller trailing behind. Teller swiped his Stetson from his head, skimming his arm across his forehead before dropping into a chair at the head of the table. "Woo-ee. I'm mighty happy autumn's a hop, skip, and a jump away."

Ben hurried upstairs to put on fresh clothes. When he came down again, Kate passed him a tumbler of tea.

Teller asked, "Now that we're assembled, what's all the hubbub?"

"I have the feeling it's not pleasant news," Kate said.

Ben and Sofia took turns describing what Mik had said. Teller and Kate exchanged glances, wearing twin expressions of bewilderment. Fear.

Kate said, "Sofia, you're thinking what I'm thinking. Adam."

"Yes."

"He's a bright fella," Teller asserted. "He'll cope."

Ben's tone was infused with conviction. "He will. I know it."

"Regardless, us fretting isn't going to influence the outcome of anything one way or another," Kate said. She drummed her nails on the table. "Zs evolving. What does it mean? Are they weakening? Dying?"

"Mik claimed they were becoming slower," Ben pointed out. "What if they're reverting to a more human-like state?"

"I reckon if they're revertin' to humans, they're gonna die," Teller posited, brow knit. "But if they don't die—"

Ben cut in, "The ramifications remain to be seen."

"What else can we do but hunker down? We remain at Mayfly Hollow until we learn more about the situation," Kate said. She clasped Teller's hand. "Isn't this precisely what we've prepared for?"

Teller's thumb stroked Kate's fingers. "Damn right. Could be months... could be forever, but we're self-sustainin' enough here."

Sofia's intestines clenched. Do it now, her intuition ordered. *Tell. Them. Now.* Taking a bracing breath, she confessed, "I know where there's a warehouse with an enormous consignment of bulk food."

CHAPTER THIRTY

"*What?*" Ben demanded. "What do you mean?"

"Remember, I mentioned my dad owned a warehouse?" Sofia turned to Teller and Kate. "He and my mom were on a cruise when everything started. They telephoned from the ship. *That* was a shitshow. Passengers were screaming and fighting and trying to take the phone. Dad told me they'd gotten word that my aunt died from the virus. They advised me to hole up at Spenser Suppliers in Mergenville until they returned home. They thought it would be safer there. I didn't have keys to the warehouse, so Daddy arranged for his manager—this creepy guy called Howard—to meet me there." Sofia choked, "But... he was already dead when I arrived."

Kate's expression was sympathetic. She removed her hand from Teller and snaked it across the table to Sofia, placing it on her arm in a gesture of support.

Sofia continued, "I didn't have the foresight to grab Howard's keys... When I considered leaving two months later, I went to the lobby for them and found he'd become a Z. Basically, I was trapped until I got the courage to kill him."

"How long were you there?" Kate asked.

"A year. I kept a tally of the days by hash marking a cinder block wall. The winter—oh God—it almost killed me… by spring, I'd had enough. I couldn't bear it anymore."

Kate asked, "You dispatched Howard?"

"Yes. No surprise… my parents never made it home."

"Praise the Lord you found your way to us. To Mayfly Hollow," Teller said. "I cannot fathom what you bore, Sofia."

"I had it better than most. Plenty of food and water. Shelter. I was… fortunate." Sofia's windpipe clogged, foretelling waterworks. She tried gulping the clog away, but her voice cracked when she admitted, "It was *unbearable*."

Kate tsked. "Nobody else knew about the warehouse?"

Sofia put her hands up. "Not one person ever showed up when I was there. It's out of view from the main road so maybe it's still untouched? We can transport some of the goods here."

Ben asked, "You couldn't confide in me, Sofia? You said you trusted me."

She swiveled her gaze to him. He looked hurt. Offended. Betrayed. "I-I—"

"You have more secrets you plan to pounce on me outta left field?" Ben queried, his tone severe. His face was scarlet. "How else have you lied to me?"

Sofia floundered, "I… haven't *lied*—"

"Bull-fuckin'-shit."

"Simmer down now, Ben," Teller chastised.

Ben glared at Teller. "Don't interfere."

Kate gently reproved, "Sofia isn't obligated to share anything she doesn't wish to. Not her secrets. Not her belongings."

"Both of you mind your goddamn business. This is between me and Sofia!" Ben stalked from the table, banging the door as he left.

Eventually, Teller drawled, "Welp. Can hear a pin drop."

Then, Maggie burst into tears, howling from her playpen. *I know exactly how you feel, kid.* Sofia laid a palm on her flaming cheek. "Should… should I go after him?"

"Let him cool his heels a mite." Teller stood, plopping his

Stetson on his head. "Fritz and Josh are fabricatin' cages for the surveillance cameras. 'Spose I'll check if they require assistance."

Kate hastened to Maggie, whisking her into her arms. She cuddled the baby until she quieted, then plunked her on Sofia's lap. "Here. You need a distraction. It's almost lunchtime, and everyone will be starving. I've got to get the bacon started."

Bouncing Maggie on her knee, Sofia indifferently watched Kate preheat the oven and place bacon strips on jelly roll pans then pop the pans into the oven. Dread lapped at Sofia's stomach lining. She identified the unpleasant acidic sensation as guilt tinged with resentment.

Switching Maggie to her other knee, Sofia concluded Kate was correct. She didn't owe Ben—or anyone—an explanation for why she chose to delay divulging about the warehouse. So why did she feel so pitiful then? Sofia groaned, blanching at the mouth-watering aroma of the bacon as it cooked. No matter how hungry she was, she'd never be able to endure lunch.

Kate scrutinized Sofia as she chopped cucumbers and tomatoes and dumped them in a melamine bowl. After adding herbs and red wine vinegar, she stashed the salad into the fridge to chill. Leaning against the counter, Kate fixed on Sofia thoughtfully. "Ben tell you about him and me?"

Sofia stared at Kate in shock, saucer-eyed.

"Ben, Ben, Ben," Kate clucked. "So, he gives *you* a rash of shit for keeping secrets, but he's got some of his own."

Apparently Kate was the woman Ben alluded to. Sofia poured more iced tea from the pitcher and took a slug to sidestep replying.

"You look terrified," Kate said, her mouth quirking. "Chill. We weren't star-crossed lovers… it was temporary. No strings."

Sofia bit her nail. "I sense a *but* coming."

Kate pulled plates from the cabinet. "Yes."

"Well, don't leave me hangin', Kate."

Kate chuckled as she arranged forks on the counter beside

the plates. "Ben caught feelings. I didn't reciprocate. Then, I met Teller and…"

"Are you telling me Ben's carried a torch for you ever since? Jesus. I don't want to hear this."

Kate sighed, saying, "I mean to reassure you, but I'm bungling it. You've heard that expression *still waters run deep*, right?"

"Yeah. What about it?"

"That's Ben in a nutshell. Cheerful, happy-go-lucky, tries to do the right thing…"

"Yeah, he's Mister Honorable. I've teased him about it before."

"He takes his role as a moral, upright man seriously yet has hidden depths. Has he let *you* see his other side?"

Sofia contemplated their nocturnal chats at her house before their journey to Mayfly Hollow. Of their encounter at Juniper Rise. When they were on the porch swing. And the tender kiss the other night after the bonfire. "A little."

Kate bobbed her head in a knowing way. "Uh huh. I thought so. Ben doesn't open himself to many people, but if he has to you… I'm just sayin', it shows he cares for you."

"I'm not so sure about that," Sofia intoned glumly. "I'm beginning to think it's one-sided."

"One-sided? Oh please, I'd have to be blind not to see there's something special between you two. No matter how hard you guys try to appear platonic, those furtive looks give you away."

"Sure, Kate." Sofia rolled her eyes. "Then why have I heard a litany of excuses from Ben about why we can't be together?"

Kate crossed her arms under her chest. "When Ben reached Mayfly Hollow, he was on the brink of death. I doctored him. During that time, he was wrecked emotionally… we all were in the early days. Anyway, he became convinced that affection and gratitude equaled love, but it didn't. It doesn't. He would've realized that he wasn't in love with me on his own eventually."

Sofia stared at Kate, mulling her words.

Kate shrugged her shoulder. "You know how people rhap-sodize over the one who got away, Sofia."

Sofia's temple pounded with a headache. Lack of sleep and the stress of the altercation in Calhoun were taking its toll. She muttered, "If you say so, Kate. All I know is that he's pissed I didn't tell him about the warehouse, and I'm exhausted."

"He's wounded that you didn't, not pissed. There's a differ-ence." Kate came to Sofia and took Maggie from her. "You look ready to drop. Go to your cabin and nap. You and Ben can have a chat later tonight after you've both gained perspective."

Sofia gave Kate a thankful smile.

One-handed with Maggie balanced on her hip, Kate assem-bled BLT sandwiches. Before Sofia stepped from the kitchen, she advised, "Be patient with Ben, Sofia. See if you can get him to reveal what happened on his trip to Mayfly Hollow. I know it haunts him."

Sofia walked to her cabin, Ace trotting beside her, keeping her company. Yawning as she lumbered up the cabin stairs to the porch, she let herself inside and shut the drapes. After unlacing her hiking boots, she collapsed on the bed and slept as if drugged.

CHAPTER THIRTY-ONE

WHEN SOFIA WOKE, IT WAS DARK OUTSIDE. SHE'D SLEPT THROUGH dinner. Her stomach gurgled, demanding food. Without turning on the lamp, she staggered into the kitchenette and got a jar of peanut butter, a slice of bread, and a butter knife. Clumsily, she slathered peanut butter on the bread and folded it, eating while standing at the peninsula counter.

The door opened, and Lark entered the cabin, flipping on the lamp at her side of the bed. She flinched as she caught sight of Sofia. "Christ, you scared me!"

"Sorry," Sofia mumbled around her mouthful of sandwich. "Missed dinner."

Lark came into the kitchenette and took a pitcher of water from the fridge. She offered Sofia a glass before pouring one for herself. "Kate called a meeting tonight after we ate. She told us what that girl in Calhoun said about the Zs."

"Was Ben there?"

"No. I haven't seen him all day. Nora took a picnic basket to his house this afternoon, then Josh went down to bring her back to the farmhouse after dinner." Lark gulped a hefty slug of water then wiped her mouth with the back of her hand. "Think she was lying?"

"Who?"

"The girl in Calhoun. Who else?"

"I'm still half-asleep," Sofia protested. "Her name was Mik. Why would she lie?"

"Fuck if I know."

"I believed her. She seemed truthful enough."

"What do you think is happening out there with the Zs? Are they mutating?"

"I have no clue, Lark, but I've got a bad feeling about it," Sofia admitted.

"If whatever it is kills off the Zs, maybe we have a chance to begin civilization again."

Sofia weighed her words before answering. "I pray that's the case." She set her knife in the sink and put the peanut butter away. "I'm going to shower. I want to go talk to Ben."

"It's almost nine. Do you think it's wise to walk down to his place after dusk?"

"I'll take a flashlight and the ax."

DRESSED in a ruffled tank and a pair of jeans, Sofia made her way up to the farmyard. The house was dark and silent. She peered at the chicken coop and the red barn behind it, then at the white pole barn further afield. Other than the rustle of the penned animals and the buzz of insects, all was peaceful.

The gravel lane meandered through vegetation, and Sofia's hold tensed on her ax, her flashlight beaming a swathe of light in the blackness. Clouds inched across the sky, revealing the moon. At last, the set of staff cabins with their lamplit windows where Fritz, Josh, Rob, Milo, and Bella lived glowed like a beacon, indicating she was mere minutes from Juniper Rise.

Occasionally, farmyard sounds echoed, carried by wind that swished her flesh like delicate silk. The moon looked immense.

Sofia was convinced if she extended a hand that she'd be able to touch it. To pull it from the ebony sky.

Mini solar lights had been pushed in the soil alongside the juniper bushes leading to Ben's front porch. Sofia's sandals sank into pebbles as she trod on the path—the pebbles were a new addition since the last time she'd visited, along with the patio furniture on the porch.

From the recesses of the house, diffused light shone. Evidently Ben had gotten his electricity functioning. Sofia pressed the doorbell, and chimes reverberated. A moment later, a shadow moved across the stained-glass cutouts in the door. The porch fixture came on.

Ben cracked the door, asking flatly, "What are you doing here?"

"We should talk."

He backed away, leaving the door ajar for Sofia. Cardboard boxes and home décor items were piled at the fireplace, a small tweed sectional sofa arranged around it. After latching the door, she set her ax and the flashlight on the floor and slipped off her shoes, following Ben down the hall. He went into a bedroom across from the bathroom. The walls were a freshly rolled pale pink, the trim not yet painted. He dipped his paintbrush into the can and drew a line of pink along the closet molding. *Days Like This* streamed over Ben's smartphone.

"You're quite a Van Morrison fan, aren't you?"

Ben shrugged.

"Am I getting the silent treatment?" Sofia leaned against the door jamb. "Don't you have *anything* to say to me?"

"Van Morrison was one of my dad's favorite singers. Makes me feel closer to Dad when I play his music." Ben didn't look at her. "If you want to talk, talk."

Sofia sighed, picking at her thumbnail. Being in Ben's house reminded her of their encounter beside the fireplace. She needed neutral territory. "Can we go sit outside? Maybe on the porch? It's gorgeous tonight."

Ben set his paintbrush on the rim of the paint can. "Fine."

He led her down the hallway and past the kitchen to the back door. There was a small wooden deck with stairs leading to his backyard. He sat on the top step, and Sofia settled alongside him, their shoulders just touching.

For a time, they were quiet, taking in the night air and listening to the sounds of nature. Sofia considered and discarded several approaches before she asked, "Have you told me all *your* secrets, Ben?" She swallowed, adding, "Of course you haven't. I know you haven't. You've given me enough crumbs to pacify me. Period."

He swiveled to study her, his mouth pursed.

"Why didn't you correct me when I introduced you to Mik as my boyfriend?"

"I don't know. I've asked myself the same thing."

"All I've heard is one argument after another why we can't be together," Sofia pointed out. "So, are we more than friends, or not? One minute you're putting out major vibes, and the next you're shutting me out, so I'd like to know."

Ben crossed his arms over his chest.

"You are such a typical man." Sofia rolled her eyes and laughed without humor. "Newsflash—if we're not in a relationship, then you don't have the privilege to demand behaviors—or confidences—from me. You understand that, right?"

"Is that what this visit is about? Professing your stance?"

"*Consensus ad idem.* I'm certain you recognize that phrase, counselor."

A specter of a smile flitted across Ben's lips. "A meeting of the minds? Is that what you're attempting to accomplish?"

"I'm sick of beating around the bush. As I've said before— you want me. I want you. And neither of us wants a relationship." Sofia waved her hand. "So let's hash it out. Either we call it quits or negotiate a… a…"

"A what?"

"An understanding. I don't need a boyfriend. I need sex. I *need* it."

"I've told you—"

"Yeah, yeah, yeah," Sofia said, waving her hand again. "I know. It's time to put up or shut up. Can you handle what I propose or not?"

"Not with someone who's dishonest. What other shit have you been withholding from me?"

"Again—I never lied to you! I didn't tell you about the warehouse because I wasn't ready to tell anyone. Either believe it, or don't believe it. I refuse to beg forgiveness because I did nothing wrong."

"You're an enigma to me, Sofia," he murmured, shaking his head.

"And you're an enigma to me." She heaved a breath. "Look, other than the warehouse, I don't have anything to hide. I've been forthcoming. Can you say the same? The difference between us is that I won't push you to share your secrets. So. Don't. Push. *Me.*"

Ben didn't respond.

"It really hurt you that much that I didn't tell you about the warehouse? 'Cause I'm at a loss here. I've never been involved with such a sensitive man before."

"Is that a dig at my masculinity?"

"Only if you think sensitivity is a sign of weakness."

"Yes, it hurt me!" Ben whirled on her. "Since meeting you..." He put his hand on the nape of his neck, massaging it. "God, you've brought out reactions in me that I didn't know I was capable of. *You* make me weak, but I can't seem to stop thinking about throwing you on my bed and fucking you senseless even though I know it's a horrible idea."

Arousal whooshed to Sofia's loins, and she shifted. "Doesn't sound altogether horrible to me."

"You're a goddamn distraction," Ben ground out impatiently as if she hadn't spoken. "Before we met, I'd come to terms with the fact I'd probably be alone for the rest of my life. I'd made peace with that. Planned another life—a simple life—building a home, raising Nora alone..."

Sofia's heart thudded so hard in her chest cavity she was worried she'd pass out. "So, I've triggered you to second guess all your plans, have I? That's the big issue? That's why we can't fuck? Jesus."

"Believe me, I've struggled with this, but I know how it'll end badly. Sex-only arrangements don't work—I won't lay myself bare to that sort of misery again."

Disappointment and frustration welled, prompting Sofia to demand, "Is that your final word on the matter?"

"It's for the best."

Sofia got up and descended the stairs, facing Ben where he remained seated on the top step, her knuckles on her hips. Narrowing her eyes, she asked, "Kate really annihilated you, didn't she?"

CHAPTER THIRTY-TWO

BEN WAS DOWN THE STAIRS AND BESIDE HER IN SECONDS, HIS FINGERS wrapping around her upper arms and his face tormented. "How do you know about that?"

"How the hell do you think?" Sofia wrenched from his grasp. "She told me you were friends with benefits until you *caught feelings*. Before we came to Mayfly Hollow you said that you were in love with another woman. Was it Kate? It was, wasn't it?"

Ben swept a hand over his mouth, pacing barefoot through the grass. "Yes, dammit. It was Kate."

"Are you," Sofia swallowed the lump in her throat, "still in love with her?"

"Yes—no—I don't know!" He ceased pacing and raked his fingers through his hair. "I wasn't prepared for this. For being put on the spot."

"Good! I think we're well overdue for some old-fashioned plain speaking. I'm tired of walking on eggshells with you, Ben." She approached him, halting when they were a foot apart. "I don't care if you're still pining for Kate. Pine away. It's got nothin' to do with us. What I won't stand for is you penalizing me for what another woman did to you."

Ben's mouth was an *O*. "You don't care if I'm in love with someone else?"

"Why should I?"

"I-I didn't count on that. Most women would."

"In case you didn't notice—I'm. Not. A. Stereotype." She smiled tightly up at him. "If you're so in love with Kate, then you can't possibly catch feelings for me, right? Because I can promise that I won't catch any for you."

Ben shook his head in awe. "You're a force to be reckoned with, Sofia. I've never known a woman your age with your level of poise and self-assurance."

"It's because I know what I want. It'll only be weird if we let it be weird. I'm not interested in flowers and candies and marriage and babies." She stepped into him until her breasts brushed his rib cage. Ben's breath hitched at the contact, proof that he was as affected as she was. She slid a hand down his taut abdomen and cupped his cock. It responded immediately to her touch, swelling to fill her fist. "This is all I require."

Sofia dropped her hand. Ben made a strangled sound, something between a tortured groan and a fierce growl.

She whispered, "This is your last chance to take me up on my offer. You don't even have to say anything. Turn around and go inside if you don't want me."

Trance-like, Ben fixated on her mouth as she spoke.

"Go on," she urged, cognizant of the moisture pooled in her panties, "and we will be finished. Permanently. No more back-and-forth. No more heated looks or stolen kisses. No more pussy-eating. I'll find myself a man who I can screw silly."

Sofia moistened her lips, and Ben blinked, his breath escaping in a wheeze.

"I don't believe I'll have a problem vetting another candidate, do you, Ben?"

Seizing her wrist, Ben hauled Sofia up the stairs and into the house. Pulse rocketing in her throat, she allowed him to drag her to the master bedroom. He kicked the door shut behind them.

There were no blinds on the windows. Moonbeams outlined the king-size bed with its down comforter.

She was wordless as Ben shucked his t-shirt and stepped from his basketball shorts. His hard-on bobbed. "Undress. Now."

Triumphant, Sofia pulled her tank over her head then shimmied out of her jeans until she stood only in her bra and panties. Head tipped to join Ben's gaze, she unhooked her bra and let it fall. She closed the distance between them, purring, "Glad you came to your senses, counselor."

Her nipples puckered with arousal as their skin touched. Sofia gasped, goosebumps pricking along her décolletage. Ben bent, sealing his mouth over hers. Their tongues tangled. His fingers explored the base of her spine, then tracked to her derriere. Gripping her underwear, he yanked them down her legs. Once Sofia kicked them away, Ben grabbed her ass and thrust her hard against his pelvis. She broke her mouth from his. Angled her head back and whimpered.

"Lay spread-eagle on the bed," he instructed huskily.

Sofia did as Ben commanded, her heavy-lidded gaze never leaving his face.

"You're even more beautiful than I imagined, Sofia. Fuck, you drive me wild." Ben encircled his shaft, stroking. "Touch yourself."

She toyed with a nipple then glided her fingers along the supple curve of her stomach. Her fingertip delved into her damp curls. Ben's eyes were riveted on Sofia as he observed her pleasure herself, his hand pumping his cock.

Knowing she was watched was erotic. Hedonistic. Carnal. Sofia fondled her clit, her eyelids fluttering as she concentrated on the sensations traveling to the soles of her feet. Back bowing, she moaned.

Ben had kneeled at the bed. "That's enough. My turn." He gripped her hips and roughly tugged until she was balanced on the edge of the mattress. He buried his face between her thighs, inhaling her before hungrily licking his way to her pussy.

"Oh God." Sofia arched against his mouth. "I'm close."

Ben's teeth were on her clit. He sucked, inserting two digits into her slit. Sofia writhed and mewled as Ben curled his fingers. Tickled her G-spot. Her walls constricted, a gush of warm liquid soaking into the comforter as delectable spasms radiated through her.

He collapsed beside Sofia, supporting his head with one hand. She turned toward him, trying to catch her breath. His eyes on hers, Ben put the fingers he'd used on her in his mouth and slurped them clean.

Sofia's limbs were heavy. Languid. But Ben's actions caused a bolt of desire to zap directly to her loins. She pushed her hair from her brow, teasing, "I guess you don't mind that I'm sometimes a squirter."

"Nope." Ben flashed her a grin, planting his lips on hers. He kissed her thoroughly, his mouth tasting of her salty juices. Fingers kneading her breast before gently twisting her nipple, he tweaked it, then trailed his nails down her torso. Sofia's sex still throbbed from her climax. Ben's touch was feathery as he rubbed her there in a circular motion, but she gasped and shivered anyway, her flesh hypersensitive. When Sofia laid a hand on his to still him, Ben chuckled. He shooed her away, continuing his ministrations while she squirmed.

"Scoot up." Ben got up on his knees. Once Sofia had repositioned, he loomed over her, putting his palm on her clavicle and forcing her against the mattress, keeping her immobilized. He caressed her, his thumb pressing her throat where her pulse raced. The moonlight silhouetted his musculature, crafting the planes of his face into savage, predatory beauty.

"You're in charge now, huh?" Sofia challenged, raising her eyebrows.

Ben laughed softly. He climbed on top of her, pinning her in place, his forearms caging her head. His engorged tip jerked against her thigh and leaked a drip of precum. The hypnotic heat of his scent—spice and musky alpha male—enveloped Sofia. He brought his lips to her ear. "There's no going back now. Are you sure, brown-eyed girl?"

She nodded, and Ben lowered his mouth to hers, nibbling her lips before readjusting himself so he was between Sofia's thighs. Hands on her hips, he tilted her pelvis. Her legs were against his chest, her ankles on either side of his neck.

Lining up at her entrance, Ben pushed through her folds gradually, allowing her walls to accommodate his girth before drilling into her, fully sheathed. He groaned at her sudden intake of breath, his fingernails digging into her skin as he set a leisurely tempo. Eyes shut, his face a study of control, he withdrew smoothly before pounding deep. Deliberate. His hips flexed as he drove into her over and over.

Her heartbeat like thunder in her ears, Sofia fingered her clit and clenched her muscles. Ben's breathing shallowed. She glimpsed up and snagged his gaze. His eyes were fevered. He rasped, "Come, Sofia."

His cock swelled, filling her. Stretching her. Intensifying her pleasure. Sofia teetered on the precipice. When Ben shuddered his release, she followed.

CHAPTER THIRTY-THREE

Ben had fallen asleep. Sofia slipped out from under his arm and collected her clothes, quietly opening the bedroom door.

There was a stack of fluffy towels on the bathroom vanity. She wet a washcloth and cleaned up then threw the washcloth in the wicker hamper at the end of the bathtub. She peered in the mirror after dressing. Her sable hair was tousled, and her cheeks were flushed. Pink marks tracked her jawline where the stubble of Ben's five o'clock shadow had abraded her while kissing.

Finger-combing her hair into order, Sofia went into Nora's room to place the cover on the paint can. Ben's smartphone still streamed music. The intro to *Brown Eyed Girl* played, and recognition dawned. Ah. So that's where her nickname originated. She powered the phone down and switched off the bedroom light before tiptoeing to the foyer. Sandals on, she gathered up her flashlight and ax before letting herself out of the house. She'd told Ben things would only get weird if they let it get weird, and she'd meant it. She was determined to prove she was cool. Uncomplicated. That she could keep their relationship informal. There would be no sleepovers—they were not a couple.

The moon hid behind the misty clouds. Dew flecked the foliage, seeping into her tennis shoes. From somewhere nearby a twig snapped. An owl hooted. Spooked, Sofia dashed back to her cabin as hastily as she could. Not turning on a lamp, she changed into a nightie in the dark, unwilling to disturb Lark.

She was tucked into bed when Lark murmured sleepily in a singsong voice, "Somebody got some."

"Huh?"

"Don't play dumb. You stink of sex."

Sofia hesitated, unsure what to reply.

Lark giggled. "About fricking time. Good for you." She rolled over and went back to sleep.

IT WAS Sofia's day to cook breakfast. Once the children had eaten and were sent off with Edna for class, the adults filed in and piled their plates with the pancakes and sausage Sofia had arranged buffet-style on the counter. Lark's face was knowing, but she didn't comment further.

Ben was the last to arrive. His hair was washed and slicked back, his face freshly shaved. Sofia dawdled at the kitchen counter, stealing a look at him when he approached to make his plate. His expression was impassive, but the corner of his mouth twitched when he noticed her scrutiny. "Good morning, Sofia."

"Morning, Ben," she said cheerfully. Before pivoting on her heel to find a seat at the trestle table with the others, she whispered to him, "I'm not wearing any panties."

His face suffused with heat but remained blank as he trailed her to the table.

Sofia picked at her breakfast, half-listening to the smattering of conversation around her and keenly aware of Ben's weighty gaze drinking her in.

Kate unbuckled Maggie from her highchair, taking her upstairs for a diaper change, and eventually everyone except Ben and Sofia left the kitchen. Cheeks flaming and heartbeat ratcheting, Sofia set about loading the dishwasher, knowing

Ben's eyes stalked her every movement. Inspiration struck, and she leaned over, hiking up the hem of her skirt to give him an eyeful of her naked bottom.

Finally, Ben finished his coffee and stood, ambling to the sink. He put his dishes on the countertop then cuddled up to Sofia, hugging her from the back with one arm cinching her waist. His free hand slithered under her sundress and skated up her thigh. She smelled the maple syrup on his breath as he brought his lips to the crook of her neck. His probing finger slipped into her slit, and he made a noise of approval. "Meet me in the garden shed in five minutes."

Ben removed his hand and stepped away, releasing Sofia. A moment later, the screen door closed after him. She steadied the heels of her palms against the counter and shakily exhaled. *Holy fuck.* Trembling with need, she swiftly finished stacking dishes in the dishwasher and began a cycle.

Sofia fetched the wicker veggie basket from the laundry room, passing Kate and Maggie in the hall.

Indicating the basket she planned to use as a pretext to meet Ben in the garden shed, Sofia said, "Getting lettuce for lunch."

"You're the early bird today. Pick some rosemary for me for dinner tonight, will you?"

"Sure thing." Sofia shot her a smile before going outside. It was a pretty morning. The sun sparkled on the dew-covered lawn, where a trio of brown and white goats munched on the overgrown grass. One goat with a star-shaped marking on her forehead—a friendly nanny called Tabitha—spotted Sofia. Bleating, she scampered up for an ear scratch, then kept Sofia company as she walked.

The shed was a whitewashed cinder block building beyond a plot of earth where they cultivated potatoes, watermelon, and squash. The twenty-foot square building housed a hydroponic garden where lettuces and herbs grew year-round.

At the door, Sofia patted Tabitha's flank. "You have to stay outside."

The interior was a juxtaposition of brightness and shadow. Fans attached to the ceiling whirred. Artificially illuminated by LED fixtures, rows of metal shelves were fitted with oversized PVC pipe. The PVC was filled with water, where plants grew without soil. Adam's cannabis took up one whole section. Sofia scanned the perimeter of the shed, gasping and dropping the basket when Ben sneaked up behind her. He stepped into her like he had in the kitchen—his chest to her back and a forearm cinching her waist. "There you are, brown-eyed girl."

"Here I am," she purred, reaching behind to bury her fingers into his hair.

Ben prodded his arousal against her tailbone, trapping Sofia against the shelf. Mouth moving against the sensitive skin at the crook of her neck, he cupped her breast, scolding, "You knew exactly what you were doing in the kitchen, didn't you?"

Sofia bit her lip, not answering. She felt deliciously wicked. Ben wedged a booted foot between her shoes, goading her to spread her legs, then he bent her over the edge of the shelf so her torso was flat against the surface. He flicked Sofia's sundress up, fully exposing her. Kneading her ass cheeks, Ben gave her a sharp spank on each cheek. Sofia flinched and moaned, her loins clenching at the sweet stinging of her flesh.

Cupping her sex from behind, Ben's fingers slipped into her wet cleft and stroked her walls. When his knuckle roughly grazed her nub, Sofia whimpered, bucking against him. "Fuck me. Now."

Breath rapid, Ben broke from her long enough to unbutton his jeans and push them down to his ankles, along with his briefs. One hand gripping her hips, he rammed his cock into her, his other around her neck. His rhythm was frenzied as he plunged in and out. Sofia climaxed seconds before Ben.

He collapsed on her back, panting. They both were slick with sweat. He kissed the shell of Sofia's ear before getting to his feet. "That was amazing. I can't seem to get enough of you."

Still catching her breath and her legs barely holding her, Sofia adjusted her dress. "Want me to come over to your place tonight?"

"Yeah. After dusk."

"Let me leave the shed first." Sofia retrieved the basket from the concrete floor, picking the veggies she needed and adding the herbs Kate had requested on top. Before she exited the building, she drew Ben's head down to give him a lingering kiss. "'Til tonight."

CHAPTER THIRTY-FOUR

OVER THE ENSUING DAYS, SOFIA FOUND THE CLANDESTINE rendezvous with Ben exhilarating. Electrifying. She felt vitally *alive*. She could think of little else than those blissful stolen moments. But, they were never enough. Sofia wanted more. Always more. Her body craved him. He was like a drug, and she was addicted. Frantic for her next hit.

The sex pact was operating flawlessly to plan. Sofia was smug. She and Ben agreed that their fuck sessions were just that, fuck sessions. Fornication was a way to pass the time. To feel good. To blow off steam. Nothing further. However, Nora's all-seeing gaze ricocheted from Sofia to Ben when they were together in the farmhouse. Sofia was nonplussed—the girl was canny. Discerning something was up, Nora made zero effort to cloak her animosity for Sofia, often glaring at her in defiance or back talking when Sofia spoke to her. Nora's frank dislike gave Sofia pause. She didn't need the aggravation, so she granted Nora a wide berth. When Nora moved into Juniper Rise, Ben and Sofia's trysts relocated to the vacant cabin adjacent to the one Lark and Sofia shared.

There had been no additional dialogue about driving a flatbed trailer to Spenser Suppliers. On Friday after the evening meal, Teller took Maggie upstairs, leaving Sofia and Kate alone in the kitchen. Sofia volunteered to help her tidy up. "So. The warehouse on the agenda?"

Kate closed the dishwasher and pressed start. Grimacing, she drummed her fingers on the butcher block counter. "In all honesty, Teller and I have been ambivalent about whether we should do it now or wait. Based on what you learned in Calhoun the... current environment is... volatile." She gave Sofia a sheepish look. "What's your opinion?"

"Well," Sofia said, wetting the sponge to wipe the stove down, "on one hand, it's not like we're low on food here at the farm. On the other, the clock *is* ticking as far as expiration dates. There are pallets of chips and crackers and soda that have already spoiled. And I wouldn't trust the bottled water anymore unless I had no other option—plastic leaches chemicals. But the rest is worth bringing to Mayfly Hollow now, even if it expired within the last month or two."

"Such as?"

"Canned and jarred veggies, fruit, meat. Pallets of pasta and rice and dried beans," Sofia said over her shoulder. "Personal care items, too. Shampoo and soap. Condoms. Feminine hygiene."

Kate perked up. "What sort of feminine hygiene?"

Sofia threw Kate a winsome smile, thinking of the lifetime supply of products on the shelves. She used a washable silicone menstrual cup for her monthly cycle, but the other women at Mayfly Hollow had resorted to fashioning maxi-pads from old washcloths and rags, which was messy. "Tampons. Pads. Go With The Flo Cups."

"No shit," Kate breathed. "I've *yearned* for tampons this last year. Who knew it would be one of the things I'd miss the most?"

"Lark has complained about the homemade pads. You should try the cup though. Bet you'd love it."

"I know Bella would like to have a new one—hers wore out,

and she had to throw it away. And she commented the other day that her cache of condoms is dwindling. We've gone through our birth control pills, and she's petrified of getting knocked up."

Sofia put the sponge on the rim of the sink. "I've got a few years left on my IUD, or I'd be freaking out about that, too."

Kate's eyebrows went to her hairline, her expression titillated. "Oh?"

Sofia snapped her mouth shut, but Kate grinned shrewdly. "Does that mean you and Ben…"

"No comment."

"Uh huh. Pleading the fifth? You two are keeping it on the down low, I see."

Shrugging, Sofia murmured, "Easier that way."

"I won't tell."

LATER THAT NIGHT, Lark came into their cabin with a cat-that-got-the-cream smirk. She slammed the door and plopped onto the mattress. "Wait 'til you get a taste of the mouthwatering tea I'm about to spill, sis!"

Sofia put the novel she was reading on her bedside table and faced Lark, her interest piqued. "Spill away."

"Major to-do. Huge blowout."

"Well?"

"Milo caught Bella screwing Josh."

"No way. Mister No Personality Josh and mousy little Bella? I don't believe it."

"Would I fib? Get this. I had just checked on Adam's pot plants in the hydroponics building and bumped smack dab into them mid-fight. Milo was screaming. Bella was screaming. Then Josh showed up and sucker-punched Milo."

"No."

"Oh yeah, then Bella shrieked that she was gonna shack up with Josh, and Milo could fuck himself. Then she stuck her tongue down Josh's gullet. Milo hollered about how Bella had always been a slut, and he should've kicked her ass out the first time she cheated on him when they lived in Upper Bremer. Then he charged Josh, and Josh slugged him again. Milo plummeted to the gravel, and Bella and Josh sauntered away. I had to help Milo to his damn feet!"

"Like sands through the hourglass... so are The Days of Our Lives." Sofia giggled, sitting up against the headboard. "But wait. Josh and Fritz bunk together in the two-bedroom staff cabin. What'll Fritz say about his new roommate?" She didn't speak her thoughts, but the speculation the Josh, Milo, and Bella love triangle was certain to cause was *exactly* why Sofia and Ben intended to be discreet.

"There's bound to be fireworks! The best part," Lark laughed uproariously, tears streaming down her cheeks. She put a palm on her chest, attempting to steady her breath, "is after I got Milo to his cabin, he asked me if I was game to move in with him!"

Sofia wagged her eyebrows. "And what was your answer, Lark?"

Lark put her head back and chortled. "C'mon, Sofia. You really think I'd mess with that pencil dick? I want a man." Her tone transformed to musing. "Since you've snagged Ben, Adam may be a contender. I might jump his bones when he returns."

Sofia pointed out, "You mean if he returns."

"Yeah. If." Lark sobered, propping against the headboard near Sofia and pulling her knees to her chest. "Suppose it's small of me to gossip about Milo and Bella."

"Don't be so tough on yourself. It's nice to see you smiling. You've been pretty pensive." Sofia plucked a stray piece of lint from the quilt over her knees. "I notice that you tend to isolate. Like, a lot. You spend most of your free time under that willow tree down past Juniper Rise ever since Adam left."

"I like to be alone. Journaling sorts my head out."

"You didn't sing for a long time after we arrived at Mayfly

Hollow," Sofia remarked, "but I heard you the other day. You *are* happy here, aren't you, Lark?"

Lark gnawed on her thumbnail, lending Sofia's question due consideration before admitting, "I am. I'm the happiest I've been in a while. I was a skeptic. If it wasn't for you insisting I give this place a gamble... I'm grateful to you, Sofia." She cleared her throat before adding gruffly, "I've never had a so-called best friend, but you're damn close to one, sis."

CHAPTER THIRTY-FIVE

SOFIA HELD A WICKER BASKET BRIMMING WITH FRESHLY WASHED clothes, balancing it on her hip as she latched the door to the staff laundry building.

"Sofia! Sofia!"

Sofia spun around, startled to see Nora rushing toward her. Her cheeks were pale and her cornflower blue eyes wide with panic. Sofia's heart skipped, trepidation sparking. "Are you hurt? Is Ben hurt? Did Zs breach the fence?"

"Ben's haying with Teller and Rob." Nora tugged Sofia's arm, urging her to follow. "Please, Sofia, come to my house!"

"O-okay." Sofia set the laundry basket inside the building then permitted Nora to grasp her hand. She accompanied the girl on the now well-worn trail to Juniper Rise. "But why aren't you in class?"

"Class is done early. Edna had a migraine. She's napping."

"You shouldn't be wandering around on your own, Nora. It's dangerous."

"I do all the time," Nora argued.

"Maybe that ought to be re-evaluated."

"Just hurry, Sofia! It's an emergency!"

The house came into view, and Nora's pace quickened. She

released Sofia's hand and ran ahead. Sofia hurried to keep up with her. Nora's sneakers crunched on the pebbled path as she sprinted along it and up the porch stairs. She disappeared into the house.

Once Sofia was inside, she glanced around. It was odd to be at Ben's house during the day. Nora was nowhere in sight. "Where'd you go?"

"I'm here!" Nora stood in her bedroom doorway.

When Sofia entered the room, Nora waited by her closet, which was ajar. She gestured to the inner recesses, indicating the floor.

"What in the world..." Sofia muttered, peeking around the louvered closet door to where Nora pointed. A white cat with tan spots was sprawled on an old towel. Sofia had seen the barn cat around. Not much more than a kitten herself, her abdomen was distended in late-stage pregnancy. She panted and whined. "Does Ben know you have her in your closet? She's probably infested with fleas."

"No. I brought her yesterday. Her name's Toffee. She's in trouble!"

"She sure is—my guess is that Toffee's in labor."

"Duh. I know that," Nora scoffed. "I'm not a dum-dum. I asked you here because Kate said you wanted to be an animal doctor. Look at her privates."

Sofia kneeled and lifted Toffee's tail. Inflamed tissue resembling two bloody sacs protruded from her. Her fur was stained red-brown with a small amount of similarly-colored discharge sullying the towel. Toffee's gold eyes peered up at Sofia. She scratched Toffee under the chin, saying softly, "It seems scary, but cats generally do alright birthing on their own."

"At first, she was crying and moving around, but she's been this way forever! I think the kitten is stuck!"

Sofia reflected more to herself than Nora, "She's not actively pushing. Maybe I should ask Rob to assess her."

"Ugh! Are you deaf? I *said* Rob's with Ben and Teller."

Sofia sat back on her heels and reproached Nora, "Hey. Knock off the sass-talk. You really think that's the way to treat someone you want to help you?"

"But—"

"You've been a real brat lately. Actually, you don't deserve my help. I should refuse and sashay out of this house, little girl."

Nora gasped. "You have to help Toffee!"

"I don't *have to* do anything," Sofia said coolly, eyebrow arched. "*I'm* a grown up."

Nora averted her gaze, her manner contrite. "Sorry, Sofia. I'll try harder to be nice. *Please* stay."

Biting her cheek, Sofia petted the cat, running a palm over her abdomen, and Toffee rewarded her with a rumbling purr. Sofia felt movement under her hand, indicating the kittens were alive. She couldn't abandon the unfortunate creature—she decided to stay and monitor Toffee. "Fine. But you owe me."

Nora hopped up and down, clapping her hands. "Thank you, thank you, thank you! I promise I'll be nicer!"

"Shh," Sofia admonished. "You're too loud, and that stresses Toffee out. She must have peace and quiet."

"I'll be quiet."

"Let's shut the closet most of the way so she has privacy and let her be."

"Can't I sit with her?"

"I'll check on her every so often, okay? Then, once haying is finished for the day, I'll discuss the situation with Rob."

"Ben said he'll be kinda late…"

"I'm not going anywhere, alright?"

Uncertainty crossed Nora's face, but she nodded.

"That's a girl. What should we do while we wait for Ben?"

Nora shrugged, frowning as Sofia pushed the closet door until it was just cracked.

Sofia planted her hands on her hips and surveyed the bedroom. It was now fully painted princess pink. A white daybed had been pushed up against the wall across from the closet along with a matching dresser, but the room was otherwise unadorned. Packages of curtains and rods were stacked in the corner alongside a framed poster of watercolor hearts. Sofia had an idea. "If you can locate a toolbox, I'll put up your curtains."

NORA ASSISTED Sofia in hanging the rainbow patterned curtains and the poster, centering it over the daybed. Nora made her bed with the purple-and-pink patterned quilt, and Sofia laid Nora's teddy bear against the coordinating pillow sham. Then, they worked on the living room, rearranging the coffee table and sectional sofa to Nora's specification.

Nora unpacked the boxes of home décor, organizing the pieces on the fireplace mantel while Sofia installed curtain rods. After they finished decorating, they gave each other a high five and flopped on the sofa, propping their bare feet on the table. "Phew! Good job, Nora!"

"It was fun. There's still all sorts of stuff in the pole barn..." She peeked at Sofia shyly from under her lashes. "Maybe sometime we can pick out more?"

"Sure." The late afternoon sun filtered through the filmy sheers Sofia had hung on the living room windows, revealing it was near dinnertime. Nora's stomach gurgled, and Sofia laughed. "Hungry, huh?"

"Yeah."

"Worked up an appetite." Sofia had looked in on Toffee several times, but her condition remained unchanged. Although Kate would be preparing the evening meal soon, Sofia didn't think it was smart to leave the cat. She tipped her head toward the kitchen. "You guys have any food here?"

"I think so. Ben brought some pans and stuff last night."

Sofia got up and opened the refrigerator door. There was a pitcher of iced tea. She poured the tea into Mason jars, handing one to Nora before pulling the earthenware bowl with raw chicken parts from the fridge, along with a tray of veggies. In the cabinets above the stove, a bag of rice was beside a variety of canned goods. Sofia preheated the oven, sending Nora outside to pick wildflowers while she assembled a casserole using the chicken, rice, sliced carrots, and canned cream soup she'd found. After rummaging through the meager assortment of spices in the cupboard above the dishwasher for garlic powder and black pepper, Sofia popped the casserole in the oven.

Nora was walking across the clearing behind the house with a massive armful of colorful flowers. Sofia went to unlatch the kitchen door, ushering her inside. She recognized cardinal flowers, bee balm, wild bergamot, and cranesbill. Relieving Nora of half of her burden, she chuckled. "You took your assignment serious!"

"Ben should transplant some of the peonies from my cabin down here. Just think how pretty the blooms would look in a bouquet with juniper berries," Sofia said, trimming stems while Nora filled large Mason jars with water. Once the arrangements were ready, Nora went around the house and placed one in every room.

There were sounds at the front door as Sofia pulled the steaming casserole from the oven. A dusty Ben appeared in the entryway to the kitchen, a surprised look on his face. "Smells great... What are you doing here cooking?"

Ben's appearance had Sofia salivating like Pavlov's canines. It was all she could do to curtail herself from launching at him. Face flushing, Sofia haltingly told him about the cat as Nora entered the kitchen.

"What's the deal with the barn cat, Nor?"

"Her name's Toffee."

"Okay, but you didn't ask my permission to bring Toffee into the house."

"She's my favorite," Nora explained meekly, "and I wanted her. We can keep her, right?"

Ben swept a palm across his forehead and rubbed the bridge of his nose. "We'll see. Run up to the farmhouse and try to catch Rob before it rains. Be polite when you ask him to come look at Toffee. Hopefully you won't be interrupting his dinner."

Wordlessly, Sofia dished up a serving of chicken and rice, and Ben washed his hands at the kitchen sink before taking a seat at the table in the dining nook. Sitting across from him, she sipped her iced tea while he tucked into his food. "This is delicious. Thanks for cooking." He glanced around the living room. "And decorating."

"I didn't overstep, did I? I wanted to distract Nora from fussing over the cat."

"You didn't overstep. Look, I know she's been a monster toward you. I've had discussions with her about respecting her elders, but the kid's savvy. She knows something's up with us."

"It's our pheromones."

"Could be." Ben grinned, a dimple emerging in his cheek. "Are your panties wet?"

She shook a finger at him playfully. "No time for a quickie."

"Shame." With a sigh of lament, Ben resumed eating.

The sky had darkened outside, signaling an impending storm. Sofia said, "Nora's at a precocious age, and with the amount of freedom she has, she could get into all kinds of mischief."

"Yeah. I've been preoccupied with the house and you." He winked at Sofia, conceding, "I'm still adjusting to full-time parenthood. My new normal."

"Speaking of parenthood, you've never shared what happened to her mother and father."

"We don't talk about the tragedies we've had at Mayfly Hollow."

"Don't feel obligated to tell me," Sofia assured him, "if it's a touchy subject."

"No, no, it's not taboo." He dismissed her objections with a careless hand gesture. "When Judy suffered a miscarriage, both her and Nora's father, Jamie, withdrew and shut themselves into their cabin. It was as if they forgot they even had a daughter. Jamie nursed Judy while Nora stayed at the farmhouse. Poor lady lingered weeks before dying."

Sofia's mouth parted. "A miscarriage left her *that* badly debilitated?"

"Pregnancy is risky during these times," Ben reminded Sofia. Pushing his empty plate away, he lifted a shoulder. "Kate was there during the miscarriage. Not many people know the gory details, but apparently Judy's fetus was infected with the Z virus. Kate saw it moving in the toilet bowl."

"What? The fetus," Sofia swallowed, her stomach churning, "*was a Z?*"

"Horrifying, right?"

"I'm sickened," Sofia admitted, shuddering. "So, Judy basically wasted away after the miscarriage?"

"Precisely. And... after dying, she turned into a Z and mauled Jamie. That was how Kate was bitten—by Jamie. She'd delivered a tray of food, and he tackled her. He got a chunk out of her."

"Adam told us about Kate, but I had no clue about Nora's parents. How awful for her."

"She's been through the ringer."

"I've got to remind myself to exercise more patience with her."

"You've been sufficiently patient in my opinion. She's tested you, but she's a helluva kid. You've witnessed her prowess with a compound bow during target practice. When that MC attacked us last year, our success was due in a large part to her."

"But she's so tiny!"

"And tough as nails. She was shot during the siege, but against all odds, she recovered."

Footfalls on the porch announced Nora and Rob. Sofia served the girl a plate of food and instructed her to eat while she and Ben accompanied Rob into the bedroom. They discovered Toffee, who was now in active labor, straining to push. Sofia tsked. "There's been no progress."

"The bloody discharge is troubling," Rob said. After briefly examining the cat, he got to his feet. "It's not like I can perform a C-section. I don't have a sterile OR or the proper instruments. I don't have anesthesia. I'm not even certain of my skills—felines aren't my specialty. My advice is to let nature take its course. Prepare Nora for the worst."

CHAPTER THIRTY-SIX

AFTER THANKING ROB FOR COMING DOWN TO JUNIPER RISE, SOFIA saw him out then lingered at the kitchen table, listening as Ben repeated Rob's grim prognosis to Nora.

Moisture accumulated on the girl's waterline, making her fair eyelashes spiky. A single tear hovered, then splattered on her t-shirt. She whispered, "Why are you talking that way? You guys are quitters then. That's not okay!"

Sofia sighed, her heart squeezing. "We're not quitting, Nora, but we can't promise everything will be alright. It's in God's hands."

"Best we give it to you straight, honey." Ben bent to embrace Nora. "Lying isn't the answer."

Nora's cries were muffled by Ben's shirt. "I don't wanna sleep tonight. I wanna be with Toffee."

"You have school tomorrow. How about if I keep Toffee company?" Sofia asked, blinking back her own tears.

"Both Sofia and I will tend to Toffee," Ben reassured Nora. He dried her cheeks with the pads of his fingers. "Are you done eating?"

Nora sniffled, nodding.

"Bath time then. Afterwards, you can take your book into my bedroom and read there until you fall asleep. Alright?"

Sofia asked, "Shall I run your bathwater?"

Nora shook her head and trundled down the hall. A minute later, the bathroom door shut, and there was the sound of the bathtub faucet being turned on.

Sofia huffed a weary breath. "Wow. You actually volunteered for this parenthood gig?"

"Yeah. It's an undertaking. You don't have to hang around, you know. I can deal with the cat."

"I gave Nora my word."

"Don't you want any dinner?"

"No, between the cat drama and learning about Nora's parents, my stomach's in knots."

"I understand." Ben scraped Nora's leftovers into a plastic storage container, then stowed the dirty dishes in the dishwasher. He tore a sheet of cling film and covered the casserole before putting the food in the fridge. After rinsing the empty pitcher, Ben measured out a scoop of pre-made drink mix from a countertop canister. "Want a glass of lemonade?"

"Sure. It's bizarre seeing you all domestic and paternal."

"What can I say? I'm a man of many talents, Sofia," Ben said easily, filling two Mason jars with ice cubes from the freezer before adding lemonade. He set the glasses on the table then stooped to kiss her. "I'm going to shower in the master bathroom. I'll return to hold vigil with you."

The ceiling fixture in Nora's bedroom was on a dimmer switch. Sofia adjusted it so the light was muted, then settled on the carpet next to the closet, her lemonade in hand. Toffee's respirations were uneven. She lay prone on her towel, half-asleep, clearly fatigued.

The bathroom door unlatched across the hall. Now dressed in pajamas with her hair wet from her bath, Nora slumped against the bedroom door jamb. "How is she?"

Sofia injected her tone with sympathy, answering, "Not great."

Crestfallen, Nora removed her chapter book from the top of her dresser and silently went into the master bedroom. A short time later, Ben joined Sofia, handing her an old magazine. "Something to pass the hours?"

"Thanks, maybe later." Putting the magazine aside, Sofia skimmed her hand over Toffee, soothing her. "She's officially in distress, Ben. I feel powerless."

"Pity we can't crush juniper berries from the bushes out front. They're toxic to cats and dogs, but in the Middle Ages the berries were used to bring on uterine contractions in women."

"How do you know that?"

"From my grandmother."

"Oh?"

"She was a plant pathologist. Lectured at Dunhaven University in Northwood. I can picture her so clearly in my mind's eye. Wish she was here." He smiled with affection.

"You were close to her?"

"Yeah. She was famous for her potions and tinctures. My grandfather teased her, calling her witchy." Ben stared into space as if lost in thought. "She always said she wanted a daughter so she could name her Juniper, but she only bore sons."

"Lovely name."

"It is. The symbolism and lore of it adds to its appeal."

"Oh." Sofia admitted, "I don't know anything about that kinda thing."

Ben winked at her, and Sofia was under the impression he was trying to sidetrack her from worrying about the cat, much as she had with Nora. "*Everything* in the natural world is rife with symbolism, Sofia."

"And I suppose you have a poetic quote by Longfellow that ties into that," Sofia said lightly.

Chuckling, Ben responded, "No. No quotes. But there is a story about why I named this homestead Juniper Rise."

"Don't keep me in suspense."

Ben settled into a more relaxed position against the wall, crossing his legs at the ankles. "I was out on the fringes of the acreage last summer and came across a thicket of juniper bushes —my eyes zeroed in on them right away. We had them at our family farm growing up. I was hit with a wave of homesickness. It's difficult to articulate," Ben's face was animated as he explained, "but every cell in my body energized. I was compelled to establish a home of my own. Building something from the ground up. I figured I'd have to chop trees and hew a log cabin myself, so it was like providence when I found this place ripe for the taking while out scavenging."

"It was meant to be." Sofia's heart panged at the passion in Ben's tone. What would it be like to be part of his vision—to build a life from the ground up—together? She cleared her throat, murmuring, "I had wondered whether the bushes lining the walkway meant something."

"I transplanted them from that thicket."

"So the rise part of Juniper Rise refers to… what? Rebirth?"

"That and the fact the house sits on a sloping hill. I liked that the word had multiple connotations—you know the adage *like a phoenix rising from the ashes*?"

"Of course. Clever." A hush fell over them. Sofia inhaled deeply. The bedroom smelled of new paint, carpet, and Toffee's feral scent, but the house seemed drowsy. Rain pattered against the windows, lending tranquility to the ambiance. Still stroking Toffee's wiry fur, Sofia met Ben's eyes. The connection was there —the ever-present awareness that linked them. It was gossamer and intricate and delicate yet unwavering.

Sofia's voice was husky when she reminded Ben, "You never told me what juniper itself symbolizes."

"Purity. Strength. Protection. It wards off evil by sheltering those who remain in its shade."

"Appropriate for the apocalypse."

Ben's gaze homed in on her mouth as she spoke, intensifying.

Twisting, he reached to cup her face. His fingertips caressed her jawline, and he leaned in to bring his mouth to hers. Nibbling at her bottom lip, he then traced it with the tip of his tongue.

Winding her arms around his neck, Sofia clung to him as he kissed her. Her fingers slithered down his torso, seeking the elastic waistband to his basketball shorts.

At the plaintive cry from the closet, Sofia stilled. Breathing heavily, she broke away from Ben, squinting at Toffee. "Oh my God... Ben, look!"

A newly born kitten lay on the towel.

CHAPTER THIRTY-SEVEN

TOFFEE SNIFFED THE KITTEN, UNCONCERNED. THE MEMBRANE encasing it had ruptured during birth, and the kitten did not move.

"She ought to be cleaning it up, don't you think?" Ben asked

"It's stiff. I think it's a stillbirth." Sofia kneeled in the closet doorway and scooped up the lifeless kitten. Using her thumb, she wiped away the blood and mucus coating the kitten's nose, but it was evident there was no reviving it. "Definitely is."

Within minutes, Toffee delivered the afterbirth and ate it.

Ben wrinkled his nose, declaring, "Nature."

"It's hardcore," Sofia agreed, sitting back on her haunches for a spell before going to wash her hands.

Toffee panted and labored for another hour, and in succession, she birthed two additional offspring—both white with tan speckles and both robust. Maternal instinct kicking in, she tore off the membranes of their sacs and cleared their faces and noses before biting through their umbilical cords. Toffee ceased straining and rested, allowing the kittens to suckle.

"Think she's finished?"

Sofia palpated Toffee's abdomen. "Pretty sure there's another one in there. I feel a lump."

"Waiting game."

Sofia smiled as she watched the kittens nurse. "They're adorable. Nora's going to be so excited in the morning. Are you letting her keep the cats here?"

Ben gave her a baleful look. "I'm a moosh, so... what do you think?"

"You'll have to treat Toffee for fleas. And worms. Are there animal meds stocked at Mayfly Hollow?"

"For the livestock, sure, but for barn cats? Highly doubt it."

"Fleas will make your life miserable, Ben. And worms? Some parasites can be passed to humans."

Ben steepled his fingers, suddenly looking drained. "I know Teller treats Ace for heartworm."

"But canine meds aren't indicated for feline use." She placed a palm on his forearm. "Why don't you crawl into bed? Haying is exhausting work, and you're about ready to pass out."

Ben glimpsed longingly at Nora's daybed. "If you're sure?"

"I'll be fine."

"Wake me if you need me."

Within minutes, Ben was under the quilt and snoring. Sofia bit her tongue to prevent giggling as she surveyed him. Such a large, masculine man tucked up in a child-size bed seemed incongruous. His legs were too long for it—his bare feet were crammed awkwardly against the footboard.

She knew him well as a lover, but being in Ben's home cast him in a new light—father. Protector. Not without flaws, but a wholly virtuous man. The type of man that would do *anything* to protect the people he loved. Something akin to tenderness squeezed Sofia's heart as she recalled the fondness in his tone when he spoke of his grandmother. How energized he'd been on the subject of building a life here at Juniper Rise. Sofia pondered how he sounded when he talked about *her*. Was he reverent? Animated? Affectionate? Or was he indifferent?

What did it matter? There was no future for her and Ben beyond their sex pact.

It was almost dawn when Toffee roused and began panting and crying again. The head of the final kitten appeared but mid-birth, Toffee wilted to the towel, listless. Her eyes closed, and her diaphragm stilled. Sofia tapped her but received no response. "Oh no..."

Sofia peeled back Toffee's eyelid. An unfocused pupil stared, unseeing. Panic clutched at Sofia as she checked the cat's gums. White. "Oh no!"

What should she do? A trickle of sweat beaded down her forehead. Sofia brushed it away. White gums meant internal bleeding. Toffee wouldn't make it. That much was apparent. Could Sofia save the kitten? Gingerly, she extracted it from the birth canal. Once it was free, a gush of blood followed, soaking the towel and the other kittens, who mewled and rooted around. Toffee was hemorrhaging. Inflamed tissue protruded from her. Sofia's eye was untrained, but even she recognized a prolapsed uterus. With no emergency surgery, Toffee was done for. "I'm sorry, kitty."

Sofia dabbed at the kitten's face with the hem of her shirt, wiping the afterbirth from its nostrils. Her actions were frantic, but it was futile. The kitten was stillborn. Sofia set it on the towel and scooted away.

Using the wall to support her spine, Sofia leaned back, staring stupidly at her hands. Unwelcome images flashed. She couldn't shake them—the torn flesh at Zac's throat. His livid, sticky blood. The gurgle as he choked on it. The metallic stink that invaded her nostrils. She vigorously rubbed her palms on her jeans. The blood was thick. Tacky. Her hands wouldn't come clean. A keening whine broke through the stillness. It came from Sofia.

She was vaguely cognizant of Ben flinging back the quilt and joining her on the carpet. His arms wrapped around Sofia, bundling her and cradling her against the warmth of his chest. She buried her fingers in his t-shirt and sobbed, her head under his chin. His voice was husky with sleep as he consoled, "It's okay, Sofia. I'm here. Let it out."

He held her for several minutes after her tears subsided, his fingers massaging her scalp and the base of her neck. Self-consciously, Sofia pulled away, wiping at her nose with the back of her hand, but Ben restrained her. "Don't be embarrassed."

"I don't know w-what's wrong with me," she blubbered. "I-I just got overwhelmed all of the sudden. Had flashbacks f-from… Zac."

Ben tsked, using the calloused pads of his fingers to dry the tracks of moisture on Sofia's cheeks, much as he had the night before with Nora. He leaned in and brought his lips to her forehead.

"It was like I was there again. The same helplessness, you know?"

Ben nodded, his eyes compassionate. "I know."

Sofia gestured to the closet. "Only two survivors. Without a mother, they'll never make it, Ben. They'll need kitten formula. And soon. Syringe feeding every couple of hours… if only there was another nursing cat here that could adopt them. Maybe we could offer goat's milk? But I don't think that has the proper nutrients."

"You know hand-raising kittens isn't a priority here. We have plenty of other barn cats."

Sofia gave him a severe look. "So we just let them starve to death?"

"It's not like we can venture outside the gates to scavenge for cat supplies," he argued.

"You wanna explain that to Nora? Hasn't that kid seen enough death already? Haven't we all?"

"C'mon. Don't make this more difficult than it already is." Ben toyed with a tendril of her hair, but she moved out of his reach. He reasoned, "Beyond the obvious hazards, Kate and Teller will never approve of us wasting precious gasoline on such an errand."

"I thought this was an egalitarian society," Sofia said pointedly.

"It is, but Kate and Teller are the only remaining members of the council. They have final say since I'm enmeshed in the situation, and Adam isn't here to vote. They'd balk, and rightly so. Resources are finite. Common sense must prevail."

"Then brainstorm a better alternative! I saw a motorcycle parked by the pole barn. With a motorcycle, we'd barely use any gas to get to the vet hospital I worked summers at in Mergenville! Can we take it?"

"Sofia. I admire you for—"

"*I'll* feed the kittens around my duties at Mayfly Hollow. *I'll* assume full responsibility... Does the motorcycle by the pole barn run?"

"No, but we have other motorcycles, and some do," Ben said. "Nevertheless—"

"I cannot *not do anything*, Ben." She shot him an imploring look. "Have I ever asked you for any favors before?"

Nora stood in the doorway, her eyes smudged from slumber and her hair rumpled. She demanded, "Why are you fighting? Where's Toffee? Is she okay? Did she have her kittens?"

CHAPTER THIRTY-EIGHT

Nora, an ordinarily stoic child, lost her composure immediately upon learning of Toffee's passing. Not even the presence of the two surviving kittens was enough to assuage her grief.

Collapsing into Sofia's embrace, she bawled pitifully. Sofia wrestled with her own emotions as she comforted Nora. She was compelled to make haste—time was of the essence. *If* she could convince Ben. She shot him an appealing look.

Jaw ticking, Ben muttered, "Told you I'm a moosh... Alright. Nora, choose some clothes. We'll get washed up and walk to the farmhouse."

Sofia latched the closet door while Nora hurried to select a t-shirt and a pair of shorts from her dresser, then Ben and Sofia left the room. Ben shut the door behind them. Without the light spilling from Nora's fixture, the hallway was shadowy. Sofia pulled his head down to kiss him. "Thank you."

"It's not a done deal yet," he reminded her. "Not 'til Kate and Teller agree."

"Still..."

Ben goaded her into the wall outside the bathroom, penning her with his arms. He bent to say against her lips, "I'll be expecting a lot more than a measly smooch after doing this favor for you."

"You'll get it."

IT HAD STORMED ALL NIGHT, leaving the footpath to the farmhouse muddy. They traipsed parallel to the trail, in the weeds, as briskly as they dared in the predawn gloom. Once they stepped on the gravel lane past the staff cabins, they were able to pick up speed.

The kitchen window glowed with yellow light, but the rest of the house was dark. Letting themselves in through the back door, they scraped their shoes on the doormat. Ben directed Nora to watch a DVD in the family room until breakfast. Lark was at the counter stirring batter in a melamine bowl, her eyelids baggy from sleep. She said, "There you are, Sofia. Is that blood on your shirt? What happened?"

Sofia filled Lark in about the cat, telling her she wanted to journey to Mergenville Pet Hospital for supplies. "Have you seen Teller or Kate?"

Glancing at the wall clock, Lark dropped a handful of blueberries in the bowl and mixed them in with a wooden spoon. "It's only five. Want coffee while you wait?"

Sofia tapped her toe, angst blooming in her sternum. As strong as her convictions were about saving the orphaned kittens, braving the real world still terrified her. The only thing she could place bets on was its predictable unpredictability. "We can't wait."

"We aren't stampeding upstairs to wake them." Ben poured mugs of coffee, adding a splash of milk from a pitcher in the fridge before handing her one. "I'm sure Kate will be down shortly. She's an early riser."

"I can't sit still. I'll raid the stockroom for what we need."

Ignoring Ben's exasperated expression, Sofia put her mug on the trestle table as he sat on the bench seat.

Lark asked over her shoulder, "Can you get me a jug of maple syrup while you're in there?"

By the time Sofia had gathered everything she wanted from the stockroom—Lark's maple syrup, along with weapons and two backpacks—Teller came down the stairs. He entered the hallway, his Stetson in hand and a drowsy Maggie on his hip. "Howdy, Sofia."

"Morning." She smiled at Maggie, who lay against Teller, sucking her thumb.

"What's goin' on? You fixin' to take a trip?"

She started to tell him about Toffee, but Ben joined them in the hallway, and she let him take over. Leaning against the wall, his thumb in his jean pocket, he calmly relayed the issue.

Teller scanned the pile of weapons and backpacks at Sofia's feet, saying mildly, "Puttin' the cart a tad before the horse. We got a system in place, Sofia. Didn't Benji enlighten you about obtainin' approval before scavengin'?"

Sofia couldn't help feeling like a chastised child despite Teller's kindly manner. She switched the gallon jug of maple syrup to her other hand, her cheeks heating. "He did."

"Where's Kate?" Ben asked, his gaze over Teller's shoulder. "Not like her to sleep in."

"She ain't feelin' too bright this mornin'. I insisted she stay in bed."

A frown passed over Ben's face. "She okay?"

"She'll do." Teller turned once again to Sofia. "Barn cats are low on the totem pole, Sofia, but I know you got a fire in your belly 'bout animals. Rearin' them kittens mean a lot to you, don't it?"

"I'm fed up with seeing death. That's all. And it's important to Nora." Her eyes slid to Ben, then returned to Teller. "I know Ben was concerned about wasting gasoline, but with a motorcycle we'll barely use any at all—Mergenville can't be more than, like, ten miles away."

Teller listened, face impassive.

She wheedled, "I'll collect whatever I can for Ace while we're there—dewormer. Flea prevention. Doc Gil had a whole cupboard of meds."

"Supplies for Ace are always useful." The tap-tap of nails sounded against the wood floor, and the shepherd loped to Teller's side. Teller shifted Maggie, slouching to scratch Ace's ears. "Did you hear us talkin' about you, fella?"

Sofia's lips thinned, impatience and lack of rest making her edgy. It was an effort to maintain a level tone. "So are you cool with us riding into Mergenville?"

"Would be a favorable time to go into town," he drawled, more to himself than anyone else. "We ain't hayin' today. Too wet. Fritz and I were gonna tinker with the flatbed to ready it for the trek to your warehouse. Anyhow, it'll be a slow day."

"Hold up. You've decided about the warehouse?" Sofia asked, her eyebrows raising. "When?"

"We discussed it yesterday while out in the field. Kate's all for it," Ben said. "It'll be next week sometime. After hay baling."

Lark peeked around the kitchen entryway, a spatula in her fist. "Didn't mean to eavesdrop, but were you speaking about Sofia's warehouse?"

"Yeah, it's scheduled for next week," Sofia said. "Why? You want to go along?"

"I think so. It'll be good for me."

"We'll be havin' a meetin' about it," Teller said. "Why don't y'all get truckin' to Mergenville. Don't dilly-dally, alright?"

"Thanks," Sofia said, bending to grasp the compound bow she'd braced against the wall. She passed it to Ben, along with an empty backpack. She had a pistol in the waistband of her jeans and had also chosen an ax from the armory.

"Meet me outside in five minutes, Sofia. I'll bring a motorcycle from the pole barn." Pack on his back and the bow slung over his shoulder, Ben dipped his chin toward Teller before exiting the house.

Teller left Lark and Sofia in the hall. After relieving her of the maple syrup, Lark searched Sofia's face, eyes perceptive. "*Staying overnight* at Ben's? Sure that's wise?"

"I told you why I spent the night. The cat."

"I just don't want you to get hurt. Be careful, Sofia."

Lark had hit too close to the mark. Irritation made Sofia snap, "Do I smell burning?"

"My pancakes!" Lark whirled and dashed into the kitchen.

The reverberation of an engine approaching rattled the screen door. Sofia looked in on Nora before going outside. She was absorbed by the cartoon on the TV screen, not acknowledging Sofia's farewell.

Ben straddled a black cruiser-style motorcycle. His bow hung from a handlebar, and the remote control to the gate was clipped to a cupholder. Sofia had speculated that he'd be on a dirt bike, which would've been too small for them both to sit astride, but the cruiser was a perfect size.

Climbing on the back of the bike, she balanced her ax across her lap and twined her arms around Ben's midsection. "Let's go!"

Once on the highway, Ben accelerated, zigzagging around obstructions on the rain-slick road. Sofia pinned the ax with her elbow to prevent it from falling. Chilly wind nipped her cheeks. She ducked her face into Ben's shoulder. The colorless sky was transforming to dramatic bands of crimson, violet, and lavender, heralding the impending break of day. *Red sky in the morning, sailor take warning.* Sofia shivered. She hoped it wasn't a bad omen.

Ben stayed on back roads. They saw nothing—dead or alive—other than a trio of whitetail deer in an overgrown field. The air smelled of petrichor—pleasant and earthy, like cold rain sizzling on a hot stone. At the outskirts of Mergenville, Ben slowed. He coasted until they were within city limits, then he idled.

With a population of fifteen thousand, Mergenville was an unremarkable and modest municipality, but Sofia considered it her stomping grounds. Until freshman year, when she'd lobbied to attend public school at Crestview, she'd received a Catholic education there at Holy Family Academy. Later, her father arranged a summer job for her with his veterinarian friend, Gilbert Palmerston.

She brought her mouth to Ben's ear. "Take a left on Roosevelt. Follow until it Ts, then hang another left. That'll be Eisenhower. Mergenville Pet Hospital's a block down."

"What. The. Hell," Ben said over the hum of the engine. His eyes were trained on the reflection in the mirror attached to a handlebar. He motioned behind them.

Contorting in her seat, Sofia's breath caught.

A group of Zs congregated on the sidewalk in front of the post office. Three men and two women. Their clothes were tattered rags, exposing more than what they covered. A man was missing an arm and one of the women had a foot-wide hole in her chest. Making no move to pursue Sofia and Ben, instead they remained in place, swiveling their heads and ogling the newcomers with unbridled curiosity.

CHAPTER THIRTY-NINE

"Why are they just *standing there*?" Sofia asked, the timbre of her voice shrill.

Ben rocketed down Roosevelt and turned left. Sofia's gaze stayed trained on the Zs, but they didn't pursue the bike.

On the corner of Roosevelt and Eisenhower, a pair of women Zs loitered beside the crosswalk. When Ben swung wide onto Eisenhower, Sofia raised her ax in case they charged. They didn't. The orb of the sun had broken fully over horizon, bathing the avenue in shafts of radiant gold and revealing the Zs' facial features in detail. They were close enough for Sofia to maintain eye contact.

Mergenville Vet Hospital was an unassuming squat tan stucco building with a red shingled roof. A small window by the reception desk had been busted out, but the hospital was otherwise undisturbed. Fixated on a dozen Zs assembled at the grocery store down the street, Sofia instructed Ben to go to the rear of the building, where the employee entrance was located.

Once Ben had cut the engine and had the kickstand down, they scrambled from the motorcycle. The only sound in the eerie stillness was birdsong. Sofia perused the immediate area. They were alone. The kennels behind the building were bolted, the ragged furry remains of dogs who'd been entombed inside littering the concrete. The windowless metal door leading inside was closed. Sofia tried the knob. Locked.

Ben's grip flexed, loosened, and flexed tight again on his bow, belying his calm demeanor. "Pass me the ax, and I'll break in. We gotta make this fast. I'm creeped the fuck out."

Instead of answering, Sofia mentally crossed her fingers and stooped to the clay flowerpot beside the door. Hands trembling, she wiggled it until it moved. The spare key Doc Gil stashed there lay in the dirt. Exhaling a jagged breath of thanks, she snatched it and unlocked the door.

The spatters of sunlight from the windows at the front of the building trickled into the interior hallway. Swallowing the lump in her throat, Sofia twisted the deadbolt and whispered, "Want to sweep the place? Make sure we're alone?"

Ben nodded, preceding her from exam room to exam room. Empty. The bathroom was unoccupied, as was the small adjoining lab and surgery. The waiting room and reception desk were located just inside the street entrance. Doc Gil's office, where the built-in wall cabinet containing the meds was located, connected to the reception area by a short corridor.

The corpse of a vet tech was slumped against a file cabinet, her skin gray and withered like a mummy. Somebody had tracked through her blood before it had congealed. Now dried bloody shoe prints trailed in a crisscross pattern, intersecting the tiled floor. Some led into Doc's office.

Balancing his stance as he inched forward, Ben clasped his bow in position, string pulled back. Doc, his lab coat stained with blood, stood stock-still just inside the door. His mouth gaped as he stared at Ben.

"D-Doc G?" Sofia asked, and his head rotated to her.

Ben released the arrow, and it hit its target—Doc's forehead. He fell, striking the corner of his desk before rolling to the floor. "Holy shit," Ben muttered, his hand shaking as he yanked the arrow out. "The Zs are clearly in a stage of metamorphosis."

Mind racing, Sofia shucked off her backpack and tiptoed around Doc's body. Unbolting the built-in cabinet that served as a dispensary, she shoveled medications into her pack. When it was so full that it bulged, she zippered the backpack and slung it over her shoulder.

Ben passed his pack over. "Be thorough. We are *not* coming back here anytime soon."

Nodding in assent, Sofia returned to the reception area where a metal display rack was stacked with pet foods and supplements. She filled Ben's pack, handing it to him so he could put it on. "I'm ready."

Sofia followed Ben through the main corridor and outside. He climbed astride the bike and started it while Sofia secreted the key under the flowerpot. Clambering behind Ben, she clung to his shirt, their overstuffed backpacks making her position awkward.

The roar of the engine punctured the silence as they sailed down Eisenhower. More Zs had amassed on the sidewalks. Like parade attendees, they watched Ben and Sofia. Patting Ben's side, she urged him to go faster.

THEY'D BEEN GONE under an hour, but between the tension of the trip, skipping meals, and not sleeping a wink the previous night, Sofia was flagging by the time Ben dropped her at the farmhouse. Leaving her with the backpacks, he went to stow the motorcycle in the pole barn.

She lugged the packs inside to the kitchen, finding Bella, Lark, and Kate at the trestle table. Kate said, "That was quick!"

"Not quick enough for my liking," Sofia murmured. She deposited the backpacks and her ax on the floor and went to the sink to scrub her hands. On the counter, there was a platter piled with leftover blueberry pancakes. Sofia made a plate, dousing it in syrup before sagging onto the bench beside Lark.

Lark raised a judicious eyebrow. "Christ. You look spent."

Between bites of food, Sofia shared news about the Zs in Mergenville until Ben arrived. After putting his bow in the armory, he poured a cup of coffee and sat in the chair at the head of the table across from Kate. He picked up where Sofia left off, saying, "I'm telling you, I've *never* seen Zs react to people that way—they were spectators, and we were the entertainment. They didn't lift their noses and sniff us, and they didn't attack us, but somehow their behavior was infinitely more sinister. We were still prey."

"I told you guys how that Z in Calhoun made eye contact with me, remember?" Sofia asked. "Get this—every single Z we encountered gawked at us. And they look more human in other ways—their posture's straighter, and their skin's less splotchy."

"Further confirmation it's what we suspected. They're reverting back," Kate said, drumming her fingers on the table.

"Their appearance may be more human, but I'm not sure what's happening," Ben pointed to his temple, "up here."

"I'm scared," Bella said, her fair cheeks pallid. She wrapped her arms around her rib cage. "Teller told me about the horde outside on the highway last summer. What if they come here again? What if they attack?"

"Then we fight them," Kate replied curtly. "Why do you think we perform weekly drills? We'll protect our home from people *or* Zs."

Bella's expression turned chagrined, and she glanced away.

Kate returned her gaze to Ben, sighing. "Sounds like the Zs are in a latency period. If they aren't interested in hunting right now, maybe we should push up the warehouse."

Wincing, Ben shook his head. "A *latency period*? You're attempting to apply logic to illogical circumstances, Kate."

"I'm gonna let you two hash it out." Sofia stood and went to load her dishes in the dishwasher. "I'm so tired that I can barely keep my eyes open."

As Ben and Kate continued debating, Lark gestured to the

backpacks Sofia had left on the floor. "You found what you were searching for in Mergenville."

"We did." Sofia opened the packs and sorted the canine meds from the feline meds, kitten food, and canisters of formula. Packing up the items for the cats, she waited for a lull in Kate and Ben's discussion, then said, "This pile is for Ace. I'll put it in the stockroom."

"Thank you," Kate replied before resuming her conversation with Ben.

Yawning, Sofia went to the stockroom, returning the ax and pistol to the armory. After stowing everything neatly, she bolted the door and asked Ben what his plans were for the day.

"I'll check in with Teller and see what needs doing. Are you going to tend to the kittens?"

"Yes. Then I'll shower, and nap in Nora's room, if that's alright."

"Of course it is. Make yourself at home."

Threading her arm through her backpack, Sofia said, "Something will have to be done with Toffee's body."

"I'll bury her this afternoon. And the kittens. Set them outside, and I'll see to it."

Mouth grim at the thought of the unpleasant task, Sofia hastened to Juniper Rise.

CHAPTER FORTY

SOFIA TRAVERSED THE TRAIL PAST THE STAFF CABINS. THE morning chill had dissolved, indolent late summer balminess replacing it. Normally, she cherished such moments of solitude. Not today. Today solitude wasn't her friend. It allowed too much time to think. To dwell on Mergenville. On the Zs.

They'd *seen* her—had locked eyes with her. Their gazes had stalked Sofia and Ben. Was it an indication of restored sentience? What was next? Speech?

And what if they developed keener abilities for tracking prey? What if they were able to locate Mayfly Hollow? It was unthinkable. Unnerving.

The threat the changing Zs posed to the sanctity of her newfound home made a scorching ball of dread form in Sofia's stomach.

She paused, the basket of clean clothes she'd snagged from where she'd left it in the staff laundry building the day before against her hip. How had that been only yesterday? Her hand went to her mouth. Would she throw up the pancakes she'd just devoured?

Perhaps they should forgo the trip to the warehouse. Why

chance leading any Zs back to the farm? Sofia would have a word with Kate. Soon.

Knees wobbly, she hurried down the path and ascended the porch stairs to Ben's house. Sofia had become an expert in compartmentalization since the apocalypse—she must shift her focus or she'd make herself sick. Taking a deep breath before going inside, Sofia sent up a prayer of thanksgiving for the protection of the security fence, entreating that it persist in safeguarding the farm's occupants.

Slipping off her mucky shoes, Sofia hurried to the kitchen sink to wash her hands, then unpacked the kitten formula and assorted supplies. She measured out powder from the canister. After mixing it with water, Sofia drew it into the smallest plastic syringe, then attached a silicone neonate nipple. On the way to Nora's bedroom, she grabbed the pet scale she'd brought along with a notebook and pen from the kitchen counter.

The kittens were where Sofia had left them, cuddled up to Toffee's body on the towel in Nora's closet. They seemed chilled. There was a walkie-talkie in the kitchen—she'd call up to the farmhouse and ask them to scrounge up a heating pad. Setting the scale on the carpet, Sofia weighed the kittens to determine how much to feed them. One was just under four ounces, and the other was just over four ounces. She jotted the weights in her notebook. Holding the tiniest kitten tummy down in her palm, Sofia introduced the nipple. The kitten didn't latch, but allowed her to dribble drops of formula into its mouth. She repeated the protracted and time-consuming process with the other cat.

Going to the bathroom to wet a washcloth, Sofia sponge bathed each kitten, mimicking how their mother would groom them and stimulating them to relieve themselves on the old towel from the closet.

There was a stackable washer and dryer behind louvered doors in the hallway. Sofia tossed a bath sheet into the dryer, heating it for five minutes. Eyes burning with fatigue, she fashioned a nest for the kittens before wrapping Toffee and her dead offspring in a bag and placing them outside the back door for Ben. Then she went to shower.

The hot water sluiced over Sofia as she shampooed her hair and scrubbed with shower gel. She was weary—her body pleaded for sleep. After thumbing through her laundry basket for a tunic and leggings, she threw her dirty clothes in the washer. Sinking into Nora's bed, Sofia dozed until the next feeding.

THE SOUND of Ben and Nora arriving home woke Sofia. She'd spent the day alternating between nursing the kittens and napping.

Nora ran into her room, her pigtails swinging. "How are the kitties? Can I help you feed them?"

Sofia budged over to make space on the bed for Nora to sit, heedful of the kittens in the towel in the crook of her arm. "I'll teach you."

Sofia caught sight of Ben in the doorway as she supervised Nora using the syringe to drip formula in the smaller kitten's mouth. He looked tired but as handsome as ever. Sofia's heart constricted as she found his gaze, and he smiled, his eyes warming. She recognized the urge to go to him. To bury her face in his chest so he could fold her into his embrace. To soak him in and let him allay her fears. She squelched the urge, looking away.

She and Ben were lovers, not a couple. Sofia had begun to rely on him too much—she must remember their boundaries. It wasn't his role to comfort her.

"Lark's on KP tonight. She sent along a casserole for our dinner," he said. "And Kate said she'll prepare breakfast tomorrow if you'd like. Just let her know."

Sofia was touched. A tear sprang to her eye at their kindness, and she blinked it away.

Nora piped up, "Kate said she remembers how much work it is taking care of a newborn."

Correcting the way Nora angled the syringe in the kitten's mouth, Sofia cleared her throat, murmuring, "It's not fair to expect others to pick up my slack. I'll bring the cats with me up to the farmhouse tomorrow."

"I thought you'd feel that way. I brought a small storage tote and the heating pad you requested. Since the guest room isn't set up yet, put everything in my room. You'll take my bed tonight. I'll couch surf," Ben said. He winked significantly, letting her know that he had ulterior motives.

Sofia's toes curled at the prospect of a nocturnal visit. She wanted to immerse herself in Ben and forget all else for a little while. Squirming at the agreeable ache tickling her center, she said, "If you insist."

"I insist. A good host assures his guest's *every* need is attended to." He threw her a devilish grin then turned from the doorway, saying over his shoulder, "I'll put the casserole in the oven. I have a few things to do outside before I grab a shower."

Sofia nodded, realizing what he meant—burying Toffee and the others. She'd ensure Nora was distracted. As she showed Nora how to stimulate the just-fed kitten's bladder, Sofia asked, "What do you think we should name them?"

"Depends on whether they're girls or boys," Nora said sagely, and Sofia chuckled.

"We won't know that for a couple weeks at least."

"This one is Sam," Nora indicated the larger cat then the smaller, "and this is Rory. Because those names are good for boys *or* for girls."

"Smart."

Ben came inside and down the hall as they finished feeding Sam. He met Sofia's gaze before he headed into the bathroom, his chin dipping almost imperceptibly to let her know the deed was done.

"We'll get Sam and Rory situated in Ben's room, then you can set the table for dinner," Sofia told Nora, "but you have to make sure you wash up really well. The cats may have parasites that can be passed to us. Once they're old enough, I'll deworm them."

Nora went out to the living room to fetch the plastic storage tote, and Sofia supervised as she plugged in the heating pad and spread it at the bottom of the tote. Sofia covered the pad with a clean towel. Once Sam and Rory were placed in the tote, they rooted until they were snuggled together. Wrapping her arm around Nora's thin shoulders, Sofia squeezed her in a half-hug.

Ben appeared just as Sofia set the casserole on the dining table. His blond hair was spiky from his shower, and he wore a tank top and shorts which exposed the well-defined musculature of his arms and legs. He bent forward, leaning on the back of a chair to watch her, the veins in his forearms appearing. Sofia's eyes tracked from Ben's biceps to his large work-calloused hands, imagining how the roughness would feel as they graced her naked flesh. She swallowed, tearing her gaze away, but not before spying his smug expression. He knew his effect on her.

During the meal, Ben made small talk with Nora while Sofia concentrated on her plate, scarcely eating. Though his words were directed at the child, Ben's scorching gaze branded Sofia. Yes. He most certainly had plans for her. That was clear. Butterfly wings flapped in Sofia's stomach, and she fidgeted.

She excused herself to feed Sam and Rory while Nora and Ben cleared the dinette and loaded the dishwasher. She was sitting cross-legged in the master bedroom nursing Rory when Ben hollered, "Almost done? I'll put a movie in the DVD player."

"No, it'll be a bit yet," Sofia called out. "You two go ahead."

"It's alright. We'll play cards 'til you're finished."

After settling the kittens, Sofia was on her way down the hall to wash her hands in the bathroom when she heard Nora timidly ask Ben, "You really like Sofia, don't you?"

Sofia came to a hasty stop, holding her breath to hear Ben's response. He didn't answer right away. She sensed he was selecting his words with care. "Sure. I like Sofia. Don't you?"

"I didn't used to. But I didn't know her then. She's nice."

There was the sound of Ben reshuffling cards. "She is."

"The kitties would've died without her."

"Yes."

"But are you, like, girlfriend and boyfriend?"

Ben laughed, and Sofia pictured him ruffling Nora's hair. "Sofia doesn't want a boyfriend, and I don't want a girlfriend. We talked about it and decided we're friends. And that's that."

Silence.

"Remember what I said way back when I talked about building Juniper Rise? It's just you and me, kid. Right?"

"Right," Nora replied, her tone uncertain, "but..."

"Don't you like her staying here? I can speak to her about returning to her cabin."

Sofia swallowed hard. She didn't want to hear anymore. Nora's reticence was telling. Was she irritated that Sofia had slept in her bed? Or maybe Sofia was simply wearing out her welcome. Making a point of coughing, she projected her voice to say, "All finished! Let me wash my hands, and I'll join you for the movie."

Ben had cued up a DVD in the player beside the fireplace and dimmed the lamp on the side table. When Sofia entered the living room, she caught Nora's gaze but couldn't read her expression. She gave the girl a smile and, trying to cover her awkwardness, sat next to Ben, one leg tucked under her.

Cartoons flashed across the television screen, engrossing Nora from where she lay sprawled on the floor in front of the sofa at Ben and Sofia's feet.

Ben's fingers reached to trace the curve of Sofia's kneecap, and she shivered. "You look cold, Sofia. Let me grab you a blanket."

Sofia shook her head and shot Ben a meaningful glance.

However, he ignored her, flinging the throw across her legs. Nora didn't glance away from the TV.

Feigning interest in the movie, Ben cozied under the blanket beside Sofia. His hand found her knee and slid up her thigh. Fingers splayed, he lazily fondled her flesh through the fabric of her leggings. Sofia was afraid Nora would notice his actions— how would Ben explain them away if she did? Sofia stilled his hand, but he mimed it was fine.

At last, the credits rolled, and Ben announced it was time for Nora to tuck up. He doused the lights, and they chorused good-nights from their respective beds—Ben on the living room couch, Nora in her room, and Sofia in the master bedroom.

Sofia wondered whether she ought to undress. Shimmying from her leggings and underwear but leaving on her tunic, she lay against the pillow to await Ben. Feathery moonbeams filtered through the curtains. She observed them dancing on the ceiling, her mind wandering over the conversation she'd overheard earlier. She wasn't sure how she felt about it. Exhaustion over-took her, and Sofia's eyelids flickered, but the click of the door locking had them fluttering open.

Ben took off his clothes and sidled into bed next to Sofia, his hand gliding proprietarily along her thigh. He leaned over and put his mouth to hers, commanding huskily against her lips, "Get up and sit on my face."

CHAPTER FORTY-ONE

"I never tire of looking at you."

The moonlight washed Ben's features, sharpening them as he watched Sofia undress, his gaze roving her body and his nostrils flaring.

Once she stood fully unclothed before him, he reached out and reverently skated his thumb along the curvature of her hip bone. It was like a spark flaming a match. Sofia's breath caught as a delicious pulse of white-hot desire blazed through her bloodstream, searing her veins with fire.

She put her hand over his and laced their fingers. He tugged her hand to his mouth, grazing her knuckles. "Climb up. I need to taste you."

Sofia told herself to forget all else, to give in to her carnal needs. She let him draw her under his spell and complied with his demand, crawling across the mattress. Using the edge of the headboard to steady herself, she straddled his shoulders and tentatively crouched above his chin. She was a big girl. What if she suffocated Ben? Suddenly unsure, she hesitated.

Hooking his arms under her knees, Ben cupped Sofia's ass and jerked her down, situating her so she hovered just above his face. He craned his neck, his nose touching her sex. Slowly, Ben inhaled her scent. With a groan, he dug his fingers into her flesh. He ground out, "Fuck. I've been salivating for this pussy all day."

He kissed her slit then moved on to her lips, the point of his tongue explorative. Sofia gasped, bracing against the headboard. Ben sank into the pillow, adjusting her closer at the same time. His tongue darted into her folds, laving them. He licked her juices as if ravenous, his enjoyment unmistakable.

She'd never been with a man like Ben before—a man who didn't hide how much he relished savoring her body. A man who never seemed to be able to get enough of her. His zeal had any lingering hesitancy fleeing.

Abandoning herself to the sensations gathering intensity at her center, Sofia tipped her head back and shut her eyes. She was an addict, and his touch was her fix—she had no choice but to chase her high.

"Mmmm." Face buried in her, Ben suckled each lip in turn before working her with his tongue. He made guttural sounds low in his throat as she gyrated her hips, her breathing ragged.

Sofia homed in on the tension mounting in her belly, her staccato heartbeat drumming in her ears. She rode his mouth, her fingertips clinging to the headboard. When Ben's teeth scraped her swollen, throbbing clit, Sofia came undone.

NESTLED INTO BEN'S SIDE, Sofia's chest wracked as she strove to steady her pulse. He lapped up her wetness left on his mouth and dragged a hand across his face, wiping the remainder away. "That was fun."

Still out of breath, Sofia watched him, murmuring, "You sure know how to make a guest feel welcome, Mr. Cassidy. But I thought I owed *you* for taking me into town this morning."

Ben turned to her, grinning at the flirtatious pitch of her

voice, a brow raised. "That's right. You do. How do you intend to pay your debt, Miss Spenser?"

Biting her lip, she slid the pads of her fingertips along the ridges of his abs to where the golden hairs formed a wiry V-pattern. His thick arousal bobbed in the silvery light, begging for her notice. She swept a digit across the head where pre-cum had beaded, smearing it.

Ben hissed, and she smiled. "I have an idea."

Sofia kneeled over him. Wrapped fingers around him and pumped. More moisture leaked from the tip of his cock, oozing on her hand. She brought her mouth to him and flicked her tongue back and forth over the tip. Ben arched his pelvis in response.

She wanted to pleasure him how he'd pleasured her. To taste him as he'd tasted her. She slurped him into the recesses of her mouth. He was rigid velvet, his flavor salty. Musky. Masculine. She sucked deeper, until his engorged length filled her throat. The soft gagging noises she made seemed to gratify him. He grasped the hair at the base of her neck, tangling his fingers in the strands as he guided her movements, her name an oath on his lips.

Sofia allowed Ben to set a rapid tempo, keeping her jaw tight and lips pursed as she sucked. He panted, perspiration sheening his skin. His heels burrowed into the mattress, his toes tensing. He was getting close. Sofia's eyes watered, yet she didn't slacken her pace. She loved the feel of him in her throat. The way he growled when he was fully sheathed, choking her.

She played with his balls, gently rolling them in her fingers. His flesh constricted. She anticipated the first sticky drop as Ben spasmed. Hungered for it. He jerked, and his warm seed flowed down her esophagus. Sofia swallowed it greedily until she had milked him dry.

After, Ben bundled her close and threw the comforter over them. They didn't speak. There didn't seem words adequate enough to accompany the intimacy stretching between them.

Sofia lay her ear against his chest, the reassuring tattoo of Ben's heartbeat lulling her. He kissed the crown of her head before drifting off to slumber. She listened to Ben's even breathing and the night sounds. Rain pattered on the roof, and wind whistled through tree boughs, rattling the windowpanes. Ben was like a furnace. Cozy. She felt sheltered by his large form. She dozed until mewling from the storage container on the floor caught her attention. Extracting herself from under Ben's arm, Sofia snuck from the bed.

He stirred briefly, and she studied him, her gaze floating across his aquiline profile and full, generous mouth. She was struck yet again by how gorgeous Ben was—he was a fine specimen of a man. The blanket slipped down his sculpted pecs as he flung a muscular arm on the pillow above his head. God, she was smitten with him. She squelched the urge to press her lips to his forehead. To caress his bristled cheek.

Why did it feel like allowing such tenderness would be her undoing?

After dressing, she took the kittens to the living room, closing the door to Ben's bedroom. The chore of syringe feeding them distracted her, but Sofia was uneasy. It was a punch to her rib cage when she recalled Ben assuring Nora that he and Sofia would never be anything other than friends. He'd sounded unwavering in his resolve.

And if Sofia hadn't announced her presence, how would Nora have responded to Ben's query about whether she wanted Sofia to leave? The girl may no longer actively dislike her—to some degree they'd bonded over the last days—but that didn't translate to Nora fancying Sofia shacking up with them. It wasn't as if Sofia aspired to be someone's mommy at twenty-one, either. Playing house had never appealed to her before.

Why, then, did it feel like something had been set in motion? That the three were forging a family? That Sofia belonged with them at Juniper Rise?

Tears pooled in Sofia's eyes, and she rubbed her temple. No.

She was overtired. That was why she was having trouble regulating her emotions. This wasn't her—ordinarily Sofia was a levelheaded person. It was only her anxiety about the Zs twisting her guts and making her second-guess her instincts.

She was being a silly, romantic fool. Of course she cared for endearingly odd Nora. And, of course she cared for Ben. What woman wouldn't have a soft spot for an orphaned waif? What woman wouldn't be weak in the knees for a sweet guy who knew how to satisfy in the sack?

This was *not* her home. Ben was *not* her husband, and Nora was *not* her daughter.

Sofia wasn't a part of this place and never would be.

She knew the score. She and Ben didn't broach the subject of a future. And why would they speak of it? There was none for them—they both knew that. Impartiality was what kept their arrangement afloat, after all.

Then why did she feel excluded? Why the fuck did she *care*?

A tinge of bitterness rose in her throat. She was merely a warm body. A receptacle for Ben's dick. A convenient hole. She instantly regretted her thoughts. That was unfair. Harsh. Ben had never made her feel dirty. She'd pursued him. He treated her with the utmost respect, and that respect was mutual. Sofia reminded herself that she'd sworn to Ben that she wouldn't fall in love with him. That she was cool. They were friends with benefits. That was all. Although they enjoyed each other both in and out of bed, Sofia had a sense that if Ben knew she was forming an attachment, he'd balk. Break things off. Her heart squeezed at the pain such realization brought.

She'd never been in love before—she didn't even know what that felt like. Were the gooey panicky feelings in her gut the vestiges of love? Had she been lying to herself?

For chrissake, Sofia, get your shit together.

Struggling to rein in her emotions, Sofia finished feeding Sam and washed her hands in the kitchen sink. Gnawing on her cheek, she sat on a stool at the breakfast bar.

It was a matter of time before Nora told Ben she wanted Sofia gone. Her scalp tingled at the thought of Ben asking her to leave Juniper Rise. Nope. No more stayovers. They blurred lines anyway. What she required—they all required—was distance.

Sofia would walk back to her own cabin, toting the storage crate with the kittens along. She'd tend to them there.

After packing her bag with supplies, Sofia slipped on her tennis shoes. She let herself out of the house, the crate on her hip and a flashlight in hand. She resolved to keep her wits when it came to Ben. Enjoy the sex and remain aloof.

Her tennies squished in the damp pebbles as she trod along the juniper-lined path. Just as she was about to turn to go up the trail to the farmhouse, Sofia detected lamplight glowing in the window of a double-wide trailer in the distance near the cold spring under the willow tree.

CHAPTER FORTY-TWO

Sofia blinked, her pulse ratcheting. A thunderclap boomed in the distance, and she flinched.

What on earth? Did the farm have a squatter? And, if so, how had they breached the security fence? They would've had to cut through the barbed wire enclosure on the far side of the pasture and tramp in from there—they never would've gotten through the main fence. Surely a squatter wouldn't be foolish enough to use a lantern at night, would they? Sofia flicked her flashlight off. She didn't want to be seen.

She'd have to investigate. She wouldn't wake Ben. There may come a day when Sofia didn't have the luxury of backup, so she may as well toughen up now. Conquer her fears and assert her independence. She'd scope the situation out and return for him *only* if necessary. Hurrying into the house, Sofia left her backpack and the storage container with the kittens on the foyer floor.

Ben kept a metal baseball bat in the hall closet. Before ducking back outside, Sofia grabbed it. She wedged her flashlight awkwardly under a bra strap, both hands gripping the bat. It was still wet outside, but it had stopped raining. The shadows of the row of tall conifers between Ben's homestead and the trailers concealed her, the damp needles strewn on the ground masking her footfalls. Along the fence line near the spring was another matter. Sofia squelched through the mud to the double-wide trailer with the lit window.

The rectangular structure had dark siding and a shingled roof. A small open porch was integrated into one end where the main entrance was located. It faced the rocky outcrop beside the weeping willow and the bubbling spring. An old-fashioned grass whip cutter leaned against the porch railing. The over-grown weeds leading to the front steps had been trimmed back. Sofia squinted into the darkness. Yes, a walkway leading up the hill was in the process of being cleaved. Somebody from the farm was obviously setting up residence. Perhaps Bella and Josh had wearied of living with Fritz and sought their own little love nest.

An eye on the window where the lamp was lit—the middle of the trailer where she presumed the living room was—Sofia tiptoed backward toward the fence, intending to leave. She didn't want to disturb the lovers.

She'd made little progress when the front door flew open. The beam of a flashlight sliced a swathe of yellow into the night, and Sofia stilled.

"I have a gun. Show yourself."

Lark. Sofia put a palm to her chest, where her heart thumped. She exhaled slowly. "It's me. Sofia."

Lark descended the stairs, slipping her revolver into her waistband. She held out the flashlight to light Sofia's course as she joined her. "What the hell are you doing skulking around out here at this time of night?"

"I thought we had a squatter. I wanted to poke around."

"Aren't you the brave one?" Lark asked drily. "You may as well come inside. I have a thermos of Irish coffee."

Feeling sheepish, Sofia scraped her shoes against the wooden porch slats to remove any lingering mud. She took them off before following Lark into the trailer, looking around with curiosity once she stepped over the threshold. A fully fitted open concept kitchen with laminate cabinetry was immediately beyond the small foyer, adjacent to a living area where a camp lantern sat on a crate next to a thermos. Lark's journal and a pen were on the seat of a folding chair beside the crate. A sleeping bag was on the floor, along with her rucksack. "Are you *living* here?"

Lark set the gun and the flashlight on the crate, then removed her journal from the folding chair, indicating Sofia should sit. Sofia put her flashlight on the carpet at the base of the chair and propped her bat against the wall. She perched on the edge of the chair, waiting while Lark poured her some coffee spiked with whiskey, using the thermos lid as a cup.

"I meant to mention that I've been thinking about it, but there never seemed to be a right time." She arranged herself cross-legged on her sleeping bag, avoiding Sofia's gaze. "You and Ben have been so hot and heavy lately that we haven't had a minute alone."

"Oh." Guilt cascaded over Sofia. She had been preoccupied and distant, neglecting her friendship with Lark. "Why aren't you staying at the cabin anymore?"

"Bella and Josh moved in next door." Lark rolled her eyes. "Sick of listening to them fuck all night."

"Oh," Sofia said again. "I thought they were staying here."

"I wish. Bella's a screamer." She changed the pitch of her voice, mimicking Bella as she moaned, "Harder, Josh. Harder, Josh. Ooooh, Jossssssh!"

Sofia giggled.

"I can't even look those two in the face anymore without cringing. Rude fuckers."

"That is tacky."

"I'm better off on my own down here anyways, even without running water and electricity."

Sofia considered her. Lark's jaw jutted out stubbornly, the tightness around her mouth telling. "Everything alright with you, Lark?"

Lark lifted a shoulder. "Life gets to me." She nodded to the journal. "Writing's always been my escape."

"I've been a shitty friend lately, haven't I?" Sofia swallowed a drink of tepid coffee, setting the cup on the crate. "Sorry."

"Nothing to be sorry for. When I get inside my head, there's nothing anyone can say or do." Lark smiled, her eyes traveling over Sofia. "You have a face like a smacked ass."

"What?"

"You're pouting. What's the problem? Trouble in paradise?"

Sofia shrugged. "Why would there be trouble? It's just sex."

"Uh huh. Sure it is, Sofia."

Sofia scoffed, "It is! You keep making comments. I wish you'd knock it off."

"Don't BS me. I've seen the way you moon at Ben."

She glared at Lark but was unable to bring herself to refute her words.

"I was afraid of this."

Anger flared in Sofia's gut. "I don't want to hear *I told you so.*"

Lark softened, throwing her a sympathetic look.

"I've had a lot of fuckbuddies, and I never got attached before. Why would I now?"

"It's happened to the best of us." Lark laughed in a self-deprecating fashion. "Good dick sometimes worms its way up to a girl's heart and clamps hold."

"I promised him I wouldn't fall in love with him, and I... I haven't."

"First time for everything," Lark said tartly. "You've gotten yourself entangled in a situationship. What does Ben say?"

Sofia didn't answer.

"Ah. If you haven't talked to him then how do you know Ben doesn't feel the same as you?"

"I don't *feel* anything."

Lark snorted, her expression a mixture of skepticism and mocking.

Sofia angled her head back to study the popcorn ceiling and sighed. "I know because I overheard him and Nora talking. He even went so far to say that he'd ask me to leave if she wanted him to." Bitterness was a sharp ache in Sofia's throat. She coughed it away. "Well, I'm not going to give him the opportunity."

"He's probably just reassuring her. Besides, she's a kid. She doesn't call the shots."

"He takes his commitment to her seriously."

"He'll come around. And she'll adjust."

"I'm not sure about *any* of that."

"You and Ben really gotta have a conversation. Clear these things up."

Sofia swung her head and regarded Lark, horrified at the prospect. "Hell, no. It'll make everything... weird!"

"Grow up, Sofia."

Sofia narrowed her eyes. "Excuse me? I *am* grown!"

"Then act like it!"

"Suddenly you're Dear Abby dishing out advice on relationships. What about you and Kyle and Tucker? *That* was screwed up." As soon as Sofia uttered the words, she wished she could call them back. Deflated, she whispered, "I shouldn't have said that."

Instead of being incensed, Lark appeared morose. "You're right. I'm no expert on relationships. But that's another discussion for another day." She ran a hand through her blonde hair. "What're you gonna do about Ben?"

"What I should've done from the beginning. Cool my heels. Back off. Stop hanging out at Juniper Rise." Sofia sat up straighter in her chair, her voice determined when she declared, "I am *not* stepmother material."

CHAPTER FORTY-THREE

Sofia's visit to Lark's new home ended shortly after her declaration. She returned to fetch the kittens and her backpack, encountering Ben in the process of getting a drink of water from the kitchen.

"Where were you?"

"I noticed a light in the trailer down the hill. I didn't realize it was Lark."

"You shouldn't have gone there alone. Why not wake me?"

"Why should I? An independent woman can take care of herself," Sofia said evenly. "In fact, I was about to head to my cabin."

"It's late. Stay here." He placed his empty glass on the counter and approached Sofia, bending to kiss her. "Come back to bed."

She was sorely tempted to allow him to lead her into his bedroom but pulled away. "I've got to be up at five to cook breakfast. I've been shirking my responsibilities around the farm too much lately."

Ben's gaze raked over her. Was she coming off *too* aloof? Sofia smiled nonchalantly, keeping the mood light as she said goodnight.

She made her way to the cabin she'd once shared with Lark, absentminded. It was unnatural to be detached in Ben's presence. He'd sensed something in her tone or in her manner. Reining herself in was like walking a tightrope. It would take determination to not show what was in her heart.

She was irritated with Lark's attitude, interpreting it as blasé. Of course Sofia's conundrum was no big deal—to her. Conundrums were never a big deal to those who weren't embroiled in them! She hadn't been there when Sofia had brazenly pursued Ben, hadn't heard her arrogant pronouncements.

Her face burned with a fresh ripple of indignity as she revisited the idea of confessing her feelings to Ben, imagining his inevitable reaction. She shook her head. How humiliating! God, she was an idiot for getting herself in this predicament.

The only thing that settled her was reaffirming her plan—remain detached, keep the mood light, and enjoy the sex.

Sofia set the bedside alarm, blearily nursing Sam and Rory before going to bed. She slept fitfully. After their four o'clock feeding, she decided to shower and walk to the farmhouse. When she arrived, Kate was at the kitchen trestle table in her nightie, a mug of tea in hand as she read from a three-ring binder.

"Not even five yet," she commented, briefly bestowing Sofia a once-over before returning to the binder.

Sofia situated the storage container on the far side of the room, shedding her backpack. "I got up to give the cats their formula and figured why go back to bed for a half hour."

"Teakettle's hot on the stove. Pour yourself a cup," Kate instructed. "I want to chat."

"Ominous," Sofia murmured as she fished a homemade tea bag from the canister on the counter and dropped it in an earthenware mug.

Kate chuckled. "Nothing to fret about. It's just I've not seen much of you lately. I'm glad you came early enough so we can catch up."

Sofia doused the tea bag with water from the kettle then sat on the bench across from Kate. "I wanted a word with you, too."

"You seem bothered. What's going on?"

She said without preamble, "What if the Zs track us back to the farm from the warehouse?"

"On foot?" Kate sounded dubious.

"We don't know how sophisticated they're becoming. What if they can communicate among themselves?"

Kate drank from her cup, peering at Sofia over the rim. Sofia kept her face blank, but Kate had a way of making her feel as if she were staring straight into her soul. Her jade green eyes were difficult to evade. "We'll be on our guard during the scavenge and on the trip home. The guys are still patrolling the perimeter of the fence daily. That'll carry on. What more can we do but be prudent?"

"There's been no sign of anything peculiar since Ben and I discovered the broken camera?"

"No. I assume a bird flew off after colliding with it, but, again, the patrols will *not* stop."

Sofia nodded, her confidence bolstered by Kate's composure. The woman had mastered poise—she seemed unflappable. "Sometimes the best explanation is the simplest explanation, I suppose."

"Yes." Kate yawned lustily. "Tonight after the kids are in bed, we're having a meeting to bring everyone up to speed about the warehouse. We'll ask for volunteers. Naturally, you'll have to go. Is that what's disturbing you?"

"No. I expected that." Sofia shrugged, suppressing a shudder. "Just those fucking Zs yesterday."

"I get it. They've always been terrifying, but we learned how to handle them. We're finding ourselves back at square one with them." Kate patted Sofia's hand. "We'll cope, Sofia."

Sofia exhaled, trying to shake off the impending sense of doom constricting her diaphragm. Changing the subject, she pointed to the binder. "What's that?"

"An instruction manual my sister Connie put together for me. Step-by-step guides for canning veggies and preserving meats. Recipes for soaps." She tipped the binder so Sofia could see the neat columns of cursive on the page. "This section is about constructing a still—she researched and then wrote notes for future reference. She and my brother-in-law intended to build one but hadn't gotten around to it. Fritz and his cousin made moonshine, so he'll be in charge of the still, but I'm trying to learn all I can."

"Why do we need a still?" Sofia blew on her tea before sipping. It was mint dried from the herb garden. Kate had used coffee filters and thread to create tea bags.

"Grain alcohol will serve as fuel. That'll be its primary use anyway."

When Kate yawned again, Sofia asked, "Stills are more important than sleep?"

"Insomnia."

They drank their tea in companionable silence until the kittens were due for a feed. Kate watched as Sofia syringe fed them, occasionally asking questions. The ceiling fixture shed bright light on her features, accenting the dark circles beneath her eyes. It seemed to Sofia that Kate carried the weight of the entire farm on her shoulders. How heavy a burden that must be. She told Kate as much.

"It is. Responsibility for the well-being of others always is." Kate shut the binder and crossed her arms as Sofia put the kittens back in the crate and went to wash her hands. "If you would've told me two summers ago that I'd be married, a mother of a toddler, and running a farm, I would've laughed 'til I pissed my pants."

"I remember you saying you owned a bakery."

"I poured myself into growing my business—I was a worka-holic. Marriage and kids weren't on my radar. In fact, I did my best to avoid letting *anyone* close. I'll bet you were a social butter-fly. You're easy to open up to."

Sofia went to grab her mug to put in the dishwasher. She ought to start breakfast preparations. "Am I?"

"Approachable."

"I have heard that before," Sofia admitted. Ben had told her the same once during a conversation at her house in Mergenville.

"How are you and Ben?"

Sofia started. Kate was astute—it was as if she had read Sofia's mind. She hadn't confided many details to Kate. Deciding discretion was the best tactic, Sofia shrugged, noncommittal. "Fine."

"Have you asked him yet about what happened on his trip up here?"

Sofia took a bowl from the cabinet, along with the dry ingredients she needed to make a quick dough for cake doughnuts. "We don't discuss much about our pasts. I don't want to pry."

Sofia could hear Kate's smile when she teased, "Busy with more pressing activities?"

Sofia didn't reply. Why couldn't people mind their own goddamn business? She kept her mouth zipped as she added milk into her dough batter and stirred with more vigor than warranted.

"I wasted a lot of time after meeting Teller. Don't waste yours with Ben."

Sofia raised her eyebrows in surprise. She turned to look at Kate. "What do you mean?"

"I don't want you to make the same mistakes I did. Remember, tomorrow isn't guaranteed."

"More unsolicited advice," Sofia said under her breath as she turned back to knead her dough on a floured cutting board.

Kate continued, "At first he seemed like a mystery to me, but Teller doesn't put on airs. My sister once told me he was the real deal, and he is. I'm more cagey. I didn't wanna allow myself to let go."

After rolling out her dough, Sofia used metal cutters to cut the dough into doughnut-shaped rounds. She rummaged around in the cabinet next to the stove for a shallow pan and set it on the burner, adding a healthy dollop of lard from the fridge. Turning the flame on medium to melt the lard, she faced Kate. "Why are you telling me all this, Kate?"

"Just helping love find its way."

"First Lark has to put her two cents in," Sofia groused. The smell of hot oil permeated the air. She carefully dropped a half dozen rounds into the oil. "Now you."

Gagging, Kate jumped from her chair and ran toward the hallway bathroom, her palm over her mouth. "Ugh."

"Kate?"

Sofia turned the burner down and followed after her. The woman kneeled on the floor and heaved into the toilet bowl. Sofia crouched down, gathering Kate's chestnut hair away from her face. When Kate was finished vomiting, Sofia pulled the towel down from the wall hook beside the sink and offered it to her. Concerned by Kate's pallor, Sofia asked, "You alright?"

After wiping her face, Kate sat against the wall opposite the toilet and brought her knees to her chest. She met Sofia's gaze and grimaced. "It was the lard. I can't tolerate certain smells anymore."

"Want me to wake Teller?"

Shaking her head, a small smile played on her lips. "It's only morning sickness. I'm pregnant."

CHAPTER FORTY-FOUR

THE KIDS FILED IN, EDNA TRAILING BEHIND STILL IN HER FLOWERED nightgown. She got them settled before heading to shower. They were a boisterous bunch, rowdy as only children can be first thing in the morning. Sofia and Kate shushed them, serving the cheese omelets and doughnuts Sofia had fixed.

As Sofia went to make more omelets on the countertop plug-in skillet, Nora bounded into the kitchen, her blue eyes shining and an overnight bag on her arm. Ben was a few steps behind, freshly shaved and as attractive as ever. Nora asked, "How're Sam and Rory?"

The crate in the corner had gone unnoticed to that point, but once the kids realized the kittens were there, they jumped from their seats and gathered around it, ohhing and ahhing and asking to pet Sam and Rory. Sofia picked up the kittens so the kids could look at them. She promised that once Sam and Rory were older, she'd allow them to take turns with bottle feeding.

Having plated Nora's breakfast, Ben urged her and her friends to sit and eat. Sofia went to close the kittens in the laundry room, and when she came back, Nora was beside Ravi, tucking a napkin in the collar of his shirt and tearing his doughnut into bite-size pieces before focusing on her own food. Ben grinned at her with paternal benevolence then snared Sofia's gaze as he reached for the coffee carafe. "How are you this morning, brown-eyed girl?"

Sofia's pulse hitched at the familiarity in his sapphire eyes, knowing he was remembering their last encounter just as she was. Reminding herself to be cool about it, she smiled coyly, using a spatula to flip the ends of the omelet. She murmured she was alright.

That was a lie. In truth, she was still reeling from Kate's news.

Assuming the pregnancy was unintended, Sofia had been shocked when Kate insisted it was *planned*. After witnessing firsthand with Toffee how dangerous giving birth was, Sofia couldn't fathom why Teller and Kate would accept the risk. When Kate reassured her that Rob was closely watching her, Sofia let the matter drop but privately speculated what everyone's reaction would be once Kate's condition was common knowledge.

Ben drank his coffee, resting against the counter near Sofia.

Kate said from her spot at the table, "Ben, can you arrange the hay bales around the fire ring in the side yard sometime today for tonight's bonfire?"

"Sure thing."

His aftershave wafted to Sofia's nose, and her body responded at once. He was sexy as sin in a sleeveless t-shirt that displayed his muscled arms and faded jeans which molded to his thighs. Should she organize a quickie before lunch? Sofia stifled a groan, hating her lack of willpower. *Chill out.*

Ben added, "Not much on the agenda today. Teller wants to drive cattle—"

"Did I hear my name?" Teller came into the kitchen, Maggie on his hip and Ace tap-tapping behind. Passing the baby to Kate, Teller bent to kiss his wife chastely on her forehead before cupping her cheek. Sofia envied their easy show of affection. She glanced over to Ben. He observed the couple, his expression indecipherable.

"I was saying that you want to relocate the cattle to another pasture today," Ben supplied casually, extending an arm in front of Sofia to filch a doughnut from the pile on a platter. He purposely brushed her breast, and she gulped.

"I'm planning on dinner alfresco. Sausages and potato salad," Kate said. "What are you making for lunch, Sofia?"

Sofia pulled herself together. "Baked ziti."

Thursdays were usually light days on the farm. Other than tending to the animals, they worked in the garden or on projects around the house.

"Children," Edna said from the doorway, now showered and wearing her customary flowered blouse and polyester slacks, "are you ready for today's lessons?"

The kids carried their plates and cups to the sink, Nora supervising. Knowing Edna was not much of a breakfast eater, Sofia prepared a mug of black coffee for her and took it to where she dawdled at the entryway to the kitchen. Edna smiled her thanks before whisking her charges downstairs to the basement where there was a makeshift classroom.

Sofia loaded the dishes in the dishwasher, listening to Teller's chatter as he stacked a tower of doughnuts on his plate and fighting the urge to set up a tryst with Ben. Soon Fritz arrived, then the others began trooping into the house—Rob, Bella, and Josh and finally, Lark. Milo was conspicuously missing.

Chewing her doughnut, Sofia felt Lark's assessing gaze on her from across the table. Annoyed, Sofia kept her face blank. She wasn't going to let Lark see anything that she didn't want her to, dammit.

Typically, Sofia loved being around people. Today, however, she tapped her foot with impatience for everyone to finish their food so she could clean the kitchen, throw together the casseroles for later, and flee. When Kate asked her to lend a hand harvesting tomatoes from the garden until lunch, Sofia agreed with reluctance.

DIRECTLY AFTER THE NOON MEAL, Sofia returned eagerly to the solitude of her cabin. She was free until dinnertime.

The kittens fed and toileted, she tidied the bathroom and washed the dishes Lark had left in the sink. It was strange to have the place to herself, but she'd make it her own. She pushed the bed to the opposite wall and dragged the dresser so it was beside the door. She rearranged the chair and ottoman so they were in the corner next to the window, leaving one of the night tables and a lamp there. Hands on her hips, she nodded with approval. Much improved flow. And now she had a comfy reading nook.

She'd placed her suitcase on the mattress when she'd moved the bed. Lower lip between her teeth, she unzipped it. The silver framed family photo was there. It was a formal studio portrait, taken the winter before Sofia went off to college. She didn't look at it often. Seeing them all together was painful. It triggered homesickness that gnawed at the pit of her stomach. A runaway tear tracked down Sofia's cheek, splashing on the glass. Swallowing past the lump in her windpipe, she used the hem of her shirt to polish the teardrop away.

Pleasingly plump, Mama posed on a wingback chair, her ankles sedately crossed and hands in her lap. She was dressed in an amber-colored silk gown that emphasized the coppery flecks in her brown irises—the same eyes Sofia saw when she looked into a mirror. Glittering citrine jewelry adorned her throat and ears. With her ebony hair coiled on her proud head, Mama was as regal as a queen.

Positioned to one side of Mama's chair, Daddy wore an

impeccably tailored dark suit, the finest money could buy. His posture was ramrod straight. Dignified. He beamed, the corners of his eyes crinkled. His weathered face conveyed kindness.

Sofia flanked her father. Her dress had been silk, too. Peach georgette silk. Scoop-necked with a fitted bodice and cap sleeves. She'd adored it. Her sable hair had been longer then, and her face was fresh-scrubbed. She looked so young.

That life seemed an eon ago, not merely three years.

Sofia sat the photo on the dresser. The gold charm bracelet they'd gifted her for her twentieth birthday was stowed in her underwear drawer. She didn't like to wear it for fear that it could become damaged or lost, but life was short. She'd put on the bracelet and treasure the pleasant memories it invoked. The clasp was tricky, but Sofia managed to fasten it on her wrist. She admired it before curling up on the bed for a catnap.

Later, after a bath, Sofia twisted her hair into a clip and pulled on a denim dress before hefting the crate and leaving the cabin. Kate expected her at the farmhouse.

They'd spread old blankets on the hay bales Ben had set in a semicircle around the firepit, balancing their supper plates on their knees. Labor Day neared, and with it, the hint of autumn. The afternoon was sunny with a slight cool breeze. Sofia counted the weeks since Adam had left, startled to realize that he'd been gone a month. When the six weeks concluded, would he be at the rally point?

A trilling laugh tugged Sofia back. Bella. She and Josh sat next to her. Draped across Josh's lap, Bella fed him morsels of sausage and whispered in his ear. Clad in a skimpy blouse and a miniskirt that bared more skin than it concealed, she was apparently putting on a display for Milo, who glowered from his seat across from them.

After the meal, Sofia and Lark went inside to start the dishwasher while the others formed into softball teams or lounged beside the unlit firepit. Their laughter drifted into the stillness of the kitchen. Sofia was still salty about Lark's advice but didn't want her to notice or remark about it. While tidying the kitchen, Sofia tried to look unbothered. When Lark inquired about her bracelet, she was relieved. She'd decided that she wouldn't discuss her and Ben with anyone anymore.

Returning outside, Sofia watched Ben pitch the softball to Nora then cheer her on when she hit it. His patience and positivity while coaching the kids gladdened Sofia's heart.

Once the sun slipped beyond the horizon, Edna and Bella corralled the kids. It was time for baths and pajamas. Nora would sleep over. The mood festive, Fritz lit the fire. He had brought a guitar from his cabin. Legs stretched to accommodate his rotund belly, he strummed it.

"You know *Cowboy's Lament*?" Teller asked, and he began to sing as Fritz plucked the strings. Sofia hadn't heard the song before. Teller sang the mournful tune with fitting solemnity. The second stanza, Lark joined in. Her melodic soprano was far superior to Teller's pitchy baritone.

Lark's singing was a treat. Those who hadn't gotten to experience it before listened with their mouths agape. When the song drew to an end, Teller commented, "I'd wondered about your songbird tattoo. Dang, you possess real talent, Lark."

Her fair cheeks were tinged livid crimson, but Lark accepted the compliment gracefully.

Bella and Edna had returned mid-performance. From her perch on Josh's lap, Bella complained, "I missed most of it. Can you sing something else?"

"Maybe something by Van Morrison?" Ben asked hopefully.

"I only have one by him memorized—*These Are the Days*."

Since Fritz didn't know which chords to play for that song, he set the guitar aside and went to fetch everyone tumblers of homemade wine. Sofia peeked at Ben while Lark sang a rendition of *These Are the Days* a cappella. The blaze of firelight revealed a half-smile on his lips. Was he remembering his dad?

When Lark finished singing, they applauded. Fritz brought

the tray of wine, which he distributed to Lark and Teller first. "Entertainment's gotta be thirsty."

"Welp," Teller said with regret after he took a healthy slug of his drink. "Best get down to brass tacks, I reckon. Anyone keen on a supply run? We leave tomorrow."

CHAPTER FORTY-FIVE

"ALLOW ME, TELLER." KATE WAITED UNTIL SHE HAD EVERYONE'S attention then explained about Sofia's father's warehouse in Mergenville.

There was a flurry of feedback around the campfire running the gamut from enthusiastic to hesitant.

"Are you sure we ought to venture outside Mayfly Hollow?" Edna asked, her gray brow furrowed. "We don't truly *need* for anything, do we? The beauty of this farm is that it's wonderfully self-sustaining."

"If it proves too dicey, we halt and hotfoot home," Teller assured her, "but from what Sofia says there's plenty we can utilize there. It's ripe for the pickin'."

Kate said, "Teller and Sofia will be primarily in charge of this run. Sofia, you know the layout of the building and where to park the flatbed. Can you sketch out a map for everyone to review? And come up with a list of items of value in order of priority?"

Sofia inwardly winced, nodding. She wasn't accustomed to being in charge of anything. Would she be able to lead? "I-It's only about a fifteen-minute drive to Spenser Suppliers. I have keys to the lobby, so I'll enter that way and then open one of the bays by shipping and receiving from inside. We can reverse the truck into the loading dock and pack it there."

"I'd say that's a mighty efficient method," Teller said in approval, which boosted Sofia's confidence.

She continued, "Thing is, the goods are in stacked wooden crates. I used a crowbar to get into the ones on floor level, but it wasn't the best tool for the job."

"Should we bring a ladder?" Fritz asked.

"No, there's one there."

"Someone'll have to climb it and break into the crates. I'll bring a hatchet or an ax," Teller said. "We'll devise a way to get the goods down once we get there."

Sofia added, "Shame we can't use the forklifts. It'll be hard work loading the freight piecemeal, but I would think with strong people, it shouldn't take more than an hour or two."

"I'm strong as an ox." Fritz smiled at Sofia. "What about you, Josh? You game to go?"

Before Josh could answer, Lark said, "I am."

"Gotta offset the numbers for coverage," Teller advised. "Kate'll stay back with Edna, Rob, and the kiddies, but best we leave some menfolk behind just in case. Benji, you willin' to stay behind?"

"Sofia doesn't venture anywhere without me," he intoned flatly from his hay bale. His arms were intersected at his chest, and his expression brooked no argument.

Oh really? Sofia raised an eyebrow. Ben wasn't prone to possessiveness when they were around the others. She shot a questioning glance in his direction, but he looked at Teller.

"Alrighty then." Teller clucked. "I know it ain't a thrillin' prospect to remain here, but someone's gotta."

Bella said, "Josh can stay with me. No way am I volunteering!"

Milo, who hadn't spoken until then, laughed in a nasty sort of way. "Big shocker there."

Bella glared. "What are you implying?"

"I'm not *implying* anything. You're lazy as fuck all. And your boyfriend," he looked pointedly at Josh, lip curled, "is a pussy."

Josh was up on his feet within seconds. He marched to Milo and knocked off his glasses. Burying his fists in Milo's shirt, he towed him up off the hay bale until they were nose-to-nose. "You wanna say that again, you scrawny four-eyed cuck? I'll lay you out just like I did last time you talked shit."

"That'll do now, you two," Teller interjected, but neither Josh nor Milo paid him any heed. Ace, who'd been napping on the grass at Teller's heels, lumbered up and stood at attention.

Milo swung wide, his knuckles connecting to Josh's chin. Sofia gasped as the two began a brawl in earnest. Ace growled, weaving around their ankles and nipping at the cuffs of their pants.

Both Ben and Teller got up to intervene, but it was Kate who reached the duo first. Placing herself between them, she put a palm out to hold Josh off. Josh complied, pausing. Taking the opportunity presented, Milo veered around Kate and slammed into Josh, shifting him off his feet. Josh snatched at Milo, and they fell precariously close to the bonfire. They jarred the metal campfire ring, and the mounded pyramid of firewood toppled, sending embers in all directions.

After wrestling on the ground, Milo disengaged, stumbling up. Sofia thought that would be the end of the mêlée, but Josh rebounded, leaping into a balanced stance. Milo charged him, and he boxed at Milo's ears. Ace lunged at Josh, barking.

"Cut it out, Milo," Kate ordered, yanking at his shirt.

"Ace, heel! Kate, let me dammit—" Teller insisted, putting an arm out to drag her away from the fracas.

It happened as if in slow motion. As Kate waved Teller aside and again inserted herself between Milo and Josh, a flying fist connected to her cheek.

She swayed before crumpling to the grass, and Ace went to her, nosing her hair and whining.

Edna cried, "Oh my stars!"

"Damn hell!" Without hesitation, Teller rounded on Milo, sucker-punching him into submission. His nostrils flaring, Teller challenged Josh, lifting his clenched fist. "Wanna take another poke, or are you done, hoss?"

Ben had gotten up and was at Teller's elbow, his demeanor making it evident that he was inclined to do whatever required, whether it be aid Teller or restrain him.

Josh glared at Milo, then, seeming recalcitrant, eyed Kate and Teller and Ben in turn. He raised his hands in surrender. His lip trickled blood. He massaged his knuckles as Bella ran to him, tsking and blotting his bloodied lip with a ratty tissue.

Milo slinked to a bale of hay like a whipped mutt and slumped down. He looked the worst of the lot—he had both a black eye *and* a swollen jaw.

Sofia sprung to tend Kate, along with Rob. She was conscious but barely. Sofia caressed Ace's ears and reassured him he was a good boy then drew him away by his collar to make more space for Rob to inspect Kate's injury. A bruise was forming on her right cheekbone. She stirred, blinking rapidly and groaning.

Once he had Milo and Josh sorted, Teller kneeled to Kate and gathered her against his chest. He praised Ace and murmured to Kate, asking if she was okay. His gaze daggered Milo, then Josh. "So help me God if anything happens to our unborn child… all y'all will be exiled from this farm, that is if I don't skin you alive first!"

The rest of the group gawked, riveted by the drama unfolding before them.

Ben looked from Kate to Teller, his face draining all color. "*Unborn child?*"

Kate, reviving, touched her fingertips gingerly to her cheekbone and stretched her jaw.

Teller boldly bore Ben's scrutiny. "Kate's expectin'."

"Are you two insane?" Ben snarled, confronting Teller with, "How could you let that happen?"

Ace's hackles rose, and he bayed. Teller hushed him, saying

to Ben, "This is between me and my wife. It don't concern you none."

"Don't you remember what happened with Connie, Kate?" Ben demanded, his voice tortured. "How could you be that careless? That reckless?"

"Connie would've been fine if Seth hadn't stabbed her," Kate protested weakly, allowing Teller to assist her up. He kept one hand wrapped around Ace's collar and his free arm around Kate's waist. She straightened her spine, the set of her jaw pugnacious. "I've thought long and hard about this, Ben! I will not stop living based on what *may* happen!"

Sofia wrung her hands, stupefied. The interchange was surreal.

"You mean the pregnancy is *on purpose*? Jesus Christ, Kate!" Ben grasped Kate by the forearm, his expression savage. Sofia wondered whether he would try to shake sense into her. Instead, he entreated, "What about the virus lying dormant in your bloodstream? Didn't you learn anything after what went down with Judy?"

Kate paled, but she lifted her chin. "It's a chance we are willing to take."

"So you're *willing* to gamble with your life? *Willing* to gamble with leaving Maggie motherless? And what about me? Have you thought at all about how *I'd* feel if you die?"

Teller slid in front of Kate, shielding her, his manner cold. "Like I say. This don't concern you none. Now, you gonna let this go, or am I gonna hafta get ugly?"

Ben shook his head in disgust and stalked away without another word.

CHAPTER FORTY-SIX

SOFIA'S ALARM WOKE HER AT FOUR. EDNA HAD AGREED TO BABYSIT the kittens at the farmhouse so she could get a full night's sleep. Though she'd slept like the dead, once Sofia woke and sat up in bed rubbing her eyes, her heart sank. It all flooded back.

The bonfire. Josh and Milo's fistfight. The melodramatic unveiling of Kate's pregnancy and Ben's angst-ridden response. How he'd strode away without even a backward glance at Sofia, ostensibly to cloister at Juniper Rise and lick his wounds in seclusion. And Lark's pitying glimpses as Fritz doused the flames and they all bid each other a subdued goodnight.

It was as Sofia feared. Ben still loved Kate. Even Lark saw it. It was as plain as the nose on her face.

Sofia hung around until everyone had dispersed. Then, alone in the kitchen, she scratched out a map of the warehouse and the list of items Kate had requested. She left the notepad on the counter and trekked to her own cabin, melancholy and disconcerted and heartsick.

For someone who'd always been in control of her sexual relationships, it was a stunning reversal. Why, Sofia harangued herself over and over as she walked down the hill, did she have to *care*?

A notion occurred to her, halting Sofia in her tracks. Had any of her fuckbuddies ever fallen for her? Doubtful she would've noticed, and they'd never said. Well, she hoped none of them had because she now knew what it meant to love someone who didn't reciprocate—love equaled suffering. Love fucking hurt. It wrecked you.

Sofia wouldn't wish such misery on anyone. Not a soul.

She closed her eyes and forced herself to breathe. She must switch gears, concentrate on the upcoming warehouse mission.

Sofia sensibly chose clothing suitable for labor. A black long-sleeved t-shirt, jeans, and rubber-soled sneakers. After scraping her hair into a ponytail, she put on a baseball cap.

Before leaving her cabin, Sofia threaded a leather belt through the loops of her jeans, buttoning on a detachable holster for her revolver. Her fingers trembled as she clipped her keychain onto her belt and stuffed her pockets with spare ammo.

Was it nerves about the run or a presentiment of foreboding about something else? Regardless, her intuition cautioned *be wary*.

Lark waited for her at the back door, her clothing similar to Sofia's. They entered the kitchen together. Kate had cooked a hearty breakfast—fried eggs, grits, and biscuits with sausage gravy—and it was arranged buffet style on the butcher block counter.

Teller was halfway through his meal, Maggie slumbering in her kitchen playpen with Ace standing as sentry. Fritz, plate heaped, was beside Teller, studying Sofia's map as he shoveled grits in his mouth. They called out preoccupied greetings.

Kate, hair disheveled and still in her pajamas, nursed a cup of mint tea and loitered at the sink. Her skin was wan, and she appeared unwell. At Sofia's probing look, she mumbled, "The smell of the food."

Lark spooned a generous serving of gravy over three eggs, forgoing the biscuits and grits. Her long blonde hair was piled messily on the top of her head, tendrils framing her face. She was as lovely as ever. "So is Ben flaking out on us or what?"

"That's a million-dollar question," Teller replied, frowning. "With how het up he was last night, he's likely sulkin'. Figure it's just you, me, Fritz, and Sofia."

While breakfasting, Sofia described the interior of the warehouse, pointing to the map. "After crates are opened, it'll be a matter of getting the boxes down. Canned food in this section'll take precedence. If we have time, personal care stuff is stored here."

"What's in the opposite corner?" Fritz asked as he wiped at his gray-streaked beard with a cloth napkin.

Sofia drained the last of her apple juice and went to put her dishes in the dishwasher. "Potato chips, crackers, baking mix, candy. Items that're past their sell-by date or are a non-priority."

"I'd kill for a bag of red licorice," Kate said, suddenly animated. She took Sofia's vacated spot, placing a hand on Teller's forearm. "If you see some, will you bring it home for me? I've had a hankering for licorice."

Teller warned, "Any we find out there will be so old you'll chip a tooth."

Kate beamed, wheedling, "But the baby wants red licorice."

Teller flashed an indulgent grin. "Welp. Then lemme see what we can—"

The screen door creaked, and they stilled expectantly.

Ben rounded the corner and came through the arched entryway, his compound bow in hand. His face was blank, but he looked worn out. Voice clipped, he said, "Sorry. Overslept."

Conversation was stilted as Ben made his plate and ate. Kate avoided looking at him. Several times Sofia snagged his gaze and held it, but she wasn't able to decipher his temperament. He didn't sulk, but he was withdrawn. She could only guess what was going through his head.

"Kate packed sandwiches and canteens. There's a backpack

for each of us." Teller nodded toward the far side of the kitchen where the packs were tidily assembled.

"I included the canvas ponchos for smearing Z blood to disguise yourselves," Kate said before adding, "Though I'm not sure that's effective anymore."

Teller put his empty coffee mug on the table. "Everyone oughta carry a gun and knife on their person as a reserve, but we gotta be quiet-like. Pick your poison from the armory. Any weapon you favor—ax, sword, bow, machete."

Ben had been reviewing Sofia's hand-drawn map. He indicated where she'd written *loading bay doors* at the rear of the structure. "What sort of foliage is back here?"

Sofia replied, "It's woodland on three sides. The parking lot is at the main lobby entry. It butts up to the woods too, but it's more sparse there."

"I see the highway egress has a security gate and a guard shack." He tracked a finger along what was denoted as an asphalt driveway beyond the front gate. A left turn on an access road a quarter mile from the guard shack led to the shipping and receiving docks. Continuing past the access road turnoff would route them to the parking lot which faced the lobby. "Seems meaningless to employ a rent-a-cop at the gate then neglect fencing the property in."

"The woods are thick enough to keep vehicles out."

"People on foot can bypass the gate by hiking through the woods," Ben said. "Not necessarily an issue before but a theoretical one now."

Teller drawled, "Possibility to consider."

"We won't all fit into the flatbed cab," Fritz said. There was the squeak of footsteps on the floorboards upstairs as Edna got the kids up for the day. It was a reminder that it was time to hit the road. "Either you or Teller can drive the truck. I'll drive the cupcake van with Sofia and Lark. That'll be the pilot vehicle."

Ben narrowed his eyes. "Like I said last night—where Sofia goes, I go. *I'll* drive the van."

Fritz lifted a shoulder. "Don't get testy. That's fine by me. We won't be leaving the highway until you walkie us that things are kosher. That flatbed don't exactly turn on a dime if we gotta bounce."

Ben unfolded from the bench. "That's settled then. Sofia and Lark and me in the van. You and Teller behind in the truck."

Teller pushed his chair back. "And if anythin' looks hinky at the warehouse, y'all haul ass, and we'll do the same. We rally here at the farm."

After they selected weapons, they slung their backpacks on their arms. Ben chose a walkie from the countertop charger, tossing another to Teller. Teller lingered behind to share a private moment with Kate. The others stepped outside.

The sun had begun its ascent. Gradient bands of lavender and coral splashed the horizon. The cool dampness hadn't yet dissipated, and the air was perfumed with wet grass and manure. Robins twittered. Freddy, their rooster, strutted past, crowing. From the henhouse, the hens roused, clucking.

The minivan with the cupcake logo on the door was parked beside the barn that housed the goats and the handful of horses they owned. As Ben got behind the wheel of the van and started it, Bella exited the barn with pans of chicken feed, waving at the trio self-consciously.

Sofia slid into the front passenger seat, and Lark sat in the middle bench seat. Ben drove the van onto the gravel driveway, idling until Fritz brought the flatbed truck from where it was stored by the machine shed. The air brakes hissed as Fritz came to a stop behind them. Once Teller climbed into the passenger seat of the cab, they were on their way.

The highway appeared as it always had—strewn with the occasional rotting corpse or an abandoned vehicle. The over-grown weeds bordering the roadway swayed in the gentle breeze. They rolled down the windows to listen, but there was no sound other than those of nature—the cadence of birdsong and insects and the unmistakable drumming of woodpeckers who hadn't yet migrated south pecking into trees.

Ben adeptly maneuvered around the stranded vehicles. Fritz negotiated them skillfully enough, but often there was not adequate space and the trailer portion of the flatbed scraped them as it inched by. Both vehicles' engines hiccupped as if in rebellion, their exhaust sporadically belching black smoke. It was an indication that the fuel was spoiling despite the additives Fritz said he'd put into the gas tanks. Sofia estimated that the warehouse scavenge would be their last until they were able to convert their engines to run on grain alcohol.

She held her breath as they neared Mergenville. Three minutes later and the ornate iron gate to Spenser Suppliers loomed. The decorative scrollwork was overrun with entangled vines that hadn't been there when Sofia locked the gate behind her that spring.

"Nobody's driven through it in a while. I should've foreseen this when you said it was wooded," Ben surmised. He scanned the bushes around them which were shaded from daylight by the canopy of trees and covered with dew. There was no movement.

Sofia unclipped her keychain from her belt loop. "The vines are thick around the hinges. They'll have to be cut back."

Ben picked the walkie up from where he'd left it in the cupholder by the radio and depressed the button. He relayed the situation to Teller, saying, "It'll take ages. You two can't sit exposed on the highway."

After a second, Teller responded, "Affirmative. And we don't have the fuel to fritter idlin'. We saw another driveway a mile back. Fritz'll reverse this rig, and we'll pull in there where we're concealed. If we don't hear from you in a half hour, we'll return to check up on y'all."

Ben switched the ignition off, telling Sofia and Lark, "I'd have one of us take watch, but like I said, even with all three of us hacking those damn vines, it'll take forever. Have your guns and knives ready."

Once out of the van, Lark stuck her pistol in the waistband of her jeans and flicked the button on her switchblade, her mouth tight. Sofia used her key to unbolt the gate's lock before reclipping her keychain to her belt. She wiggled the gate to confirm that the vines restricted passage.

Casting frequent glances over their shoulders, they used their blades to lacerate the glossy vines. It was painstaking work that took far longer than they preferred, especially when stinky, gelatinous liquid seeped from the cut vegetation, making the task a slippery one.

At last, when they deemed the vines were severed enough, they sheathed their knives. Grabbing at the vertical fence pickets, they hoisted the panel in tandem until the few remaining bits of vegetation tore. With a collective sigh of relief, they propelled the gate fully open.

The driveway stretched to the warehouse five hundred yards ahead. The putty-colored cinder block structure was tucked behind a row of aspens and barely visible from their vantage.

Sofia skimmed the weedy prairie with patches of scrub that ran along each side of the drive. Further afield, densely clustered pine trees dotted the landscape as far as the eye could see.

Lark used the back of her hand to wipe sweat from her brow. "That sap stuff is making my skin itch."

Ben hastened to the van, and they followed suit. "Kate usually puts a wet washcloth in a zipper bag in the packs."

Starting the engine, Ben pulled slowly through the gate. "Suppose I should radio Teller…"

From the periphery of the asphalt driveway, a figure appeared, a semi-automatic weapon raised. It was a filthy, craggy-faced woman with icy eyes. She stepped in front of the van, her gun trained on Ben.

Uttering an oath, Ben braked, putting his palms up.

Another figure emerged from behind a tree, advancing to

Ben's side of the van. A string of dead rabbits was attached to his belt. He was swarthy with black bushy hair and a full beard. He held a hunting rifle pointed at Ben through the open driver's window. Sofia gasped as she recognized the self-satisfied smirk the man wore. Tucker.

There was a whistle from behind Sofia. She whirled in her seat, blanching when she became eye level with the business end of a double barrel shotgun. Kyle grinned at her through his shaggy facial hair, a finger on the gun's trigger and the butt braced against his armpit. He lifted his free hand and waggled his fingers. "Hey, sweetness."

CHAPTER FORTY-SEVEN

SOFIA STARED AT KYLE. HE MUST'VE BEEN TICKLED BY HER expression. Throwing his head back, he cackled.

"Shit, I wondered if I'd ever clap eyes on you again." His lips stretched against his yellowed teeth as he sucked them, then he said, "I been waiting for this."

"What—" Sofia's voice cracked, and she cleared her throat. "What are you doing here?"

"Would you believe we're just passing through?"

Her gaze was calculating as it flew over his body. He'd gained weight and now sported a potbelly—it strained against his grubby shirt. "No, I don't believe that. How'd you find this place?"

"Wasn't rocket science. The keychain of the car we borrowed said *Spenser Suppliers, Wholesale Vendor.* Even had the address. There's more food there than we could possibly eat in a lifetime. You're a sneaky one."

"*I'm* sneaky? You didn't borrow my father's car, you *stole* it," Sofia argued coldly.

"No one owns anything in this world." His voice hardened. "We're past that. Now the spoils go to those with the most firepower."

Ben spoke up from behind her, saying, "Why don't you put those weapons down? Firing them will draw Zs. Anyway, we don't have a beef with you, and we don't want a war."

Kyle's eyes didn't leave Sofia's, but he snapped, "Shut. The. Fuck. Up. The days of kowtowing to your arrogant ass are over —you're not top dog no more. I'm conversing with Sofia here."

The vein in Sofia's temple pounded, matching the rhythm of her pulse. She felt woozy. Trying to ignore the shotgun leveled at her, she moistened her lips. "So you're living at the warehouse now?"

"Yup."

"Whatever. We'll leave. You can have it."

Kyle leered as he considered her. "Nah. I don't think so. Ain't that simple."

A ball of flaming dread formed in Sofia's gut. "What do you want, Kyle?"

Putting his palm over his fly, he adjusted himself. "You know what I want. Maybe I'll let you go after. Depends."

Sofia felt rather than heard Ben tense in his seat. The air crackled, the friction of the hostile energy robbing the oxygen from the atmosphere. "D-depends on what?"

"Whether you spit or swallow."

Bile rose in Sofia's throat. From the bench seat, Lark swore under her breath.

The woman lowered her gun, marching around the hood of the van to Kyle. Her expression aggrieved, she grasped his arm. "You told me I was—"

"Git, Sadie. I got a score to settle." Jerking away, Kyle shook her off.

"Stop! Kyle, no—"

Kyle brought his arm back and punched Sadie hard, square in the face. She reeled back, almost losing her footing. Blood poured from her nose, which was clearly broken.

"Now shut up, or you'll get worse," he ordered.

Tears streamed down her cheeks. Holding her nose with one

hand, Sadie retreated to the weeds. She stood as if in shock, her weapon dangling at her side.

Tucker spoke for the first time, saying, "Do I see my songbird in the backseat? Well, well, well. Two for the price of one. We got us a genu-wine BOGO up in here."

Kyle opened the sliding door, motioning to Lark with his shotgun. "Out. In fact, all of you out. And leave your guns. No funny business now."

Stomach cartwheeling, Sofia unholstered her revolver and placed it on the floor of the van. Ben did the same. She quickly met glances with him before unlatching her door. His face was grim—he understood the gravity of their predicament as well as she did.

They were fucked.

Legs jelly, Sofia slipped from the van and sidestepped until she and Lark were shoulder to shoulder. Lark's ragged gasps revealed her terror. She was on the verge of a meltdown. Sofia reached out to lace their fingers, giving Lark what she hoped was a reassuring squeeze. She silently implored God to help Lark keep her wits about her, or their dilemma would escalate in the blink of an eye.

Tucker nudged Ben with his rifle as he walked around the rear of the van. "Your fearless leader can watch Kyle and me take turns. You always had a soft spot for Sofia, so we'll save her for last—we'll wanna take our time pleasuring her."

Kyle closed the distance to her and Lark, and Sofia held her breath to see what he would do. He seized Lark's wrist and hauled her to him. Clinching her against his chest, he ground his pelvis against her backside. Lark stiffened, whimpering. She scrunched her eyes shut.

Sofia knew they needed time to formulate a plan. She must do something. "Kyle, please—"

"You'll get your turn," Tucker promised.

"We have resources—meat, fresh milk," Ben said. "Let me barter with you for our freedom."

Kyle laughed, his hand snaking under Lark's t-shirt and up to her breast. He pinched her nipple, and she cried out. "You must have resources if you're driving. Nobody has gas anymore."

"Squeaky clean *and* well fed," Tucker observed. "We'll strike a bargain about your freedom later. After."

Kyle's eyes became lidded. His ruddy cheeks suffused scarlet, and he slathered his tongue down Lark's neck, apparently aroused. "Mmm. I'm gonna make the songbird sing."

How much longer until he ripped Lark's clothes off and raped her in front of them? Sofia's appalled gaze skated to Lark's face. She was yielding to Kyle, but her eyes opened, appealing to Sofia. Sofia's brow knit.

What was Lark trying to communicate? One of her hands was in her pocket. What was she doing? Her switchblade! She must be counting on Kyle's distraction to extract her knife!

Had Ben discerned what Lark was up to? Sofia side-eyed Ben, and he winked. Yes. He'd noticed. They'd practiced numerous potential scenarios during drills at the farm. Now they would see if their training had been fruitful.

Shifting, Ben spoke in a low tone to Tucker. Another distraction technique. Sofia assessed the setting as she'd been taught. Lark would take on Kyle. Ben had Tucker. That left Sadie for her.

There was no time to second guess the plan.

Sadie's eyes were lasered with rapt attention on Kyle's face, her weapon held loosely by a hand on the fabric shoulder strap. Her other hand hadn't budged from her nose.

Lark's switchblade was liberated. She gripped the handle as Kyle moved to unbutton her jeans. With a war cry, she arced her arm smoothly up and in, jabbing the blade into Kyle's neck. It sank into his jugular. Removing it, Lark pierced his neck with repetitive stabs.

Sofia launched at Sadie where she stood at the side of the road. Kyle's spurting blood sprayed her shirt as she sped past. Head down, Sofia drove for Sadie's midsection. Outweighed and caught unprepared, she was easily tackled with a throaty *Oof.* Wresting the gun from her, Sofia kneeled on her hip and aimed it at her before checking to see how Lark and Ben fared.

Kyle was on the asphalt, bewildered and mumbling to himself. His fingers were jammed into the holes in his neck, but he was bleeding out. Lark's face was streaked with the carnage of his lifeblood. She resembled a Viking shield maiden—a warrior—victorious after a battle. Smiling, she bent to take his shotgun before training it on Sadie.

Sofia eased up, staggering to her feet. Adrenaline caused her to tremble. She gulped, scrambling to comprehend, to calculate her next move. Ben and Tucker tussled for his rifle, the veins on Ben's neck bulging. He was beefy and barrel-chested, but Tucker had fifty pounds on him.

"Not an inch," Sofia shakily advised Sadie before duck-walking to Ben and Tucker, head down in case the rifle was discharged during the scuffle.

Raising the butt of Sadie's semi-automatic weapon, Sofia aimed at Tucker, but he and Ben swayed and reeled as if in a complicated, choreographed waltz—it was impossible to get a fix on her target. She captured Ben's eye. As soon as Tucker was in position, Ben loosened his grip on the rifle. That threw Tucker. He fumbled. Sofia shoved her gun into the small of Tucker's back as forcefully as she could.

With a yelp, Tucker abandoned the rifle and grabbed at his back. He fell to his knees.

Sweat ringed Ben's armpits, his face beet red. Expression feral, he stooped to recover the rifle. Putting a booted foot on Tucker's spine, he pushed Tucker so he lay prone on the driveway. Holding him in place, Ben struck Tucker's head with the rifle.

Whack. Whack. Whack.

Rooted to the blacktop, Sofia numbly observed Ben repeatedly ram Tucker's skull until it was nothing more than a flattened mess.

CHAPTER FORTY-EIGHT

Sofia wobbled to the side of the driveway and retched into the weeds. Her ears buzzed, and her vision blurred. Shock, her mind whispered, you're in shock.

She sat back on her heels, putting a hand to her stomach. A rivulet of Kyle's blood seeped toward her. Before it soaked into her jeans, she recoiled with a squeak, springing away from it.

My God. What have we done?

The buzzing ceased, replaced by the monotone hum of insects and the wheezing judder of Sofia's panting. From the interior of the van, Teller's disembodied voice came over the walkie Ben had thrown on the dashboard.

Ben stood hunched over Tucker's body with his palms on his knees and, head hanging, fought to catch his breath. His t-shirt and jeans were splattered with sweat and blood and brain tissue. Straightening, he paced, exhaling, "Fuck... Fuck... Fuck!"

Sofia chewed her lip, looking to Lark, who still held the shotgun on Sadie. Sadie erupted a great whooping wail, the sound warring with the squawk of the walkie. Lark shook her head and tucked the shotgun in the crook of her armpit. Cupping her hands over her ears, Lark's distressed gaze landed on Sofia. Her eyes were wide with stark realization. Gone was the victorious warrior. The adrenaline rush that had propped them up had dispelled, leaving them shivering. Nauseated. Perplexed.

Tears mixed with the vomit and snot dripping from Sofia's chin. She swiped it away with her sleeve, clamping her teeth on the inside of her cheek. She marched up to Sadie, nudging at her shin with her sneaker. "Are there more of you?"

"Y-yes."

"How many?" When Sadie didn't answer, Sofia dug in her foot. Sadie abruptly quit wailing and curled into a ball. "How many, dammit!"

"S-six. Two men and four women." She sniffled, shielding her head with her arm. "They're in the warehouse. P-p-please, don't hurt me!"

"Don't force us to," Lark ground out, her eyes enormous in her face.

There were zip ties in Sofia's backpack. She darted to the van and grabbed a handful of them before returning to kneel beside Sadie. Arranging Sadie's hands behind her back, Sofia unsteadily zip-tied her wrists together. "I apologize for this. Just comply, okay? I don't want to hurt you, I swear."

Ben, stone-faced, snatched Tucker's rifle from the blacktop and rubbed it against the overgrowth to clean it. While Lark guarded Sadie, Sofia grabbed the walkie. Sweeping her gaze furtively from the rearview mirror to along the sides of the driveway and up toward the warehouse, she pressed the button on the side of the walkie and spoke into it. "Teller?"

Teller's reply oozed relief. "Thank the Lord you finally answered. What's goin' on? Y'all alright?"

He knew about the brothers—Ben had mentioned them when they'd arrived at Mayfly Hollow. She refreshed Teller's memory and briefly relayed what had happened without detailing the brutality of the encounter. "We overpowered them... both the men are dead. And we have a hostage. Thing is, she said there are more of their group up at the warehouse."

"Nuh-uh. Ain't worth it," Teller stated unequivocally. "Bail. Now."

"But... what about our prisoner?" From the corner of Sofia's eye, she saw Sadie perk up to listen.

Teller didn't reply right away. Sofia held her breath. If he decreed they should kill Sadie... she wouldn't be party to that.

"Unwise to leave an eyewitness who can lead her group to us..."

Sadie, comprehending the implication of Teller's words, began to stir. Lark warned, "Be still."

"Wait," Ben commanded. He unlatched the van's lift gate and deposited the guns in the trunk. Going to the front passenger side, he rummaged in the glove box until he unearthed a travel-sized pair of binoculars. "I saw something on the hill."

"Where?" Sofia gasped, squinting. The morning sun behind the warehouse obscured details.

"By the access road." Huffing with impatience, Ben edgily tossed the binocular pouch aside and lifted the binoculars. He fiddled with the dial at the bridge of his nose to focus, stepping from the van but remaining slouched behind the open door for cover. "We're like sitting ducks. Get out of sight."

Lark pushed Sadie over and hunched down beside her so they were camouflaged by the foliage.

Feeling conspicuous, Sofia huddled behind the steering wheel. "Should I start the van in case we have to peel out?"

"Sofia?" Teller's voice crackled over the line. "I best get an update, or I'm comin' in with guns a blazin'."

Ben snorted in disbelief. Putting his index and middle finger to his mouth, he whistled sharply. A whistled reply drifted to them. Hand extended, Ben gestured for the walkie, and Sofia passed it to him, her forehead furrowed in puzzlement. A dark figure stepped out from the corner of the building and waved, but he was too far away for Sofia to discern his identity.

"Teller," Ben breathed into the walkie. "You're never gonna believe who's here."

Sofia grabbed the binoculars Ben had discarded on the passenger seat and brought them to her eyes. She whooped.

"It's Adam, isn't it?" Lark demanded, rising.

Feeling giddy, Sofia laughed. "It's Adam!"

"Hey!" Lark yelled. She brought the shotgun up, aiming at Sadie who sprinted toward a copse of trees.

Ben put the walkie on the dashboard, instructing Lark, "Let her go. She doesn't have a weapon, and her hands are bound."

They piled into the van and drove to where Adam waited for them by the turnoff to shipping and receiving, a dazzling smile on his face. He waved in greeting as they got out of the van. Lark flew into his arms for a hug, then he and Ben embraced. When Ben stepped away, he had a tear in his eye.

"Hello, Sofia," Adam said. He held his arms out.

Sniffling, Sofia allowed Adam to enfold her in his arms. He was unwashed and his hair was matted and he smelled foul, but she couldn't disguise her delight in finding him alive and unharmed.

After Adam released Sofia, Ben motioned to Kyle and Tucker's corpses down by the gate. "Sorry about your friends."

"Those assholes were no friends of mine," Adam replied mildly.

"They ambushed us," Lark told Adam, her jaw clenched. "Held us at gunpoint. If we hadn't put them down, they would've raped me and Sofia."

"I believe you," Adam assured her. "We heard the commotion in the warehouse, and I recognized the van." He scrutinized them. "Are you okay, psychologically?"

"We will be." Ben rubbed his face, looking exhausted.

Did Adam's eyes linger on her? Swallowing, Sofia whispered, "They were the brothers I told you about. The ones that stole my dad's car."

Adam nodded. "I figured—when I met them I put two and two together. Small world, eh?"

Sofia asked, "How did you ever get hooked up with them?"

"I encountered other members of their group collecting fresh water in a stream in the woods a few weeks back. The brothers were none too pleased that they hadn't been consulted ahead of time before I was brought to the warehouse."

"That's because you're Black," Lark spat. "They were racist jerkoffs. They deserved to die."

Sofia scanned Lark's mulish expression. Was she trying to convince herself, or was that really how she felt?

"What about us? They discuss us at all?" Ben asked.

"No. They mentioned in passing that they stumbled across the keys to this place after nicking a car—which was confirmation to me that they were the ones you told me about."

Lark hitched a thumb over her shoulder. "That chick Sadie took off. Think she'll be a problem?"

Adam scratched his eyebrow, then tossed his machete from one hand to another, considering. "I don't believe so. She was Kyle's girlfriend, although he treated her abominably."

Scoffing, Lark didn't comment.

Sofia said, "We planned to load up a truckful of food and provisions to take home. Teller and Fritz are nearby with a flatbed—"

"You prepared to come home today?" Ben interrupted, his face intense. "Are any of the others in the warehouse candidates, or are they cut from the same cloth as the brothers?"

"There's a middle-aged couple—Jan and Kevin—and a mother and daughter named Trina and Nese."

"With you, that's five. What about the sixth person?" Lark asked.

"Marta. No, she isn't getting an invitation. Too rough around the edges. I wasn't sure Sadie would integrate either although that's a moot point now."

Fifteen minutes had elapsed. Sofia thought of Teller and Fritz. They'd be chomping at the bit. "Teller and Kate were clear that they aren't willing to start a war over provisions that we can live without. As far as I'm concerned, the warehouse doesn't belong to me anymore. Do you think this Marta would barter for supplies?"

Adam considered Sofia's request, wincing. "She's a tough customer. Once she learns about Tucker and Kyle's deaths—and that Sadie's absconded—I'm afraid she won't be reasonable. Even more so when I exclude her from the invite to Mayfly Hollow."

All three regarded Sofia, awaiting her verdict. Kate and Teller had said that she was leading the run. They'd been adamant that their safety was paramount above all else. Sofia rendered an executive decision that she hoped she wouldn't regret.

"Forget it then." Sofia just wanted to go home and wash the stink of death from her skin. "I'll inform Teller that he and Fritz can leave. Go on inside and talk to the people you want to bring to Mayfly Hollow. We'll stand by."

CHAPTER FORTY-NINE

ADAM WAS BEHIND THE STEERING WHEEL, BEN IN THE PASSENGER seat next to him. The remaining six people—Sofia, Lark, Trina, Nese, Kevin, and Jan—were packed like sardines in the bench seats. With Adam as a go-between, Sofia had negotiated with Marta after all, trading a gun for a box that included menstrual cups and licorice. It rested at Sofia's feet amongst their backpacks, innocuous and everyday. It seemed bizarre. The incongruity of it taunted her.

When they'd passed by Tucker and Kyle's bodies, she'd swiveled her head, refusing to bear witness. The images were already seared into her brain—Tucker's head *gone* and Kyle sprawled in a congealing pool of blood. It was a grisly tableau. Sofia was defiled by it.

The drive home was somber. The pungent iron tang of the slaughter clung to her hair and clothes. When she linked gazes with Lark, the woman was defiant, silently challenging Sofia to disagree with her. To debate that they had been wrong to kill. Sofia couldn't. In her rational mind, she surmised that they hadn't been wrong—they'd been in circumstances where they'd had no alternative but to act. Nevertheless, that didn't mean that Sofia wasn't mourning their actions. One thing she was certain of was that she was unwilling to participate in a bullshit circle jerk meant to soothe instead of confront the seriousness of what happened.

Of course Tucker and Kyle were vermin. Of course Sofia would do anything she must to survive. That didn't mean she'd flout the moral implication of slaughtering another human.

Ben's reflection in the side mirror showed that he too was shaken. Adam kept checking on her in the rearview. Sofia closed her eyes. All she could picture was the savage expression on Ben's face as he smashed Tucker's skull, the shattered bone and bits of brain matter raining across the blacktop like macabre confetti.

Adam took pity on Sofia, dropping her at her cabin, saying he would get the new people settled and debrief Teller and Kate himself.

Murmuring that she'd be up to the farmhouse later, Sofia slipped from the van and rushed up the porch steps without glancing back.

She wanted solitude.

THE SUBSEQUENT WEEKS BLENDED TOGETHER. Sofia robotically performed her duties around the farm, pasting on a pleasant smile and pretending everything was hunky dory. She felt like a fraud, supposing that the others saw through her façade. When she was around them, she longed to be by herself, but upon fleeing to her cabin, she discovered that she wasn't happy when she was alone either.

Lark and Kate had tried in turn to broach the subject of the brothers with Sofia, but she'd shut them down. She just didn't have the strength to discuss the maelstrom of emotions swirling through her. Adam, in his erudite and undemanding way, had left a care package of wine and a dozen joints along with a thoughtful notecard on her porch. Ben had granted Sofia space, too. When he'd wanted to arrange a rendezvous a week after the incident, she begged off, and he hadn't pushed.

Fluctuating between conflicted and jaded, Sofia knew undeniably that she was changed—she wasn't the woman she'd once been. What terrified her was that she'd never return to her normal self again. At night, sleep elusive, she sat on a plastic chair on her porch. She smoked joints and drank apple wine and listened to the farmyard noises, feeling broken. Like she no longer belonged. Not at Juniper Rise. Not at Mayfly Hollow. Not anywhere.

Sofia and Ben had no future. She'd lost her humanity participating in murdering Tucker and Kyle. There was no coming back from that. She didn't recognize herself anymore.

Was the biological drive to survive worth the interminable struggle?

She was depressed. Was it chronic or would she begin to feel more like herself if she just gave it more time? It made her itchy to do something drastic. Though it was an absurd notion, Sofia considered leaving the farm.

But where was there to go?

The routine of caring for Sam and Rory grounded her. Soon they were old enough to be weaned off the kitten formula and litter trained. They'd been dewormed and were eating kibble procured from the vet's office. Cognizant that she was unable to put off the task of delivering the cats to Nora any longer, Sofia loaded them in their crate with their supplies.

Ben flipped the hallway light on when she arrived at Juniper Rise, opening the front door to receive her. "I didn't expect to see you tonight, brown-eyed girl."

"Where do you want me to set up their food dishes and litter box?" She indicated the crate, keeping her voice low since Nora was surely already in bed.

He gestured dismissively as he ushered her into the foyer. "I'll take care of that in a bit. Want a mug of tea? I was just steeping one for myself."

Nodding, Sofia went into the living room and sat on the sofa. Ben had lit a fire in the fireplace. It took the evening chill from the air, spicing it with woodsmoke. It was homey. She scooped Sam out of the crate and kissed her before placing her on the carpet. She meowed in dismay, searching for Rory. Sofia put Rory next to her sister, petting her. The white and orange kittens whizzed around the room, investigating and sniffing furniture and trying to climb the curtains.

Ben closed Nora's door before carrying steaming mugs of tea into the living room, handing Sofia one before sitting beside her on the sofa. "I can't wait to see Nora's face in the morning when she realizes you've brought the cats."

Sofia blew on the surface of the tea before taking a sip. Chamomile and rosehip, spiked with whiskey. It was good.

"Haven't seen much of you lately." The firelight flicked over Ben's features, accentuating his probing eyes. A lick of desire prickled over Sofia, the first in weeks.

"Have you missed me?" She held her breath pending his rejoinder, studying her mug and playacting that his answer didn't matter.

"How could I not?" He relaxed back into the opposite corner of the sofa, his gaze contemplative. "You've been blaming yourself about Tucker and Kyle, haven't you?"

"I wish I would've kept the warehouse to myself," she admitted quietly.

"Woulda, coulda, shoulda." Ben shrugged. "What's done is done."

"How can you be so... offhand?"

"I'm not being offhand."

"Well, I'll never get over what happened. Never."

"Nobody is suggesting you *get over* it. But you've got to find some measure of peace, Sofia. We can all see it's eating you alive."

Sofia's eyes filled with tears. "Doesn't it bother you at all? Jesus, it has to. You're not heartless."

"I keep forgetting how young you are," Ben tsked. "A degree of trauma is part of life now."

"And you claim you aren't being offhand." She sniffled. "It is my fault, you know."

"How so? You couldn't possibly have any idea they'd taken up residence at Spenser Suppliers."

"Not that." Sofia took a big swig of the whiskey-laced tea. It bolstered her. "The night before the brothers stole my father's car... Kyle picked the lock to my bedroom."

Ben straightened, twisting toward her. *"He what?"*

"Yeah."

"That motherfucker!"

Sofia shushed Ben, cautioning, "You'll wake Nora."

"And?"

"I pulled my revolver on him. Threatened him. Stated that I planned to tell you that he'd broken into my room. That I'd be calling a meeting. He got the message—he and Tucker were about to be ousted at best. They knew not to screw with you."

Gaze narrowed, Ben demanded, "Did he touch you? Hurt you?"

"No! But don't you see? *That* was the score Kyle wanted to settle—his rationale for why he and Tucker were going to assault Lark and me. The way I handled that last night... it provoked him and ruined any chance of reasoning with him."

"You cannot seriously be browbeating yourself over this. Kyle was in the wrong when he picked the lock to your bedroom door, and he and Tucker were wrong when they ambushed us. There's no justifying their behavior. You weren't culpable."

"I mean, I *understand*," she pointed to her temple, "in here."

"I'd gathered that it was your first time being in such a situation." Ben reached over and interlocked their fingers. "But you didn't kill them—I did. Lark did."

"It's not that cut-and-dried," Sofia argued. "I have blood on my hands regardless, Ben."

"Why didn't you confide in me about Kyle?"

"It wasn't important at the time. Later, it was even less so. How was I to know that we'd come up against the brothers again?"

Ben put his mug on the floor then grazed her cheek with the back of his hand. "The thought of either of those guys touching you..."

She closed her eyes as radiating warmth spread across her chest.

"I want you to promise that you'll never hold anything back from me again. Can you promise me?"

"I-I'll try." When she opened her eyes, she identified compassion. She let it infuse her. Reveled in it. "Sometimes I need to sort things out in my own head before I can verbalize. I mean, I've never even slapped anyone before, much less been an accessory to their death."

"Fair enough." Ben smiled, his sapphire eyes softening all the more as he surveyed her. "Rest assured that the ethical dilemma you're grappling with is natural after seeing that degree of brutality firsthand. It's... expected, even healthy. I'd be more concerned if you *weren't* conflicted. The first time is always the hardest."

"Was yours?"

Ben's face transformed, becoming aloof. Sofia felt him retreat emotionally. It pissed her off. "I'd rather not get into that tonight, Sofia."

She pulled away, putting space between them. "I confess all to you—put myself on the line and be vulnerable—but you won't return the favor? That's not cool."

He sighed. "You're right. It's not fair. Fine. I'll tell you about the first time I killed someone."

CHAPTER FIFTY

BEN GOT UP AND STOOD AT THE FIREPLACE. HE STARED INTO THE flames, his expression brooding and unreadable. The crackle and pop of the flames in the grate punctuated the hush of the room. Sofia waited for him to speak, her stomach knotted with trepidation.

Ben's tone was low, introspective. Leaning forward, Sofia strained to hear. "At the outset, what people had difficulty grasping was the sheer implausibility of the news reports. The consensus was that the media was manufacturing hysteria. Even as people were falling ill and dying in alarming numbers, there were naysayers. It was merely the flu, right? Except I was friends with the Deputy Commissioner of Public Health, and she set me straight in no uncertain terms—it was *bad*. When the president announced the shelter-in-place order, I telephoned my folks and told them to contact the immediate family, who were all local. We'd meet at my parents' farm on the outskirts of Clayton's Corners and hole up there together.

"My mom and dad, my three sisters and their families, my brother and his family... and me. The farm was out in the country, remote. For a couple hours, we were unaffected by the insanity in town. We camped around the TV, flipping from channel to channel, anxious for the latest. Then," Ben's voice broke, "that night, my folks started showing symptoms. Their decline was... quick. They passed within twenty-four hours, along with two of my sisters, a niece, a nephew..."

"Ben," Sofia whispered, "I-I don't know what to say."

"My story is no different than anyone else's story. We've all been touched by the virus."

"Don't do that."

Ben turned to her, eyebrows raised. "Do what?"

"Minimize your ordeal so matter-of-factly."

He lifted a pragmatic shoulder. "I'm not minimizing, Sofia, just pointing out the irrefutable. I'm not special. Scores of people had their families die in front of them."

"I didn't."

"Then you're luckier than most."

"I know. Believe me."

Ben paced the room. Sam and Rory, roughhousing, tumbled in his path. Crouching, Ben picked them up. He handed Rory to Sofia and sat on the sofa, stroking Sam, the look in his eyes far away. "Then my nephew, who'd been dead for hours, woke up and attacked my brother. I had to put him down. My brother died from the bite. I had everyone who wasn't yet sick quarantine in separate parts of the house, but in the end, I was the only one who remained standing."

"How'd you avoid getting the virus?"

"I don't know. I should've been infected. I'd been exposed countless times... the whole fucking thing is a blur. I'd learned what killed them was destroying their brains. As a preventative measure, I-I stabbed my family through their eyes after they passed—I couldn't have them turn into... could I? Part of my soul died. Christ." He ran a hand across his face, then went on, not waiting for Sofia's answer, "Staying there with their corpses *fucked me up*. I remember looking out the window, and my blood ran cold. Zs were massing outside. That snapped me out of my stupor. I had shotguns and a handgun, but I couldn't hold them off by myself for long if they stormed the house."

Rory purred contentedly in Sofia's lap. She petted him, shivering as a chill overcame her.

"I'd been able to reach Kate, and she extended an invitation to Mayfly Hollow. I plotted the route on an old map my dad had. It was a two-hundred-mile drive. I packed food and water and extra bullets for my handgun. At first light, I snuck out to the barn, where my dad stocked spare cans of gasoline. The Zs heard me or smelled me. There were probably ten of them. They chased me to the barn. I was sure they'd bust through the door, but they didn't. By morning, they'd forgotten about me, scattering enough for me to make a break for the Jeep. I got into the driver's seat as they vaulted on the hood and roof. I put the pedal to the floor and, eventually, they dropped off. I'd never been so scared in my life. I thought I was having a heart attack."

Rory had fallen asleep. Ben placed Sam on Sofia's lap next to her sister. Sofia rubbed the gooseflesh from her arms, considering Ben. "That's what? A three-hour trip?"

"Took all day. The interstate was gridlock, so I detoured on the fly. Driving in the dark wasn't safe. I parked in an out-of-the-way place that night, but I didn't sleep. I was functioning on fear and NoDoz."

"Were there a lot of Zs on the interstate?"

"Every so often I came across a lone Z, or a cluster of them. I'd plow through. My Jeep was pretty beat up by the time I entered River Heights. I was *almost* to Mayfly Hollow."

"It happened at River Heights?"

"Outside city limits. A woman ran into the road. Blocked me. She was holding a little girl and crying—begging—for assistance. I couldn't *not* stop. I got out of the Jeep, offering her a ride. Mister Honorable, right?"

"I would have done the same," Sofia assured Ben.

His sober gaze spoke volumes when he met her eyes. "It was a foolhardy mistake, stopping and rushing up to her. I'd been tricked—it was a ruse. A man with a gun stepped out from behind a stalled vehicle and told me they were taking my Jeep." He paused, swallowing hard. "I'll spare you the details, but suffice to say, I wasn't about to go down without a fight. We had words. I tried to talk sense into him. He shot at me. I didn't dive fast enough and got hit. You've seen the scars on my side."

Sofia nodded her assent. She had seen them. She'd traced tentative fingertips over the ridges and wrinkles of the puckered scar tissue, speculating how the injury had come about but loath to ask.

"I was lightheaded. Stunned. It hurt like a sonofabitch. I unholstered my gun and fired back, emptying my magazine—" Ben put his face in his hands, bending at the waist to prop his elbows on his knees. His voice was muffled and chock full of pain. "I missed the guy... I shot the girl instead. The bullet went through her skull and into her mother's chest." Sitting up, Ben turned to Sofia. "I fucking killed them both. And it's tormented me since."

"Ben..." Sofia murmured as he jerkily got to his feet and resumed pacing, ignoring her.

"I passed out, and when I came to, the guy and the Jeep were gone. He didn't stick around to see if my wound was fatal. Almost was. I shuffled around what seemed eons, combing the countryside for Mayfly Hollow. I was out of my head with fever... I don't recall much except that I was terribly thirsty. I don't know how I found the farm in the state I was in. I don't know how the Zs didn't get me."

"It was a miracle."

Ben halted, sitting on the stone hearth. "Maybe."

"Kate nursed you back to health?"

"Yes, for weeks. She and Teller had to go foraging in town for heavy-duty antibiotics. She and this place have been my salvation. I owe her everything. Everything."

No surprise he loves Kate, Sofia thought, after all that. She supposed in fraught circumstances indebtedness could cross lines with affection and be conflated into love. Apparently, that love hadn't diminished in the meantime. Throat constricting, Sofia kept her mouth zipped.

"I almost couldn't believe it when I saw Nora. She resembled that girl so closely... same blonde hair, same big blue eyes. She needed someone, so I took her under my wing. I owe it to the universe to give back."

"To what—to atone?"

"To make amends. Over time, I've come to care for Nora as if she were my own kid." Cheeks pale, Ben took a deep breath. "Now that you know the truth about me, I suppose you think I'm a monster. Do you hate me?"

CHAPTER FIFTY-ONE

DURING THE WALK HOME THAT NIGHT, SOFIA SECOND-GUESSED HER reaction to Ben's revelations.

Put on the spot, she'd tripped over her words as she endeavored to clarify her jumbled thoughts—that knowing about the death of the child in River Heights put to rest the questions she'd had about why he felt so obligated to adopt Nora. That her beliefs about what type of person he was had been further cemented. Ben was a principled man. A man who always persevered to do the right thing. *Mister Honorable.*

No, she didn't think he was a monster. Did she hate him? That was ridiculous. Laughable. She didn't hate him. How could she? She loved him. But Sofia kept that tidbit to herself, telling Ben that she was honored he trusted her enough to share the gritty details of his journey.

The frown on his face revealed that she hadn't reassured him adequately. He'd waved Sofia's declarations aside. The mood shifted, causing a curious awkwardness between them that churned her gut. They'd finished their tea, and Sofia bid him farewell, feeling very much that no matter what she said, it wouldn't be enough.

Ben's kiss at the door had been as ardent as usual. If they had nothing else, she thought, at least they still had that connection.

Over the ensuing days, both Sofia and Ben, along with the others, were swept up into the busyness of Mayfly Hollow. They had no time—or energy—for even a quickie. Now officially autumn, the impending frigid temps and snow of winter spurred the group as they hustled to wrap up projects.

Completing the still was the primary goal, and to a lesser degree, converting engines to run on alcohol. Teller had established a timeline—the still in full production distilling grain alcohol before snowfall so they could stockpile a surplus. Engine conversion would be tackled after sowing the spring crops.

They were out of fuel for the tractor. Josh and Ben and Milo hooked an antiquated plow to the horses and tilled the fields. Once that task was done, manure was spread to enrich the soil. When Ben wasn't prepping fields, he helped Lark set up solar panels on the roof of her home.

It was apple-harvesting season. Lark and Sofia and Bella led the new people to the orchard with wicker baskets and galvanized metal pails. Trina, a friendly woman in her forties, was an ideal match for Mayfly Hollow. She had grown up on a farm and was knowledgeable about gardening and canning and food preservation. Sofia liked her sunny disposition. Trina's teenage daughter Nese seemed shy. She assisted Edna in the mornings with the kids' schooling. In the afternoons she worked in the kitchen or the garden. Sofia wondered about the girl—she felt Nese's eyes tracking her like a hawk during meals.

When they arrived at the orchard, Nese stayed close to Sofia, quietly loading her basket with ripe apples. After a while, she asked, "You're *TheRealSofiaS*, aren't you?"

Thrown, it took Sofia a beat to formulate a response. "Uhh... I was."

Nese's face brightened. "I thought so! My cousin was in your Western Civ class at St. Belfridge."

"Oh?"

"I followed you. You had the best clothes!"

Sofia looked down at her ratty sweatshirt and jeans, smiling ruefully. "*Had* is right."

"Don't you, like, miss it?"

Removing another apple from the branch, Sofia put it in her basket. "I miss my parents and my friends."

"But I watched your vlogs. You had an amazing life!"

Surveying Nese, Sofia estimated she was four or five years older than the girl but felt ancient in comparison.

When Sofia didn't respond, Nese asked, "Wasn't it amazing?"

"At times." Influencing was a deceptive art, presenting a fictionalized, filtered standard of living. Her vlogs and social media posts displayed a slice of life that wasn't truly representative of the whole. Sofia would've never been caught dead uploading a photo without flawless hair and makeup. Even her candid shots had been mindfully posed to display her in the most flattering light. She'd been sponsored by two brands but hadn't earned enough to employ a PA, so she'd juggled her content around school and life. It wasn't all fun and games. It had been a job. There'd been days when the last thing she wanted to do was be *on*. Sofia had wearied of the inauthenticity of influencing and considered quitting as a birthday present to herself.

Kevin, Jan's husband—Sofia would've never pegged them as a married couple if they hadn't said so—set up the ladder he'd carried over one shoulder to the orchard. He was in his fifties, and everything about him was average. Ordinary. He wasn't talkative. Lark had posited that Kevin was *slow*. Perhaps he was self-conscious of his ill-fitting dentures. When he did talk, they slipped and gave him an unfortunate lisp. "Jan," he said, "pash me that empty bashket."

Jan bustled to fetch it for him. As Sofia continued on to another apple tree, she theorized about opposites attracting. Jan and Kevin seemed an unlikely pairing. Where he was soft-spoken and reserved, she was giggly and chatty. Her chatter was incessant.

Lark strolled up to Sofia, eyeing her bushel basket. "Full enough," she announced. "Let's you and me head back to the farmhouse."

Sofia glanced at Nese's bucket, finding it wasn't filled. *Good.* The girl alternated between starstruck and nosy, asking intrusive questions. Sofia likened it to the Spanish Inquisition. She needed a reprieve.

They walked through the pasture, leaving the others to finish up. Lark said, "I had to get away from that blabbermouth. She's given me a splitting headache."

"Jan? I've resorted to tuning her out. Nodding when appropriate."

"She never has anything important to say anyway. I'm not a fan of her nicey-nicey fake shit. She's *too* chummy."

"It's like I'm babysitting when Nese is around. She wears me out," Sofia admitted, tiredly rubbing her eyes. It had been a day, and it wasn't over yet—she'd agreed to prepare dinner.

Lark snorted then said in a singsong voice, "Sofia has a fan girl."

"Ugh."

"Hey, preferable to Jan."

Sofia laughed, switching her basket to the other hand. Lark's trailer came into view, the late afternoon sun hitting the recently installed solar panels on the roof. "We shouldn't be unkind. No doubt she's trying to fit in here. She's probably nervous. I was."

"My BS-meter is swinging into overdrive." Lark paused as they approached her house. "Her teeth skeeve me out, too."

"They must bother her. Rob said he'd try extracting them if she wants—she told him they rotted because of poverty and lack of food when she was a kid."

"She's made up for that since, hasn't she?" Lark asked tartly, hitching a thumb toward her double-wide. "I'm fixing up my bedroom. Wanna see?"

The walls of Lark's bedroom were painted a restful blue. A wooden dresser was between two windows—she'd hung crisp white lace curtains—and a metal bed frame was centered in the middle of the room. Sofia complimented Lark on her décor choices.

Lark said, "I sorted through the mattresses in the pole barn. There's a memory foam one, but I couldn't carry it by myself."

"I'll help you bring it down tomorrow." Sofia's stomach growled. "The pork shoulder I have in the roaster will be done cooking by now."

Once they reached the farmhouse, Lark and Kate placed trays of apples wrapped in tissue paper on shelves in the root cellar beside bins of squash and potatoes while Sofia finished dinner preparations.

Everyone raved about the *hornado* Sofia served—a version of her mother's Ecuadorian roasted pork recipe—along with potato patties and salsa.

The meal was celebratory. Fritz declared the still completed. He and Teller had fired it up that afternoon to ensure that the welds held. The construction had been a feat that they'd shared in detail at the dinner table over many a meal. Sofia had heard enough about copper sheets and vapor cones and condensers to last her a lifetime.

"Will you make moonshine?" Jan asked, squinting as she brushed her blonde hair from her face with a plump hand. She'd explained that her eyeglasses had broken, joking she was blind as a bat.

"It's more for practical uses—fuel and disinfectant," Fritz replied, "but I've been known to partake in a jelly jar of moonshine."

"You said it's a hundred-ninety proof." Kate laughed, her cheeks pink. "Please tell me you cut it with water."

Fritz winked and smacked his sternum. "Puts hair on your chest."

"Yeah, no thank you." Kate gave him side-eye. Her morning sickness had vanished as her pregnancy progressed. She was the picture of health—clear-skinned and glossy-haired—sporting an adorable baby bump. Forehead scrunching, she asked Jan, "Did you work at the Save-A-Bunch?"

"No. I was assistant librarian at the public library in Upper Bremer."

Kate was convinced she knew Jan from *somewhere*. Every day she suggested a place where she could've encountered Jan before, without success.

Kate shook her head. "Give me a day or two, and I'll remember. It's on the tip of my tongue."

Jan scooted from her seat on the bench. "Can I take everyone's plates?"

While Bella, Kevin, and Jan cleared the table, Kate said she wanted to go over the tasks for the following day. "I've written a list."

"My wife and her lists," Teller teased.

Kate rolled her eyes at her husband. "We have plenty of apples stored in the cellar now, so priority one is making applesauce and canning pie filling."

Sofia yawned.

Lark told Teller, "Kate's teaching me and Sofia how to can."

"Freezing broccoli, cauliflower, and Brussels sprouts will be the day after tomorrow. Then we'll till the gardens," Kate said before pushing her chair back.

"Are we playing board games tonight?" Nese asked hopefully.

"Oh honey, everyone is pooped," Trina said, giving her daughter a side hug. "Another night."

Ben went to the family room to check on the kids, who'd eaten earlier and were watching a DVD. He returned to the kitchen, saying, "Nora's conked out on the couch next to Ravi."

Kate wrapped leftovers in foil. "Let her sleep here tonight. It's no biggie."

As Ben thanked Kate, his and Sofia's gazes locked. He lifted an eyebrow in query, and her pulse accelerated in response.

Cheeks blooming with heat and exhaustion forgotten, she mouthed, "My place?"

CHAPTER FIFTY-TWO

SOFIA DASHED TO HER CABIN TO SHOWER, BREATHY WITH anticipation. She flicked on the lamp on the table beside her reading chair and closed the curtains to set the scene for romance. The lamplight was mellow. Dreamy. After hunting in a drawer for a match, she lit a scented candle and then took off her bracelet, laying it on her dresser before shucking her clothes. If she hurried, there'd be enough time to shave her legs.

She'd pulled on a fuzzy robe and combed her wet hair when there were footfalls on the porch. Crossing the room, she unlocked the bolt and swung the door wide before he could rap on it. Ben's large frame filled the doorway. He was dressed in a flannel shirt over a long-sleeved tee and faded jeans, the jeans tented at his crotch. Sofia quirked a brow suggestively. "Is that so?"

Flashing a wolfish smile, Ben's eyes narrowed on her. She was his quarry. He stepped inside, kicking the door shut with a booted foot. Tread purposeful, he stalked her, cupping her head in his hand and bending to seal his mouth to hers.

Tongue insistent, Ben guided Sofia until she was trapped against the kitchen wall. Making a growling noise in his throat, he untied the sash to her robe, slinging it aside.

He trailed the pads of his fingers across her naked hip to the apex of her thighs. When Ben's thumb grazed her clit, she broke away, panting. His breath was hot as he bit the apple of her cheek, then kissed her ear. Raspy-voiced, he murmured, "I need you, Sofia. Now."

His words sent a jolt of lust zooming with lightning speed directly to her core. Weak-kneed and fingers tremulous with urgency, Sofia sought the waistband of his jeans and unbuttoned his fly. He wasn't the only one needing—she craved Ben. Burned for him. She could think of nothing but him buried deep inside her.

Yanking his jeans down his corded thighs, Sofia fondled his swollen length through his briefs. Precum leaked through the fabric. Ben exhaled harshly as she circled her thumb on his tip.

Slanting her head back, she studied his face, which was fixed in intense concentration. She held his hooded gaze as she dragged his briefs down. When his cock sprung free, Sofia wrapped her hand around him and pumped once. Twice. His flesh was rock hard. Responsive. Ben's pupils dilated.

Palming her ass, he ran his hand along Sofia's leg and hooked her right knee around his hip. He pressed his body close, his left palm braced on the wall beside her head. Adjusting himself, he drove into her.

Ben understood Sofia's body. How to please her. He knew the exact angle to tilt his pelvis to hit her G-spot, each stroke geared to maximize her gratification. She was consumed by him, her senses engulfed with his tangy aftershave and musky skin as he pounded into her. By the sixth thrust, Sofia came. It was sublime.

Then, with a groan, Ben spilled his seed.

If he hadn't propped her against the wall while they caught their breath, Sofia would've crumpled to the floor. "Wow."

His chin rested on the top of her head. "You have no idea how many cold showers I've taken these last weeks. I'm as randy as a damn fifteen-year-old."

Sofia nibbled her bottom lip, feeling naughty. "Do you ever fantasize about me while you jerk off?"

The rumble of his chuckle had her grinning. He asked, "What do you think?"

"Oh you nasty."

Still chuckling, Ben led Sofia across the room to her bed, tugging at her to join him. He undressed and laid down. When she stretched out next to him, he scooted into her. Spooning Sofia, he slung his arm around her midsection and curled his hand around her breast. "I wanted to give you time. Respect your boundaries."

Boundaries, Sofia thought. Her soul delighted at Ben's closeness, but she reminded herself to hold back and safeguard her heart. They didn't typically engage in pillow talk. She didn't know how that worked. Tentatively, she asked, "Are you... satisfied... with our, uh, no strings arrangement?"

He kneaded her breast, grinding into her. His arousal poked her backside. "*Satisfied* isn't in my vocabulary when it concerns you."

Sofia didn't reply. Closing her eyes, she submitted to his touch. He kissed her shoulder blade as his fingers plucked her nipple.

"It won't be quick this time," he whispered into her hair.

AFTER, they dozed. At ten, Sofia got up and washed. Dressing in yoga pants and a sweater, she then put her bracelet on and blew out the candle on the dresser. Ben snored, an arm thrown over his head.

Settling cross-legged on her chair by the window, she picked up her novel. She reread the same passage multiple times. It was futile—she couldn't focus.

To her, what just transpired in her bed wasn't fucking. It was lovemaking. How could she not develop an emotional attachment? What would Ben say when asked his opinion about whether they had *made love*?

"Come back to bed."

She acquiesced, perching on the edge of the mattress yet feeling brittle.

"Maybe it's only me," he said gruffly, lacing his fingers with hers, "but you seem disconnected. I wonder, are you tiring of me?"

Sofia's brow pleated in confusion. "Tiring of you? Why do you say that? I enjoyed every minute. I thought that was obvious."

"Physically, yes. I can't put my finger on it, but you've been different." He swallowed, his face shuttering. "It's what I told you about River Heights. It's changed us, hasn't it?"

"What? No!"

"Then what? Talk to me, Sofia."

"I've changed. *We* haven't changed," she insisted.

"Do you mean the warehouse? Are you still wrestling with it?" Ben sighed when she disengaged her hand. "You're becoming agitated. Why're you acting evasive? Why can't you talk to me?"

"Why are you pressuring me?"

"We had a connection once. Now, the more I try to connect, the further you retreat. Even during sex, I can feel a wall between us."

Sofia's cheeks stung as her anxiety hitched. She didn't know what to say. What tact to take. Frustration was the easiest to pounce on. "You didn't have to react the way you did when you found out about Kate's pregnancy."

"What does Kate have to do with *us*?"

"Please. Stop playing. It's clear you're still in love with her."

"No, I'm not *in* love with Kate. Not anymore. Haven't been for ages, but I do love her and always will. I owe her my life."

"Not *in* love with her? That's not the impression I received. Why did you freak out at the bonfire?"

"Because I was angry! Procreating during the zombie apocalypse—when there aren't obstetricians or emergency rooms—is fucking asinine!"

Sofia slid from the bed, arms intersecting over her breastbone. She averted her gaze. Everything was screwed up. She'd lost control. Logic eluded her. "It doesn't matter. I have no claim over you. We agreed when we started this."

"*You* set the terms, remember? You swore you needed dick, not a relationship."

"I didn't. I don't!"

Ben now stood behind her. The warmth of his naked body radiated. "Then why do you sound resentful?"

Her voice was unnatural to her own ears when she asked, "Why does a connection matter if it's only sex? Why do you care?"

Taking hold of her upper arm, Ben swung her around. His expression was dark with irritation. He crouched until their gazes were level. "For fuck's sake, I'm tempted to shake you until your teeth rattle," he barked. "Talk. To. Me."

Shouting from outside. Somebody banged relentlessly on the door.

"Shit," Ben muttered, releasing her to scoop his jeans from the floor.

"Sofia? Ben?" A man.

Sofia nudged the curtain aside and peeked out the window as Ben stepped into his jeans. The porch light illuminated Kevin, his body language panicky. Flustered. He hopped from foot to foot as he knocked.

"Hold up!" Ben buttoned his fly and unlatched the door. "Kevin, what's the trouble?"

"Fire!" Kevin gesticulated wildly toward the hill. It was dark, but Sofia saw Bella and Josh running helter-skelter up the lane.

The acrid stench of smoke wafted through the doorway and to Sofia. Ben pulled on his shirt. "Put your sneakers on, Sofia."

Kevin's dentures slipped when he replied, "Shtill blew! It shpread to one of the outbuildingsh already! Hurry!"

Ben ordered in a clipped tone as he laced his boots, "If nobody has done it yet, go hook the garden hose to the spigot by the kitchen door, Kevin. We'll be up shortly."

Turning on his heel, Kevin hastened down the porch steps and loped in the direction Bella and Josh had gone.

Sofia slipped into her sneakers then twisted her hair into a clip, her hands shaking. Ben had tied his bootlaces and was ready to go. He held his hand out, and she grasped it. Before stepping over the threshold, Ben pivoted to her, his face earnest.

"We aren't done talking, Sofia. Not by a long shot. I'm gonna get to the bottom of what's going on with you if it's the last thing I do."

At the crest of the hill, orange and yellow flames blazed against the onyx sky, the inferno devouring a corner of the machine shed. Figures rushed to and fro, their voices echoing as they shouted. Gulping away her unease, Sofia kept pace with Ben as he raced up the gravel lane.

CHAPTER FIFTY-THREE

THE BLAZE BLASTED THEM WITH SIZZLING HEAT AS THEY VALIANTLY struggled to contain it, smoke hazing their vision.

Spare hoses had been coupled to lengthen the garden hose enough to reach the machine shed. Teller trained the spray on the roof of the shed, but the stream flowing through could not touch where the flames devoured the shingles on the rafter. He instructed Milo, "Get me a ladder!"

The lean-to enclosing the still was engulfed by a hungry inferno, sparks flying. Ben, face smeared with soot and eyes watering, threw a wooden bucketful of water on the grass to quench the flames trailing from the lean-to and to the machine shed.

Fritz shouted, "What about the still?"

"The still is fucked," Ben yelled back as he exchanged his empty bucket with the full one Fritz held. "We've gotta douse the machine shed!"

A gust of wind carried a plume of biting smoke toward Sofia. She, along with those flanking her, shied away. They coughed and sputtered in unison. Her eyes smarting, Sofia took the galvanized metal pail of water from Lark and passed it to Kate, amplifying her voice to ask, "Are you sure you ought to be out here, Kate?"

"If the machine shed burns, the equipment inside will burn. Can't have that. I'll be alright," Kate assured her as she handed the full pail to Trina, swapping it for an empty one.

At first, caught unawares, they'd run in circles like a flock of decapitated chickens. Then, they conquered the chaos, fetching pails and forming a human chain—a bucket brigade. Empty buckets were exchanged with full ones to keep a steady supply of water traveling to the front of the line.

Josh dipped a bucket into the water trough outside the pole barn. It went from him to Rob, then Bella, to Nese, to Adam, then to Lark who passed it to Sofia. Kate was next in line. She forwarded it to Trina, who transferred it along to Fritz. Fritz was behind Ben, who was at the helm.

Kate coughed, then hiked the neckline of her pajama shirt to cover her mouth and nose. She switched buckets with Sofia. "Edna stayed at the house in case the kids wake up."

"Hey," Lark said. Her eyelids were rimmed red, and tears tracked down her cheeks. "Didn't I see a commercial-grade fire extinguisher in the livestock barn?"

Sofia nodded, wiping the sooty grime from her eyes. She handed another empty bucket to Lark and then a full one to Kate. "I'll get it."

"Hurry, for chrissake!"

Sofia jogged along the gravel toward the barn behind the farmhouse, picturing where she'd last seen the fire extinguisher. It hung inside the door on a metal hook. She'd grab it and rejoin the battle.

The smoke dispersed a bit as she closed the distance to the barn. The air was cold, a shock to her system. It made her lungs ache. Pausing, she hacked up black phlegm. As she spit on the ground, she sighted a vehicle parked behind the house. It was the cupcake van, doors ajar. Why was it there? Were her eyes playing tricks on her? Sofia rubbed them and blinked. The van wasn't a mirage.

"What the..." Sofia went to it and peered inside. The keys were in the ignition. She glanced over her shoulder and down the lane where the fire raged. Forehead wrinkling in consternation, she climbed the concrete stairs and entered the house. "Edna?"

Every light in the house appeared to be on, but there was no response. Should Sofia get backup?

Muted barking from upstairs. A thump.

Without further thought, she ascended the stairs, two at a time.

Edna was sprawled face down on the landing, her nightdress around her thighs. Blood soaked her gray hair. It puddled under her cheek.

"Oh no!" Sofia gasped, stooping to examine her. Edna was alive, her breaths shallow. Sofia placed her fingers on Edna's throat to assess her pulse. Thin. Thready. "Edna, it's Sofia. Can you hear me?"

A cry broke through the stillness. Then, more muted barking. Sofia leaped up. The noises originated from the bedroom at the end of the hall—the room the boys shared.

Tiptoeing, Sofia slinked down the narrow corridor. The door was cracked, the ceiling fixture on. Her jaw dropped in disbelief. Jan stood at the window, holding Maggie in her arms. Maggie's face was screwed up and flushed with the promise of an impending wail. The other four children were lined up along the wall, gagged and bound. Ace whined from inside the closet. The door bounced in the jamb as he jumped against it, trying to free himself.

Sofia demanded, "What the *hell*, Jan?"

The floorboards creaked behind Sofia, and she spun around.

Kevin. His eyes gleamed with malevolence.

He raised a tire iron. The end was painted with Edna's blood.

Stomach lurching in horror, Sofia retreated into the bedroom, hands up. "Wait—"

Advancing, Kevin brought the tire iron down, thwacking Sofia in the temple. She staggered.

Astonishment and pain mingled, rendering her senseless. Sofia's vision doubled. She touched her temple, then brought her fingers to her nose. Red. Wet. She was bleeding! A wave of dizziness overcame her. Sofia slumped onto the bed. Head throbbing, she was aware of her wrists being zip-tied behind her back. Blood trickled in her eye. It saturated the blanket under her cheek.

Maggie let out a lusty howl, and the kids writhed against their shackles. Ace resumed barking, frenzied to break loose from his confines. Muzzily, as if she were in a nightmare, Sofia observed Jan cram a sock in Maggie's mouth. She counted the other kids. They were all there—Nora, Ravi, Gretchen, and Ted—gawping at Sofia, wide-eyed with terror, mutely beseeching her to save them. Sofia lamented her choice to not get backup. She whispered to them, "I'm sorry."

"What will we do with her? Leave her or take her?" Jan asked Kevin over the cacophony of Ace's noise. Maggie screamed into her gag, her eyes bugging.

"The baby," Sofia protested. "Please, pull the sock out!"

Kevin thumped Sofia on the butt with the tire iron in warning, but Jan adjusted Maggie's gag. He told Jan, "May ash well bring her along. She'sh a shcore."

"You're right. She *is* a score," Jan replied, nodding and beaming, her rotted teeth on display. She grabbed Nora by a flaxen braid and pulled. "Up! You behave yourself or the baby gets it. That goes for all you brats."

Kevin prodded Sofia in the spine. "On your feet."

Sofia was lethargic. Her muscles refused to obey.

Jan snatched Maggie's arm and wrenched it. Maggie flinched. Jan sneered, "Shall I snap it?"

"No, no," Sofia cried. "Please, no!"

"On. Your. Feet," Kevin repeated, and Sofia scrabbled to comply. "Fat bish."

Maggie on her hip, Jan descended the stairway, pilot of the procession. The kids were sandwiched between her and Kevin. Kevin had stuffed a onesie from a basket of clean laundry into Sofia's mouth before putting her in a headlock. Still wobbly, blood in her eye, and her air restricted, she prayed she wouldn't trip as she clumsily traversed the steep stairs.

Sofia twirled out of Kevin's grasp when they reached the van, vacillating between wanting to run and not wanting to abandon the kids. She couldn't ascertain whether the fire had been extinguished—the air was clouded by thick smoke. Yelling drifted to the farmhouse. With her gag, she couldn't call out for aid. Why hadn't someone come to check what had delayed her? Hadn't she been absent long enough for them to notice?

Kevin shoved her into the rear of the van, then tossed the kids on top of her before getting into the driver's seat. Jan slammed the sliding door, rounding the van to hop into the passenger seat, dragging Maggie with her like a rag doll.

The kids were mounded on Sofia, compressing her thorax. They flopped around like fish, trying to right themselves. Moaning into her gag, Sofia hauled herself from under the pile and to her knees. The plexiglass window was opaque. She couldn't see anything, but she feared that by the time the others realized they were gone, it would be too late.

"Enough of thesh damn thingsh," Kevin said as he started the van. He removed his dentures and threw them on the dashboard.

As Kevin accelerated down the lane and away from the house—away from where Ben and the others fought the fire— the engine hiccupped. Sofia craned her neck to eye the fuel gauge. An eighth of a tank. She held her breath, waiting to see if the engine would stall. The trusty van chugged along.

Shit!

The side windows afforded little vantage. The sky was too

dark. Too smoke-filled. Sofia's heart sank. There was no search party. No hero to rescue them. Nauseous, she slumped against the bench seat, disheartened.

They were at the main entrance. Punching the remote control on the visor, Kevin idled until the gate opened. He sped through it and into the abyss.

CHAPTER FIFTY-FOUR

THE VAN STOPPED FIFTEEN MINUTES LATER. KEVIN AND JAN HAULED their captives out and dumped them unceremoniously on the ground. The kids stayed in a huddle, shaking and sniffling. Even Maggie, who was unrestrained, didn't wander.

Rolling over and getting onto her knees, Sofia hobbled closer to them, hoping her presence consoled them. If necessary, she'd shield their bodies with her own.

Scanning their surroundings, Sofia was startled to recognize the squat tan stucco building they were parked beside—Mergenville Pet Hospital.

There was scuffling of boots on the blacktop. Their steps neared, flashlight beams haloing a circle of gold over their path. Coming to a standstill three feet from the van, they swept their flashlights over the kids and Sofia. Eyes downcast, she tried not to draw their captors' attention.

"Y'all are proving to be our top producers. Plump ones are rare," the man on the left said. He shook hands with Kevin and clapped him on the back. Then he kissed Jan on the cheek. "And children are an indulgence indeed."

"We lucked into the opportunity, Tommy," Jan replied, brushing off his praise. "We would've arrived a lot sooner, but we had to bide our time. The ones in charge at that place were shrewd. Woman even claimed to know me from somewhere. Kevin had to start a fire to distract them so we could leave before she recalled me."

"You made it home, darlin'. That's all that matters. Six is a number to be proud of," the other man complimented. He had the crackly, gravelly tones of someone of advanced age.

"Anybody else back?" Kevin asked as he went to unlock the van's rear liftgate.

"Covey brought two women. Ernest and Ida provided four more," Tommy replied.

Jan preened, "We *are* the top producers."

"Indeed you are. You'll be treated like royalty, honey," the elderly man said, side hugging her. "Kevin, what are you doing back there?"

Kevin rummaged around in the van's trunk area behind the farthest bench seat. When he rounded the van he had an armful of wine bottles. He'd filched homemade wine from Mayfly Hollow's storeroom. "More where this came from."

"Anyone still awake?" Jan asked. "We can celebrate our bounty. Party hearty."

"Rog, why don't you and Jan roust the gang while Kevin and I take care of," Tommy inclined his head toward Sofia and the children, "this?"

Kevin handed Jan and Rog the bottles of wine. They strolled to the building, chatting and laughing. Kevin told Sofia, "C'mon."

As Sofia clambered upright, Tommy kneeled to collect Maggie. He was a slight man with sandy hair, pock-marked skin, and a scruffy beard. Maggie's eyes were enormous in her tiny face, but she didn't resist as he hoisted her. "All y'all come along now."

Sofia chafed at how meekly the kids followed Tommy's orders, but what else could they do? Cooperation would buy

Sofia time to strategize. It was up to her to figure out how to get them out of this mess.

Kevin's rough hand snaked around Sofia's forearm. He escorted her around the building, Tommy and the kids filing behind them. Clouds covering the moon coasted away. Sofia's pupils adjusted to their environment. What had originally been homogenous inky blackness was now cast in distinctive shades of silver and black. The half-dozen L-shaped kennels were straight ahead. They weren't about to stash them *there*, were they?

Tommy had a keychain hooked to his belt loop. He twisted a key in the padlock at the chain link panel that served as the entrance to the kennel nearest the clinic.

Kevin prodded Sofia. Knock-kneed, she stepped inside. Tommy reached for her gag. Her saliva had dried, fusing the fabric to her lips. Her skin tore as Tommy yanked the onesie from her mouth. He pitched it into the kennel. "Nobody around to help you here so no use hollering. I'm holding you account-able for keeping these kids in line. We hear a ruckus, we'll cut out all y'all's tongues. Savvy?"

Sofia nodded, mouth pursed.

"Speak!"

"Yes," Sofia croaked.

"Turn." Taking a penknife from his pants pocket, Kevin sliced the zip tie from her wrists before jostling her deeper into the kennel.

One by one, Kevin cut the kids' binds and removed their gags before shoving them into the enclosure with Sofia.

Tommy held Maggie out to Sofia, and she seized her, bringing the toddler to her chest. Maggie shivered.

"Sofia." Nora was at her elbow. She whispered, "I have to go to the bathroom."

"Latrine over yonder." Tommy pointed to the shadowy part of the kennel, then closed the padlock, locking them in.

He and Kevin left them, entering the vet clinic through the back door and slamming it behind them.

Sofia licked her lips, dying for a drink of water. She imagined the kids were, too. Maggie burrowed her face in Sofia's sweater, her chest wracking with silent sobs. Verging on tears herself, Sofia looked down at her charges. They stared back, their eyes solemn.

Five children depended on her to provide safety and comfort. Their well-being was a tremendous responsibility. Daunting. If anything happened to them, Sofia would have a lot to answer for, especially if Maggie was injured... or worse. Swallowing hard, she visualized explaining to Kate and Teller. Her head pounded, causing a cramp of nausea. Feeling faint, Sofia touched her temple. The wound was sensitive but no longer bled. A scab had formed.

She swayed, sagging against the chain link and clinging to Maggie. *Think. Think.*

"Sofia," Nora whispered, "you better sit. You're super hurt."

"I-I'm okay.

A low voice intoned, "Hi."

Sofia started, wheeling around. A petite Asian—perhaps Japanese—woman emerged from the recesses of the enclosure. Her shoulder-length hair was tangled, and her clothes were wrinkled.

"I didn't mean to frighten you. I'm Himari. May I give you a hand?" Himari gently assisted Sofia as she folded into a sitting position.

Head spinning, Sofia murmured her thanks.

Himari squinted at her temple. "That's recent."

"Uh huh."

Himari tsked. "Needs stitches. I'd be concerned about concussion as well."

Sofia bit back a hysterical cackle. "I think that's the least of my problems right now, Himari."

Nora clenched her knees together and fidgeted. "I really have to *go*, Sofia."

"I can show you." A stooped woman with a buzz cut melted from the shadows, followed by another woman, and then another. In addition to Himari, there were five women of various ages and ethnicities. When Sofia's gaze landed on a craggy-faced one with dirty blonde hair and dirt-streaked clothes, she froze.

Sadie.

CHAPTER FIFTY-FIVE

SADIE FRANKLY REGARDED SOFIA, HER EXPRESSION MOURNFUL. SHE said nothing, but by the way she slouched, Sofia comprehended. Sadie wasn't spoiling for a fight. She was browbeaten by her circumstances.

"Grace," said the stooped lady who'd offered to show Nora to the latrine, then the rest spoke in turn, identifying themselves.

"Francine." Tall, willowy.

"Jo." Dark-skinned. Skeletal frame. Sympathetic eyes.

"Beth." Average height, wide-hipped.

Sofia introduced herself and the children. Grace put an arm around Nora and ushered her into the far corner of the kennel.

The women took seats alongside Sofia, huddling for warmth. They encouraged the children to sit on their laps. Sensing kindness, the kids settled in. Cold seeped into Sofia's bones. The air was chilly, as was the concrete pad beneath them. They all shivered.

Poor babies, Sofia thought sorrowfully as she scrutinized their night attire. Toddler Maggie and little Ted—four years old —wore footed pajamas. Everyone else had on either nightgowns or garb wholly unsuitable for camping outdoors during September in upstate NY. Most didn't even have socks.

Ravi was in Francine's lap, teeth chattering. His t-shirt provided insufficient protection from the weather. Francine rubbed her palms on his bare arms, then gathered him to her bosom.

Maggie sneezed. Sofia lifted her sweater and stretched it over Maggie so they were skin-to-skin. She asked the women, "How long have you been here?"

"A day and a half," Francine replied. She indicated Beth, who cuddled seven-year-old Gretchen. "A guy called Covey accosted us in the woods outside River Heights."

"We were tricked into coming to this place yesterday," Himari said, "by a couple who'd joined us last week. Me, Sadie, Grace, and Jo had been traveling together. We were managing. We never should've trusted them. Ida and Ernest."

"They were talented liars," Sadie spat.

Jo added, "They claimed they had an idea for where we could possibly spend winter, in Mergenville. Ida said she'd been a bookkeeper at a vet clinic. That keys were hidden under a flowerpot."

"I worked here summers during high school," Sofia said, "but that name isn't familiar."

Grace and Nora came back. They joined the group, lowering to the concrete.

"Alright?" Sofia asked Nora, and she nodded. Sadie snagged Sofia's gaze. Lungs still irritated from the fire, Sofia coughed up a glob of phlegm. She rotated away to spit through the chain link before inquiring of Sadie, "You didn't return to the warehouse?"

"You two know each other?" Grace breathed from beside Sofia. "How?"

"Month ago we crossed paths," Sadie answered while Sofia hacked again. "Her people and my people... clashed."

Jo tilted her chin. "What's this about a warehouse?"

"My father owned it." Sofia paused to catch her air. "I took my group to scavenge supplies, not realizing Sadie's people were occupying it."

"Supplies... like *food*?" Jo demanded.

Sofia said, "Yes."

Jo asked Sadie, "You knew where there was food? Why didn't you share that information with us?"

"Because I thought they'd taken over the warehouse! I wasn't messin' with them—they murdered two guys," Sadie growled, then asked Sofia, "You didn't stay there?"

Nobody seemed outraged by Sofia's people killing Sadie's people. Sofia supposed turf wars were par for the course these days. She said, "We have our own place—a nice place. Adam's one of us. He goes out to recruit... to bring survivors to our farm. Nese, Trina, Jan, and Kevin came home with us."

"Not Marta?"

"No. Adam didn't believe she'd be a fit."

"I didn't have an issue with her. Marta doesn't eff around, but you know where you stand with her." Sadie lobbed Sofia an irate look. "If I'd realized you guys went away, I woulda gone back to the warehouse. And I wouldn't be here."

Sofia was contrite. "We never meant you any harm, Sadie. Tucker and Kyle forced us into a position where we *had* to defend ourselves—remember, we were willing to back off."

Sadie sighed. "Yeah. Well. Who cares anymore?"

"So," Sofia said, gaze roving over the women. "Why have we been abducted? Why are we in this kennel?"

Francine shrugged. "We hardly see them. When we do, they don't acknowledge us. At sundown yesterday, a girl delivered a wooden bucket of water and tossed us a sack of apples. Same as tonight. Guy with a gun accompanied her to discourage us from trying anything."

"Water?" Sofia asked, perking up. "Any left over?"

"Sorry."

Sofia exhaled, crestfallen. Her eyes stung. She wiped charcoal-colored grit from her eyelids. "How many of *them* are there?"

Beth used her fingers to count. "Five? Six?"

"Plus Jan and Kevin, who abducted us," Sofia said.

Sadie looked at Sofia, taken aback. "Jan and Kevin *abducted you?*"

Sofia inhaled swiftly. Her brain was so disordered that she'd not thought to interrogate Sadie about her connection to them. "Yes. Any idea why?"

"No." Sadie hitched a shoulder. "Those weirdos seemed harmless. I barely knew them."

Sofia's gaze probed her. No. There was no dishonesty there. Shrugging, she said to Himari, "If only we could overpower our abductors."

Himari shook her head. "Not feasible. We'd have to free ourselves from this pen first, and they have weapons."

"Sofia," Jo said, "we spent all night trying to pull a post from the cement—there's a spot where it's loose. No dice."

"We've been over every damn inch of the chain link, checking for weak points," Sadie added. Her face scrunched as if she were about to weep.

Sofia tipped her head, surveying the metal canopy that roofed the kennel.

"Forget it," Francine said. "Hopeless. This place is like Fort Knox."

Maggie's respirations evened out. She'd fallen asleep under Sofia's sweater. Ted yawned. Nora's eyelids fluttered.

Fatigue dragging at her and head throbbing, Sofia murmured, "I can't think."

"Let's get some shut-eye," Beth suggested. "Tomorrow's another day."

THE NIGHT WAS AGONIZING. Never ending. Between the nippy temperature and the hard, cold slate of the concrete slab beneath them, they all felt rough when they got up at dawn. They stretched and groaned, looking worse for the wear.

Muscles protesting, Sofia lapped the perimeter of the kennel like a caged lioness. L-shaped, it measured approximately fifteen feet by five feet in the elongated portion of the L and seven feet by five feet in the shorter part. The bucket serving as the latrine was located in the shorter section. The dog carcasses Sofia had seen before when she and Ben came for kitten formula were heaped into a corner across from the bucket.

The exercise warmed her. She studied the chain link panels, the metal fasteners that attached the panels to the posts, and the roof. She tested the post Jo had referred to. It wiggled, but Sofia doubted it would loosen enough to allow egress. Without tools, they'd never breach the enclosure. Despondency welled. She kicked the post with her sneaker.

Jo paced with Maggie, who articulated *hungry* in baby sign language to Sofia. She knew a handful of words but hadn't learned how to string them together. Since the trauma of the kidnapping, Maggie communicated exclusively via signing. Sofia's heart squeezed in pity at her regression, understanding Maggie's confusion. When Jo soothed her, Maggie repeated *hungry* while whimpering.

Rubbing her forehead, Sofia spun, unable to watch any further. If she'd had any moisture left in her body, she'd cry, but she was dehydrated. They all were.

Sofia steepled her fingers and prayed to God for Ben to find them, somehow. Her thoughts spiraled. What if her friends hadn't been able to quench the fire? What if it had spread from building to building and all that remained of the homestead was ash? Had everyone perished?

"They extinguished the flames. They saved the machinery in the machine shed. The fire didn't spread. They're alive," Sofia said aloud. She'd manifest it to reality.

In her mind's eye, she envisioned Kate finding Edna when she went upstairs to look in on the kids. The panic of realizing the children were missing, along with Jan, Kevin, and Sofia. Everyone congregating in the kitchen, weary and lungs full of soot, trying to wrap their heads around it. Kate would be frantic —everyone would be, especially Ben. Sofia knew he'd be freaking the fuck out.

Sofia closed her eyes. *Please let me have the chance to see Ben again.* She'd fall on her sword. Lay herself bare. Be vulnerable. Admit she was in love with him. Say she was sorry to complicate their relationship and would leave it in his hands. If he wanted to break up, so be it, but she couldn't die without confessing the truth to him. And Lark. She owed her an apology, too. She'd been annoyed with Lark's advice although it had been sound. Sofia's annoyance was because deep down, she knew Lark was right. She needed to grow up.

The day stretched on, tummies grumbling from hunger, and nothing to occupy their minds. Sofia unfastened her bracelet and gave it to Maggie to entertain her. Nora and Gretchen played tic-tac-toe on the cement pad, dragging fingertips through the dust. The women were generally quiet, putting on a brave face. Their predicament weighed on them, but they wanted to be upbeat to spare the kids as much as was in their power.

When the sun had set low on the horizon, the clinic's rear door creaked open. A teenage girl had a five-gallon pail of water and a mesh sack of apples. The pail was heavy. Every few feet, the girl sat it on the sidewalk before continuing toward the kennels. Tommy joined her, a pistol in his grip.

Sofia's eyes went round at their approach. The teenager was no stranger.

CHAPTER FIFTY-SIX

THE GIRL'S GAZE CONNECTED WITH HERS. HER HAIR HAD GROWN, but it was definitely Mik Chalmers, from Calhoun. Before Sofia could utter a word, Mik slightly shook her head.

Sofia frowned. Mik did not acknowledge her. Instead, she schooled her face with a blank expression and unlocked the padlock. Tommy glared, menacing them by pointing the gun indiscriminately into the kennel while Mik placed the water pail with a ladle just inside the enclosure. She emptied the bag of apples onto the cement pad before backing away.

After Mik fastened the padlock, she and Tommy strode back to the clinic. She didn't look at Sofia again until Tommy was indoors. Her gaze conveyed a warning. Then, she disappeared inside.

The kids fell upon the apples. Using the plastic ladle, Sofia drank thirstily from the bucket. She felt like her soft tissues were a sponge absorbing the water. Her headache eased after eating the meager meal, but her mind raced as she came to terms with seeing Mik with their captors. She'd seemed like a decent girl. Not evil. What was her association with them?

Propped against a post, Sofia dozed in fits, snuggling Maggie. The group clustered together to conserve body heat—it was colder than the night before. She dreamed of Ben and her parents. Of happier days.

When the sky transformed into the misty somber gray of predawn, a voice beside her intoned, "Sofia?"

Sofia jolted awake. Mik crouched outside the kennel. "Oh my God. Mik?"

"Yup." She put her hand up to still Sofia.

"But I don't get it," Sofia whispered hoarsely, not wanting to wake the others.

"They think I'm one of 'em, but I ain't. I know all about them motherfuckers. I sneak away and search Mergenville Drug when I can. I'm tryin' to find some kinda sleeping pill I can crush into a powder. Then I'm gonna," she slid a finger across her throat, "once they pass out."

"Whoa." Sofia's eyebrows inched up her scalp, which made her injury smart. She winced. "Who are they? Why'd they abduct us?"

"You don't know? They're roamers, Sofia. They want to eat y'all," she muttered grimly, her blue eyes doleful.

Mouth gaping, Sofia stared at Mik. *No.*

Mik grimaced, presenting her teeth. She tapped a brown incisor with a grubby fingernail. "They think I'm a roamer too 'cause of my dentals. They can't sniff us out no more, and some of 'em are kinda dumb. Kicker is, although they can eat regular food, they're hungry for people. Tommy brought a woman last week. They chopped her up."

"*What?*"

"Yup. That's when I started my trips to the drug store. I gotta kill 'em. No question." She pressed her lips together in distaste, then confided, "They can't chew good, so they chopped her up in teeny tiny pieces. Foul."

"You ate *human flesh*?"

"Shh." Mik's gaze darted to the clinic. "No. I ain't no cannibal! They share the regular food, but say I gotta earn my place at the table for *that*—I'm not in the inner circle yet. I do chores for now."

Sofia reeled from the onslaught of information, her brain sluggish.

"I'll go again today if I can. They're talkin' about *feastin'* again, so time's short. Once I can slip the medicine into their wine, and they're unconscious, I'll bring the key out here and unlock the padlock. Kevin said the van's on fumes. Think it'll get you home?"

"I don't know."

"I'll bring the key fob anyhow."

A thought occurred to Sofia. "Mik," she said urgently, grabbing the chain link, "listen. Don't bother with the town pharmacy. Doc Gil stocked a variety of medications in his office. Look through the built-in cabinet behind his desk for a tranquilizer in pill form."

"Got a brand? A name?"

"No, sorry. Liable to be grouped with sedatives though."

"I'll do my best, Sofia," Mik vowed, then grinned. "Told ya I owed ya, right?"

Sofia returned the grin, hope blooming in her chest. "You did."

"If I can find something, I'll try to dose 'em at supper, okay? I got to go now." She briefly clasped Sofia's hand through the chain link. "Hang in, alright?"

* * *

SOFIA VIBRATED with nervous energy the remainder of the day.

Mik had chutzpah. Sofia admired her, every bit of her optimism hinging on Mik's scheme. The group's morale plummeted as the day wore on. Sofia yearned to tell the others about Mik but thought it wiser not to.

Maggie had cried herself out. Sofia held her until her arms ached. Hollow-eyed, the kids cowered together against the chain link. The sun's rays offered a modicum of relief from the cold, but the entire group was glum. For Sofia, it harkened back horrendous memories of her winter spent at the warehouse.

They ran out of water by mid-day, despite strict rationing. Without extra diapers, Maggie developed a wicked rash from sitting in a soiled one. Sofia removed it and fashioned another from the onesie Kevin had thrown into the kennel. Using the latrine bucket was both gross and humiliating—they had no toilet paper. They were filthy, stinky, ravenous, and freezing. Nobody was happy.

Sofia fantasized about arriving home. Into Ben's arms. There'd be a delicious meal. Then, once she ate, she'd take a bubble bath in Ben's jetted garden tub. Wash her hair. Scrub her fingernails. After, she would dress in her pajamas and lay on the couch with a blanket, drinking tea and watching a DVD with Ben and Nora. Once the movie concluded, they'd tuck Nora into bed. Sofia would seduce Ben. They'd sleep together in his bed, spooning, and when they woke, she and Ben and Nora would have pancakes. Like an actual family.

She closed her eyes. If Mik found a tranquilizer. If she was able to mix it into their drinks. If the dose was enough to conk them out. If they didn't awaken and foil Mik's plans.

If. If. If.

"Where are you from?" the lady named Beth asked.

Sofia's eyelids flickered open. "We have a farm. It's in Colliers Junction, on the River Heights side."

"You said it was nice."

"The nicest," Sofia said, her eyes pricking with unshed tears. "You see, there's a man there."

"Ah," Beth said.

"I..." Sofia trailed off. "Ben. I love him, but I've been a coward about telling him. Now I may never get the chance to."

"Do you have a faith, Sofia?"

"You kidding? I was raised by a devout Catholic mother. I

had to beg to transfer to public school when I was a freshman. You?"

"I believe in God," Beth said, head against the chain link and ankles intersected. "Tell me about this Ben."

Sofia described their meeting. "He said he was too old for me, and he thought he had feelings for his ex. But I convinced him."

"You won him over."

Snorting delicately, Sofia said, "My smoking hot body did."

Beth laughed.

"If I survive this, I'm telling him how I feel, even if it's one-sided."

"Not love a pretty girl like you? I can't imagine that." Beth smiled at Sofia. There was no guile there.

"If we get out of here, would you like to visit my home?"

"I'd be honored. Maybe you can introduce me to your Ben."

At sunset, Mik brought another sack of apples and took the pail inside, refilling it while Tommy lingered at the door of the kennel, aiming his gun. He seemed to get perverse pleasure from frightening the children.

Before they returned to the clinic, Mik chucked a significant glance in Sofia's direction.

It was on.

CHAPTER FIFTY-SEVEN

GUTS CHURNING, SOFIA PICKED AT A HANGNAIL AND CROOKED HER neck to assess the moon's position. It was way past midnight.

The women snored, leaning on each other, the children in their laps. Maggie was bundled under Sofia's sweater in a fitful slumber. The cold was unrelenting.

Waiting for Mik to appear with the keys to the kennel that night had been nothing short of agony. Sofia was tense. Edgy. Her gaze rarely strayed from the clinic's door. Eyes burning, she shut them for a minute, willing Mik to creep out, tiptoe to the gate, and unlock the padlock. They'd gather the children and run to the van. Peel away from this goddamn nightmare. As hours passed, and Mik didn't appear, Sofia started panicking.

What if she'd been caught spiking the wine? What if the Zs had hurt Mik? Murdered her?

No matter how restless Sofia was, she didn't dare get up and pace the kennel. She'd wake the others. There would be questions. Instead, muscles griping, she stayed seated and watched the door.

Movement by the clinic registered, and Sofia jumped, her palms dampening with sweat. Maggie twitched, and she patted the toddler's back until she settled again.

Was it time?

The furtive figure did not walk down the sidewalk, which was the most direct course. *Fuck*. If it was Mik, that wasn't a good sign.

Sidestepping along the edge of the clinic, they sprinted across the narrow strip of grass to the far side of the kennel, following along the perimeter.

"Sofia?"

Taking care not to jostle Maggie, Sofia turned to face the chain link. Mik crouched on the other side. "Have they passed out? Do you have the keys?"

"Naw." The dark obscured Mik's features. She sounded remorseful when she disclosed, "It didn't work. Some of 'em got sleepy, but no one passed out—I had to wait for 'em to fall asleep before comin' out to talk to ya. Ya think I used the wrong pills?"

Sofia's rib cage constricted. *It didn't work*. "I don't know. Which kind did you use?"

"Sacyerax malate I think it's called. Ya heard of it?"

"No."

"Shoot. I split the powder between three bottles of wine... they guzzled all the wine, but like I says, it didn't work."

"Meds lose potency if they're old."

"I made sure it wasn't expired. Could be it's not a strong one."

Sofia wrapped fingers around a section of chain link, her other hand supporting Maggie's rump. "So, now what?"

"There's another I can try. It's somethin' called Esepimazine. We're outta the wine Kevin brought, but there's a bottle each of whiskey and bourbon left. I'll put it in those. They always drink at night." Mik halted. Sighed. When she spoke, she was near tears. "I-I don't know if I should tell ya..."

Foreboding tinkled over Sofia. "Please, don't pull any punches with me."

"Earlier tonight, Rog and Tommy was talkin'. They decided they're gonna choose someone tomorrow... for *feastin'*." At

Sofia's sharp intake of air, Mik's chin fell to her chest. "They're tryin' to decide who. Debatin' it."

"Well?" Sofia asked. "Who are the contenders?"

Mik sniffled. "Tommy wants a kid."

Sofia's ears rang. She felt dizzy. Unable to breathe. They planned to eat one of the children, and there was nothing she could do. *Nothing!* She was fucking powerless.

"Oh man. You're hyperventilatin'." Mik covered her face with her hands to muffle her sobs. Her shoulders shook. "I shouldn't have said anything. Now you're gonna drive yourself crazy all night."

"No. You did the right thing," Sofia reassured Mik, her voice quavering. She was hit with a surge of pity for the girl. How awful it must be to live alongside the Zs, to witness their horrific behavior, to put on an act. Mik's existence was in jeopardy, too. Sofia extended a finger, and Mik hooked hers with it. "If you hadn't warned me, I-I'd be blind-sided."

"I'm so sorry, Sofia."

She combatted the helplessness and dread swirling in her chest, saying, "Me too, Mik."

"Maybe they'll change their minds." When Sofia didn't respond, Mik said, "I ain't givin' up. I never will. I promise. I'll mix the Esepimazine into the liquor when I go inside. If it's strong enough, it'll work. I know it."

Sofia nodded, hardly believing the plucky teenager held their lives in her hands. Fortifying herself, she straightened her shoulders. She met Mik's gaze. "Once they lose consciousness tomorrow night, don't kill them until you come and get me. I want to help you do it."

"You alright, Sofia?" Beth asked that afternoon, her blue eyes inquisitive. She French-braided Gretchen's waist-length brown hair. "Something ailing you?"

Sofia had been jumpy all day. It came as no surprise that somebody had picked up on the tension exuding from her. She pointed to her head, fibbing, "My, uh, cut hurts."

Sofia couldn't tell Beth the truth—that she expected Tommy to step from the clinic at any second and snatch one of the kids.

She watched Nora and Ravi whisper amongst themselves as they played a version of hopscotch at the opposite end of the kennel. Ravi was Nora's best friend, but she had been a big help with the younger kids, too. Ted had grown particularly attached to Francine. He just wanted to be cuddled. He lay an ear against Francine's breast, his skinny forearm around her abdomen, and his hazel eyes observant. Maggie was insistent about never leaving Sofia's lap. Despite Sofia's efforts, the toddler was sneezy. Between her cold and her diaper rash, Maggie was miserable. At least the afternoon sun warmed the concrete under them. That was something.

Sofia's brain continually circled back to the question that had dogged her during the night, when sleep was elusive. *Who would be chosen?*

Sofia begged God to take one of the other women rather than her or the children. Anyone but them. Did that make her a selfish person? A terrible person?

"Shall I braid your hair?" Beth asked.

Sofia dragged her gaze from where it had been zeroed on the clinic door. "Hmm?"

"Your hair. I can braid it," she said. She smiled, and a dimple by her lip appeared. "C'mon. It'll pass the time."

Sofia scooted in front of Beth, the clinic in full view by design. She adjusted Maggie, tucking the toddler's feet under her sweater.

Avoiding the cut on Sofia's head, Beth gently massaged her scalp before braiding. The pads of her fingers worked magic on the knots of tension at the base of Sofia's neck. When she groaned, Beth laughed. "You retain a lot of stress here."

"I can't imagine why I'd be stressed," Sofia murmured wryly. "Where did you learn how to do this?"

"I was a massage therapist." After she kneaded Sofia's shoulder blades, she skimmed her fingers through Sofia's hair, working out tangles at the ends of the strands. She separated the strands into sections and weaved, keeping tight to Sofia's scalp. When she finished, Beth said, "Pity I don't have an elastic."

With a lusty creak, the clinic door burst open. Tommy stepped out, Mik trailing him with a bag of apples. Conversations ceased. Nora and Ravi rushed to join the women where they sat by the kennel entrance. Sofia stiffened, her hold on Maggie tightening.

Tommy strutted to the kennel, swinging his keyring around his index finger. His gun was in a holster attached to his belt. He slid the key into the padlock. Before opening the gate, he put the keychain into his jean pocket. Unholstering the gun, he motioned for Mik to empty the apples onto the concrete. "Since we have festivities planned tonight, supper'll be early for y'all."

Mik's skin looked pasty, and her mouth was pinched, as if she were ill. Her gaze skated to Sofia as she poured the apples out of the sack and bent for the empty five-gallon pail. Before turning to get a refill of water, she allowed Sofia to see her anguish.

Sofia's heart lurched as Mik went for the water, attempting to decipher her expression. Tommy was role-playing gunslinger, training his firearm on one person and saying "Pow" before aiming at the next. They sat rigid, not risking movement.

Mik lugged the full pail down the sidewalk and placed it inside the enclosure, averting her gaze. Sofia didn't blame her when she hurried back to the clinic.

Tommy hadn't closed the gate. His eyes narrowed, and he pointed the gun at Gretchen. "You. Up. Let's go."

CHAPTER FIFTY-EIGHT

IMMOBILIZED, THE GROUP HELD THEIR BREATH AS GRETCHEN unfolded from Beth's lap and stood.

She wavered. Took a step.

Sofia blinked, incredulous. Lips parting to protest, she reached for Gretchen's wrist. Someone must act. Someone must stop this madness!

Tommy scowled with impatience. "Not you, kid. No meat on your bones." He leveled the gun at Beth. "You. Now."

Sofia snatched Gretchen to her. Relief flooded her veins, made her light-headed. Gretchen trembled, flopping against Sofia.

All eyes skittered to Beth. Face ashen, her mouth moved as she recited the *Lord's Prayer*.

"Not like you were my first choice," Tommy scoffed. When she repeated the incantation rather than abide by his command, his tone turned icy. "I don't have time for crap. Up!"

"Please," Francine pled. "Please. Have mercy."

"You want to take her place? I didn't think so." He cocked the gun and fired it into the concrete at Beth's feet.

They all shrieked. Some covered their ears. Others ducked.

Beth sat frozen. Insensate. A chunk of concrete had flown in her face, nicking her forehead. Blood dotted her skin.

Everyone scooted or crawled away. The pail of water spilled. Apples scattered haphazardly.

Sofia scrambled up, yanking Gretchen with one hand while clutching Maggie to her chest with the other. She scurried to the far corner of the enclosure. The group tagged along, except Beth.

"I'll go," she said in a mechanical voice dripping with resignation. She got on her knees then awkwardly to her feet. Before leaving the kennel, she looked back at Sofia and smiled sadly.

"Beth—" Sofia called, but she didn't respond.

Tommy instructed Beth to secure the padlock, then he shepherded her into the clinic.

In the kennel, people cried and hugged, seeking solace in each other. Sofia cradled Maggie, standing at the side of the enclosure, her gaze on the clinic door. She curled her fingers around the chain link, increasing her grip until her knuckles were white.

There was a bloodcurdling scream, then silence.

Nora came over, nestling her face into Sofia's side. She sobbed.

Jaw hurting from clenching her teeth, Sofia whispered, "I'm going to murder that bastard."

THE WATER HAD SPILLED. Apples were smashed into the cement. There would be no meal that night. It was okay. They had no appetite anyway.

Francine lay in a ball, hugging the chain link and weeping. Unsure what she could do to alleviate Francine's grief, Sofia knelt beside her. She placed a palm on her back to let Francine know that she was there. The others sat around them, embracing. Sofia was compelled to discuss Mik's plan—to offer hope—

but what if the girl hadn't been able to put the tranquilizer into the liquor bottles? What if the tranquilizer was too weak?

How much more could they bear?

Nora and Gretchen held hands. They sat next to Sofia and Maggie. Sofia had taken off her charm bracelet and handed it to Maggie, but she grasped it dispassionately.

"Sofia," Nora asked. "Is Beth dead?"

Brushing Nora's hair from her fair brow, Sofia linked gazes with her. Hesitating, she eventually said, "I won't lie to you. Yes. I think Beth is dead."

Nora swallowed, dusk darkening her cornflower blue eyes. "Are they going to… to kill *us*?"

"I hope not."

"Are you scared?"

"Yes," Sofia admitted. She gathered Nora and Gretchen close and kissed the crown of Maggie's head. "And angry. Nobody has the right to hold us against our will. To terrorize us. *Nobody*."

From inside the clinic, raucous laughter wafted. The party was under way. Francine flipped around to glare in the clinic's direction. Lifting a hand, she gave a middle finger salute.

Sofia didn't expect to sleep, but with negligible rest the previous night and the stress of Mik's visit and Beth's death, her body demanded it. With Nora and Gretchen snoring on each side of her, and Maggie slumbering under her sweater, Sofia napped.

"Hey."

Sofia jerked, disoriented. She blinked. Mik was beside her, balancing on the balls of her feet. Tommy's firearm was in a holster on her belt, along with a dagger. She had a Bowie knife, too. Sofia's pulse thrummed as she asked, "The tranquilizer worked?"

Mik nodded, beaming. "It did. They're knocked out. You still wanna…"

Her tailbone smarted. Sofia sat up. "Yes."

"You're positive?"

"Mik, those assholes aren't people. They're Zs." Her voice was husky. She coughed. "And two of them know how to find my home."

"Alright."

Sofia carefully laid Gretchen and Nora on the concrete, then lifted her sweater. Maggie's nose was clogged. She wheezed, sleeping deeply. She didn't wake when Sofia arranged her between the girls.

"Sofia?" Francine croaked. "What's happening?"

Jo stirred, sitting up.

Shushing them, Sofia quickly explained about knowing Mik. About the tranquilizer tablets and spiking their jailors' liquor.

Mik said grimly, "We're going inside to finish them."

"And get the keys to my minivan. You're free to leave if you'd like." Sofia worked the kinks from her spine. "Or you're welcome to come home with me."

"I want a knife," Francine said, lurching to her feet. "I'm coming with you."

Sofia nodded.

"Go on. I'll stay back with the kids," Jo offered. Mik passed her Tommy's pistol.

Before they left the kennel, she gave the Bowie knife to Sofia, then unsheathed the dagger for Francine. Taking a switchblade from her jean pocket, Mik headed to the clinic, Francine and Sofia hot on her heels.

The hallway inside the windowless door was dim, light spilling from the end of the hall where the waiting room and reception desk were located. Refuse littered the tile floor. Sofia picked around the trash. The metallic tang of fresh blood hung in the air. Mik shut a door halfway down the corridor.

Sofia knew that room was a combination lab and surgery space. "Is that where they butchered Beth?"

Francine blanched.

Mik nodded. "Everyone's in the waiting area. There are seven of 'em."

The space was illuminated by camping lamps placed on the reception counter. Card tables held leftover food, plastic dishes, and empty liquor bottles. The broken reception window Sofia had seen on her prior visit had been patched with cardboard and duct tape. The plate-glass window and main door were covered with old newspapers. It stank of unwashed bodies, feces, and stale liquor.

The waiting room had been lined wall-to-wall with stained mattresses. Jan and Rog lay on one, Kevin nearby. Tommy was asleep in the receptionist's chair. There were three others Sofia didn't recognize scattered on other mattresses.

"Covey. You sonofabitch," Francine hissed. He was young. Dark-haired, with a beard. She strode to him, dagger in hand. Falling on her knees, Francine stabbed him in the rib cage.

Sofia shared a glance with Mik. She said, "Go through the eye sockets. It'll pierce their brains."

Mik advanced on Jan and Rog.

With no hesitancy, Sofia went to Tommy where he sat with his head drooping on his chest. Gritting her teeth with disgust, she grabbed his hair and pulled his head back until he was in position. She lined the tip of the Bowie knife in the middle of Tommy's eyelid. Slid the blade in. There was little resistance until the hilt butted against his frontal bone.

Sofia pulled out the knife. The viscera on the blade was red and smelled of human blood. Turning, she found Mik had finished Rog and Jan and was working on Kevin.

Francine hadn't stopped stabbing Covey. She panted, her skin and clothes blood soaked. Sofia went to her, speaking soothingly. She stilled Francine, then guided the dagger to Covey's eye socket. Together they pushed the blade.

Mik stood between the couple Sofia hadn't recognized. They must be Ernest and Ida. They looked like ordinary people, but looks were deceiving—Ernest and Ida weren't people. They were monsters. After dispatching them, Mik said, "We're done here."

Sofia and Mik were unsullied—a blade in the eye socket was

a clean kill. Mik went to the reception desk and rooted in a back-pack lying on the computer keyboard. She pulled out a pair of sweatpants and a t-shirt, handing them to Francine.

"Where are the van keys?" Sofia asked Mik as Francine changed her clothes.

Mik opened a desk drawer then tossed her the minivan's key fob.

Sofia caught it. As she marched down the hallway to the back door, she said over her shoulder, "Mik, this time, you're coming home with me. No arguments."

CHAPTER FIFTY-NINE

SOFIA LOOKED UP AT THE SKY, BOWIE KNIFE AT HER SIDE. NOT YET dawn. Darkness had transformed to hazy gray, allowing her to see the outline of the kennels ahead.

Figures moved inside the enclosure as the women roused the children. There was the murmur of conversation.

Nora's sleep-smudged eyes widened as Sofia, Mik, and Francine stopped at the kennel gate. "Sofia, where were you?"

"Getting the keys to the van," Sofia said, flashing Nora a smile. Her breath vaporized in the chilly air.

Maggie used the chain link to get to her feet, toddling toward Sofia. Sofia bent to pick her up and kissed her cheek. Adrenaline made her shaky, urging her to hurry. To get into the van and leave.

Handing Maggie to Mik, Sofia turned to the women who now stood with Gretchen, Nora, Ravi, and Ted. They didn't seem to know what to say. They surveyed Sofia wordlessly, their eyes drifting to Mik.

"Our jailors are dead," Sofia assured them. "They don't pose a threat anymore, but that doesn't mean we're safe. They weren't people. They were Zs."

There were gasps, mutterings of skepticism. Astonishment.

Sofia put her palm up to stave off any additional dialogue. "I met Mik," she angled her head to the teenager beside her, "months ago. We recognized each other after I was brought here. She's *not* one of them—she was trying to kill the Zs and release you before I arrived. Our freedom is thanks to her. She's coming home with me. You all are invited, but you don't have to come."

Sadie stepped forward. Her chin jutted. "No way, lady, would I go *anywhere* with you. You're cursed—you pop up, and people die." Sadie strode from the enclosure, intentionally bumping into Sofia as she left.

"Maybe you're the one who's cursed," Sofia muttered under her breath at Sadie then mentally shrugged. "Kids, let's hit the road."

"I'm coming," Francine said.

Sofia nodded, tapping her foot. The urge to leave was immense. "Grace, Jo, Himari?"

The children eagerly followed her to the van. Sofia unlocked the doors with the fob and got behind the wheel as the women piled in and set the kids on their laps. Francine closed the sliding door. Everybody except Sadie had elected to come along to Mayfly Hollow. The atmosphere was thick with tension. They trembled from nerves and cold.

Would the van start?

When Sofia turned the key, grinding noises came from the engine, but the van fired up. The fuel light dinged. They *were* on fumes. Putting the gearshift in drive, Sofia pulled from the parking lot, uncertain whether they'd accomplish the fifteen-minute voyage. The van belched. Shuddered. She clung to the steering wheel, whispering to the engine, "Please don't stall."

Sofia drove through Mergenville proper and onto the highway, speeding up. The engine smoothed out. *It's gonna be okay.* She switched on the defroster and the heater to high, and blessedly warm air filled the cabin. Everyone jointly sighed with pleasure.

"What's that?" Mik asked from the passenger's seat. She

peered through the windshield, then used her sleeve to wipe away moisture on the inside of it. "It's a guy and two ladies. Holy cow, I think they're handcuffed."

"Floor it," Jo said from the rear of the van. "It's nothing to do with us."

"Imagine if somebody had helped *you* when Ida and Ernest handcuffed you at gunpoint," Sofia said.

"I ain't standing by doin' nothing." Mik ordered, "Pass me the pistol, Francine."

Sofia pulled the van alongside the trio, who were traveling on the weedy berm. Mik lowered the window, letting them see the gun she casually palmed. "Hey. What's goin' on here?"

The man was grizzled and toothless, his face heavily scarred. He held a machete in his grimy hands. He regarded Mik as if she were a Martian in a spaceship. "What concern is it of yours?"

The girls who accompanied him were roughly Mik's age with matted hair and torn, mud-spattered clothing. Wrists tied in front of them with scraps of fabric, their eyes were imploring. Mik said, "Plenty to concern me if them two are your prisoners, pal."

"Want out of those restraints?" Sofia asked the girls, and they nodded. "Come around to my door."

They met glances, then by unspoken agreement, took a step.

"No you don't," the man protested, moving to waylay them.

Mik trained the pistol on the man. "Let 'em go, and give me your machete, handle first."

When the girls approached Sofia's window, they faltered, their manner distrustful. "We were kidnapped and just escaped. You want a ride?"

Eyes wide, they shook their heads and backed away.

"You're smart. Here, these are yours now." Sofia took the machete from Mik and threw it on the asphalt, along with the Bowie knife. "Be suspicious of everyone you meet, and spread the word—the zombies have changed back into people."

Identical looks of wariness flittered across their faces, then one girl scooped the Bowie knife from the ground. She sliced her friend's binds, then her friend returned the favor. They tendered their thanks, picking up the machete and disappearing into the woods.

Sofia rolled the window up again. Mik was kneeling on her seat, half-hanging out the window and yelling at the retreating man, "That's right, you better run, dirty stinkin' roamer!"

Putting the van in gear, Sofia accelerated, an eye on the gas gauge. Idling had wasted fuel, but it had been worth it to give those girls a second chance.

Face set in determination, Sofia navigated the van around obstacles in the road. They came across no other people. At last, the highway turn off for Mayfly Hollow loomed.

They made it five hundred feet down the lane before the van sputtered to a stop.

"We'll have to walk," Sofia said. She took the remote control for the gate from the visor, opening her door. The others joined her on the gravel road.

"How far is it, Sofia?" Himari asked as she grasped Gretchen's hand.

"Maybe a quarter mile? Once we're inside the gate, we'll bear right. There's a circular lane up the hill to the farmhouse—it loops around, leading back down to the gate."

Nora and Ravi linked hands. Francine picked up Ted. Sofia carried Maggie.

As they hiked along the overgrown driveway, Sofia told them about Mayfly Hollow. The fence with the entrance gate came into view. The gate was latched. Sofia looked up at the security camera attached to a metal pole and waved in case anyone was watching. She clicked the button on the remote. They waited until the gate closed behind them before continuing right, where the driveway curved.

The three wooden cabins with their green roofs were a welcome sight. Sofia pointed to the middle cabin, explaining that was where she lived. She said, "Kate will figure out where everyone will sleep. If I stay at my friend's place, someone can use my cabin."

"You can stay with me and Ben," Nora said.

Francine asked, "Who's Kate?"

Maggie pumped a tiny fist at Kate's mention. Sofia smiled, feeling giddy. She hugged the toddler. "Maggie's mom."

Sofia continued telling the women about the farm. They gasped at the concept of hot showers, plentiful meals, and comfortable beds. Himari and Jo cried. As they climbed the hill, Sofia looked to the right. The machine shed stood, the roof half-charred and the walls streaked with soot. But it stood. Sofia breathed easier. *Thank God.*

They bore left, to the crest of the hill. The brick farmhouse was bathed in the glorious shades of daybreak—rose and mauve and indigo. Sofia's heart sang. She'd done it.

The back door flew open. Ace bounded out. Kate descended the concrete stairs, followed by Teller, Lark, Fritz, Josh, Milo, Rob, Nese, Trina, and Bella. They raced down the lane to meet the newcomers.

Adam was missing. And Edna. Where was she—convalescing in bed? Sofia's gaze didn't deviate from the farmhouse. She waited for the most important person to materialize. He didn't.

As her friends reached them, joyful and excited and gathering them into hugs, Sofia watched the farmhouse.

Where was Ben?

CHAPTER SIXTY

Sofia washed her hands in the bathroom sink, then wet a washcloth, gingerly wiping at the dried flakes of rust-colored blood on her face.

The reflection in the mirror showed eyes that were ringed from stress and lack of nutrition, but Sofia's body hummed. After praying so fervently to set foot on Mayfly Hollow soil once again, it was mind-boggling that she'd actually made it. She couldn't believe that she was home. That she was safe.

In the flurry of answering questions, Sofia hadn't been able to ask any of her own. She'd caught Nora inquiring about Ben but hadn't heard Lark's response.

The adrenaline which had shored her up was dissipating, leaving her pulse fluttery. Bracing her hands on the sink, Sofia inhaled and exhaled. She wasn't conflicted about dispatching the Zs. Not in the least. She'd do it again if necessary. What was a mind fuck was the normality of Mayfly Hollow juxtaposed with the horrors beyond its borders—it was like she was on another planet.

"Sofia?" Lark asked through the bathroom door. "Time to eat."

Lark and Bella served breakfast in the farmhouse kitchen. It was the largest grouping of people they'd ever served at one meal. Fritz and Josh had to bring folding chairs from the basement to accommodate the new arrivals.

As soon as everyone's plates were heaped, Sofia asked, "How's Edna?"

Kate replied, "Was touch and go for a while, but she's upstairs recovering."

"Head trauma," Rob spoke up from the other end of the table. "is tricky. I'm keeping a close watch on her. I'll examine your injury after breakfast, Sofia."

Sofia nodded at Rob, asking Kate, "And Ben? Adam? Where are they?"

"After the fire was under control, and we realized what happened, Ben was *wild*—you know how he gets." Kate spooned a piece of biscuit with gravy into Maggie's mouth. "The camera footage was useless with the smoke, and we were all filthy and exhausted, but he insisted on grabbing his bow and trying to track you on foot."

"Wouldn't even wait 'til mornin'," Teller drawled. "Adam tagged along 'cause we couldn't reason with him." He quirked a shoulder. "Like Kate said, you know how Ben is when he's het up."

"Yeah." Sofia didn't bother to conceal the specter of a smile that played over her lips. She knew. She shoveled in a forkful of sausage and chewed. "When they due back?"

"Any day," Lark said. "He took a walkie, but he's been out of range every time we check in."

Nora set her fork on her plate, her expression fretful. "Ben could be hurt."

Sofia put an arm around her. "He'll be fine. He's smart, and he's strong."

"I've been taking care of Sam and Rory while you've been gone," Lark told Nora. "They've missed you."

While they ate, Sofia detailed their tribulations over the last days. When she revealed the truth about their captors, a hush fell over the room.

"How do you know they were Zs?" Fritz asked.

"Their penchant for human flesh was the first clue," Sofia said. "But Mik's more an expert on them than I am."

Mik swallowed a huge mouthful of scrambled eggs, then responded, "They look normal except their teeth are lousy. That's how I blended in."

"Sure," Fritz said. "But how did you *know*?"

"They yap about it." Mik rolled her eyes. "They're kinda dumb and don't remember much about when they were roamers, but they know what they are."

Kate smacked the table. "That's why Jan was familiar! I saw her *twice* in River Heights—once by the post office and then at the pharmacy when Teller and I went looking for medication to treat Ben's infection. She was a Z! I've been wracking my brain to figure it out, and it just now came to me."

"Dang," Teller said as he used a biscuit to sop up the remnants of gravy on his plate, "it's more perilous outside Mayfly Hollow now than it ever was."

"We won't be leaving the farm," Kate declared. "Not until further notice. We're stepping up the fence patrols, too."

She didn't receive any arguments.

Sofia apologized about Maggie's cold and her diaper rash as Kate wiped the toddler's nose with a napkin. Kate hadn't set Maggie down since taking her from Sofia upon their arrival.

"I saw it when I changed her diaper... I slathered her bottom with cream. It's nothing that time won't remedy," Kate said, flouting Sofia's apology. "I know you did everything you could for her. That's not in dispute."

Grace said, "Sofia did a wonderful job caring for all the children."

"I couldn't have managed without your support," Sofia said, emotion clogging her throat as she looked from Grace and Jo to

Himari and Francine. She reached across the table to touch Mik's hand. "We wouldn't be here without you."

Himari regarded Mik with admiration. "You're one of the most fearless girls I've ever met."

"I'll admit," Sofia said, "there were moments when I wasn't sure we'd make it."

"But you brought our kids home safe and sound," Teller replied softly, "and we can never begin to repay you for that. All of you."

Broadcasting a bright smile over the table, Kate said, "You five have a home here for as long as you want it."

"Josh and I will move back in with Fritz to free up the smaller cabin by Sofia's place," Bella offered as she cleared the table. Fritz grimaced.

"And I can take a few people," Lark said, "although I don't have any beds for my guest bedrooms yet."

Mik shrugged. "A sleepin' bag'll do me."

"I'm bunking at Juniper Rise until Ben returns," Sofia said, "so my cabin's up for grabs. I just need to pack a bag first."

It was decided Mik would stay with Lark. Francine and Grace would share Sofia's cabin, and Jo and Himari would take the one Bella and Josh were vacating.

Kate got up from the head of the table and took her dishes to the sink. "Now that accommodations are sorted, I'm bathing the kids and tucking them into bed. I suggest you all do the same—bath and bed."

Sofia hugged and kissed Gretchen and Ravi and Ted. Bellies full of food and their cheeks rosy from the warmth of the kitchen, they yawned. The abduction and Beth's murder had left them all shell-shocked, but Sofia prayed for resiliency.

"There are extra clothes for our new people in the laundry room," Kate said as she waited for the kids. "And take a box of provisions when you go to Juniper Rise, Sof."

Sofia thanked her as Rob bent to inspect the injury on her temple.

"Nese," Trina instructed as she stacked the dishwasher, "go up and help Kate, honey."

Nese and Kate shepherded the children upstairs, and Bella went to pack bags for her and Josh to move to Fritz's cabin.

"Give me a minute," Sofia said to Himari, Jo, Grace, and Francine. She longed to shed her burdens and, unencumbered, slip away to Juniper Rise with Nora. "And I'll walk with you down to your cabins."

Fritz and Josh and Milo went outside to tend the livestock while Lark fetched the laundry room first aid kit for Rob, along with the extra clothes.

"It's healing nicely." Rob swabbed disinfectant on Sofia's cut then opened the kit, taking out a stack of gauze bandages and a roll of tape. He handed them to her. "Wear one of these when you shower—they have a layer of plastic. Otherwise, let the air at your injury."

BELLA WAS STILL PACKING when Sofia escorted Himari and Jo into the cabin. Sofia was relieved to place the women in Bella's hands. Grace and Francine sat on the porch until Sofia came out, then they trailed her to the other cabin. Setting their crates of clothes on the unmade bed, they stood in the center of the room, speechless and looking overwhelmed.

Sofia showed them around before pulling her suitcase from under the bed. Francine poked in the kitchen cabinets as she packed. "You'll find an extra set of sheets in the bathroom closet. There's a communal laundry room up by the barn... we'll give you a tour in a few days."

After peeking into the bathroom, Grace said, "Wow. This is amazing. Thank you, Sofia."

"Try to decompress. You've been through a lot." Sofia zipped her case. What if Ben arrived home while she packed? "If you need anything, there's a walkie on the counter."

Mik, Lark, and Nora were by the henhouse. Learning Ben hadn't yet shown up, Sofia wilted with disappointment. She was desperate to reach Ben's home. To surround herself with his belongings. To play his music. And, to sleep in his bed.

It was no substitute for having Ben back in her arms, but in the meantime, it would have to suffice.

CHAPTER SIXTY-ONE

ONCE THEY REACHED JUNIPER RISE, SOFIA PUT HER SUITCASE DOWN on the pebbled pathway, informing Nora she wanted a moment alone with Lark.

"It's okay, Sofia. I'm not a baby. I can shower on my own," Nora assured her. Looking amused, Lark passed her the crate of provisions she'd packed. Juggling it, Nora staggered under its heft as she walked down the path.

"I won't be long." Before Nora closed the front door, Sofia cautioned, "Be careful not to slip in the tub!"

Lark went inside her double-wide to show Mik to the bathroom. While she waited for Lark, Sofia perched on the top step of the diminutive porch, craving a moment of solitude.

The morning was crisp and cool, rife with birdsong. It was lovely. Over by the fence, the spring bubbled on the rocky outcrop beside the weeping willow. Lark spent a lot of her free time there—a patio chair and side table had been positioned under the tree. Sofia imagined her writing in her journal while drinking iced tea, the wind ruffling the branches as it carried the scent of wildflowers.

It was easy to appreciate why Lark treasured her spot beside the spring.

The door opened then closed behind Sofia. Lark plopped on the step beside her. For a spell, they didn't speak, then Sofia said, "Sorry for being bitchy that night when you told me to talk to Ben."

"Sofia," Lark replied drily, "friends argue."

"But you were right! I thought about it a lot while in Mergenville—I didn't have much else to do but think. I'm mad at myself. Should've listened to you. I still have a lot of growing up to do." Her sinuses prickled, foretelling tears. "You think they'll make it home?"

"Yeah," Lark said. "Like you told Nora, Ben is strong, and he's smart. So is Adam."

Sofia chewed her bottom lip. "When I... that is, if he..."

Lark nudged her with a shoulder. "Jesus, fuck. Spit it out."

"Can I have your spare guest room... if things don't work out with him?"

A laugh burbled from Lark. She tipped her head back and hooted.

Sofia's mouth dropped. "What? What the heck is so *funny*?"

"Don't be a dumbass," Lark said. "Listen, you didn't see him when you were AWOL. I can promise you—a guy doesn't react the way he did unless he's in love."

"He probably was going ballistic over Nora's disappearance."

"That's horseshit."

Please let Lark know what she's talking about, Sofia thought.

Her gaze perceptive, Lark asked, "Weird for you, isn't it? Being back, I mean."

"It's just... a lot, you know? I pleaded with God to get me home. Then, when I finally am, no Ben. I don't know where I stand with him—I don't even know if he's alive. And the whole Zs reverting to people thing..." Sofia buried her face in her hands.

Lark placed a palm on Sofia's back. "You're tired."

"Tired isn't the word," Sofia said, her voice dull.

"Like Teller always says—what matters is that *we live to see another day.* You should be focusing on putting your feet up. Worry about tomorrow, tomorrow. Now, for crying out loud, will you go shower? You're rank as fuck."

WHEN SOFIA LET herself into Ben's house, she found Nora in the kitchen, fresh-scrubbed and wearing a powder blue sweatsuit. She unpacked the crate of food, neatly grouping items on the countertop. From the hallway closet, the stackable washer glugged. "You want a cup of tea, Sofia? I can put the kettle on."

Sofia clucked. "What are you, like thirty years old?"

Nora tucked wet strands of hair behind her ear and regarded Sofia, nonplussed. Sam and Rory rolled across her bare feet as they roughhoused. "I'm eleven. And three quarters."

"Can't forget about the three quarters," Sofia ribbed her. Though she hid it well, Nora must be anxious about Ben—Sofia wanted to keep the mood light. Shooing her from the kitchen, she said, "I'm here to take care of *you*, little girl. Pick up your cats and put a cartoon DVD in the player or something. Be a kid, for goodness sake."

Sofia's gaze fell on the pile of apples on the counter. Sweeping them into the crook of her arm, she went to the side door by the dinette and pitched them into the grass—let the squirrels have the apples. Sofia couldn't stomach the sight of them. She stowed jars of canned veggies and fruit in the cabinet before heading to shower.

As she scrubbed the dirt from her fingernails under the steamy spray, her heart panged with maternal realization. Much as it pained her to think of Ben failing to return... if he didn't, she would move to Juniper Rise permanently. Adopt Nora.

She combed her hair and, after lotioning her body, dressed in yoga pants, a sweatshirt, and fluffy slipper socks. Before exiting the bathroom, Sofia peeled the bandage from her temple, inspecting her cut in the mirror.

Joining Nora in the living room, Sofia sprawled on the sofa and sighed lustily. Observing Nora drag a piece of string across the living room carpet for Sam and Rory, her lips curved into an affectionate smile. There was no doubt—Sofia had grown attached to the girl. Was she capable of providing Nora the childhood she deserved?

"Uh, Nor?"

The girl turned to look at Sofia, her finely etched eyebrows raising expectantly. Shafts of morning sunlight shone through the window beside the fireplace, sparking the golden highlights in Nora's flaxen hair.

"I... I love you, sweetheart."

Without a beat, Nora replied, "I love you too, Sofia."

Later that afternoon, once they'd napped, Sofia and Nora picked late-blooming wildflowers in the clearing behind the house—bellflowers, asters, and anemone—and arranged them in Mason jar vases. Then they tidied the house. Nora emptied the cats' litter pan outside before refilling it with sand. Sofia dusted and vacuumed.

They listened to Ben's music while they ate the breaded pork chops, baked potatoes, and green beans Sofia prepared for their dinner, then they lounged on the sofa with books. Nevertheless, there was an element lacking—the home didn't have the same vitality without Ben.

When it was time for bed, Sofia sent Nora to brush her teeth. She flipped on the porch light for Ben, then went to turn down Nora's purple-and-pink quilt. Climbing into bed, Nora clutched her teddy bear to her slight body. Sofia was reminded how young she was.

"Sofia?" Nora asked. "Will you sleep with me?"

"Sure." Her arm around Nora, and Sam and Rory curled at their feet, Sofia contemplated Ben and Adam. Where were they this cold night? It didn't seem fair to be snug in bed when the men were likely freezing somewhere, sleeping rough, their well-being uncertain.

Nora snored beside her. Sofia smoothed her hair and recited a prayer as she drifted off that Ben and Adam would be home when she woke.

CHAPTER SIXTY-TWO

SOFIA AWAKENED WITH A START, HER CHEEKS WET WITH TEARS. RORY nibbled her toe. Sitting, she scooped the kitten up, scratching under her chin. Rory rewarded Sofia with a rumbling purr.

Rain pelted the roof, the light seeping through the curtains gloomy. It was late. They'd missed breakfast at the farmhouse.

Nora slept. Sofia jockeyed out of bed, mindful not to disturb her. The house was silent. Unoccupied. Another day without Ben, Sofia thought, her mouth turning down.

She brewed chicory coffee and took a mug outside, sheltered from the downpour by the canopy of the front porch. Lightning flashed, followed by a crack of thunder. Sitting on a patio chair, Sofia wrapped her fingers around the mug and trained her gaze on the muddy, rain-soaked hill. If only Ben would appear.

Rainstorms usually lulled her, but today Sofia brooded— she'd been plagued with nightmares of Beth screaming for Sofia to stop Tommy as he dismembered her into pieces with a meat cleaver. The imagery had been lurid. Distressing.

Poor Beth. She'd been a good person. Someone who wouldn't have hurt a fly. What purpose did her death serve the universe? It made no sense. Why, Sofia questioned, did God allow the destruction of beauty and goodness yet permit evil to endure? What was the lesson to be gleaned?

Her nightmare set the tone for the day—Sofia's mood was as murky as the weather. When hours passed and Ben didn't appear, it shifted from dismal to desolate.

Kate walkied at lunchtime. "Coming up to see us today?"

Sofia looked to Nora where she colored in an activity book with washable markers and picked at a ham sandwich. She shook her head, and Sofia replied, "If it's cool, we'll hang out here today."

"Of course it's cool."

"Heard from Ben?"

"No. Sorry, Sofia."

After lunch, she and Nora played a card game, then put a puzzle together while listening to Van Morrison. When the intro to *Brown Eyed Girl* came over the smartphone's speaker, Sofia fought tears. The lyrics hit home, haunting her.

Nora clicked a puzzle piece into place. "That's you."

Collecting herself, Sofia asked, "You know about Ben's nickname for me? How?"

"He told me."

They didn't have much appetite at dinnertime. Sofia heated a jar of home-canned beef stew, but they couldn't force themselves to eat. They ended up giving their bowls to Sam and Rory. Sitting at the dinette with their chins propped in their hands, Sofia and Nora bleakly regarded each other.

Sofia sighed. "We should be around people. Tomorrow we'll spend the day at the farmhouse. Plenty of work to be done there anyhow."

"I'd rather wait here for Ben."

"I get it, but we've moped enough."

"There won't be school if Edna is in bed," Nora pointed out. "I can stay home."

"Yeah, but Nese may be teaching from Edna's lesson plans."

Selecting her words carefully, Sofia asked, "Do you want to discuss what happened in Mergenville?"

"Why? It's done with."

"Because you witnessed serious stuff. Grown up, upsetting stuff."

"The bad guys are dead. I don't think about them."

"Hmm." Sofia deliberated Nora losing her parents and the battle waged with the motorcycle gang resulting in the injury which almost killed her. "Has that technique worked well for you?"

"I guess." She bent to pet Sam. "Why are you worried about me?"

"Because I care about you."

"I know. You tell me every day."

"You're very mature, but things can build up on a person. I want you to know that you can talk to me anytime about anything."

Nora nodded, meeting her eyes. "Okay, Sofia."

Sofia pushed her chair back and picked up the soup bowls from the floor. As she loaded the dishwasher, she said, "Maggie and Ted will likely forget about Mergenville because they're young, but Gretchen and Ravi are another story. They may be struggling to process it all—I know I am, and I'm an adult. Why not keep the kids company tomorrow? In case they want to open up to you."

Nora mulled Sofia's words. "I'd feel bad if I didn't help my friends, so I guess I'll go. Now can we watch a movie?"

ONCE NORA WAS ASLEEP, Sofia slipped from her bed and left the room, softly closing the door. Flipping on the porch light for Ben —it was becoming a nightly habit—she decided to read. She stretched on the sofa, Sam and Rory napping on the cushion beside her.

Three chapters in, Sofia yawned. Setting the novel on the carpet, she dimmed the lamp on the side table and pulled on the crocheted afghan from the arm of the sofa. She dozed for several hours.

A door clicking shut permeated her consciousness. Sofia abruptly sat up, her breath stuttering. She twisted on the cushion, squinting into the foyer.

Ben.

He stood in front of the door, his clothes drenched from the rain. His face was heavily creased with fatigue. Rivulets of water streamed down his cheeks and dripped from his chin. Setting his compound bow on the tiled floor, Ben's gaze sharpened as he caught sight of Sofia.

She threw the afghan aside and wobbled to her feet. Her gait was unsteady as she negotiated around the side table and into the foyer. She felt like she was in a trance. Was Ben a figment of her imagination? The product of a vivid dream? When she was directly in front of him, Sofia stopped. She searched the sapphire eyes she knew so well.

Ben dropped to his knees, head bowed. He pulled Sofia close. Arms encircling her, he nuzzled his face in her thigh as if he were drowning, and she was a life preserver. He trembled. Exhaling a shuddering breath, he held tight but didn't speak.

Tenderly, Sofia skimmed his hair back from his forehead. Smoothed it on his scalp. Caressed his shoulders. She lowered her body to the floor so they were kneeling face-to-face and whispered, "I wasn't sure if you were real."

"I'm real." Ben brought up a hand, brushing her jaw with calloused knuckles. He frowned at the cut on her temple. "You're hurt, brown-eyed girl."

A tear teetered on her waterline, then coursed down her cheek. "I don't feel anything except gratitude right now." Emotion choking her, Sofia murmured, "You have no idea how much I prayed for this moment."

He asked gruffly, "Nora asleep?"

She nodded, sniffling. "Do you want to wake her up?"

"Later." Ben dragged a thumb to dry her tears then cradled her head in his hands. Heavy-lidded, he peppered her face with gentle kisses. When Sofia's breath quickened, he responded by tangling his fingers in her hair and placing his lips on hers. "Kiss me."

The heat in Sofia's loins kindled. Sparked. She ran the tip of her tongue along his lower lip, then sucked. Ben groaned, deepening their kiss until they were both panting.

Climbing to his feet, Ben held a hand to Sofia, assisting her up. He led her into his bedroom and locked the door.

CHAPTER SIXTY-THREE

THEY WERE NAKED, THEIR WET CLOTHES DISCARDED ON THE FLOOR. Ben was between Sofia's thighs, her legs around his waist. He hovered over her, his tip teasing her entrance, but he made no move to penetrate her folds. Pinning Sofia's wrists to the mattress, Ben immobilized her, his breath raspy.

Sofia squirmed, bucking her pelvis. "Please…"

"No," he said, eyes glittering, "not until you tell me."

"Tell you what?"

"I want you to reveal," Ben kissed her collarbone, his whiskers chafing her skin, "what the fuck you've been hiding from me."

Sofia's limbs tensed. She wasn't prepared. He had her at a disadvantage. She was defenseless. Closing her eyes, she swallowed, her senses too muddled to form a reply.

"Sofia." Ben rested his forehead against hers. "Don't do that. Don't disengage."

"Not now," she beseeched. "Let me have this moment. We'll talk after."

Ben's fingers constricted on her wrists. He demanded unevenly, "Have you cheated on me? Are you in love with someone else?"

Sofia's eyes flew open. "What? No!"

Putting his mouth to the shell of her ear, he mounted her, his tip wedging into her slit. "You do want me. *This.*"

She gasped, arching her spine. "Yes. Yes."

"Then tell me, dammit," he growled.

"I love you!" Sofia turned her head away, steeling herself for his inevitable negative reaction. In the foyer, she'd been strong, and he'd been weak. Here, in bed, the power had shifted. Ben was in charge.

His throaty chuckle was the last thing she expected.

"That's why? You've been conflicted because you *love me?*" Ben questioned, tone indecipherable.

"Yes! Now will you fuck me?"

He pushed into her until he was fully sheathed. Rocking his hips, he set a leisurely rhythm. The friction of their chests abraded Sofia's nipples with each stroke. They pebbled, shooting pleasure to her center. She mewled. "Tell me again, Sofia."

Her fingers roved over the rigid musculature of Ben's back as he filled her. His flesh was hot. It singed her. Branded her. They were so close that his breath was her breath—she couldn't tell where he ended and where she began. Reaching to palm the taut curve of Ben's ass, Sofia gripped him. She was brought to life by the way he moved. Slowly. Methodically.

He took everything from her but gave back more.

As Sofia homed in on the frenzied tension intensifying in her loins, Ben slowed to a halt. She whimpered in exasperation.

"If you want to come," he coaxed raggedly, ardently, "tell me again."

Her blood pounded in her ears at his command. She breathed, "I love you."

Ben resumed his pace then pummeled into her, his strokes so long and so deep that Sofia was sure she'd split in two. She felt him swell. He grunted, and the first sweet spasm caught, building into a dizzying crescendo.

Afterward, they collapsed on the mattress, spent.

BEN HAD FALLEN ASLEEP. Sofia arranged a blanket over them then lay beside him, her fingers interlocked on her stomach. She was thoughtful. Nothing was truly resolved between them, yet Sofia didn't wish to disrupt Ben. She understood how stressful it was while outside the fence—the danger, deprivation, and hunger took a toll. How exposure to the elements without proper clothing shattered the psyche. Depleted strength.

The toasty, cozy bed must be like a balm to Ben's soul. It was something Sofia would never take for granted again. A few hours respite would rejuvenate him, then they'd have a heart-to-heart.

Reflecting on how Ben had turned the tables on her by demanding answers during the throes of passion, Sofia stifled a laugh and shook her head. That was an underhanded tactic. Not malicious yet nonetheless sly. And effective. That rascal knew she'd be at his mercy. What piqued Sofia's curiosity was Ben's reaction—not ambiguous, yet vague enough to provoke her. Discovering her feelings for him seemed to feed Ben's desire. Did that mean he reciprocated them?

In the early morning hours, Ben snaked an arm under Sofia's neck. She jumped. She'd been engrossed in her thoughts, not grasping that he had woken up.

"I stopped at the farmhouse. Teller brought me up to speed." He pulled her into him, until her cheek was on his chest. "Are you alright? I mean really truly alright?"

Sofia traced a fingertip across his pec. "I think so. I'm working through it."

"The way you killed those Zs was badass as hell. You never cease to surprise me."

She scoffed. "Are you saying I'm not capable of bad-assery when the circumstances call for it?"

"Not at all. But brutality can throw a person off balance. Most of us aren't built for it. Are you having any doubts about your actions? Regrets?"

"Not about that. What I regret is Beth's death. I regret whatever scars it'll leave on the kids. Nora's coping well, thankfully."

"She has experience with suffering. It's shaped her into who she is today."

"I'd decided that if you didn't return," Sofia confided in whisper, "that I'd move here and raise her myself."

Ben smiled. "I appreciate you watching out for her."

"You shouldn't have gone looking for us, Ben. It's too dangerous out there."

"You're right. It was a fool's errand," he acknowledged, "but I was rabid. I couldn't sit here with my thumb up my ass. I had to *do* something."

"I understand the compulsion. Knowing the Zs are reverting to people again... aren't you scared about what the future holds?"

Ben was pragmatic. "We can defend the farm if it comes to that. Closing ranks is a sound plan." He flipped on his side so they faced each other. "I don't want *you* to be scared."

"Mik says they're dumb, so we have that going for us..."

"Fuck the Zs. Let them try to breach the fence. There's something else that interests me far more. Us." Ben murmured, "So, somebody *caught feelings*."

Sofia flushed with embarrassment, concealing her face with her hand.

"You swore up and down that you'd be able to maintain boundaries."

"I was really confident, wasn't I?"

He snorted. "Very."

Feeling sheepish, Sofia recalled the quote *confidence is the food of the wise man but the liquor of the fool*. She couldn't fault Ben for calling her out. She deserved it. "Do you want to break up with me?"

"Why would I want that?"

"Nothing has to change," she assured him. "We can continue on the way we have been."

Ben grabbed her wrist and pulled her hand from her face. Bringing her palm to his mouth, he kissed it. "You misunderstand."

Her heart leaped with optimism. "Do I?"

His eyes drank her in. "While I was out combing the countryside for you and Nora and the rest of the kids, all the pieces fell into place."

"Oh?" she asked weakly.

"You know that I wanted you from the moment I saw you."

"Yes. Same."

"That attraction has grown into more than I could've ever possibly anticipated, Sof."

Emotion blossomed in her chest. "What are you saying?"

"I'm saying that although we did things differently than most people," Ben slid his thumb across Sofia's bottom lip, "in the end, you and me—we found love."

Covering his hand with hers, she laced their fingers.

"You belong here at Juniper Rise with us."

Sofia's heartbeat thudded in her chest. "Are you serious?"

"I want us to be a family. Will you be mine, forever?"

"Yes," she said, misty-eyed. "I love you… and I always will."

Ben captured Sofia's mouth in a sweet kiss. "I love you, my brown-eyed girl."

The future held uncertainty, but there was one thing Sofia could rely on—for her, Ben and Nora meant home.

EPILOGUE

Six Months Later

The alarm clock sounded on Ben's bedside table and, with a groan, he hit the snooze button before flopping back on the bed.

Sofia stirred. Gathering her into the crook of his arm, he kissed her on the forehead. "Happy twenty-second birthday."

Yawning, she snuggled into her husband's side, her fingertips skimming down his muscled abdomen. Ben's breath quickened at her touch, his flesh as responsive as ever. She fondled his balls, then lightly raked her fingernail up the silken length of his arousal. His cock jerked against her palm. Emboldened, she bit her lip. "May I have my present now?"

"Tonight. Kate's keeping Nora so we can properly celebrate."

Sofia twisted away from him and to the edge of the mattress. Shimmying out of her pajama bottoms, she then crawled across the bed. Tossing the blanket covering Ben aside, she climbed on top of him, straddling him. "I think you forget that it's our anniversary today, counselor."

"Oh, that's right. Our two-month anniversary." Ben grinned devilishly, the dimple appearing in his cheek. He ran a thumb between her breasts to her belly button, then lower, a gleam in his eye. "Just so we're crystal clear... what's happening here is *my* anniversary gift?"

"Mmm hmm. Except it has to be a quickie."

"When I balance you over my knee tonight for your birthday spanking, I'll be taking my time," he promised, fingers working her nipple until it was a hardened peak. "Your ass is mine."

Head thrown back, Sofia rode Ben while he fingered her clit. When she climaxed, he watched her, his pupils dilating. Switching positions, Ben flipped Sofia on her back. Breathing uneven, she wrapped her legs around his waist, meeting his thrusts until he shuddered his release.

SOFIA DRESSED QUICKLY. Nora would be waking soon, and they were due at the farmhouse for breakfast in an hour. She brewed a pot of chicory coffee while Ben showered, taking a mug out to the front porch to enjoy daybreak. After the long winter, the milder temperatures heralded rebirth. Spring.

She descended the stairs. Pauline and Sally, their pair of nanny goats, ceased chomping on the grass sprouting in the front yard. They bleated a greeting, trotting toward Sofia. Ben had attached leads to their collars, staking them so they couldn't demolish Sofia's flowers. Crossing the yard, she scratched their ears before inspecting her flower beds at the base of the porch. She'd planted bulbs last fall—daffodils, hyacinths, and lilies—and checked the progress of the tender shoots daily. Another week, possibly two, before they began to bud. The peonies they'd transplanted from her cabin would take a couple seasons to flower, but that was okay. There was no hurry.

The early morning rays felt delicious. She lifted her face to bask in them, closing her eyes. When she opened them again and sipped from her mug, Sofia's gaze caught on her silver wedding band. Ben had handcrafted it from a chunk of metal. Two months married, she thought. It seemed like yesterday he was placing the ring on her finger.

The wedding had been a simple affair, their vows recited in the clearing behind Juniper Rise as soon as the snow had melted. They'd worn everyday clothes. Adam had served as their officiant. After, they'd celebrated with wine and a cake Kate had baked.

They'd fixed the guest room up for Mik, and she'd become part of their family. Although Sofia had entreated her to stay at the farm, where they remained untouched by the outside world, Mik had a wandering spirit—she wasn't a person to stay in one place for long. She'd bid them farewell the day after Sofia and Ben's nuptials.

Sofia thought of Mik as she finished her coffee. The girl had sworn she wasn't frightened of the Zs. She wanted to learn more about them. She promised to return by autumn. Sofia recited a prayer for Mik's safety beyond the confines of the fence.

"Sof," Ben peeked out the door. "You about ready to go?"

Nodding, Sofia went inside to put her mug in the dishwasher. Nora came out of her room with a wrapped package. "Happy Birthday, Sofia."

Grinning, Sofia tore the paper. It was a framed photo of the three of them taken in the clearing after the wedding ceremony. "Aww."

"Kate printed it on the office printer. I decorated the frame," Nora said, pointing to the glued gems bordering the photo. "Gretchen helped."

Sofia hugged Nora. Since Mergenville, she'd watched Nora—and the other children—for any indication their abduction left everlasting scars. The children proved resilient. "I love it. You two did a beautiful job."

"We have to hurry," Ben said, opening the door. "Lark is making you French toast."

They walked up the trail together.

Fritz stepped from his cabin as they approached it, Trina and

Nese behind him. He and Trina had begun dating in October. By Christmas, she and Nese had moved into his cabin. They'd formed a family of their own.

"Howdy," Fritz boomed.

They chorused good mornings.

"Shall we keep you company?" Trina asked, and they fell into step together, chatting about nothing in particular.

When they reached the farmhouse, Bella was scattering chicken feed to the hens. She joined the group as they closed the distance to the house.

Ben held the door, and they filed into the kitchen. He winked at Sofia. The others were assembled there. After making their plates and settling around the table, they serenaded Sofia with *Happy Birthday*, handing her homemade gifts. During breakfast, she thanked them for making a fuss over her.

After they'd eaten and everyone left to attend to their various chores, Lark and Sofia cleaned the kitchen while Kate sat at the head of the trestle table, her hands folded over her stomach. Maggie played with blocks on the floor beside Kate, chattering to herself. Kate said, "I'll bake you a cake later today."

"You don't have to do that," Sofia replied, knowing that it was hard for Kate to be on her feet when so heavily pregnant.

Waving a hand dismissively, Kate asked, "White cake with white buttercream and blackberry filling?"

Flattered that Kate remembered her favorite flavors, Sofia nodded. "Yes, please."

The intercom in the hallway sounded, indicating somebody buzzing at the front gate. Lark and Sofia froze, trading a look. Mouth pursed, Kate lumbered to her feet and went to the hallway.

Trailing behind Kate, they watched as she pressed a button and spoke into the wall-mounted unit. "Yes?"

A masculine voice answered, "Is this Sofia?"

Kate swiveled to meet Sofia's widened eyes.

"Who the fuck can that be?" Lark hissed.

Sofia shrugged, her mind racing.

"No," Kate replied into the speaker. "This isn't Sofia."

"Kate then?"

"Who are you?" Kate demanded.

"Mik Chalmers sent me. Said to ask for Sofia or Kate." He was deep-voiced. Self-assured.

Kate raised an eyebrow, but she was canny enough to remain guarded. "Okay… what can I help you with?"

"I think I'm the one who can help you. I met Mik six weeks ago out on the road. We struck up a friendship. When she learned I was a mechanic, she shared that you've been trying to convert engines to run on grain alcohol. That's something I know how to do. I'm looking for a place to settle long term."

"Stand by," Kate said slowly, turning to Sofia and Lark. "Can you two go check the camera feed on the computer?"

Sofia and Lark brushed past Kate as they hurried to the office. Sitting on the manager's chair in front of the computer desk, Sofia used the mouse to select the camera positioned at the entrance gate. The black-and-white image popped up, filling the screen.

A tall, handsome man leaned nonchalantly against the fence. He wore a t-shirt, jeans, and boots. A leather jacket was slung over his shoulder by a crooked index finger. In another life, he likely rode a motorcycle. Raven-haired, his exposed skin was patterned with tattoos. He looked up at the camera, his manner radiating confidence.

"Fuck," Lark breathed. As if he guessed he was being watched, the man grinned, showing a set of perfect teeth. "He's a smokeshow."

Sofia considered Lark, finding her attention riveted to the screen and her expression titillated. "He's cute."

"*Cute*? He's built like a brick shithouse." Lark's gaze swung to Sofia. "Think he's on the level?"

"C'mon. You know Mik wouldn't have sent him here if there was any doubt. She knows what's up."

"I'll walk down to chat with him in person."

"Want me to tag along?"

Lark's face flushed scarlet. She fanned her cheeks then pulled the elastic from her hair, fluffing the strands. Reaching into her shirt, she adjusted her boobs. "Nope. I got this."

Sofia's lips curved into a smile. *Well, this ought to be interesting...*

THE END

AUTHOR'S NOTE:

I hope to release Lark's story next year—it's tentatively titled *Songbird Spring*. If you enjoyed *Juniper Rise*, I'd appreciate a review on Amazon and Goodreads. Thank you for supporting indie authors!

ROMANCE AT KINGFISHER COVE
ALL NET PROCEEDS BENEFIT BREAST
CANCER RESEARCH

Chapter One

KINGFISHER COVE, SOUTH CAROLINA
Summer, 2008

"POSTURE, KATRINA," Grandmother admonished, dabbing her lips with a linen napkin.

My face prickling, I straightened. At Grandmother's nod of approval, I forked a chunk of lobster into my mouth. The maid came through the swinging door connecting the kitchen to the dining room, a fresh bottle of chilled chardonnay in hand. She topped off Grandmother's wineglass, then rounded the table to Granddad's spot to refill his.

"Can't I have a little wine, Grandmother? To try?" I begged, adding, "I'm eighteen now."

It was a balmy June day. The ceiling fan above spun lazily. Dean Martin's velvet baritone crooned over the ancient record player on the sideboard. Golden late afternoon sun streamed through the window, kissing Grandmother's rouged cheeks. She picked at her plate of cold seafood salad—light fare was an absolute must when summering on the island—and arched an eyebrow. "Barely, considering your birthday was only last week."

"Oh come now, Frances," Granddad coaxed, winking at me. "Kitty Kat's old enough for a sample of vino."

Grandmother sighed. "Very well. I lack the strength at present to battle you both." She waved a hand at the maid lingering at Granddad's chair. "A *scarce* pour, Sarah."

After leaving a splash of liquid in my goblet, Sarah placed the bottle on the sideboard and fussed with the platter of fruit and cheese that would be served for dessert. I sipped my wine, feeling the epitome of sophistication. I let the flavors saturate my taste buds before swallowing. Unfamiliar but agreeable. Heady. Heat bloomed on my skin.

After everyone retired to bed, I'd sneak into the kitchen to filch a glass. I'd take it down to the beach and listen to the sea. Stargaze. Reflect. I had plenty to contemplate with starting Stayton University in the autumn.

"Sarah, would you mind mixing me a G and T with extra lime?" Granddad downed his chardonnay. "I could use an after-supper cocktail."

"Certainly, Mr. Dumont." Sarah exited the room, heading toward the parlor where the drinks cart was kept.

Grandmother threw Granddad a pointed look. "Dinner. The evening meal is *dinner*, Charles."

"Bah." He turned to me with a twinkle in his eye, grinning mischievously. "I'm a low-class fella. I can't put on airs—it'll always be *supper* to me."

"And I believe you've had quite enough spirits already. You need a clear head," she continued, "when Geoffrey phones later to review our financials."

I smiled at Granddad, thankful for the thousandth time he wasn't hoity-toity. He'd rejected Grandmother's decree we dress for dinner, his attire a simple, faded polo, and a pair of creased khakis. He didn't care whether he used the wrong fork at meals or rested his elbows on the table. Forty-odd years of marriage to a Randcliffe couldn't shake Granddad's indifference. Refusing to bow to conventions was a testament to Charlie Dumont's humble roots.

A curious tension was building in the room. Watching my grandparents' non-verbal interplay, I twirled the delicate stem of my empty wineglass, my stomach flip-flopping. Granddad was his usual carefree self, but something simmered between him and Grandmother I didn't understand. Something terse. Disturbing. Was she angry he'd spent another afternoon at the dog track on the mainland?

Sarah returned, ice tinkling in the tumbler she placed beside Granddad's plate. He rubbed his hands together in anticipation. "Your gin and tonic, sir."

"For pity's sake, Katrina! Will you *stop slouching*," Grandmother snapped, and I sat to attention, threading my hands in my lap.

Sarah collected the dirty dishes and retreated to the kitchen, the skirt of her starched uniform swishing. Evidently, I wasn't the only one feeling the friction hovering like ether.

"Franny," Granddad chided.

The song on the record player finished, the needle bouncing in the stillness of the dining room.

"I detest nicknames." Grandmother's upper lip stiffened. She glared at Granddad. "The least we can provide the child is impeccable manners. The very least, wouldn't you concur?"

She was often taciturn, even severe. Nevertheless, her resentful expression baffled me. Granddad flushed. He looked nervous. Guilty. Their bickering was commonplace but never with this kind of bite. My gaze swiveled between them, my palms dampening.

What was going on?

Granddad patted my arm. "How would you like to take the wagon into town and buy yourself a sundae, Kitty Kat? Or go for a swim at the club?"

My mouth dropped, surprise displacing my unease. I'd received my license at sixteen but rarely drove, especially alone. An offer to escape Randcliffe Cottage to explore the Cove on my own, this near to dusk? The notion was more intoxicating than the wine I'd consumed. "Really? Can I?"

He shifted forward and pulled his wallet from his back pocket. Thumbing through the bills inside, he took out a twenty, passing it to me. "Don't stay out too late though, honey."

I chanced a glance at Grandmother. She appeared displeased yet said nothing.

Pushing my chair back with eagerness, I hurried to my bedroom—the room that had been my mother's when she was a teenager. Sarah had left folded stacks of clean laundry on the canopy bed. I found my swimsuit, a pair of shorts, and a peasant blouse. Dressing quickly, I gathered my hair into a ponytail.

On my way to the kitchen, I detoured to the parlor to say goodbye to my grandparents. They now sat on the sofa, heads bent close. They didn't notice me—their conversation seemed intense, and their voices were hushed. Something was up, but I wasn't about to let the opportunity for independence slip through my fingers.

Ignoring the weird gnawing in the pit of my belly, I tiptoed away.

Chapter Two

THE ANTIQUATED STATION wagon's brakes were spongy from disuse. I drove with care along Sand Dollar Way past the gracious, low country-style cottages with their pastel-hued siding and wraparound porches. A seagull kept pace with me, sailing alongside the car, the tips of its wing brushing my window. With a short squawk, the gull changed course and flew away.

I turned onto Starfish Avenue, and the residential district morphed into upscale storefronts and eateries. The gelateria adjacent to the fishmonger we frequented was mobbed with sightseers in resort wear, a line forming which stretched to the public access beach. Gelato didn't interest me, and the country club was on the ritzier side of the island, the eastern side.

Silber Sound was on my left, peppered with vacation homes and budget-conscious summer rentals overlooking the water, the mainland beyond. I cranked my window down all the way, the wind whipping my ponytail. Scents rolled in—the tang of fish and the sweet, briny earthiness of kelp abundant in the shallows.

The entrance of the four-lane suspension bridge spanning the Sound loomed ahead. The isle's tangible connection to the mainland, its construction in 1950 transformed Kingfisher Cove from an exclusive haven for the filthy rich to a vacation mecca within the grasp of the average family.

A dented minivan zoomed from behind me, cutting me off, then slowing. I stomped on the brake, and the wagon shuddered. The minivan careened onto the parkway bridge. Frowning, I mimicked what Granddad often grumbled in such situations, "Tourists!"

Regardless of the disdain they received, tourists became the lifeblood of the Cove since my great-great-great-grandfather built our cottage in the early nineteen-hundreds. The summer home and the Cove were part of me. Part of my DNA. I was *not* a tourist. I'd been staying here every June since infancy and knew the history—an English mariner happened upon the uncharted land mass in the late 1650s while on a surveying expedition. He claimed the island for the crown, naming it after the profusion of small charcoal-gray-and-white birds with untidy crests and dagger-like beaks—the Belted Kingfisher.

There had been few human inhabitants on the island until an industrialist chose to build a retreat here more than two hundred years later. In its heyday, the highest echelon of society flooded his sprawling estate, Shoreside, for functions. In time, it fell into disrepair, and a development company purchased the estate. Now, Shoreside was a fancy private resort. Framed photographs of parties through the years decorated the walls of the reception area—photos prominently featuring *my* forebears.

The next stoplight past the base of the bridge went from amber to red. I idled, waiting for traffic. Starfish Avenue wound around the entire island. If I stayed on it, I'd find myself back by our cottage. My intent? To check out Upper Kingfisher, the working-class section where the servants of the wealthy visitors settled at the turn of the twentieth century.

Passing a supermarket vastly different from our trendy Lower Kingfisher grocer, I glanced around, fascinated. A shrill shriek of a tool drifted from a gas station garage. There were no tasteful souvenir shops or overpriced confectioners. No throngs of vacationers in pricey clothes toting designer lattes while window shopping. Instead, the people here wore jean cutoffs and sneakers, striding purposefully as they went about their business.

Adjoining the marina, a grizzled fisherman with a ginger beard filleted his catch of the day on a makeshift plywood countertop. A copper-haired girl in a tube top sold the fisherman's wares by the seawall, looking bored. I recognized the name on the peeling sign above her as that of our fishmonger—O'Flaherty's. These digs were distinctly less extravagant than the shop we bought from.

The majority of the crafts docked at the wharf were working boats. A weathered crabber chugged into the harbor, its pots teeming with blue-tinted crustaceans, a flock of greedy seagulls in its wake. Rather than Coppertone and sugar perfuming the tourist area, the air here was imbued with gasoline and fish guts. Mere miles from home, but another world.

My gaze skated over cafés, restaurants, and a dive bar called The Shanty. Then there were rows of single-family homes shoved together with the narrowest of strips of grass linking them. I cruised through the modest neighborhoods, up a street then down another. In a yard, kids played tag while their father grilled burgers. I wasn't hungry, but my stomach growled at the wafting scent of charred meat.

The sun was beginning to slide down the horizon. The tides would soon recede. My mood turned gloomy. On a whim, I decided to drive to Hollby Lighthouse and take in the sunset.

One lone vehicle remained in the parking lot when I pulled in —lighthouse tours had concluded hours ago. I locked the wagon, my sandals clacking on the blacktop as I walked. The red-and-white edifice was at the northernmost tip of the island, a cement walkway cleaving a path in the patches of seagrass and scrub leading to it. Thick rope woven through posts bordered the path.

I bypassed the lighthouse and the attached addition housing the gift shop, veering left. A wooden bench afforded an obstructed view a short distance from the roped-off cliffs' edges. Breeze lifting my hair, I stood at the precipice, chewing my lip. Here, the cliffs weren't so much cliffs as an outcrop of dark stone. If a person was super cautious, they could use the boulders as a stairway. Sitting nearer the lapping water seemed divine.

With a glimpse over my shoulder to ensure I wasn't seen, I gingerly stepped over the rope onto a boulder. Determining it safe, I lowered to another.

Halfway down to my destination, I lost my footing.

Chapter Three

I LET OUT a cry of alarm, my arms flailing as I fell.

Skidding down the embankment, I splayed my hands. Grabbed at the plumes of oat grass sprouting from between the rocks. My right foot found a sturdy stone. I braced my sandal against it, then curled my fingers around the boulder beneath me.

My left leg dangled over space, and my sandal slithered off. I froze, closing my eyes. One wrong move, and I'd plummet into the drink after it.

This is what you get when you step out of your comfort zone and break the rules. Now what are you going to do, genius?

"Hold on!" a deep voice intoned from above.

Eyes squeezed shut, I concentrated on staying in place. My temples throbbed from holding my breath, but I didn't dare shift an inch.

The man descended the embankment, promising in a calm tone, "Almost there."

Strong hands hooked under my armpits and towed me into a solid chest. I rotated, clutching at the man. My limbs trembled, but he held me tight. His shirt was smooth beneath my cheek, the thud of his heartbeat comforting. I exhaled and drew a shaky breath. "Th-thank you."

"What on earth were you thinking bypassing the stanchion and climbing down the embankment? Didn't you see the signs posted?"

I raised my head, opening my eyes. The sun washed him in a tawny aura, causing me to squint. Our gazes met. His irises were moss-green flecked with hazel. Around my age, he was gorgeous —muscular. Bronze-skinned.

Awareness tinkled over me, and I averted my gaze. Pulling away, I shook my head, embarrassment scorching my face. "I-I wanted to sit b-by the water, and I slipped on a rock."

"Lucky I stayed late tonight to do inventory," he said, flicking his shaggy sun-bleached hair from his eyes. His red polo shirt had a lighthouse insignia embroidered in black, along with a name—*Jace*. "I was leaving when I heard you scream. Can you stand?"

"I-I think so." I inhaled through my nose and blew slowly out my mouth.

Unfolding from the boulder, Jace held out his hand. I grasped it, allowing him to help me to my feet. I put my palms on my kneecaps, dizzy.

"Whoa," he murmured, grasping my forearm. "Let's get you on land."

We made our way up the embankment. My legs wobbled—I couldn't make them quit wobbling. Jace must've noticed. Mortified, I fought tears. *Why am I such a weakling? God. I'm a loser. A loser!* Swallowing hard, I murmured, "I-I should p-probably go."

"You're in no condition to drive," Jace pointed out. His hand was clasped on my forearm. Clearing his throat, he released me. He hitched his thumb toward the gift shop. "Wanna rest inside?"

"I-I better not."

"Yeah, you don't know me," Jace said. "You're smart to be careful."

Wow, he's really good-looking. I had limited experience with the opposite sex. Was I woozy from losing footing or because I found him attractive? "The bench is fine."

"After all your trouble, I wouldn't want you to miss the sunset." Jace led me to a rock bed bordering the lighthouse, flashing a smile that displayed a pearly set of teeth. "This spot'll be perfect. Better than the bench."

Once I was settled, Jace took a keychain from the pocket of his jean shorts. Winking, he said he'd be back in a second. I craned my neck to watch him walk away—the urge to check him out was irresistible—my eyes locking on his butt. *Daaang!* Unbolting the door to the gift shop, Jace disappeared inside. I was still blushing when he returned with two bottles of beer in his grasp.

"My boss keeps a six-pack in the staff fridge." He twisted the cap off of one and passed it over. "He won't care."

"But I'm not twenty-one."

"Neither am I. Go ahead. It doesn't matter."

I accepted the beer and took a drink, grimacing at the taste.

We sat side by side with our backs to the lighthouse, wordless. It was as if we were in our own bubble, insulated from the world. The breeze was cool and thick with salt, the crashing of the surf against the cliff punctuated by an occasional seagull cawing. Jace drank his beer, the movement of his arm exposing the edges of a tattoo along the cuff of his polo.

I removed my sandal and brought my knees to my chest, my heels sinking into the pebbles underneath us. I held my beer by the neck but did not drink.

By degrees, the orb of the sun vanished, the sky saturated with dramatic smudges of apricot and orange and purple. Jace's shoulder brushed mine when he tipped his bottle to drain his beer, and my skin tingled through the thin fabric of my blouse. We were close enough that I could smell the soapy scent of his cologne. I peeked at him from under my lashes. He had a nice profile—a strong brow, a nose straight as an arrow, and a squared jaw. I marshaled courage. "I'm Katrina."

He turned to me, dusk darkening his eyes. "Jace."

"I know." I nodded to his shirt, and we shared an awkward laugh. "Thanks again for, uh, saving me before."

"Well, it's kinda my job." At my blank look, he elaborated,

"Not here. My other job. It's my first summer lifeguarding at Shoreside."

"Oh." *Aren't you the witty conversationalist?*

"Haven't you heard of it? It's pretty well known on the Cove."

"Sure, but I've never stayed there."

"Most vacationers haven't." Jace put a hand up, rubbing his thumb against the tips of his other fingers to indicate *big money*.

"I mean, I've been to the pool," I clarified. "Just not recently. I like the beach better."

"Last two years I was a lifeguard at Cleary Beach, south of the Sound. You know it?" Jace paused until I assented, then continued, "Shoreside's got a waitlist for lifeguards. I was about to cave and apply for busboy in one of the restaurants when I got their call. Glad I held out—lifeguards make bank over there."

I recalled Granddad leaving a hundred-dollar tip at brunch the weekend before last at Shoreside's casual dining bistro, The Seafarer. "You should be a waiter."

"They only give those jobs to frat boys from the mainland. Lifeguarding or caddying is the only option for guys like me." Jace tossed his head, unconcerned. "Where you stayin'?"

"My family has a house on the island. Lower Kingfisher."

He whistled. I sensed his manner becoming reserved.

Lower and Upper Kingfisher did not mix.

ROMANCE AT KINGFISHER COVE is a sweet and steamy novella featured in the charity anthology *Love is in the Air*. You can find *Love is in the Air* at www.books2read.com/loveisintheair

ABOUT ANNE LUCY-SHANLEY

CRAZY CAT LADY. FAN OF THE OXFORD COMMA. AUTHOR.

WITH DEGREES in education and psychology, Anne Lucy-Shanley is a novelist based in the American Midwest. An enthusiast of all things romance, she also dabbles in dystopian, young adult, and non-fiction writing. As a firm believer in happily-ever-afters, contemporary romance remains her favorite genre.

. . .

SOME OF ANNE'S pastimes include drinking whiskey, sharing dirty memes, and coming up with captivating storylines while soaking in the tub. When not embracing the quiet life with a book and a cat on her lap, she occasionally travels with her husband of twenty years.

ANNE LOVES CONNECTING with her readers! Come join the fun at her Facebook group, Saucy Society. Sign up for her monthly newsletter The Saucy Gossip at www.annelucyshanley.com. You'll receive updates on her books, info about giveaways, and reading recommendations delivered straight to your inbox.